DANCING AT D'AVENCOURT

by

Iris Lloyd

Published by New Generation Publishing in 2021

Copyright © Iris Lloyd 2021

First Edition

ISBN
Paperback	978-1-80031-225-8
Ebook	978-1-80031-224-1

Cover artwork by Nigel Perrin of Three Marketeers, Hungerford, Berkshire

www.newgeneration-publishing.com

 New Generation Publishing

About the Author

Photo by Nigel Perrin

Born in Clapham, London, in 1931, Iris moved to Queensbury, a newly-built north-west London suburb, with her parents and younger brother before the war. They survived the first night of the Blitz, while visiting her grandparents in Clapham, and shortly afterwards were evacuated with her father's firm to Chesham, Buckinghamshire. They had been there about ten days only when an enemy plane dropped bombs along the road, killing a woman just a few houses away. While there, Iris attended Dr. Challoner's Grammar School in Amersham (then co-ed.)

On returning home at the age of 14, her sister was born. Iris trained as a shorthand/typist and worked in various companies, including the BBC and as secretary to the Editor of Children's Books at Macmillan's publishing house.

Having taken dancing lessons since the age of three, she joined the chorus of a small touring professional pantomime company at the age of 17, and later wrote, choreographed and directed eight pantomimes for her church youth club and another nine in co-operation with a friend for his amateur dramatic society.

Marriage followed and a move to Berkshire, then the birth of two daughters and three grandchildren, and early widowhood. During those years, she taught ballet, tap and acrobatic dancing to children and later tap dancing to adults.

Voluntary work has included being an active member of her church community wherever she lived; an adviser at the Citizens Advice Bureau; editor of the monthly church magazine and of the local talking newspaper for the visually impaired; chairing three creative writing groups; on the team at the local Foodbank; and latterly a waterways chaplain on her local canal.

She continued writing, including being correspondent for three villages and dance critic for the local newspaper, the Newbury Weekly News.

Attaining the age of 70, Iris decided it was time to write her debut novel and based it on an archaeological site on top of the Berkshire downs north of Newbury that she was helping to excavate. And so the story of BRON began in the late Roman era and continued through five novels, all of which were self published. Three stand-alone novels followed.

Now aged 90, Iris hung up her tap shoes several years ago but continues to write and hopes you will enjoy her ninth novel, Dancing at D'Avencourt, the story of Ingaret.

Previously published in paperback and as e-books

BRON
Part I, Daughter of Prophecy   *ISBN 978-1-906206-07-9*
Part II, Flames of Prophecy   *ISBN 978-1-906206-23-9*
Part III, The Girl with the Golden Ankle   *ISBN 978-1-8380600-0-8*
Part IV, The Scarlet Seal   *ISBN 978-1-907499-89-0*
Part V, Pearl and Amber   *ISBN 978-1-8380600-1-5*

Flash Black   *ISBN 978-1-78003-811-7*

Hunterswick Green   *ISBN 978-1-8380600-2-2*

My Lady Marian   *ISBN 978-1-78955-335-2*

Author contact:
e-mail: iris@irislloyd.co.uk
website: www.irislloyd.co.uk

CONTENTS

PROLOGUE

I switch on the coloured lights and step back. Happily, each bulb is alight. Perfect! The lit Christmas tree brightens that corner of the living room.

Then memories fill me with nostalgia – the string of bells I bought in the Christmas shop in a small town in New England; the silver star from Tirana, Albania; glass icicles from Alaska and a set of small coloured lanterns that always hung on our tree at home when I was growing up. All happy memories in a long life.

My group of nativity figures in the stable – the holy family, the shepherds with their sheep, the three wise men approaching – is displayed on the table in the hall. The greeting cards, as they arrive, are being hung on strings secured to the dark oak beams crossing the ceiling. They are decorative but tidily out of the way and don't keep falling over like rows of dominoes every time the front door is opened and cold air blows through the cottage.

Now there is one last job to do. I fetch the stool from the kitchen and, climbing up, remove a floral painting from its hook on the wall to one side of the fireplace. I wrap it carefully in newspaper and put it away in the hall cupboard. Then I retrieve a similar sized package and carry it to the living room. Sitting on the couch, I unwrap it, put aside the newspaper and look at the picture, as I have done for so many Christmases past.

I love that picture! Strange that I can't remember from which antique shop I bought it and exactly when. The print, measuring 10½ by 6 inches, with a wide gold mount and in a gilt frame, has always intrigued me.

There is an old label on the back, displaying the name and address of the framer in Sunderland, and informing the reader that the title of the painting is *After Midnight Mass, Fifteenth Century*, that it was painted by G. H. Boughton and exhibited at the Royal Academy in 1897. It records, further, that it was in the private collection of Mr. W. Knox D'Arcy.

I discovered, when researching him, that he had been given a licence to prospect and drill for oil in Persia, had struck lucky, and had later founded BP.

The original painting measured – measures – 50 by 96 inches, a mammoth four feet by eight feet. I wonder where that painting is now. It is too large to have got lost!

The artist is showing the viewer the west door of a huge cathedral, from which is emerging a crowd of worshippers, dressed in clothing of the medieval period. Torchbearers light their way, revealing that it has been snowing heavily.

At the front of the crowd is a beautiful young lady in an oyster cream gown and wearing a wimple with double peaks. Two young pages look as though they are enjoying carrying her train. By her side is an elderly companion, dressed soberly but also wearing a double wimple. The label describes the scene:

"The eye is at once attracted to the lady of high birth, slender in form, youthful and elegantly clad, who is stepping lightly over the snow-covered ground on her return to her home. Torch-bearers make sure of her way, and by her side is an elderly attendant, while groups of respectful and interested spectators mark their sense of her importance."

In front of the crowd watching from a distance is a young man with shoulder-length yellow hair, who seems to be stepping forward. Does he recognise her? Who is he?

And who is that beautiful young lady of high birth with her elderly attendant?

My lady, who are you? What is your name? Why are you there, leaving the cathedral, and where is 'there'? I ask her these questions every Christmas but suppose that I shall never know the answers. *My lady, I care that your delicate shoes are robust enough to keep your feet warm and dry in the snow.*

So, once again, I am clambering up onto the stool to hang the picture on the hook at the side of the fireplace. There! It is in pride of place again.

I know that I will be looking up at it many times over Christmas when my lodger, Pam, has left to spend the holiday with her family and I am on my own with only the television for company.

I step back to admire you, quite forgetting that I am standing on a stool, and I am falling backwards. I hear the crack! as my head hits the glass top of the coffee table behind me, then black shadows blanket out my consciousness…

PART I

THE VILL

SOUTHERN ENGLAND

SPRING, IN THE YEAR OF OUR LORD

FOURTEEN HUNDRED AND NINETY-ONE

CHAPTER 1

"Whoever you are, behind that bush! I bid you good morrow!"

There was no answer.

"I know you're there. I spied you through the trees. I know you're there."

She did not move.

"I won't hurt you," he wheedled. "I just want to talk to you."

Now she was peeping through the branches.

"There! You moved! I saw you! Come out. I'll stay over here. I promise not to come any closer."

Still no response.

"I order you to come out! I am a Lancastrian and you have to obey me!"

A very small girl crept out from behind the bush and immediately lowered her eyes and dropped a curtsey.

"You're not very big."

He stared at her, at the mass of tangled chestnut curls, the colour of his rouncey's mane, probably crawling with lice. At the indiscriminate jumble of dirty and stained clothing that hung on her slight body. He was glad he had said he would not go any closer.

"What's your name?" No reply. "Come now, tell me your name!"

The name was mumbled indistinctly, as if the word might offend him.

"I didn't hear it. Say it again!"

She looked as though she might be about to cry.

"Ingaret."

"In-gar-et." He said the name slowly and liked the way it sounded in his mouth so repeated the syllables and repeated them yet again. The girl was still looking down at her filthy feet but he caught sight of a tentative smile.

"Don't you want to know my name?"

Ingaret shook her head then seemed to regret her denial and nodded.

"I'll tell you if you look at me."

For a moment longer she hesitated, then raised her head and regarded him with steady concentration.

Taken unawares, startled by the intensity of that look, by the depths in her violet eyes, he was surprised when something in his chest jumped about alarmingly and a spider ran down his spine.

"My name's – my name's – it's Robert," he stammered.

"Good morrow, Robert," she said shyly.

He was ashamed at being off-footed by this scrap of a girl, whom he should not be engaging in conversation. But she intrigued him.

"How old are you?"

"I killed my mother six summers ago."

"Then you are both to be pitied, but how young you are! I am four summers older."

Someone shouted and the boy turned his head then looked at her again.

"Do you live in the vill?"

She nodded. "You can come and see, if you like."

"Come and see – me? Step inside one of those hovels? I don't think so! Don't you know who I am?"

She shook her head. "But I could visit you, then I would know."

Robert laughed.

"I live in the manor, that's where I live, and you wouldn't get past the dogs!"

"I would if you held on to their collars."

She trusted him! Robert was sorry that he had laughed at her. There were no guard dogs. It was left to his father's pack of hunting hounds to raise any alarm, which they did without fail when strangers approached.

There was another shout.

"William's becoming impatient. I will have to go before he comes looking for me and finds me talking to you, little peasant girl. Stay well, Ingaret."

He turned from her and sped back the way he had come, between the trees, thrashing the undergrowth with his whip as he passed. When he swivelled round to look for her, she had vanished.

Pendragon, was cropping the grass at the side of the track when he returned. William was still adjusting his clothing.

"I needed that!" William declared. "Must have been the fish at dinner. Foot in the stirrup, young sire, and I'll help you up."

Robert decided to say nothing to anyone about his encounter with the peasant girl in the forest and several days later it had faded from his memory. But sometimes his dreams were disturbed by a fleeting glimpse of trusting violet eyes, and then he would remember Ingaret and smile.

CHAPTER 2

Ingaret retrieved the large bundle of kindling she had dropped when the boy had sent her scurrying behind the bush and took the path leading to the settlement on the edge of the vill, the only place she knew as home.

On the way, she thought about that boy from the big house. She had heard talk about the lord's sons. Some of the girls in the vill seemed to know a lot about them, although Gunnora, her mother – or, rather, the miserable woman her father had told her and Jethro to call 'mother' – said they knew a lot less than they pretended.

So now she had met Robert D'Avencourt, though she could never tell anyone because no one would believe her – except Jethro. Jethro, her older brother, would believe her, he always did. He always took her side when their younger sister and brother, Alice and John, went crying to their mother, saying Ingaret had pinched them or hit them with the wooden spoon or pushed them into the stream. All falsehoods, of course, but it made no difference. She was punished anyway and tied to a tree for a day to go hungry and thirsty and to be made ashamed by soiling herself.

He had been kind, that boy, and asked her name. Once she had told a tinker passing through that her name was "Insect!", which she believed at the time, after he had bought her for two tin pans from the woman who was beating her. She had gladly clambered into his covered wagon when he had promised to give her a new dress, but Jethro had run to tell their father, who was working in the forest. He had caught them up a mile away down the track, had punched the tinker in the jaw then the belly, and had brought her home.

Her father had always blamed her for killing her mother when she was born, which Ingaret was very sad about but did not understand. If she had killed her mother, she hadn't meant to, and didn't know how she had made it happen when she was only a little baby.

She loved her tall, strong father, Noah, with his dark brown eyes and hair as black as crows' feathers, and longed for him to notice her but he had never paid her much heed. So she was not surprised that evening when he had given her and Jethro some bread and sent them off to spend the night in the forest.

When they came home early next morning, the woman he had brought to live with them could not see out of a blackened eye. She said she had tripped and hit her face on a rock, which Ingaret thought very strange because she could not see any rocks anywhere.

"Father still loves us," Jethro had whispered.

If he loves us, thought Ingaret, *why did he send us to sleep in the forest all night?*

CHAPTER 3

After that, the woman's dislike of Ingaret changed to loathing, though she was careful not to reveal her feelings in front of the child's father. Ingaret tried hard to please her and do as she was told but was constantly in trouble.

Now seven years old, she had prepared the pottage for their evening meal and had sent Alice and John, her younger sister and brother, to bed near the fire that burned in the depression scooped out in the earth floor. She knew that the warmth of their bodies, as they cuddled up together beneath their flimsy coverings, would keep them comfortable until it was time to wake them at dawn.

When both had fallen asleep, she cleaned their wooden spoons in the water in the bucket then gathered up the remains of their bread trenchers and threw them outside for the stray dogs or rats to eat, and the birds, if anything was left by morning, which seldom happened.

Meantime, their mother was sleeping on the raised platform against the far wall. Her lank hair, the colour of pale straw, and her thin arms lay on top of the sheepskin covers. She was pregnant again and complaining of a headache and the need to rest.

It was April and the days were beginning to lengthen. Although sunny all week, the nights were still laying down a hard covering of frost.

Ingaret joined her father and brother on their stools by the fire. She took up a log from the woodpile and threw it onto the flames and watched as the smoke drifted lazily up towards the roof, searching for a way out between the thatch.

"How does that work, Father?" nine-year-old Jethro asked, raising his pot of ale to his lips.

"It means we would plant two strips with wheat and leave the third fallow, rotating the crops year by year."

"But we only have two strips."

"I know that, son. But that may change."

"How change, Father?" asked Ingaret.

"This is men's talk," Jethro admonished her. "It's not for girls."

"But I want to know."

"Let her be," said their father. "The two strips next to ours are planted by old Isaiah. He says he has passed his three score years and ten, and we know he is failing."

Isaiah died not long afterwards, about the time that their baby brother James was born, and Lord D'Avencourt allowed Noah to take over one of the vacated strips of land. It carried with it the usual condition that his lordship should receive one-tenth of the yield.

Busy with the new baby, their mother, for once, left Ingaret in peace as long as she carried out her chores. However, she was not too busy to go round boasting to the women with their noisy children in the nearby hovels that her husband was adopting the new three-field system.

On occasions, Ingaret was sent with the two younger children into Lord D'Avencourt's fields to blow whistles, shake rattles, beat tin pans and bang blocks of wood together, to shout and wave their arms about and scare the black kites and other scavenging birds away from the ripening wheat. Then the birds would rise up like a swarm of bees and circle the field before settling down among the wheat stalks again, when the performance had to be repeated.

It was after one such day, when she was ten years old, that Ingaret found the button.

"I'm going home by way of the high road," she told Alice, younger than her by a year and a half.

"You'll be late home," observed John, who was younger still, the first son of her father's second family. "You'll get a beating."

"I won't if you don't tell."

"What will you give us if we don't tell?" he asked, prompted by his sister.

"What do you want me to give you?"

"A story," said Alice. "A story about King Arthur."

"I'll be King Arthur!" John decided.

"If I promise to tell you a story tonight, you won't tell on me, will you?"

Both children shook their heads.

"Cross your hearts."

With their forefingers, Alice and John solemnly drew a cross on their chests above where they thought their hearts rested.

"And hope to die," prompted Ingaret.

"And hope to die," the children chorused.

"That's settled, then," Ingaret agreed. "Stay here till the sun goes behind that tree then wait for me by the church, so we all arrive home together."

"Why do you want to go up on the high road?" John wanted to know.

"I like it up there," Ingaret replied. "Things happen up there!"

If she was honest with herself, very little happened up on the high road, but there was always the chance that something might. If carriers were taking goods to and from Fortchester, that was the way they drove their ox carts. Sometimes shepherds walked their sheep to market along there or farmers their cattle; there was an occasional pilgrim on his way to the cathedral and occasionally messengers rode by on their horses, clods of mud flying from beneath their hooves.

Once, a long time ago, she had seen a covered wagon pulled by two brown horses with a bodyguard on horseback riding on each side, swords in their scabbards, and a lady had looked out. When Ingaret had asked her father about the beautiful lady, he said she may have been going to the manor house to visit Lord and Lady D'Avencourt.

Today, however, there was no one in sight. She dawdled there for a while, looking across yellow fields of ripening wheat and the green of fallow fields, which stretched away to the horizons on either side.

Then she smiled to find herself humming a song that old Isaiah used to sing at the annual May Day gatherings in his deep mellow voice that had been likened to dark brown liquid honey:

> *Fair maid – nay, beauteous beyond fair –*
> *Wilt let me loose your silken hair*
> *And take your hand? Please say me 'Yea'*
> *And walk with me a little way.*
>
> *Young sir, I durst not say thee 'Yea'*
> *Till we are wed – so not Today.*
>
> *You shall of me have everything –*
> *Fine dresses, shoes, a golden ring –*
> *And we will marry in the Spring.*

The girls in the vill said that a good marriage was the only way to escape their poverty. Ingaret thought that, if a handsome young man promised her fine dresses and shoes and a ring of gold, she would gladly walk with him and even let him hold her hand. After all, Spring was never more than a year away and it would be worth the wait.

She decided then and there that she would try to find a handsome young man who had the wealth to buy her pretty things – someone like Robert, Lord D'Avencourt's son, though he was far beyond her reach. It would have to be someone else, though there was no one else, only the boys in the vill, and their families were just as poor as hers.

But, she reflected, the fair maid in the song might after all be wise, because when she said again that she durst not go with the young man until they were wed, he promised her even more riches –

> *Your toes and fingers I'll bedeck*
> *And clasp fair jewels about thy neck*
> *And songs of Paradise I'll strum*
> *If thou wilt come, fair maiden – come.*

9

Yes, Ingaret decided that she would certainly have gone with him in the hope that he would keep his promise and marry her. She touched her neck and in imagination felt the jewels lying there, rising and falling with every breath, and became so optimistic that she lifted her arm and swung her rattle round and round her head. This so alarmed all the birds in the vicinity that they flew up above the trees, making such a cacophony that she laughed out loud.

She had just decided it was time to cross the track and make her way down the slope and so to the church when she saw a glint from something half hidden in the mud. She dropped her rattle and walked towards it.

The rays of light from the setting sun seemed to be searching it out, pointing to it, drawing her attention to it. She trampled the grass to have a better look then bent down and picked it up.

It was a button, perfectly round, with tiny flashing points of coloured lights set in a gold metal. She didn't think the jewels were real – they couldn't be – there were so many of them.

Ingaret caressed the button, rubbed it against her cheek and blinked again at the coloured lights; she was tingling with excitement.

One day, she thought, she would own a button like this – many buttons. But their jewels would be real. They would run in a line down the back of her gown where everyone could see them but so unimportant that she wouldn't even know if one had fallen off.

Clasping the button tightly, she picked up her rattle and set off down the hill. She would have to hide it, of course, or that woman would take it from her or the children would play with it and lose it. But where to hide it? It wouldn't be safe in the house, so where?

Alice and John were waiting for her by the flint church with the square tower, which the ancients in the vill said was three hundred years old and which everyone attended at least once every Sunday and on holy days to repent of their sins and partake of the blessed bread and wine.

"Your cheeks are red," John said critically as she joined them.

"I've been hurrying to get here."

"Did you see anyone up on the high road?" asked Alice.

"Not a soul."

"But you're still going to tell us a story, aren't you?" John demanded.

"Before you go to sleep," Ingaret promised, "if mother lets me."

She felt sure that their mother would allow her to tell them a story. John, her first son, was her favourite child and always got his own way. On the other hand, a story always lulled the pair of them off to sleep, as well as three-year-old James and toddler Megge.

By the time they reached home, she had made her decision. She would get up during the night and bury the button in the strip of land her father was leaving fallow this year. It would lay undisturbed there. Then, next time she was sent to the stream to fetch water, she would find a secret hiding place in the forest, perhaps in the roots of a tree. Yes, that was a clever plan.

"Tonight's story is about a button," she told the children. "It's about a button made of gold and jewels and it fell off the gown of a princess and a knight found it and gave it back to her and then they married."

"What was the princess's name?" Alice wanted to know.

"Ingaret – like mine. She lived in a castle, built of stone not wood, and she was the favourite daughter of her father, King Arthur…"

CHAPTER 4

Jethro should be here soon, to help her carry the water home. Once he had not bothered and had left her to carry both buckets all by herself. It had taken a long time, with many stops along the way, and she had been sent to bed that night with nothing to eat as punishment for tarrying so long.

Her brother could not forgive himself and had never abandoned her since then.

Before he arrived, though, she had a very important task to carry out – she must hide her button. For the past hour, she had been carrying it inside her mouth, fearful of swallowing it, because she had nowhere else to hide it. Now she extracted it and looked around for tree roots that she would recognise again.

She found nearby the gnarled and twisted roots of an old oak and soon the button was buried deep in the soil. There was no chance that she would not be able to find its hiding place again because the tree was close to the shallow part of the stream where she always came to collect water.

Now she hitched up her skirt and waded into the stream, gripping the handle of the wooden bucket. On this warm summer's day, the water was refreshingly cold as it swirled around her feet and ankles.

She bent over to lay the bucket on its side and the stream splashed her playfully as it tumbled over small boulders heaped along its winding channel. Ingaret laughed with pleasure and imagined it was gurgling to her about the happy times away from that woman's prying eyes – skimming pebbles where the water lay a murky green-brown beneath overhanging trees; scrambling up through the branches, vying with other children from the vill; or running around the trees, playing tag or hide-and-seek.

She sighed then. There was little leisure for these games for any of them. Occasionally, though, just occasionally, they stole time out of the day when their parents were otherwise preoccupied. Then they would gather in the forest, the foliage muffling their shouts and laughter, though their parents would hear nothing, so absorbed were they with their fighting cocks or watching the dogs tearing a badger to pieces. The challenge was to be back home before the grown-ups returned, a challenge they always met.

Once her bucket was full, she tugged it out of the stream, fighting the flow that never wanted to release the intruder. Then she lay the second bucket on the stones. That, too, she heaved out onto the bank when it was full.

Then she heard Jethro calling and turned to welcome him. His coming always made her smile. Although only two years older, she felt safe when he was near, this big brother of hers.

Today, she was surprised to see that he was not alone.

"Ingaret! Look who I've brought with me!"

Ingaret saw a boy with yellow hair that reached his shoulders, who was about the same age as twelve-year-old Jethro. She had seen him in the vill before. His family had newly arrived, brought in by Lord D'Avencourt to work the mill after the previous miller had hanged himself by tying a rope round his neck and jumping off a stool with a sack of grain in his arms.

The miller's family had been evicted and news came that they had made their way to the great cathedral city of Fortchester, where both sons hoped to find work.

"Come and meet Elis. He's my new friend. You must be friends, too, Ingaret."

"Well met, Jethro's little sister," the boy greeted her.

"Well met, Elis," Ingaret replied then asked in awe, "Are you an angel?"

"An angel?" Elis repeated and both boys looked at each other and began to laugh, to Ingaret's extreme discomfort.

"What nonsense are you talking?" Jethro managed to ask between snorts of laughter. It was not like him to make fun of her, especially in front of a stranger.

Elis must have seen the look on her face because he stopped laughing.

"What makes you think I'm an angel?"

"He's far from being an angel!" Jethro chortled.

"Why, Ingaret?" Elis persisted.

"It's your hair," Ingaret mumbled. "Father once visited the cathedral in Fortchester and said the glass in the windows had been painted with stories from the Bible and the angels had long yellow hair down to their shoulders, like yours."

"You see, Jethro," Elis said, turning to him, "your little sister has good reason for thinking I might be an angel."

Jethro snorted again.

"No, I'm not an angel, Ingaret. That would be fun, though, being able to fly anywhere, wouldn't it? But I can't. I'm just the miller's son, and Jethro's friend – and yours, now."

"This isn't getting the water home," Jethro said, picking up a bucket. "Elis, an angel – whatever next?" and he started off along the path, still sniggering.

"I'll take the other bucket," Elis offered.

"It's very heavy," Ingaret warned him.

"Not to me," he replied cheerfully, lifting the bucket easily. He looked at her and nodded. "Though I can see that it could be heavy for a little girl like you."

Ingaret was about to retort that she was ten years old and used to carrying a bucket of water but reflected that, if he was going to carry it for her, she was not going to argue with him.

They walked together, Jethro leading the way and pushing aside the wild pink and white dog roses that stretched across their path. Shyly, she peeked at her companion. He was a little taller than her brother and had a kind face, heart-shaped and not pock marked.

When he suddenly turned his head, she averted her gaze, but he was smiling and his blue eyes were full of mischief, and Ingaret then felt happier than she had felt for a long time – not since she had found a robin with an injured wing and had nursed it until it had been able to fly away.

After that day, Elis became her friend as well as Jethro's and he walked to the settlement to see them whenever his father could spare him from duties at the mill.

Her step mother seemed not to mind his being around and surprisingly told him that he was welcome any time. Ingaret guessed it was because he helped Jethro and their father with work about the place, chopping logs for the fire, trapping rabbits in the fields then helping to skin and joint them for a shared meal, cutting reeds to renew the thatch, or rushes to strew over the floor.

He soon became like a brother to them both.

CHAPTER 5

Four years went by very quickly because they were all so busy. Ingaret was now fourteen years old. Two more babies had arrived in the cottage, Henry and Lizzie.

Ingaret was well aware how babies were started and had often lain awake, listening to the strange noises of her father's passion for that woman coming from behind the hanging curtain.

She and Jethro used to giggle about it in the morning but, since reaching puberty, she had not found it so funny and now they never discussed it. Next morning, if their eyes met, Jethro would give her a knowing look then turn his head away.

Somehow, brother and sister were not as close as they once were. Ingaret grieved for this loss of intimacy and increasingly began to look to Elis for the companionship she missed. He never turned her away, always speaking the word of advice or comfort she needed.

Their mother started complaining about the absence of Jethro of an evening but all their father would say was, "He's growing into a man. Leave him be."

"Ingaret," her mother said one morning after the wheat had been harvested in both Lord D'Avencourt's fields and their own strips, "our flour will be ready to collect but his lordship keeps your father too busy. Go over to the mill and ask them to deliver it. Tomorrow is baking day and I'm running short."

"I'll go," Alice offered eagerly.

"No, you won't. I need you to pull up some carrots and prepare the vegetables."

"Ingaret can do that. Let me go to the mill."

"I said 'No'. Off with you, Ingaret, and don't stay gossiping with Elis. I need you here to take the last of the bread to your father and Jethro for their mid-day meal."

Alice began to complain in that annoying whine she adopted until their mother slapped her across the face and silenced her.

Ingaret was glad to escape. She liked Elis's family. Although there were also eight children in the mill, his parents always seemed in good humour, quite unlike her own family, and they were always glad to see her.

The track through the forest led her to the edge of the heathland where the trees had been felled. She crossed the heathland and then the marsh and came to the river and began to follow it as it wound its way towards the mill, part of it bordering the grassy slope leading up to the big house.

She looked up towards the manor, its red bricks glowing in the morning sun like the embers of a burnt-out fire, and wondered how many rooms it held. One room was enough to live in so what did Lord D'Avencourt and his family do in all those other rooms?

Her thoughts then turned to Robert D'Avencourt. He would be eighteen years old now. Perhaps he was in one of those rooms, looking out of a tall window and wondering who was that young girl walking along the bank of the river and staring up at his house.

She passed the specially constructed dam and followed the mill race, the narrow channel that forced the water over the wheel. For a while she watched, fascinated, as the buckets on the paddles continuously filled with water then descended because of their weight, so turning the wheel and draining the water back into the river.

When she thought she had spent enough time idling away the morning, she entered the ground floor of the mill. Here, the great iron shaft from the wheel was effortlessly moving cogs and wheels, so turning the great granite stone that was grinding wheat on the bedstone.

All the men working there knew her and greeted her by name.

"Are you looking for Elis, little lady?" one of them asked and she nodded.

"You'll find him in the yard, loading up the cart."

Ingaret thanked him and wandered out into the yard. Elis didn't notice her immediately and she watched him for a few moments, watched as the muscles in his upper arms flexed and relaxed as he swung the sacks of flour into the cart, and something inside her fluttered alarmingly. To her, he was still the angel she had always thought him since they first met.

"Hello, Ingaret," he called when he saw her. "Have you come about your flour?"

She nodded. "How many bags this harvest?"

"Five plus one for the manor."

"Father will be pleased."

"So he should be. His three-field system is working well."

She walked across and kissed him on the cheek.

"I've several cottages to visit," he said, "yours among them. Fancy a ride?"

"Please, Elis. May I?"

"Of course. You can mark my tally stick when I deliver the sacks. I'll leave yours till last. You don't have to go straight home, do you?"

"I should but I'll take the risk."

"Then we won't dally." He looked at her, smiling. "I'm glad you came."

"Mother sent me. One of us wanted desperately to come."

"And who was that?"

"Alice, of course. I wouldn't be here if she had had her way. Who did you think it was?"

He shrugged and continued loading the sacks.

"You didn't think it was me, surely, Elis? You can't have thought that. We're like brother and sister, you and I."

"You've got four brothers. You don't need another one."

Ingaret wondered why he sounded so grumpy.

"I have only one real brother – Jethro – and I don't see so much of him these days. He's never at home."

"He's got a girl in the vill – didn't you know?"

"No, I didn't, though I guessed as much, but he's never said. There was a time when he told me everything. Who is she?"

"You're getting in my way."

She jumped to one side. "Sorry."

"Her name's Thomasyn."

"Not the blacksmith's daughter? But she's so plain."

"No, she's not. You're just jealous."

"No I'm not. Doesn't she work up at the manor?"

"Sometimes. She talks about it as if she owned the place – and his lordship's five sons, of course."

"What about Lord D'Avencourt's sons?"

"How much attention they pay her, especially the young one, Robert."

"I met him once," Ingaret mused.

Elis stopped what he was doing and turned to her, the last sack slung over his shoulder.

"You never did, Ingaret. You're making it up."

"Honestly. I knew you wouldn't believe me."

"Where did you meet him?"

"In the forest. I was six years old."

"You're telling me that he noticed you, and you were only six?"

"He asked my name."

Elis roared with laughter.

"Now I know you're playing games with me. Why would Robert D'Avencourt be interested in you?"

"You just said he was interested in Thomasyn, or at least, she said he is."

"That's different."

"Why is it different?"

"Because she's sixteen and you were only six – or so you say –"

"Or so she says."

"Or so she says, but her story is more believable than yours."

He swung the last sack into the cart and kissed her lightly on the nose.

"Ingaret, you have to live in the real world. Look closer to home. Come on, hop up beside me and we'll be off. I'm not getting the flour delivered while I'm chattering to you."

He rambled on as he helped her up onto the seat beside him, took the reins in one hand, flipped them over the horse's back, and they were off at an ambling pace along the path leading away from the vill.

She suddenly had the urge to kiss him again and leaned across and pushed aside his hair and nuzzled his ear.

"What was that for?"

"To say 'thank you' for being such a good friend, Elis. You really are, you know, to all of us. It's no wonder our Alice thinks she's in love with you."

She moved closer and put her arm through his and snuggled up to him. He put down the reins and turned towards her. However, seeming to change his mind, he picked them up in both hands and absentmindedly flipped the horse's back again.

"Ingaret, behave! I can't control old Dobbin here with you sitting so close."

Chastened, Ingaret moved away from him.

"You can be such a grouse sometimes, Elis," she complained and received in response such a broad grin that she had to laugh.

CHAPTER 6

Robert D'Avencourt struggled out of bed, his head throbbing, wondering at the commotion that had awoken him. Then he heard the blast of the hunting horn and went across to the window. Pushing open the shutters, he peered down into the courtyard, which long ago had been the protective moat around the house. There the hunt was assembling, the horses whickering and stamping their hooves impatiently on the gravel, the hounds barking in unison as they strained at their leashes, and servants running hither and thither in confusion at his father's and older brothers' whims and shouted commands.

He called down his apologies for not being with them but no one heard him.

Withdrawing from the window, he yawned. His father and brothers would already have attended Mass and eaten a light meal. Crossing to the bedside table, he rang the handbell. Before he had time to replace it, Stephen was in the room.

"There you are, Stephen. Why didn't you wake me? I intended joining my father."

Through the window came the sound of clattering hooves as the hunting party moved out through the archway in the curtain wall and into the countryside.

"Now it's too late."

"Sire, last night you gave me instructions not to waken you this morning. You may remember that you were very late to bed, sire."

Robert suddenly felt the warmth of plump pink arms around his neck.

"Oh, yes, so I was. I had forgotten. Now that you're here, you can help me wash and shave and get dressed. If I can't follow the hounds and the scent of the deer, I will follow my own nose and the scent of another prey."

He washed with the water Stephen brought in a basin, cold and fresh from the well. Then he sat motionless while his youthful beard was carefully trimmed before being helped to dress in his underwear, hose and murrey doublet, the purplish-red colour of which suited him well. Finally, Stephen combed and styled his thick, dark brown hair of which he was so proud.

"Stephen, see if you can find that sketch of the iron gate my father wishes to order for the rose garden. It'll be on his writing desk. Then find William and tell him to bring Pendragon round."

"Yes, sire."

After a quick meal of bread, an apple and a tankard of ale brought up from the kitchen, Robert D'Avencourt was ready to be helped into his riding boots.

"Your hat, sire?" queried Stephen.

"I'll wear the hat with cockerel feathers and Stephen, if my mother asks, I'm paying a visit to our esteemed blacksmith. Hopefully, I'll be gone all morning."

"Yes, sire."

Once mounted on Pendragon and in high good humour, Robert dug his spurs into her sides and rode out through the arch, taking the path down to the vill.

The blacksmith's forge was at the far end of the street. Robert pulled his hat low over his forehead in the hope that no one would know for sure which D'Avencourt brother was paying them a visit, but everyone he passed recognised his rouncey and saluted him or curtsied deferentially and bid, "Good morrow, master Robert."

Halting the mare outside the forge, he took his feet from out the stirrups and slid off her back. The blacksmith's assistant hurried out to take the reins and tie the horse to the wooden rail provided for that purpose and the blacksmith came out to greet his visitor.

"Good morrow, master Robert."

Robert pushed his hat further back.

"Morrow, blacksmith."

"Is it shoeing the mare that you'd be wanting?"

"Not today. My father has set his heart on an iron gate for the rose garden he has just had planted. I have the design here."

He felt inside his doublet and brought out a piece of leather, scored with the desired design.

"There, is that possible?"

"Well possible, your grace. It's a handsome design."

"How long, blacksmith?"

"A week, no more. I'll send word when it's ready."

"No need. I'll ride over in a week."

He made no move to leave, passing his gauntlets from hand to hand and looking about him.

"Is there something else I can do for you, sire?"

Robert hesitated then said abruptly, "Yes, there is. The ride over has given me a thirst."

"Then let me offer you a jug of my wife's home-made barley wine."

"Thank you, yes. I'll wait under the tree."

He sauntered towards a table and chair that stood in the shade of a tall beech tree, patting Pendragon's neck on his way past.

"Do you think she'll come, Pendragon?" he whispered in the mare's ear. "I can hardly ask him to send his daughter out but she's the only wine I need."

He sat and waited, pushing the fallen brown and yellow beech leaves from the table with his arm then fidgeting again with his gauntlets before throwing them to the ground. Then he sat forward, arms resting on his thighs, before finally standing and walking backwards and forwards beneath the branches.

He need not have been so anxious. He saw her coming from the cottage, hips swaying, tray in hand and in danger of splashing the liquid over the sides of the jug. He sat down again, thinking how well formed she was for a girl of only sixteen.

"Ah, Thomasyn. I was hoping you would be bringing me what I needed."

"The wine, sire."

"That, too."

She put the tray on the table and poured the wine. He drank only a few sips from the pot she had filled to the brim.

"I thought you were thirsty," she commented.

"Hungry more than thirsty."

"Shall I bring you bread?"

"It wasn't bread I was thinking about."

"Oh, and what were you thinking about, sire?"

He looked at her. "You know very well."

"Then I regret that you will have to go hungry, your grace."

"My lady is cruel."

"No, sire, but the whole vill is watching."

He looked along the street and, indeed, there did seem to be a gaggle of folk about.

"It seems that my father is not working them nearly hard enough."

"They work hard, sire, but they so seldom see anyone from the manor. They are interested in you."

"I came to order a gate from your father."

"Then a gate you shall have – the most cleverly crafted gate in the whole of King Henry's kingdom."

"I don't doubt it."

He drained his pot of barley wine and she poured him another, which he also drank, then wiped his mouth on his sleeve.

"You enjoyed my mother's wine?"

"There is much here that I enjoy – or would, if my lady..."

"I will tell her. She will be pleased."

He bent and retrieved his gauntlets.

"Then my business here is finished for today?"

"It is."

He strode over to Pendragon and used the nearby wood block to mount her, with other thoughts in his imagination. He rode the horse across to Thomasyn and looked down at her.

"I shall take the path through the forest."

"Then I wish you a pleasant ride, sire."

"You could make it so, my lady."

She hesitated before saying, "You should know that I already have a suitor."

He laughed.

"Good God, girl, I'm not asking you to marry me!"

She flushed and had no answer to make.

"One of my father's serfs, no doubt?"

"Yes, of course."

"Of course. We all know our place in life."

He turned his horse.

"When will you next be skivvying up at the manor?"

"Whenever her ladyship sends for me."

"Very soon, then," he replied and set off at a trot, the feathers in his hat fluttering in the breeze, and many heads turned to see him leave.

However, somewhere in the depths of his heart, he was ashamed of himself for so humiliating her.

Thomasyn's mother hurried over as her daughter stood, gazing after him, her cheeks burning.

"What were you talking about all that time?"

"He wants to bed me, mother."

"Then you must let him."

Thomasyn turned to face her mother.

"Must I, indeed! What about Jethro? He loves me. I believe that Robert D'Avencourt wouldn't know what love was if it rose up and knocked him off his high horse!"

"Fie!" said her mother dismissively. "What can Jethro do for you except give you too many babes? Jethro can wait. That young man you have just sent away could make us all rich."

"And damaged," Thomasyn said with mature foresight.

Her mother was insistent. "Nonsense! You'll do what he wants. For the good of all of us. Your father works too hard, pleasing all and sundry up at the manor. He'll work himself into an early grave. Have you heard him coughing over that fire? Don't you love your father?"

Thomasyn did love her father, very much. "I'll think about it," she agreed reluctantly.

"You'll do more than that, my girl!" replied her mother. "I'll go and tell your father our fortunes are made."

"It's too soon," Thomasyn protested.

"It's not soon enough," her mother said and hurried into the forge.

CHAPTER 7

Meantime, Robert had urged his horse from a canter to a gallop. As he bent low over the animal's neck, avoiding the low hanging branches of the birch trees, he was swearing under his breath, then exclaimed out loud, "Curses on the whore! There's no other girl in the manor who refuses me!"

In his heart, though, Robert recognised that Thomasyn wasn't a whore – in fact, just the opposite – simply a peasant girl he had not been able to seduce – yet.

He simply wanted to be one conquest ahead of his older brothers, all of whom had noticed Thomasyn as she worked around the manor house. There was little enough he could achieve ahead of them, being the youngest, never likely to inherit any part of the estate unless they angered their father so much that he disinherited all four, which was very unlikely as they had so much to lose. Perhaps the plague would return and kill them all though, of course, it might kill him, too; there was always that possibility.

Indulging in these dark thoughts, which he did not honestly espouse as he was fond of his brothers, he was not concentrating on his progress. Rounding a bend between the trees at full gallop, in disbelief, he saw a horse and cart coming the other way. He jerked on the reins, shouting a warning, whereupon Pendragon whinnied in fright, reared up and threw him off her back.

Unable to control his flight through the air or where or how he landed, he hit the ground with such a force that it drove all the wind out of him and shook every bone in his body, probably breaking a few. He lay there, his right leg twisted beneath him, trying to recover his composure but not succeeding.

The cart horse had come to an abrupt halt and stood, quivering with fright. The driver immediately dropped the reins and leapt down from the cart.

Rendered speechless, Robert was unable to hurl at him the stream of invective swirling about in his head but, as the young man came nearer, he partially regained his voice and gave it full expression.

Ignoring the loud and venomous curses directed at him, the man apologised profusely and held out his hand. Robert took it roughly, tried to rise, slipped on leaves newly fallen, then fell back.

"I can't get up, you idiot, you dolt! I think you've broken every bone in my body!"

"*I've broken…?* You've only yourself to blame! Whatever were you thinking, riding through the trees at that speed? You could have killed us all! Do you want my help or shall I leave you lying there so you can make your own way back to the manor?"

Recognising his helplessness, Robert quietened.

"I'm sorry. The fall has shaken me up. Just give me time."

The girl had been soothing the cart horse, talking to him softly and stroking his muzzle, her mass of chestnut curls falling over her face.

"You, girl, bring my hat over here!"

He was used to giving orders, expecting to be obeyed, and this was the only way he could re-establish his authority after his utter humiliation.

She turned her head slightly, hesitated for a moment, then walked across to where his hat lay in the dirt and picked it up.

Offering it to him, she observed, "I regret, sire, that your horse trampled it and the feathers have snapped."

He took it from her without thanks and muttered, "Along with a great many of my bones, I suspect."

"I am very sorry if that is so, but until you stand, we shall not know for certain."

He began dusting the dirt off his hat by vigorously slapping it against his thigh, hiding his burning cheeks in so doing and giving himself time to regain some semblance of dignity in the face of her utter lack of respect.

Then something about her voice stirred a distant memory and he looked up, straight into those violet eyes, and felt a surge of excitement course through his body.

"In-gar-et?"

"You've remembered, sire?"

"I remember a little scrap of a girl with a tangle of hair, a grubby face and filthy feet." He took pleasure in regarding her ankles below her kirtle. "You now wear shoes, I see."

"And my hair is combed and my face is washed."

"A considerable improvement," he commented with amusement, quite forgetting his embarrassment of a moment ago. "You were six years old but you had the grace to curtsey to me."

"And you were ten, sire, and I have not lost the respect."

She dropped him a curtsey then and he laughed.

"And my name?"

"Robert, sire."

"And does the invitation to visit you in your – your –"

"Hovel?" she suggested.

"The invitation to visit you in your – cottage – Does that still stand?"

"It does, sire, if you will hold off your dogs so that I may visit you in the manor."

He clucked his tongue and shook his head. "I deeply apologise for my previous lack of manners, mistress."

"And I for my ignorance of the ways of the world, sire."

He held out his hand to Elis, who had been standing in the background, mouth open, listening to their conversation.

"Help me up, fellow."

Elis said nothing but held out his arm, which Robert D'Avencourt grabbed without looking at him, as he was still looking at Ingaret. He allowed himself to be hoisted to his feet or, more accurately, to one foot. Elis let go of him and he winced.

"Robert, you're hurt. Elis help him."

Elis stood his ground and did not move. Robert looked across to him.

"So, who is he, this fellow? Your brother? Your lover?"

"He's my friend," Ingaret said hurriedly before Elis could respond.

"Hmm."

Robert was again looking at her closely and she returned his inspection with an unwavering study of *his* eyes and *his* mouth. He wondered what she was thinking. As for him, he thought she was the most enchanting creature he had ever met. All thoughts of Thomasyn had flown out of his head. Those eyes! *If I live to be a hundred,* he thought, *I will never again look into such eyes!*

"Seems to me as though you're not going to be able to get yourself back to the manor," Elis observed, "so we had best take you there."

Robert understood that it had been Elis's intention to break the tension pulsating between Ingaret and himself. The fellow was obviously only too aware of the effect that Ingaret's eyes could have on a man, young as she was.

Elis hadn't finished.

"Ingaret, get up on the driving seat and take the reins and steady old Dobbin while I help our passenger onto the back of the cart and hitch up his horse to follow."

Friend! thought Robert. *He purposes more than friendship – making sure Ingaret and I have our backs to each other while she holds the reins and I sit here, legs dangling over the edge, unable to look at her. Still, I can't blame him. I'd do the same in his position.*

He winced again as they began their journey and the movement jolted his spine.

"Shall we deliver our flour first?" Ingaret asked.

"No." Elis was emphatic. "We'll drive to the manor and then I'll take you home."

So, he's not going to let me see where she lives, Robert deduced.

"My mother will be furious that I've been gone so long," Ingaret worried and Elis said that he didn't think she would mind when they told her where they had been.

25

Robert gave them a rueful look. *And my father's likely to strangle me when he finds out what's happened. I could have killed Pendragon. Hopefully, though, they'll get me back to the manor before the hunting party returns. I can make excuses for not joining the family at their meal and perhaps I'll feel better by morning.*

"Can't you make your nag go any faster?" he complained irritably.

"No, I can't," Elis rejoined. "I should have thought you'd had enough speed for one day!"

They arrived at the manor house an hour later. Elis drove the cart through a side arch in the thick wall, across the courtyard and to a door in the east wing, as instructed, then there were enough servants to help Robert from the cart and take care of Pendragon, who was limping slightly.

At the door, Robert, still hopping along on one foot and supported by Stephen and another servant, turned to express his appreciation to Elis and take another look at Ingaret.

"I won't forget," he said and was mortified to know that he meant it.

CHAPTER 8

Ingaret was right, her mother was furious when she eventually arrived home and she would have been beaten soundly with anything that could have been laid hands on if Elis had not intervened and explained about their detour to the manor.

Ingaret had begged him not to say anything about her previous meeting with Robert D'Avencourt so it was not mentioned. Jethro was about to ask her if their patient had remembered her but Ingaret sent him a warning look and he remained silent.

On the following day, the family was greatly surprised when Alice ran into the cottage gabbling that there was a gentleman on horseback outside their door asking whether Mistress Ingaret lived there.

"A gentleman?" asked Ingaret.

"Who is he?" demanded their mother, wiping her hands on her dirty apron.

"You'll find out," squeaked Alice in great excitement, "because he's getting off his horse."

A moment later he was knocking at the door. When Ingaret opened it, a young man in the blue livery of the manor was standing there, holding a brace of pheasants in his hand.

"Mistress Ingaret?"

"Yes, sir, that's me."

He held out the pheasants. Her mother came from behind her and took them from him with a nod of the head.

"Master Robert sent me," the young man explained. Ingaret was speechless. "I am to tell you that they've been hanging for several days so are ready to pluck."

"Ingaret, thank the gentleman!" her mother admonished her.

"Please thank your master, sir," said Ingaret. "We haven't eaten meat in weeks."

The young man raised his eyebrows as though he didn't believe her and said he would deliver that message.

"I didn't know he knew where I lived," Ingaret said as he turned to leave.

The manservant turned back and smiled. "You were not difficult to find," he said.

"But it is Elis who should be thanked – Elis Miller – because he took Master Robert home."

The man nodded. "Indeed, and I have just delivered a brace of pheasants to the mill. I bid you good afternoon, mistress."

With that, he turned again, mounted his horse and rode away.

"For once, you've done something useful, my girl," her mother told her. "Come and help me pluck and draw them. You, too, Alice."

"Ugh! They'll stink so!" Alice exclaimed.

"Then clip a peg on your nose, miss! I can't see you making such a fuss when we come to eat them!"

"Wasn't he handsome?" cooed Alice, changing the subject.

CHAPTER 9

Several days later, Ingaret arrived home with a basket full of clean, wet garments to find her parents arguing again.

"I need her here!" her mother hissed. "Take our Alice instead."

Alice was peeling and slicing potatoes for that evening's pottage. Never one to let an opportunity pass, she nodded vigorously.

"I'll go with you, Father!" she said, her light brown eyes bright with anticipation.

"Alice can go with me some other time," her father replied, just as acrimoniously, ignoring his daughter. "It's time Ingaret saw life outside the vill. Broaden her mind and it will help me."

"Broaden her mind?" repeated her mother scornfully. "Nothing will improve that girl! And what about me? I can't do without her."

"Yes you can!"

"No I can't!"

"You'll have to! She's coming with me!"

It was not like her father to champion her and oppose this woman so openly and it warmed Ingaret's heart.

They stopped shouting at each other when they noticed her in the doorway. She put the washing basket on the floor.

"You done all the washing?" her mother asked.

"Yes, all done."

"You've been gone long enough! Gossiping, I suppose."

"There were a lot of us at the river, it being such a fine day. Yes, we were chatting."

"Not telling the whole world our business, I hope."

"I told them that father is going to Fortchester for Lord D'Avencourt."

"What have you done to your hair?" Alice enquired.

"I took the chance to wash it," replied Ingaret, "and washed myself at the same time."

"Were any of the men around?" her mother demanded suspiciously.

"No, mother. I wouldn't have gone in the river if there had been."

Ingaret was surprised when her father again spoke up for her.

"My daughter's not what you're suggesting."

"Just because she's your daughter doesn't make her a saint!"

Alice came across to stroke her sister's curls, the rich chestnut quite unlike her own light brown, and raised strands to her nose to sniff it.

"Rosemary?"

"And rose petals. I'll wash yours, if you like."

"Would you? Before Elis calls tomorrow?"

"Ingaret won't be here tomorrow," her father interrupted them. "I said she's coming with me."

"To Fortchester?" asked Ingaret in disbelief. "You really are going to take me with you to Fortchester?"

"Yes, if you'd like to come."

"I'll go, if Ingaret doesn't want to," Alice interposed shrilly.

"You'll stay and help your mother. It won't hurt you to take over Ingaret's chores for three days."

"Three days!" Ingaret echoed, hardly able to believe what she was hearing.

"It'll take that long," her father said. "A day getting there, a day to do his lordship's business and a day to come home. We'll sleep in the cart."

"I don't know why you can't take Jethro with you. He'll be of more use loading and unloading those heavy fleeces," her mother said.

"Jethro can't be spared. He's too busy repairing the manor's gates and fences."

Ingaret left her mother complaining and went outside to spread the clean garments to dry on the grass, hoping they wouldn't be trampled by the pig or the chickens.

She was so excited at the prospect of the journey to Fortchester that she hardly slept all night and lay awake listening to the snuffles, snores and other noises made by the family during the hours of darkness.

It was still dark when Jethro arrived home just as they were setting off for the city. Her father had been to the manor already to load the cart, which was now full of unwashed, smelly fleeces for sale in the market at Fortchester.

"Jethro, his lordship wants you up at the manor," their father said. "Have something to eat then go up there straight away."

"You been down at the vill all night?" Ingaret asked him.

"None of your concern," said their father sternly. "A young man's got the right to sow his wild oats."

Jethro looked crestfallen. "None sown last night," he complained. "I slept all night in a hayrick."

"I thought you'd gone to see Thomasyn," said Ingaret.

"I did go to see Thomasyn but her mother wouldn't let her out of the cottage, don't know why. I don't think she wants me hanging around."

"Never mind, son. Plenty more wild flowers in the fields."

"Not for me," moaned Jethro gloomily.

"See you when we get back," their father said and they were off.

"Poor Jethro," empathised Ingaret. "I think he's really in love with Thomasyn."

"Is he that serious?"

"He could do worse, Father."

CHAPTER 10

The sky gradually lightened as they rode through the forest, dark grey shading through a hazy pink to a milky blue as the sun rose behind them.

The birds were enjoying their freedom after the busy seasons of nesting and bringing up their families and were singing lustily in the hedgerows.

"Isn't that a robin?" Ingaret asked her father, who could distinguish one happy chirruping bird song from another.

"Yes – and that is a blue tit."

"You know so much, Father."

Shambles, the horse pulling the cart, was faster than old Dobbin from the mill, but not much. It would take them all day to reach Fortchester, about twenty miles distant, taking into account the stops along the way to rest the horse and eat the bread and hardboiled eggs prepared by the cook at the manor.

The steady movement of the cart, the regular swishing of Shambles' tail, the contented calling of the wood pigeons and the physical closeness of her father next to her on the driving seat, his old woollen tunic smelling of woodsmoke, lulled Ingaret into a pensive mood.

He had never shown her any affection, had not even seemed to notice her throughout her fourteen years. Recently, though, he had begun to take her side when she provoked her mother's vicious tongue, which had surprised her and unnerved her not a little, because she was not used to it.

They had covered about a mile without talking when he said, almost to himself, "Jethro reminds me of me at his age."

Ingaret emerged slowly from her own thoughts to pay attention to what he was saying.

"Father?"

"I told him that there were more wild flowers in the field but there aren't, you know, if you've met the right girl. There is no one else."

Her father had never spoken of her mother before. Ingaret knew nothing about her and had wanted to know everything but was always too timid to ask.

He looked at her and smiled.

"You have always reminded me of her, Ingaret, more so as you've got older. I've tried to ignore it all these years but the likeness won't go away and I have to face up to the pain."

Ingaret was still. This was a father she had never known, a whisper of a father she had always dreamed about. A father who might love her.

31

"You have her smile, the way your eyes light up when you're happy – not that I see very much of that except sometimes when Elis calls. She had violet eyes too, dark violet, like yours."

He paused then added softly, as if the words caused him unutterable sorrow, "It wasn't your fault that you lived and she died. There was nothing you could have done about it – nothing any of us could have done about it – not the midwife, nor your grandmother, nor me. It happened. It wasn't your fault."

Ingaret didn't know what to say so said nothing. Her father had blamed her all these years. Was he sorry now for this burden he had laid on her young shoulders? Was he now admitting he had been wrong and was saying so?

His voice lightened. "We met at the fair, beneath the maypole. She was holding a violet ribbon – the colour of her eyes – and I had been given a blue one and there were other children holding different colours, and a small band was playing recorders and drums, and we had practised many times, but we all got tangled up. Everyone thought it was carelessness but it wasn't. I had noticed the girl with the chestnut curls and couldn't think of any other way to meet her." He laughed. "It disgraced us in front of the whole vill, and we were all in trouble afterwards, but it was worth it. There was no doubt in my mind that she was the girl I was going to spend my life with, no doubt at all."

They had passed the church some time ago and were now climbing towards the high road, where the going was easier in good weather. The ground fell away on either side of them and the undulating land stretched out to the horizons like a green and brown feather quilt that had been vigorously shaken up and had not quite yet settled down again.

"I was a firebrand in those days," her father recalled. "Always ready for a scrap. Picked fights for the joy of fighting. Never needed no solid reason. But your mother cured me of all that. I had her and Jethro to think about and then you were on the way. I was no use to her with black eyes and damaged hands. Must admit, though, that I still got out of control on occasions, especially if anyone threatened the family." He sighed. "She was so gentle. Long time ago now."

Ingaret's eyes blurred with tears as visions of her mother filled her imagination and the sorrow of loss filled her heart – her father's loss, and hers and Jethro's throughout their years of childhood.

She wanted to thank her father for confiding in her at last but she didn't know what to say and he seemed not to expect any response. She reached out and touched his arm then quickly withdrew her hand, but he grunted and that seemed sufficient for both of them.

They were now passing a trader with a couple of sacks on his back. The man called out a greeting and offered them trinkets, such as the necklaces made of sea shells he wore about his neck, but her father said they had no money.

"Then God be wi'ye," said the man and trudged on.

After travelling two or three hours, they stopped by a wayside stream to let Shambles drink and refresh themselves.

Her father said he would stretch his legs and walk a while. Ingaret took the reins and urged Shambles forward. She enjoyed being in charge of the big horse and cart with its valuable load.

After a couple of miles, her father climbed into the cart while it was still on the move and clambered over the fleeces, sending up a cloud of flies, and back onto the driving seat.

They were still travelling through open country but the folds in the landscape had risen to form gently rounded hills so that the road occasionally dropped them down into valleys with narrow winding rivers and tiny settlements.

As they drove through, people came out of their cottages to wave and try to sell them local beer or home-made meat or fruit pies, but her father shook his head and said they hoped to have money on the way home, when they would stop and buy.

As they drew nearer to the city, the traffic on the road increased. Merchants passed in carts and on foot and offered them skins and leather goods, fruit and vegetables, tin pans and pewter plates.

They had to move over to the side of the road when they were about five miles from the city, to make room for a carriage drawn by two black horses, its curtains pulled to hide the occupant.

That set her to thinking about the button she had found, which must have come from a lady's gown. She dug it up sometimes to once again enjoy its beauty, but always returned it to its hiding place in the earth by the roots of the old oak.

They breasted a rise and saw the ancient walls of Fortchester ahead of them. Ingaret clapped her hands delightedly. She had never before seen such a sight as those great walls and wished Jethro could be with them to share her excitement. Even her father's breathing had quickened. He had been to Fortchester before but once only.

"The Romans built the walls," he explained in answer to her question.

They passed through a narrow archway in the solid walls and entered the city.

Ingaret had never seen so many people all in one place at one time nor heard so much din. There was a drinking trough just inside the gateway and Shambles, ignoring the tug on the reins, made his way over to it and began to quench his thirst.

It gave Ingaret and her father time to look round. There were other horses at the trough, their owners calling greetings to each other or standing and waving arms and cursing a driver who had edged his way in.

On all sides were traders selling wares from the packs on their backs or from rickety stalls, their customers inspecting the quality of the goods or handing over coins. Stray dogs were scavenging among people's feet and getting kicked out of the way.

Ingaret found the sights, sounds and smells utterly overwhelming.

"Which way now?" she asked.

"We have to find the sheep market," her father replied, at last turning Shambles away from the trough. "We'll make for the centre of the city then I'll ask someone."

The streets were very narrow, the mud baked hard in the sun. Wooden-framed houses towered above them, some as high as four storeys, their tiled roofs almost touching the roofs of the houses opposite, crowding out the sky.

At ground level, more street sellers called out their wares and craftsmen competed with each other's sales patter. Some had balanced wooden boards across the tops of barrels to display their goods while others were using window shutters that were lowered during the day and raised at night for security.

Ingaret's stomach rumbled and she wrinkled her nose as she caught the aroma of fish and newly-baked bread. They passed a small side street where the pungent smell of urine rose from a vat in which a tanner was soaking animal hides to soften them. Further along, through an open door, Ingaret glimpsed a weaver bent over his loom while children played outside with mud pies.

Emerging from a side road, they found themselves in a large paved square and Ingaret gasped in awe at the sight of the great cathedral, glowing amber in the late afternoon sun. It stretched the whole length of the square, dominating and dwarfing the houses on the other three sides.

"Magnificent, isn't it?" asked her father. She could only nod in agreement.

"I'll take you inside tomorrow, once we finish our business."

He found space to leave horse and cart beneath the shade of a tree. There was a fountain in the centre of the square with a large basin surrounding it, full of clean water, and he went across to fill the bucket they had brought with them. He set the bucket down by Shambles' feet then hung a net of hay from one of the lower branches of the tree for the tired horse to munch.

"He'll be happy until we return," he said. "We'll find something to eat then come back to the cart to sleep."

By now, the cathedral bells were ringing for Vespers and the tradespeople were beginning to pack up their wares but Ingaret and her father had time to find the large market and buy bread, some sweet, juicy red apples, a lettuce, carrots and ale, and they returned to the cart in high spirits.

After their meal, they made themselves comfortable on woollen blankets on top of the fleeces and both were able to spend most of the night in sleep, in spite of the comings and goings through the square, the regular calls of the night watchman and the cathedral bells ringing at intervals, calling the monks to prayer.

CHAPTER 11

Dawn was breaking as they awakened, overlaying the grey sky with pale yellow. Already traders were putting up their stalls and awnings.

Ingaret stretched and lay there in a state of happy anticipation, listening to the unfamiliar noises of a waking city.

She had never been far from their vill before and was overawed by everything she saw. She was especially happy to be spending this time with her father, who was taking such good care of her.

They finished the leftovers from the previous evening's meal then relieved themselves in the shelter of the tree and washed as best they could in clean water collected in the bucket.

Having accomplished that, Ingaret's father enquired of a woman who was carrying a basket of cherries on her head where was the sheep market. She pointed to one of the streets and told them it was behind the fruit and vegetable market.

It was not difficult to find and Ingaret stayed in charge of the horse and cart while her father went to look for the agent with whom Lord D'Avencourt had arranged the sale of the fleeces. The pens were full of sheep and their noisy bleating deafened her. She decided she would be glad when it was time to leave.

Her father returned and took over the reins, guiding Shambles to an area where the fleeces could be unloaded, tallied and stacked. Ingaret saw money changing hands.

His lordship's business accomplished, her father took charge of the cart once more and they left the sheep market and returned to the same place in the square beneath the tree. He brought more water for Shambles and refilled the hay net.

By now, the sun was overhead and the masonry of the cathedral glowed golden. The bells began to clang their invitation to mid-day prayers.

"Would you like to join the monks for Sext, Ingaret?"

She nodded eagerly and they made their way across the square to the cathedral doors. There were three entrances and her father led her through the door to the right.

This entrance was not as large as the main entrance but was identical in design, the heavy wooden door surrounded by stone niches displaying statues of the saints, with elaborate stonework supporting flying angels and rising to a pointed arch overhead.

Ingaret and her father joined the crowd of worshippers making their way inside. They took their turn in dipping their fingers in the holy water kept in a marble basin just inside the door and each made the sign of the cross from forehead to chest, shoulder to shoulder. Ingaret's heart was beating fast as she gazed around her.

They were standing at the beginning of the central aisle, beneath the great west window, which was throwing pools of coloured light onto the floor about them. The aisle, or nave, was lined on each side by rows of grey marble columns, set in pairs, that directed her gaze up to the vaulted ceiling with its ornate and intricate pattern of fan shapes above the chandeliers.

At the far end of the nave stood the altar, its tapestry frontal a blaze of colour in reds, greens, blues, yellows and browns depicting the grain, fruits and flowers of the harvest.

Towering above the emaciated figure of Jesus hanging on a golden cross were three coloured glass windows. On the altar were vases of white lilies next to tall candles, their flames fluttering in the draughts.

Running parallel to the main aisle was a side aisle on right and left. Each side aisle offered privacy in tiny chapels protected by wrought iron partitions and doors, with myriads of votive candles clustered round statues of one of the saints or the blessed Virgin Mary or Jesus on the Cross.

Between the marble columns were several chantry chapels with ornate canopies above stone tombs upon which lay effigies of knights, their feet resting on lions, and their ladies, their feet on dogs, the animals offering protection in the afterlife. On the wall were plaques promising a various number of days' pardon for the priests who were being paid to say prayers for the souls of the departed and their family members.

A column of monks in their black habits was processing along the aisle to their right, heads bowed, on their way to the Choir stalls to recite the service of Sext.

Ingaret followed her father and the other worshippers over the blue and red floor tiles to join the monks and there they intoned the words of the service, as much as they were able, using the little Latin they knew. When they reached the reciting of the Virgin Mary's song, the Magnificat, altar boys swung smoking incense burners over the altar, the perfume rising like prayer to the throne of the Almighty.

It was then that Ingaret looked up at the coloured glass windows. The one on the left told the story of the birth of Jesus – and there were the angels, as her father had described them, with golden hair reaching to their shoulders, in the way Elis wore his hair. Ingaret smiled as she felt a warm glow steal over her. She wished Elis were here with them now and looked forward to telling him, when they arrived home, that she had seen his likeness in the beautiful cathedral windows.

The short service concluded, they stood as the monks left the Choir stalls, then followed the other worshippers into the Chancel. Here there were two arms reaching to left and right.

"I have been told," explained Noah, "that the whole building is in the form of a Cross. The nave runs front to back – where we came in and walked towards the altar – then these transepts, as they are called, form the arms of the Cross."

For a while they sauntered around the building, admiring every detail, overwhelmed by the beauty of stonework, windows (the glass was stained with colours, not painted, they were told), tapestries, carved wooden decorations, paintings, and figures of the saints and the holy family. Ingaret's father gave her a coin to drop in a collection box.

They eventually arrived back where they had started but in the opposite transept, and were interested to see a mason working at a trestle table. He was carefully rubbing a pumice stone over the neck and shoulders of a carved angel's head until they gleamed like pearl.

Ingaret's father asked if they were disturbing the young man. He looked up and grinned and replied that he certainly wasn't disturbed, but he couldn't answer for the angel. Ingaret laughed and asked whether he was the carver of that beautiful face with its crown of curls. The young mason smiled again, his teeth gleaming through the white dust that covered him from head to foot, making him appear supernatural, and said that no, the angel's head was his father's work.

He continued working as he answered her father's questions. The stone was limestone and, when he had finished smoothing then polishing the surface, he would be taking the head aloft to fix it in place high up in the roof.

Ingaret craned her neck to look upwards, to where he was indicating.

"You take all this care when no one will be able to see it?" she asked.

"God will see it, every day," he said. "Only the best is good enough in God's house. Any craftsman will tell you that."

"Do you work in the cathedral all year round?" her father asked. "There must be a lot to do here, a full-time job."

"I come and go as they need me. The urgency now is that everything is completed by the time the old century leaves us in six months' time. The cathedral will be at the centre of a great celebration."

"Then what will you do?" asked Noah.

"I will travel to wherever someone is willing to hire me, but work in the cathedral always takes precedence. If I failed here, there are many others waiting to take my place. There, that's done. Now I have to leave you for my other workplace – up there. Once the angel's head is in place, I have to repair some damage to a floral swag."

He placed the angel's head in a leather drawstring bag, drew the string and tied it firmly, then passed the loop over his head so that the bag hung at his side and left his hands free.

"Why not use the winch?" asked Ingaret's father, having noticed the arrangement of scaffolding with ropes dangling above their heads.

"I would if it was any heavier but the head of an angel is a light burden."

The young man crossed to the scaffolding then turned.

"Sir, would you and your daughter like to come up with me?"

Seeing her father hesitate, he added, "It's safe enough if you're careful, and there's nothing like the view from up there."

"I can well believe that."

"Oh, Father, may we?" asked Ingaret.

"I'll go ahead and you can climb up after her."

"Please, Father."

"Very well, but be careful, Ingaret."

"Is that your name? Ingaret? Mine's Roldan."

So saying, he turned again to the scaffolding, placed his foot on the first rung of the wooden ladder and began to climb to the first platform.

Ingaret's fourteen-year-old legs found no problem and she was not far behind the mason, climbing up each rickety ladder to the next platform, hand over hand, up and up and up. Her father was slower but not far behind them.

At last they reached the final platform. Roldan tied one of the fixed ropes round his waist then stepped out onto a wide ledge.

"Stay on the platform," he advised them, "and only look down if you won't feel giddy. Steady, now, hold on tightly to the rails."

Ingaret took a deep breath, gripped a wooden rail with both hands, and shut her eyes, only opening them when she felt she was ready.

"Ooh!" she said. "Father, do look. It's such a long way down. The people look like insects."

Her father also looked down, then up to the apex of the roof. The carved limestone around them was breathtaking.

"It's another world," he said.

"If I fell from here," mused his daughter, "I'd be smashed to pieces on the tiles below," and she drew back from the edge.

Meantime, Roldan was fixing the angel's head in place using a filler paste. Then he turned his attention to the floral swag that looped low along the wall and extended round the half-circle area of the altar, which Roldan called the apse.

"Kestrels sometimes build their nests up here and damage it," he explained, "but by the time I've finished with it, no one will be able to tell that it's been repaired."

As he caressed a lifelike white rose, a small piece broke off one of its leaves. Roldan bent to pick it up and held it out to Ingaret.

"A reminder of your day in the roof of Fortchester Cathedral," he said.

Ingaret had never been given a gift before, not by anyone, and was enchanted. She thanked him profusely and said she would treasure it. She knew exactly where she would keep it – with her button, hidden in the ground by the roots of the oak tree in the forest.

Again, the visitors marvelled at the exquisite work of flowers, leaves and fruit in the garland, noticing the seeds in the flower heads and veins in the leaves.

"It's time for us to go," stated Ingaret's father after they had watched Roldan for a while, "and leave you to your work."

"I'll come down with you," Roldan said. "I'm hungry."

Ingaret was pleased when her father invited the young mason to eat with them, an offer he accepted with alacrity.

Once on firm ground again, they walked outside into the sunshine. While her father went off to check on Shambles and buy food for their meal, Roldan crossed to the fountain to wash the limestone dust off his face and hands, while Ingaret found a place to sit on an area of grass on one side of the square.

Roldan was back first. He carried his dusty smock over one arm. His face was still glistening wet and his hair, which Ingaret could now see was a medium brown, was plastered to his scalp where he had plunged his head into the water in the fountain's basin. She noticed that it was beginning to dry in natural waves.

"My father thinks you are very young to be a master mason," she said as he sat down beside her.

"My father was a mason before me," Roldan explained, "and he taught me which chisels and hammers to use and how to employ them to good effect." His voice became animated. "As a very young child, I watched him birth the baby Jesus out of a block of limestone, like freeing him from his mother's womb. He told me he could hear the baby's cries as he chipped away at his limestone prison. I regret that I will never be as skillful as he was."

"Is he still alive?"

Roldan shook his head. "No, he fell," he said simply.

Ingaret did not know what to say but was saved from an embarrassing silence by a sudden noise from the other side of the square – shouts and whistles and catcalls. A crowd of men and a few women were gathering round a young man who was standing on an upturned wooden box. He was shouting to them and gesticulating and whatever he was saying was being met with a chorus of cheers and boos.

"What's going on?" Ingaret asked.

"It's the Yorkists," Roldan said. "They're often here, stirring up trouble."

"Who for?"

"Any Lancastrian families who live in these parts. Don't be anxious. They're not out to harm us ordinary folk."

Ingaret was happy to see her father approaching. He was carrying a bulky sack over his shoulder, which he set down before joining them on the grass.

"Don't look so anxious, daughter. They're blowing out a lot of hot air. Nothing to do with us."

"Aren't the D'Avencourt family Lancastrians?"

Her father looked at her in surprise.

"Where did you hear that?"

Ingaret recalled young Robert D'Avencourt announcing that fact when they first met in the forest but then she didn't understand what 'Lancastrian' meant and, anyway, had never said anything to her father about that meeting.

"I heard it somewhere," she explained lamely.

"You're right, they were and still are I expect, and some of his lordship's brothers fought at Bosworth when King Richard was killed."

"I've seen King Henry," said Roldan between mouthfuls of crusty bread. "He came to the cathedral shortly after he married Princess Elizabeth of York. They were visiting all the cathedrals. I was in the crowd."

"Is she pretty, the Queen?" asked Ingaret.

"Not particularly but I didn't get a good look, there were so many people – hundreds of them – and the King and Queen were surrounded by guards, some on horseback, some on foot, and Fortchester city officials and lords and ladies-in-waiting."

"What was she wearing?" persisted Ingaret.

"I don't know," replied Roldan, shrugging, "but it was all very splendid."

"More to the point, their marriage brought us peace," said Noah. "Lancastrian King Henry VII marrying a Yorkist princess – the white rose and the red rose – after they had been fighting for most of my life. Our king is no fool."

"What do you think happened to her two brothers," asked Roldan, "after they were sent to the Tower of London for safety?"

"No one knows that," replied Noah.

"If they turn up –"

"That is hardly likely after seventeen years."

"But if they did," persisted Roldan, "young Edward would become the rightful king, Edward the fifth, a Yorkist, and our Lancastrian King Henry with Elizabeth, the queen, their sister, would have to abdicate."

"No one seriously thinks they will put in an appearance now," said Noah, "and it is best not to speak of it. If they had been alive, their uncle Richard, their protector, would never have been made king, and he cannot now tell us the truth since he died at Bosworth. As I said, it is better not to guess. It could be considered treason to speak of it."

They enjoyed their meal together and found out a lot about each other. Roldan supported his mother and two sisters in a house on the outskirts of the city.

He asked the name of the vill where they lived and Ingaret explained that it was too small to have a name but they were serfs on the D'Avencourt manor.

The crowd of noisy protesters having dispersed, and their meal finished, Roldan was taken across the square to meet Shambles, then he said he must get back to work. However, he seemed reluctant to say goodbye and offered to show them round the city and take them to meet his mother, perhaps tomorrow, but Ingaret's father regretted that they would be on their way home early next morning.

He held out his hand to Roldan, who shook it firmly and expressed his pleasure at having met them. Noah smiled and turned to retrieve the net of hay and the bucket and unhitch Shambles from the tree.

Ingaret also held out her hand and the young mason took it gently and held on to it for a while before covering their grip with his other hand.

"It is my hope that we meet again, Ingaret," he said.

"Perhaps," she said, knowing that the likelihood was remote.

"I will remember the maiden with the violet eyes," he said, "and who knows? One day I may find you again in a block of limestone."

"And I will remember you, Roldan, every time I look at the gift you gave me."

"Ingaret, come!" her father called.

"Coming!" she called back, withdrew her hand and went over to climb onto the driving seat.

After a tour of the city and another night sleeping in the cart, they left early next morning for their drive home.

CHAPTER 12

It was late in the afternoon, three days after they had left, that they arrived back at the settlement. Ingaret knew that her mother would not show any interest in their visit to Fortchester, but she was aching to tell Jethro all she had seen, all that had happened to them, most of all the excitement of climbing up to the roof of the cathedral.

"I don't know where he is," her mother said when she asked. "Been out since yesterday evening."

Her father laid a pile of coins on the table. Gunnora scooped them up in her apron.

"That all there is?" she asked. "Where's the rest?"

"It's enough," her father replied. "We had to eat. I'm going up to the big house to take Shambles and the cart back and give his lordship his money for the fleeces."

"If you ask me, he's lucky you came home with it."

"And have you all thrown out of the cottage? The family was his ransom. He knew I'd come back."

"More fool you!" she exclaimed but, for the first time ever, Ingaret thought she actually looked pleased.

Ingaret left the cottage that night and slept outside on a bed of fallen leaves on the edge of the forest, not able to tolerate the sound of her father making love to her mother behind the curtain, or this substitute who posed as her mother. It seemed a betrayal of the girl he'd fallen in love with beneath the maypole.

Jethro did not come home all night and Ingaret guessed he was down in the village with Thomasyn.

In spite of a lack of sleep, she was awake and up at the usual time, knowing that her chores would not get done by themselves, and was very happy to collect water from the stream. She buried the tiny piece of limestone leaf, her gift from Roldan, by the side of the button before her young brother John arrived to carry the water back to the cottage.

Jethro finally came home from his work that evening, looking like a wild man from the forest. His dark hair was unkempt, his face ashen and his eyes were underlined with dark shadows.

"Jethro, whatever has happened to you?" she asked in alarm.

"I'm all right," he mumbled.

"Clearly you're not," Ingaret retorted.

"Are you ill?" demanded Gunnora. "We can't afford for you to be ill and not working."

"I'm well!" he replied irritably.

"It's nothing that a good meal and a night's sleep won't cure," their father said, but Jethro pushed his wooden plate away and would not eat but went outside again.

After their meal, their father also went out and the pair were sat on the wooden bench talking earnestly until the moon was high in the dark sky and a cold wind began swirling dead leaves about the yard.

"Do you know what's wrong?" Ingaret asked her mother.

"No idea but it's probably got something to do with that girl at the smithy," was her sour reply. "I hope the young fool hasn't got her in the family way and she's pushing him into marriage."

Jethro came in to sleep inside the cottage at the insistence of their father, but he was gone again long before the rest of the family were awake.

"What's wrong with the boy?" asked Gunnora. "At least it's saving me having to feed him."

"It's that girl," confirmed their father. "She's gone up to the manor."

"What's she doing up there?" asked Ingaret.

"Skivvying for her ladyship, so her mother says, but Jethro has heard talk."

"What talk, father?" Alice, as always, was greatly interested in tittle tattle.

"Just talk," repeated their father. "Alice, haven't you got jobs to do? If not, I'm sure I can find you something."

"She's got jobs," growled their mother. "Alice, clean out the ashes and lay the fire."

Alice pouted. "That's Ingaret's job."

"And now it's yours," answered Ingaret, her anxiety for Jethro sharpening her tone.

"What talk?" persisted their mother when Alice had stomped off to take the ashes to the ash heap.

"Jethro said he's heard that a horse and cart came for her, to take her to the big house."

"A horse and cart for a skivvy?" repeated Ingaret in disbelief. "*For a skivvy? Why didn't they let her walk up there?*"

"We'll know in time," Gunnora predicted. "The servants will talk. Servants always talk. Until then, we shall go on guessing…"

Each morning, Jethro went early to his work on the manor estate. Ingaret knew that he hoped to catch a glimpse of Thomasyn at a window, but he was always disappointed and came home each evening with a long face and drooping shoulders. He had showed no interest in Ingaret's visit to Fortchester and she did not bother him with her story.

However, she found in Alice a willing and interested listener who plied her with many questions, especially about the young master mason. The

44

only detail that Ingaret withheld was hiding the limestone chipping from the floral swag, the gift of that young mason.

Both girls were very glad to see Elis arrive at the cottage several days later to ask if there was any help he could give as he knew Jethro was busy at the manor and was not around during the day.

Their mother sent him into the forest to drag home by chains, with John's help, any logs he could find and they spent several hours journeying back and forth, fortified the while by a constant supply of home-made bread and ale.

He came to the cottage as often as he was able and on several occasions contrived to speak to Ingaret but Gunnora always called her away to carry out some chore or another. Ingaret wondered how her mother always seemed to know when they were alone, and if she really was a witch, until she caught Alice spying on them.

However, one evening, when Alice was fully occupied kneading dough for bread the next day, Elis took the opportunity to beckon Ingaret outside and they sat companionably together on the wooden bench.

"Oh, Elis, I've been dying to tell you all about Fortchester and the cathedral – and I saw you there, in the beautiful windows – the glass is stained, not painted – and I saw the angels, like father said, with their hair down to their shoulders, just like yours, the same colour, and I met Roldan – he is a master mason although he is so young – and he took us up into the roof and we looked down –" and she rambled on and on. "Elis, are you listening to me?"

"Did you miss me?" he asked. "I missed you."

"Oh, Elis, you would have so enjoyed it there. Yes, I did miss you." She touched his hand lightly. "I'm glad you're here."

They sat in a comfortable silence for a while then she asked, "Have you heard any news of Thomasyn? It is a strange circumstance."

"Not so strange," he murmured. "I understand it."

"Well, I don't," she said, "and nor does Jethro."

"I think he does," Elis answered, "and that's why he's in the state he's in."

The family was surprised one evening about two weeks later, when there was still no news of Thomasyn, to hear a knock on the door. Jethro went to open it and said the blacksmith's assistant was there, asking to see their father.

Noah went to the door then closed it behind him and they could hear the murmur of a conversation outside. When he returned, he looked very pleased about something.

"What?" asked Gunnora.

"He was here on behalf of the blacksmith," Noah replied. "John, you are being offered an apprenticeship. He is looking for a boy and wondered whether you would be interested. I said you would and you are to pay him a visit in the morning to see if he likes you."

"Will he be paid?" Gunnora asked.

"In kind – he is offering board and lodging and learning."

"Then you'd better give a good account of yourself," warned their mother, "or don't come home."

"I will, mother," said twelve-year-old John eagerly. Such a position would raise the standing of the family in the estimation of their neighbours as well as making life easier for all of them.

Neither Jethro nor his father earned a wage when working for Lord D'Avencourt. It was part of their duty to their lord, who gave them the cottage they lived in, the garden they planted and the land they worked to support themselves. He also provided their security, though his intervention was seldom required.

"One less mouth to feed, Noah," Gunnora calculated. "Has the blacksmith come into some money that he can suddenly afford to take on an apprentice?"

"It would seem so," he replied.

Jethro suddenly left the room, banging the cottage door after him.

Ingaret was beginning to understand why.

CHAPTER 13

Gunnora frequently sent Alice to the smithy to find out how John was faring. Her daughter's report was always that he was very happy there, enjoying the work and being well fed and "they seem to like him," she added.

Alice would linger in the vill, passing the time of day with anyone who would stop and chatter with her, always keeping her ears open for any gossip to take home.

After one visit, she announced that she had seen Thomasyn, who had come home to bring some pig's liver for her family.

"She was wearing a clean skirt and a bodice that laced up the front. When she caught me staring, she said one of Lady D'Avencourt's maids had passed it down to her."

When her mother did not respond to this piece of information, she continued, "She asked after Jethro."

"What did you say?" Ingaret enquired.

"I said he was all right. I didn't say how bad tempered he was lately. I said he worked up at the manor sometimes and she said she knew, she had seen him, but had not had the chance to go out and speak to him. She gave me a message for him."

"Which was?" asked their mother.

"She asked me to tell him to forget her. I told her he already had."

"You know that's not true," remonstrated Ingaret.

"But it's for the best," said their mother. "You did well, Alice."

CHAPTER 14

Winter was approaching and it hadn't rained for ten days. It was about the time of year Ingaret had been born. The exact date had not been recorded but Noah said they had put her mother in the ground at the time the leaves were falling.

A year had passed since her visit to Fortchester and Ingaret was now sixteen years old.

Nothing much had changed in the settlement and vill. There had been a few births, a few deaths and a few marriages but life had gone on in much the same way. John was very happy working at the smithy and was being given more and more responsibility, in spite of his young age.

Thomasyn had not been seen in the vill for a long time and Jethro no longer mentioned her. He sometimes spent time in the company of other girls but these friendships lasted weeks rather than months.

Alice was even more deeply in love with Elis but he had eyes for no one but Ingaret and most people, even Ingaret herself, assumed that they would marry one day, though she had not settled to the idea.

"But I want to see more of the world," she complained when he broached the subject one evening as they dawdled by the river bank. The water lulled her senses as it flowed swiftly and musically towards the mill race.

"What more is there to see?" he asked her.

"That's just it. I don't know."

"There *is* no more, not for the likes of us. My family loves you and we would live well at the mill and one day I will take over when my father gets too old. Ingaret, sweetheart, don't you love me? You will break my heart if you say 'No'."

"Yes, I do, Elis. There is no one else."

"Well, then. My mother says she will give us her wedding ring. Let me put it on your finger soon."

"One day, Elis, but not yet."

"I'll wait, though it's killing me. I'll wait."

"You always were my angel."

He turned on her then, his fists clenched.

"I'm *not* an angel, Ingaret, I'm a man and you're a young woman, a very beautiful one. We're both flesh and blood and I can't endure not having you for much longer!"

With that, he threw his arms round her and pulled her to himself and kissed her with such passion that he frightened her.

"Elis, no, don't. Let me go!"

But he wouldn't and pulled her to the ground.

She pleaded with him, "Elis, dear, not like this! Elis, please –"

Her pleading must have reached a part of him that lay deeper than his passion because he let go of her so suddenly that she fell back on the grass, banging her head on the hard earth.

She lay there for a moment, trying to regain her senses. She was trembling from the sudden onslaught of his passion and from the realisation of where it could have led. He was right! This Elis was not an angel. He was a man with a man's desires and she recognised that a fire inside her, which she had not known was there, had begun to rise to meet his.

He was standing over her, wiping his mouth with the back of his hand, then he reached down and helped her to her feet.

"Ingaret, I'm sorry, I'm so sorry!" he mumbled but then, without waiting for her response, turned and strode off, calling over his shoulder, "Actually, I'm not! Find your own way home!"

After that episode, he visited the cottage less frequently.

One evening, when she was getting the younger children ready for bed and was wondering where Alice was, she heard voices outside and went to investigate.

By the light of the harvest moon, now nearly full, she found Elis sitting with Alice on the bench. He had his arm round her waist and she was giggling.

Elis had heard the door open and looked over to where she stood, watching them, but she was unable to motivate her legs to turn and go back inside.

"Hello, Ingaret," he said, "Alice was just telling me about …" His explanation trailed away into silence.

Ingaret wanted to say something inconsequential but nothing came to mind.

"Sorry if we were making too much noise, Ingaret," Alice was saying, "when you were trying to get the children to bed. Elis and I have decided to go for a stroll down by the river. Isn't it a lovely night? There's almost a full moon so we'll be able to see what we're doing – I mean, we won't be falling in the river or anything like that."

Ingaret's legs suddenly jerked her into action. She turned immediately and went back into the cottage. The scene she had just witnessed had struck her like a hammer blow. Was she being like the proverbial dog in the manger, not giving Elis the answer he craved, but not wanting anyone else to take him from her? And her own sister? Silly young Alice?

Not so silly, she thought. Alice never missed an opportunity and she had been in love with Elis for years. But she, Ingaret, was also in love with him – wasn't she? Didn't her heart beat faster whenever she saw him approaching? Then why did she keep refusing to give him the answer he wanted above all else to hear? What more could he give her than his heart and his life? What more did she want? What else was there?

Unbidden, the melody of old Isaiah's folk song came back to her and, as she mechanically cleared away the meal they had eaten earlier in the evening, she began to sing the words in her head:

> *You shall of me have everything –*
> *Fine dresses, shoes, a golden ring –*
> *And we will marry in the Spring.*
> And there was more:
> *Your toes and fingers I'll bedeck*
> *And clasp fair jewels about thy neck…*

Ingaret remembered thinking when she was young, very young, that she would try to find a handsome young man who had the wealth to buy her pretty things. At the time – it was the day she had found the button – she had dreamed about Robert D'Avencourt, though even then her common sense told her that he was far beyond her reach and it would have to be someone else – but who was that 'someone else'? And where did love fit into this picture in her head?

> *And songs of Paradise I'll strum*
> *If thou wilt come, fair maiden – come.*

She went across to where her four youngest brothers and sisters – James, Megge, Henry and Lizzie – were tumbling about on their mattress. Gunnora was dozing by the fire, her feet stretched towards the flames.

"Tell us a story, Ingaret," the children chorused. "Yes, tell us a story!"

Ingaret was not in the mood for telling stories. "If I start it, you can finish it," she said. "There was once a very handsome prince who lived in a big castle…"

CHAPTER 15

She was only part way through describing the scene unfolding in her imagination when their father banged open the door. He had been outside, using the pit that was shared with the other ten families in the settlement, and was still pulling up his breeches.

"Strange, but I can smell smoke," he said. "Ingaret, come outside and tell me if you smell it, too."

Ingaret rose from her stool.

"Now, you finish the story for yourselves," she told the children, ignoring their protests, and followed her father out into the autumn evening.

There was no need for him to ask what she thought. A strong smell of smoke and a few grey wisps, dancing like ghosts in the moonlight, were being blown towards them on the evening breeze.

"Perhaps it's that last field of wheat that hasn't been harvested. It could have heated up and set itself alight, or someone's set fire to it," she suggested.

Her father sniffed the air again. "That's not the smell of burning grain," he said.

Gonnora joined them and she also took a deep breath which caused a fit of husky coughing. Their neighbours were also appearing at their doors, discussing the cause of the black smoke that lanterns revealed was beginning to billow above them.

"Do you think the forest is alight?" someone asked.

Then a yellow glow lit up the horizon, turning red as they watched it.

"I don't like the look of this," Noah said. "I'm going to find out what's on fire."

He was about to set off with several other men when they heard the pounding of hooves and a man on horseback galloped between them, narrowly missing one of the women.

"The manor's on fire!" he shouted. "All of you, get up there! Take buckets!" and he was gone, heading for the vill.

Without needing further bidding, everyone sped indoors to collect buckets and pans and lanterns and a crowd of men and a few women with their older children set off running in the direction of the manor.

"Gonnora, stay here with the little ones!" shouted Noah. "Ingaret, fetch the cooking pot and come with me!"

She ran indoors, grabbed the pot and joined her father outside, where she tipped out the small amount of uneaten pottage. He was carrying two buckets.

"Stay close," he said, "and run!"

As they headed towards the manor house, they were joined by their neighbours. An occasional rider overtook them and there were one or two carts that picked up people along the way, mostly the elderly, who were getting left behind.

They traversed the heathland and marsh and came to the river, streamed across the hump-backed bridge, then ran up the grassy slope to the archway in the wall through which Elis had driven his cart on the day of Robert's accident. Now, however, the archway had been widened as someone had demolished part of the wall to make more room for the crowd to get through.

Ingaret looked across to where the fire was consuming the east wing and, as she watched in horror, the roof collapsed, sending up a ball of flame and hot orange sparks in clouds.

They assembled two lines, one of people passing containers of water from the river to the house and the other returning the empties back to those standing in the river. Noah took his position at the head of the first line and was heaving water through what had been a window from bucket after pot, and pan after bucket.

More and more lines were forming, silhouetted against the light of the inferno, as people arrived from the vill. Ingaret passed utensils until her back was aching and she thought her arms were about to drop off.

The flames roared a steady background of deafening noise so that the shouts and orders from those in the lines were barely heard. A little black dog was running about, getting in everyone's way and squealing as several of the men kicked out at him.

Soon, however, the shouts died down as everyone got into the rhythm of passing utensils to the next person in the line, and no one spoke, their faces grim, so that all that could be heard above the roaring fire was the clanking of bucket handles.

"Take a break," her father said as Ingaret passed yet another bucket of water to him. "I think we're getting the fire under control but it will take a long time."

Thankfully, she dropped out of the line and moved away. Other exhausted people were also dropping out of the lines all the time and were being replaced by newcomers.

Servants began bringing out torches and pushing their long sticks into the ground. A torch was planted close by a solitary woman who was sitting on a chair well away from all the activity. Her face was lit by its flame and Ingaret saw, with concern, that she was crying. Everyone else was too busy to notice.

Ingaret made her way across the gravel and knelt by her side.

"My lady," she said, "I couldn't help noticing that you are crying. Is there anything I can do to help? Is this your home?"

The woman nodded and wiped her eyes with one of the wide sleeves that reached to her wrists. Her gown was of the finest silk and shimmered peacock colours in the flicker of the torch. However, her hair, rich silver, had escaped its hairpins and was as untidy as Ingaret guessed her own must be, and strands were plastered to her face where her cheeks were wet with tears. Ingaret knew there was only one person she could be.

"My Lady D'Avencourt?" she asked tremulously.

Her ladyship nodded. "Lady Margaret."

"They are containing the fire," Ingaret said sympathetically, not knowing whether this was true or not, "and that wing can be built again. I am sure Lord D'Avencourt will build it again."

"But my beautiful tapestries – and all the carpets and furniture in the solar – all gone. It can never be the same again – and I don't know where Lancaster is."

"Lancaster?"

"My spaniel. I haven't seen him."

"Is he a little black dog?"

"Yes. Have you seen him?"

"There was a little black dog with long ears running around the lines of people."

"That's him! Would you go and find him for me?"

"I'm not sure –"

Ingaret was distressed to see the lady sobbing again.

"All right, I'll try."

"Bless you, my dear."

"Mother?"

Ingaret looked up to find Robert's grimy and concerned face peering down at his mother.

"Robert, my dear. You're not hurt?"

"No, I'm fine. Who brought you out here? Where's Mistress Aldith?"

"She's gone to fetch me a shawl. Robert, dear, meet my new friend. She's going to find Lancaster for me."

Robert now looked down at Ingaret.

She looked up at him and, as always, he seemed unnerved by her glance as he stammered, "Ingaret? I didn't expect to see you here."

She stood. "I was in the lines but father told me to take a break."

"You know this peasant girl?" asked his mother in surprise.

"Yes, we bump into each other from time to time," he answered, recovering his composure, and grinned, pushing his hair out of his eyes and leaving a sooty streak across his forehead. Ingaret was struck again by how handsome this young man was.

"I find that very strange, Robert. However, she has been very kind to me and has seen Lancaster."

"I saw him, too," said her son. "I'll send one of the servants to find him. It's not for Ingaret to go looking for him."

He beckoned to a lad who was passing on his way back to the manor and despatched him on the errand.

"Robert, where are your father and brothers?"

"They're in the thick of it. I think we're getting it under control, mother, there's no need to fret. Stay here and you'll be safe. Ingaret, will you stay with her?" She nodded. "Please don't go till I get back."

"I'll stay with her," Ingaret promised as he disappeared into the smoke.

"So you know each other," her ladyship mused. "None of my sons, like their father, can see a pretty girl without at least finding out her name. Where did you meet?"

While Ingaret was telling her about their first meeting when she was very young, then the unfortunate accident in the forest two years ago, her ladyship's companion, Mistress Aldith, returned with a woollen shawl, which she gently put around her mistress's shoulders, then handed her a goblet of wine.

"Drink it, my lady, it will ease your throat after breathing in all this smoke and soot."

Lady D'Avencourt drank gratefully and handed back the empty goblet.

"Aldith, you must meet my little peasant friend here – Ingaret, isn't it?"

Ingaret and the other woman nodded to each other. She was in her fifties, Ingaret thought, well rounded from easy living, with eyes that were constantly surveying the scene about her. Ingaret guessed that there was little that she missed.

More and more torches were being brought out and pushed into the ground as the fire died down and people began to slacken the pace or drop out of the lines altogether.

They saw the young lad coming towards them, pulling a little black dog tied with a piece of rope, and soon it was on her ladyship's lap and licking her face and she was hugging it and laughing as she thanked the boy.

"He's my baby," she said as her companion removed him and placed him firmly on the ground and told him to sit.

"And he needs a wash," remarked Mistress Aldith. "I'll make sure someone takes him down to the river tomorrow."

"But the river's so cold," objected her mistress.

Now his lordship's seneschal was directing operations as trestle tables were brought out and erected on the gravel. He watched as servants struggled from the house with barrels, flagons and crates of wooden and pottery drinking vessels, which they were setting out on the tables in rows.

The seneschal shouted, "Ale all round!" and the shout was taken up by dozens of dry, dusty throats so that the invitation echoed and re-echoed around the courtyard.

Men who were starting to head for home returned and came over to the tables, bringing their wives and sons and daughters with them. They were tired, dishevelled and grimy and all smelt of smoke but they were in high spirits at the success of their efforts and were toasting each other as the foaming ale was poured and drunk, gallon after gallon.

Ingaret looked for her father. She saw Elis and Alice before she found him in the crowd, then noticed Jethro talking to Thomasyn in the distance. Her father waved but none of them, if they saw her, would come over to where her ladyship sat, and Ingaret began to feel like a leper. However, she stayed with Lady D'Avencourt, though Mistress Aldith said there was no more need.

"I promised master Robert that I would stay," she said in explanation.

She was surprised, though, at the realisation that she would rather be with her own people than in the rarified air of the nobility. Her thoughts were interrupted when Mistress Aldith sent a passing servant to bring the three of them some ale.

"In clean leather goblets," she insisted, "not one of the pots those people are drinking from."

"Those people," countered Ingaret, "have just saved your home from burning down!"

In that moment, she was deeply conscious of the gulf that separated their world from hers.

Then she saw Robert hurrying towards them.

"Good, you're still here," he said, with evident pleasure.

"I said I would stay," Ingaret retorted, a little more severely than she intended.

"I thought you would tire of waiting for me," he said, "but you haven't."

He smiled at her so radiantly that instantly she was glad she had stayed.

"Mother, I've seen father and the boys and they are not going to leave until they are sure the fire has burnt itself out, but it's too hot for them to get anywhere near the debris as yet. I've sent a servant over with ale for them."

"Thank you, dear."

"And father says Mistress Aldith is to take you to bed. They will stay up all night, if necessary, and you will be quite safe. He says they will all sleep in tomorrow and will not wish to be disturbed."

"Yes, dear, I understand. Aldith, I *am* tired."

"Then I will take you to your room, your ladyship."

"Don't leave me till I am asleep."

"I promise I won't, but you can't have Lancaster on the bed with you tonight, he's too filthy and smelly."

"I don't mind. Get one of the servants to find a collar for him and cut that dirty piece of rope off his neck."

"Yes, my lady."

"Good night, Robert, and good night, Ingaret. Thank you for your kindness."

Ingaret dropped a curtsey and said she was pleased to have been of service, and Lady D'Avencourt left on the arm of Mistress Aldith, who was promising her a drink of wine mixed with honey before she retired.

"And *I* thank you, Ingaret, for your kindness to my mother. She is – er – fragile and we have to take care of her."

"She was crying when I found her."

"She cries a lot. My father is sometimes very intolerant but her life with him has not been easy. But, enough of them. Come, walk with me a way. We keep meeting but as yet I have never had a proper conversation with you."

If she could have divined his thoughts, she would have known that conversation with her was his last intention. She had looked up at him as she knelt by his mother and the violet shade of her eyes, tonight with flickering flames reflected in them, prompted the violent reaction in his body he always experienced whenever he was near her.

"Sire, it will not be of any service to you to be seen talking to me. Your mother hinted at it."

Robert laughed. "Everyone looks the same this evening – thoroughly disreputable – and no one knows, or cares, who is who or where they come from. So come, walk with me."

He left their pots on the gravel for someone else to clear away and took her arm and she didn't resist. Then, with his arm round her waist, he led her in silence down to the river and, as it was so crowded with his father's workers returning to their cottages, he guided her further along the bank and stopped on the far side of a willow tree, where the drooping branches hid them from sight. Not that anyone was taking notice. They were all too tired and obviously had only one thing on their minds and that was getting home and to their beds.

"So, my Ingaret, what have you been doing with yourself since we last saw each other – apart from growing more beautiful by the hour?"

"I'm not your Ingaret, sire –"

"Oh, for heaven's sake, I've got a name as you well know, and it's Robert. So, whose are you? Are you going to marry that miller?"

"I don't know. He's asked me."

"Of course he has. He's no fool. Have you turned him down?"

Ingaret caught hold of a handful of swaying fronds and pressed them to her face, to cool herself down and hide her flushed cheeks.

Her reply was muffled. "Not exactly."

Robert gently pulled away the foliage.

"Has he made love to you yet?"

"No."

"Then he *is* a fool, after all."

"He tried."

"Of course he did."

"Robert, I should be getting home. They will be wondering where I am."

"Stay with me a little longer. I don't want to have to set fire to the manor house again to get you to myself."

"How did it happen – the fire? Do you know?"

"Not for sure but we guess it was the work of the Yorkists. There are a lot of them in the area. They won't accept that the war is over."

"I once saw a crowd of them in Fortchester."

"And very cleverly, you have drawn me away from my favourite subject – my lady Ingaret."

So saying, he put his arms about her and pulled her to him. She was surprised at the emotions churning in her mind and body. She wondered what it was like to be kissed by dashing Robert D'Avencourt and knew she was about to find out.

She was surprised at how much she enjoyed his kiss at first. His mouth was soft and moist and gentle for a few heartbeats but then he took breath and his kiss became more urgent as his lips pressed harder against hers and his hands slid down her back to press his fingers into her buttocks and pull her into him, and she felt his body convulse, revealing beyond doubt the extent of his desire.

But she was not so lost in his passion that she did not count the cost, and with a supreme effort, she pulled herself away from him.

"Robert, no!"

"Ingaret – I love you!"

"You only think you do but you don't! You can't! We can't!"

"Why not? What's to stop us loving each other?"

"This isn't all there is to love –"

He made a lunge for her but she sidestepped him.

"So do you think you're any better than Thomasyn?"

"What's Thomasyn got to do with anything? Doesn't she serve your mother?"

"By day, maybe, but by night there is someone else she services."

"Then go to Thomasyn if she gives you what you want!" she threw at him.

"Me?" He laughed harshly. "I don't get a look in."

So, thought Ingaret unhappily, the rumours the girls in the vill gossiped about Thomasyn were true.

"Your four brothers?" she asked, in disbelief at what she was hearing about the girl Jethro loved.

Robert did not reply but Ingaret had heard enough. She turned and fled.

"You don't know the half of it!" he called after her.

She didn't hear any more as the water swirling round her skirt was making too much noise and there was a pounding in her ears that deafened her and in her imagination all she could see was the gentle face of Lady Margaret D'Avencourt.

CHAPTER 16

When Ingaret looked back across the years, with the benefit of hindsight, she recognised it was the manor fire that set in motion wheels that ran away with the rest of her life.

Nothing in the east wing had been spared by the flames, which was the obvious outcome to anyone who witnessed the conflagration.

Plans for rebuilding began and Noah and Jethro kept the family informed of the steady progress being made.

First came a gang of men from the vill who took several days shovelling up the debris and taking the mess away in carts. Then work began on cleaning the whole manor, which had suffered greatly from the smoky effects of the fire.

Meanwhile, Lord D'Avencourt's bailiff despatched messengers backwards and forwards to Fortchester and one day a covered wagon arrived with a group of professional men with a chest containing measuring sticks, scrolls of vellum, pots of ink and quill pens that had to be continuously sharpened by their young apprentices, and they spent several days with his lordship and his eldest son, heir to the estate, poring over designs and plans and conducting endless discussions.

When the design of the new wing had been decided, quantities of pale red bricks that matched the existing building arrived from a kiln in the locality. Bricklayers from the city had been hired by the bailiff and they began cementing in row upon row of bricks in neat order, with two courses of blue-grey bricks running along a central horizontal line to create a different pattern and break up the regularity of the main walls.

Sometimes Ingaret and her father would take time to walk up to the manor to watch the work being carried out, slipping through the side arch, which had now been repaired.

Gradually a new east wing, on two floors, was taking shape. Spaces in the brickwork were left for a greater number of windows than previously, and it was not long before the walls were ready to take the shingle roof. Woodcutters had split shingles from wood taken from forest oaks, which Noah and Jethro had helped to fell.

A spell of rain prevented completion of the roof but, once the storms had passed, the roof went on.

In a mood of euphoria, Lord D'Avencourt invited to a feast all who had fought the fire and those who had helped construct the new extension.

Tables were once again set up in the courtyard and, as before, the ale flowed freely, but this time, from his kitchens were brought whole sides of venison, wild boar and mutton as well as pike and trout caught in the river, accompanied by bread in abundance.

The seneschal encouraged the manor's guests to help themselves to copious amounts before taking their bread trenchers with them to sit on the grassy slopes and enjoy his lordship's bounty – food such as they had never eaten before.

Ingaret learned of this from the rest of the family as she had declined to go with them, making the excuse that she was feeling sick and would not be able to eat a morsel.

In truth, she baulked at seeing Alice making a fool of Elis. He seldom called at the cottage these days, though Alice was often missing of an evening, and Ingaret guessed they were out roaming the heath and forest paths together.

Alice, now fourteen years of age, had left childhood behind. Her body had rounded and filled out and Ingaret had to admit that she was growing into a pretty young woman. Her lips were full and sensuous and her brown eyes held a challenge whenever she looked at Ingaret. Sometimes of an evening she unloosed her hair and then it would fall in light brown waves down her back, so long she could sit on it.

Ingaret sensed in her a subtle air of maturity and wondered whether she and Elis had lain together though, on the few occasions she and Elis were in each other's company, she felt his eyes following her and could not look at him, not wishing him to see the unbidden tears in hers.

Another reason for not attending the feast was that she didn't want to meet Robert again and risk a repetition of their last encounter. She had controlled Elis's outburst but did not have the upper hand with Robert. He was much too experienced and devious in his treatment of her and she was not sure that she could resist him for long. So she stayed away.

The settlement was eerily quiet now that everyone had left for the celebration. There was no need to prepare an evening meal and she was not sorry to have this time to herself. So she pulled her straw mattress over to the fire and lay down and was almost asleep when the door opened and Noah came in.

"Father!" she exclaimed, sitting up. "I didn't expect you home so early."

"I wouldn't be home but I've brought someone to see you, daughter – someone who hasn't stopped talking about you since I met him this evening. Come in, young man!"

Apprehensively, Ingaret got to her feet then gaped in astonishment.

"Roldan!" she exclaimed. "What are you doing here? I didn't expect ever to see you again!"

"I'll leave you two to catch up," her father said. "I'm missing a lot of ale-drinking time!" and he was gone.

Roldan came further into the room. He was nervously twisting his hat in his hands.

"I'm so pleased to see you Ingaret," he said, holding out his hand. "I've thought so much about you."

When she also stretched out her hand he took it and kissed it.

"Come and sit with me by the fire," she said, smiling, "and tell me why you're here and what you've been doing since we last met."

He sat beside her on the bed, his legs stretched towards the fire, and she sat with her legs curled up between them.

"I'm here," he explained, "by arrangement with Lord D'Avencourt's bailiff, at his lordship's request. Now that the new wing is finished, he has employed me to carry out work inside."

"What work?"

"To build fireplaces on both floors, decorated however her ladyship desires. Her first request is to have lions on each side of the hearths, supporting shields with the D'Avencourt coat of arms. I hope I am equal to the task, as his lordship says she is to have anything she wishes, no matter the cost."

"I'm so happy for you, Roldan."

"And I'm very happy to be here. Perhaps we will be able to see each other from time to time, as my work allows."

"I would like that. But it is such a coincidence. How did Lord D'Avencourt find you?"

"Through my work at the cathedral. I was told that your father recommended me to his lordship's bailiff, who came to inspect my skill."

"Father did?" asked Ingaret in surprise. "He never said."

"I am very grateful to him."

"And how long will you be here?"

"Many months. I'm not going to rush my work. I will carry out all the whims and wishes of my lady, and his lordship will have the best I can give him."

"He could not have chosen better," Ingaret assured him. "So where are you staying while you are here?"

"In the new wing. This is usual for me. I have brought tent and mattress. If the weather warms up, I will take the tent outside and sleep on the grass, though I doubt that will happen – it looks like snow is coming."

For a while they watched the fire in silence, the flames sending both their shadows dancing on the wattle and daub walls of the cottage. When Ingaret said she would put more logs on the embers, he said, "Let me," and crossed to the woodpile to collect a couple to throw on the fire.

Then he told her about the places he had visited and the work he had created in churches and manor houses and gardens since they last met.

"Gardens?" queried Ingaret.

"Above entrance pillars," he explained, "in fountains and on pedestals. Statuary – that's what I enjoy most because I can let my imagination roam free."

"And have you found me in one of your blocks of limestone?" Ingaret teased him. "You said you might."

He shook his head.

"No, not yet – but I will one day."

Then Ingaret told him about the fire that had burnt down the east wing, and they talked of the crowd of Yorkists they had seen in the cathedral square, and the time passed quickly.

So it was with some surprise that they were still talking together when the family came home. Noah introduced Roldan and everyone seemed pleased to meet him and he to meet them.

Finally, he took his leave and said he hoped to see them again, and Noah said he must come to visit whenever he pleased.

Alice came home later than the rest of the family and was told about their visitor. Ingaret knew that an account of this new friend would go straight back to Elis and couldn't make up her mind whether she was pleased or sorry.

However, whatever she felt for Elis, she looked forward to seeing Roldan again and hoped it would not be too long before he found his way back to the cottage.

CHAPTER 17

He appeared again two days later, towards the end of the afternoon.

"I have agreed two designs with Lady D'Avencourt," he told Ingaret excitedly as he got in her way while she was feeding the chickens, "and I begin work on the first floor fireplace as soon as the blocks of limestone arrive. Would you like to see my plans?"

Ingaret said she would, and they sat together on the bench in the yard so he could spread out a scroll of vellum and show her the fireplaces he had drawn there.

"I see you have given her ladyship the lions she asked for, holding the shields bearing the D'Avenourt coat of arms," Ingaret observed.

"As part of the jambs – and much more," said Roldan. "See the foliate corbels –"

"Corbels?" she queried. "What are they?"

"The supports for the mantelpieces. And the surrounds are decorated with swags of fruit and flowers, and his lordship's seal is engraved on the hearthstones. And see here, where I have left a space in the hood, which will reach the ceiling. Her ladyship has asked for a carved likeness of the family at ease before a fireplace that is a copy of the one I have built. I will have to design that later. It will not be easy." He hesitated then added, "I want to please her. I want to see her smile. She always looks so sad."

"I met her," Ingaret said, "while the fire was raging. She was crying and I thought it was because of the fire."

"I think she has much to endure," he mused, then shrugged, "but the gossip has nothing to do with me. I am here to build fireplaces and to finish them before the Christmas season is upon us."

"His lordship is so fortunate to have found you," said Ingaret. "They are such beautiful designs."

He carefully rolled up the vellum and put it away in his satchel then took her hand.

"And I have been fortunate to find such a beautiful living and breathing design," he said.

"But you haven't yet," she reminded him, laughing and withdrawing her hand. "I'm still frozen in a limestone block somewhere, crying to be set free – you said so yourself."

"It's true," he said, standing and looking down at her. "Meantime, I must get back to the manor or I will be scolded by cook because my meal has cooled. Do you need help in shooshing the chickens into the hen house for the night?"

"No, thanks, I can manage that myself."

"I would like to take you up to the manor as soon as I have something of my work to show you," he said, retrieving his hat and preparing to leave. "Will you come?"

"Of course I will."

Hesitantly, he took her hand again and Ingaret thought he was going to kiss her but, hearing a movement, both turned, embarrassed to have been found standing so close to each other.

"I can't see anyone," whispered Ingaret.

"Neither can I, but somebody's there."

Roldan held her hand tightly while they both continued to stare into the gathering shadows. Then there was a faint and stifled moan.

"Who's there?" called Roldan. "Come out so we can see you."

A figure dressed all in black with a veil hiding her face came forward two steps.

"Ingaret –" said the figure.

"Yes, I'm Ingaret," she answered. "You obviously know me but I won't know who you are unless you show us your face."

The figure did not move.

"What do you want?" Ingaret asked.

"Is Jethro at home?"

Ingaret thought she recognised the voice, although the person spoke very quietly and apprehensively.

"Jethro's out," Ingaret informed her. She was going to add more but thought better of it. "What do you want with my brother?"

"I – he – I just want to talk to him. I mean no harm."

"Thomasyn, is that you?" Ingaret asked and, feeling no friendship towards her, added harshly, "He's out walking with the girl from the chandler's," thinking that what was good for the goose was acceptable for the gander. "You've no business with Jethro. I don't even think I'll tell him you called."

Then Thomasyn moaned and sank to her knees and began to sob. Ingaret was at a loss to know what to do but let go of Roldan's hand and was about to cross to her when it so happened that Jethro walked into the yard.

"What's going on?" he asked. The girl was now holding her stomach and rocking backwards and forwards on her knees. "Who is it?" he asked his sister.

"It's Thomasyn."

The disturbance had brought Gunnora, Alice and the children to the door and their neighbour's door also opened.

"What's going on?" Gunnora wanted to know. "Ingaret – Jethro – who's making all the noise?"

"It's all right, mother, Jethro will deal with it," Ingaret said quickly. "Take the children inside. It's nothing he can't deal with."

Then Noah was standing behind Gunnora.

"Jethro –" Gunnora began, but Ingaret ushered the family inside, with difficulty, then pulled Roldan after her and shut the door.

"If that was Thomasyn, I'll not have that girl in my house," Gunnora ranted. "From what I've heard about her – and her mother's no better, sending her up to the manor to work – what work, I'd like to know. In my day, sweeping and washing floors was never paid for with bolts of cloth and legs of mutton!"

No one seemed to have noticed Roldan until Ingaret brought him forward, when Noah apologised for the rumpus, and Roldan said they shouldn't be embarrassed on his behalf and he was happy to meet them all again.

"Though I should be leaving," he said but was persuaded to stay and eat with them.

Now all was quiet outside. They ate their meal in silence and the younger children had been put to bed and were asleep before Jethro returned. His face was haggard and his dark hair looked as though he had been running his hands through it for the last hour.

Without uttering a word, he walked over to his bed and gathered up the coverings, then stood as if wanting to give some explanation but not knowing what to say.

"Well, son?" asked Noah. "What's all this upset about?"

"Father, may I speak to you outside?"

Noah nodded and they went out into the yard together, Jethro distractedly trailing his bed covers.

It was some time before Noah returned. He pulled up a stool and joined the others by the fire.

"Well?" asked Gunnora.

"It's not good," he said, "but he's made up his mind and nothing I can say will change it."

"Where is he?" demanded Gunnora.

"He's gone."

"Gone where?" asked Ingaret.

"To Fortchester."

Gunnora, Ingaret and Alice all spoke at once but he held up his hand for silence and they were quiet.

"You'll waken the children," he warned, "and the fewer ears that hear this the better. Roldan –"

"I will leave if you wish, but nothing you say will go any further, I swear it."

"Husband, you're not making sense," complained Gunnora. "Jethro is bound to Lord D'Avencourt. He can't go anywhere. Tell us plainly."

So Noah told them. "The girl *was* Thomasyn. She's four months with child and has been dismissed by the bailiff."

"What?" demanded Gunnora. "You mean that your dolt of a son is running away with a girl whose baby is plainly not his? He should send her home!"

"She went home and her mother threw her out. They're making for the high road. They intend to sleep in the forest tonight and start walking in the morning, and hope someone will pick them up."

"How stupid he is," said Gunnora, "going away with a girl like that and expecting to support her and her bastard child. Which of those boys is the father – I suppose she doesn't know?"

Noah didn't answer. Ingaret felt a pain in the pit of her stomach then remembered that Robert had said he wasn't having anything to do with Thomasyn. 'I don't get a look in' were his exact words, and she believed him. So the baby wasn't his.

"Does she know?" asked Alice, intrigued.

"She knows," said Noah.

"Lord D'Avencourt will send his bailiff after him to bring him back!" declared Gunnora. "Then we shall all be in trouble! We could be thrown out. Has he thought of that? How could he do this to us?"

"He loves her," said Ingaret simply. Gunnora snorted unsympathetically.

"I doubt that his lordship will find him in the city," said Noah, "if they get that far. Though I wonder whether he will even look for them."

"And why should that be, may I ask?" demanded Gunnora. "Of course he'll look for them! As long as they're found within a year and a day, he can bring them back – in chains if need be."

Again Noah said nothing.

"Father?" Ingaret enquired. "Mother's right."

"Of course I am," said Gunnora, "and I don't need you to tell him so, girl."

Still Noah remained silent.

"Husband, have you nothing to say?"

Finally, he spoke. "You may as well know the truth. It's his lordship's bastard. I guess he will be glad that she has gone."

The three women stared at him.

"Roldan, have you heard any gossip?" Noah asked him.

Roldan looked very uncomfortable. "I haven't been here long but I have heard something of the sort, though I didn't know which of her ladyship's servants they were talking about."

Gunnora said slowly, "That puts a different light on the matter. If that baby is Lord D'Avencourt's, he's part of that family, a noble family. Jethro may not be so stupid, after all."

"His lordship will never acknowledge the baby as his," said Noah, stirring a log with his foot. "Of course he won't."

"But we'll know different," said Gunnora.

"If you can believe what Thomasyn says," suggested Alice.

"Oh, I believe her," said Ingaret, "and I don't suppose she had any say in the matter. Father, I have an idea to help them get away."

"Nonsense!" exclaimed Gunnora.

"Let her have her say, wife!" Noah admonished her, and she remained quiet while Ingaret outlined her plan.

"I could go to the mill and ask to borrow Dobbin and the cart. Of course, I will have to tell Elis why I need it. There is time for me to overtake Jethro and Thomasyn – they won't have got very far – and Jethro could drive us to Fortchester. If I slept in the cart during the night, I could bring the cart back tomorrow. As you know, I can handle old Dobbin."

"What if he needs his horse and cart tomorrow?" asked Alice. "Elis is not going to beg his father for this favour just because it's you asking, Ingaret. It's all over between you and Elis now!"

Her sister flushed. "I think Elis will listen to me because Jethro is his friend."

"Ingaret, you shouldn't drive all that way back from Fortchester on your own," Roldan objected. "Let me go instead."

"If anyone goes, it should be me," interrupted Noah, "but I would be missed, and so would you, Roldan, but thank you for the offer. If we decide to do this, it will have to be Ingaret who brings the cart back."

He turned to her. "But I'll not have you going alone to the mill. I'll go with you, daughter, and speak to Elis's father and, if he agrees, I will drive us both to look for them. Once we find them, I'll walk home from wherever that is."

"Then let's go now, Father. Roldan, you must return to the manor and Alice, please shut the chickens up for the night."

"Why me?" sulked Alice.

"Because there is no one else to do it," Ingaret said, fetching her shawl from her bed.

"And don't make a noise about it," Gunnora said. "We don't want the neighbours suspecting anything."

CHAPTER 18

"So how will you deal with Lord D'Avencourt, Father?" Ingaret was beside him on the driving seat of the cart as they left the mill and made for the high road. "He will have to be told that Jethro has gone. Won't that get *you* into trouble?"

"I think not, as things stand," replied her father, "but I will have to tread carefully."

They agreed that everyone should carry on as normally as possible. However, he would request to speak to the seneschal, with whom he had a nodding acquaintance, and ask him to take the message of Jethro's absconding to his lordship. Men would be sent out to look for him and, as Thomasyn would also be missing, some lie would have to be told to her ladyship.

They drove on in silence, the sides of the path lit by the lantern that Ingaret was holding above her head, both of them peering to right and left.

They had not got as far as the high road when she thought she saw a movement ahead of them, though there was nothing to be seen by the time they reached the spot. Noah reined Dobbin in.

"Jethro!" Ingaret called. "It's Father and me! We've come to take you to Fortchester!"

She had to call two or three times before a figure scrambled up the embankment from the ditch.

"Jethro!" Ingaret called again and he approached the cart.

"Is that Father with you?" he asked suspiciously.

"Son, we've brought you the miller's cart. Thomasyn shouldn't be walking all that way in her condition."

"We're here to help you," Ingaret said again. "Where's Thomasyn?"

"I'm here," a voice said quietly and her tired face appeared above the edge of the ditch.

"Help her into the cart, son," said Noah, "and take the reins. I will walk home. Ingaret will bring the cart back tomorrow."

Jethro could not thank them enough and soon he was on the driver's seat and both women were curled up on the floor of the cart between coverings brought by Ingaret.

"Drive carefully," Noah said. "Send us word if you can, to let us know how you are faring. Off with you now. Ingaret, I'll see you tomorrow some time."

Jethro bent down to clasp his father's hands, then took the reins, and they moved off at Dobbin's measured pace.

Jethro drove carefully but there were times when he could not avoid the cart's wheels bumping over deep ruts in the highway. Soon after they set off, Thomasyn crawled across Ingaret's legs and, kneeling up and clutching the top slat, was violently sick over the side of the cart.

Ingaret had thought to bring a leather flask of water filled at the mill race and now put it to Thomasyn's lips then cradled the girl's head in her lap until she fell asleep. Ingaret was then able to sleep herself, waking only occasionally, and the remainder of the journey passed without event.

As they neared the city, Jethro reined in Dobbin and the cart came to a stop, which woke both women. Dawn was creeping across the sky behind them.

"We'll walk from here," said Jethro and jumped down from the driving seat. He unfastened the back of the cart and helped the women climb down.

"I cannot tell you how grateful we are," said Thomasyn, hugging Ingaret then accepting Jethro's embrace.

"Yes, sister," said Jethro. "We've been through some adventures together, haven't we? But none like this. I'll reverse the cart for you."

This took a while longer than expected as Dobbin wasn't the cleverest of horses and appeared not to want to go home just yet, but eventually Jethro got him and the cart facing in the opposite direction.

"Do take care of yourself," Ingaret said, in tears as she hugged him. "Send us a message if you can. Good luck with everything and take care of the baby. We'll meet again one day, soon I hope."

"Soon," repeated Jethro. "We'll watch you go."

They stood and watched until Ingaret turned for a last wave and was lost to sight in the distance.

CHAPTER 19

The return journey was without incident. Ingaret had muffled herself in the bed coverings she had brought with her and no one she passed would have guessed that the hooded figure driving the cart pulled by an elderly horse was a young woman.

She returned the cart to the mill and Elis insisted on driving her home. He did not go as far as their cottage but dropped her off nearby. Ingaret said nothing about his escorting her home when she faced the many questions of Gunnora and Alice.

"There is nothing to tell," she said. "They are safely hidden in the city and I am safely home. Not a word to anyone. No one must know. We will all carry on as normally. We don't want to attract attention; it will only cause trouble."

"Jethro must love her very much," mused Alice, a faraway look in her eyes. "Almost as much as Elis and I love each other. We're going to be married one day."

"Is that so, young lady?" asked her mother. "Is that your idea or his?"

"It's both our ideas. He's sort of asked me," said Alice, "and when he does, I shall bring him to speak to father. Of course, he won't be able to afford a ring but that doesn't matter."

Ingaret noticed that Alice had not mentioned his mother's wedding ring, which he had promised Ingaret if she accepted him.

"Whoever I marry will be able to afford a ring," she countered, the pain in her heart making her words cruel and dismissive.

"So who do you know who is rich enough to buy you a ring?" Alice asked. "If you have all these impossible dreams, sister, you're never going to find a husband."

Ingaret wondered if that were true, but was it herself or Alice who was dreaming the impossible? She was talking about marriage to Elis but Ingaret had not been unaware of the way he looked at her both yesterday evening and again today when he drove her home. She longed for the easy friendship she had had with him when they were children, but those times were long past, and here was Alice talking about marrying him.

Noah arrived home that evening, having spoken to the seneschal. Lord D'Avencourt had asked to speak to him personally. Noah had told him that Jethro had surprised them by saying he was running away with one of the servants from the manor. They had begged him not to be so foolish but he would not listen to reason and had gone, they did not know where. His lordship had asked many questions but Noah had professed ignorance of any details. His lordship had informed him that men would be sent to find the couple and bring them back, when both would be severely punished. Noah had replied that it was what they both deserved and finally had been sent back to his duties.

After that, they heard no more.

Neither did Ingaret hear any more from Roldan. Two weeks went by and still no visit from him. She wondered whether he did not wish to be involved in the unsavoury situation in which the family had found itself; whether the favour of Lord D'Avencourt was too fragile to jeopardise.

Another two weeks went by and still no news. She asked her father if Roldan was still working on building the fireplaces and her father said her ladyship kept him very busy with extra work in the manor house and gardens.

Then one afternoon, he appeared unexpectedly at the front door of the cottage, in the height of a snowstorm. He beamed when he saw Ingaret and she felt herself beaming back at him.

"Roldan! I thought you had forgotten me!" she exclaimed. "Come inside, out of the cold."

"How could you think that?" he reproached her, stamping his feet to rid his shoes of snow and shaking flakes from his hat. "I've been so busy but my work here has finished now and I shall be leaving soon to return to Fortchester."

The smile faded from her face. "You're leaving us?" she repeated.

"Quite soon," he affirmed, nodding. "But I couldn't go without taking you up to the manor and showing you my drawings come to life. Will you come?"

"I have chores to do here. Mother, may I go if I promise to finish the mending when I come back?"

"I suppose so, if you must," grumbled Gunnora, "but that mending needs to be done if you stay up all night."

"It will be," Ingaret replied happily and went to fetch her shawl and to tie sacking round her shoes.

"If you're late coming home, I won't do the mending for you!" Alice announced.

"I won't be late. I'll be home in time," Ingaret stated and followed Roldan into the yard then stopped in astonishment. Waiting there very patiently in the snow was a brown and white pony between the shafts of a small cart. She turned to Roldan in surprise.

"Meet Patches," he said, laughing.

"Whose is he?" she asked.

"He's mine," Roldan answered. "I walked here from Fortchester but was determined I wasn't going to walk back." He added, "His lordship has paid me well."

71

Ingaret crossed to the pony and stroked his muzzle. His fringe and mane and tail were white.

"Hop up, my lady," laughed Roldan and helped her into the cart, wiping dry with a cloth a space for her on the bench. "I would not have you walking far in this weather."

Fortunately, the snow had stopped falling by the time they reached the manor and the sun had come out from behind the dark clouds. Roldan helped Ingaret from the cart and they entered the new wing.

Men were standing on wooden platforms built on scaffolding in order to plaster the ceiling of the downstairs solar.

Roldan took Ingaret across to the fireplace and she saw, indeed, that the designs in his imagination had been brought to life in the soft grey colour of the stone. There were the lions and the coat of arms, the fruit and flowers, and Lord D'Avencourt's seal engraved in the hearthstones, and an engraving on the hood of the seven members of the D'Avencourt family seated round a fireplace that was a replica of the original.

Ingaret was speechless with admiration.

"Come and see the fireplace in the sleeping room upstairs," he said and led her up a staircase to the room above the solar, where his second design had been translated into limestone, this time in a slightly bluer shade.

The ceiling here had already been ornately plastered and the floor tiles laid in patterns of pale blue and white.

"Her ladyship must be so pleased with your work, Roldan."

"She is," he beamed.

He looked out of the window, which was fully glazed.

"The sun is shining," he said. "Come with me now into the rose garden."

Ingaret was intrigued.

"Why the garden?"

"Because I have been working out there as well. My lady gave me a very special commission to carry out in her rose garden. It has taken me a long time but it was finished this morning. Come!"

Ingaret followed him from the door in the new wing to an archway in a dark green hedge, through a tall black metal gate and so into the rose garden, where there were still a few straggling flowers surviving the winter.

The rose beds were laid out in a circle with paths between them, at the convergence of which, surrounded by a black shallow basin of snow melt, was an object covered by a large cloth.

"Apart from its black colour, the basin is quite different from the limestone of the fireplaces," Ingaret commented.

"That's because it's marble," Roldan replied, "as is this!"

So saying, he reached up and whipped off the cover and Ingaret found herself staring at the figure of a young girl seated on a pedestal, her legs curled up beside her beneath her gown. Her colouring was all black with a soft grey vein running throughout, and the figure was gleaming in the sunshine.

Ingaret walked round the outside of the basin that prevented any admirer from getting too near the sculpture, until she came face to face with the young girl. Her curls fell to her shoulders and her gown, in softly flowing folds, had slipped from one shoulder to reveal a glimpse of the swelling of one breast.

Ingaret gasped. "It's – it's –" she stammered.

"Yes, it's you," said Roldan. "I said I would find you one day and there you were in a block of black marble. I just had to let you out."

"But I'm not as beautiful as she is," protested Ingaret.

"Oh, but you are," countered Roldan, "at least to me. See, I have remembered exactly your mouth and nose – and, of course, those eyes."

"I don't know what to say," murmured Ingaret. "Roldan, you are a magician. I don't deserve this."

He took hold of her hand. "I think you do." He paused, then said, "Ingaret, when I return to Fortchester, come with me."

"Go with you?" she repeated.

"Yes. You've nothing here worth staying for. Come with me."

He went down on one knee in the snow.

"I'm asking you to marry me. Will you let me speak to your father this evening? I will be leaving in a day or two. My darling, please give me leave to go and speak to your father tonight."

"Please get up, Roldan, or your knee will freeze and you won't be going anywhere and, yes, I will tell my father that you are coming to speak to him tonight."

Roldan stood and took her in his arms.

"Does that mean you're saying 'Yes' to my proposal?"

"Yes, I think it does."

Their kiss was interrupted by a discreet cough behind them and they turned to find Mistress Aldith watching them.

"Yes, my lady?" asked Roldan, releasing Ingaret but not letting go of her entirely.

"I am sorry to disturb you, master mason, but her ladyship has asked me to take you to her."

"Of course," he said and let Ingaret go. He retrieved the cloth and threw it over the statue again. "We are unveiling it officially tomorrow," he explained to Ingaret, "and I expect her ladyship wishes to talk to me about the informal ceremony. My dear, wait for me in the new wing and I will drive you home as soon as her ladyship has dismissed me. Lead the way, Mistress Aldith."

Ingaret watched them go then turned back to the statue, now hidden again beneath the cloth.

"Well," she said to her black marble self beneath the cover, "life is full of surprises. It seems that I am engaged to be married. Well!"

Well, indeed! She had said 'Yes' with little thought. That Roldan was deeply in love with her, she had no doubt. That he would always take care of her, she had no doubt of that, either. He would take her to the heartbeat of a city, to its strange sights and sounds and smells and its people. Her imagination raced ahead. She would bear their children in their own home – something more than a dilapidated cottage. Above all, she would be escaping life here, no longer a serf in a long line of serfs stretching back into forever, but respected as the wife of a man of some standing in the eyes of cathedral and community. Yes, there could be no doubt that her decision had been the right one… but then she thought of Elis. Elis, whom she had always loved. But what could Elis offer her? Only more of what she had already and it would never be enough, she knew that, and her nagging dissatisfaction and resentment would destroy them both, and she cared about him too much to drag him through all that. She had to let him go for his own sake.

Her reverie was broken by the sound of heavy footsteps crunching through the snow on the path behind her and, when she turned, she was confused and not a little apprehensive to see Robert D'Avencourt approaching with a determined look on his face that did not bode well.

"Robert!" she exclaimed. "How long have you been standing there?"

"Long enough," he said. "I came across with Mistress Aldith and who knows what we might have seen if she had not interrupted master mason?"

"There is no need to speak of him in that offensive manner!" Ingaret protested, then wondered at her temerity.

However, he strode on past her, reached across the basin to grasp the cover and pulled it off, letting it drop in the water.

"So!" he said. "It is finished! I have watched you taking shape in the new solar these past few weeks and now here you are, displayed on this pedestal, for all to see – for me to see –" he hissed. "Have I to spend the rest of my days knowing you are here, as cold and black as you are in real life? My lady black heart – the right name for you!"

The vehemence of his outburst astounded her. "Robert, you've no right to say such things. I have never caused you any mischief –"

"You don't know what you've caused me!" he thundered back at her.

"Then you'll be pleased to know that I won't be in your way for much longer!" she spat back at him, equally incensed. "I am going to Fortchester with Roldan. We are to be married. Then you can forget all about me!"

"Forget you, when you are here, every time I come into the rose garden? Every time I glance out of a window? When you will always be looking at me with those murderous eyes? Forget you?"

He grabbed hold of her wrist and dragged her to him. His other arm went round her back and he pulled her closer. He kissed her hard, his tongue and teeth seeking her mouth, then just as suddenly roughly pushed her from him and strode off, breaking a rose from its stem as he passed and dashing it to the ground.

Ingaret regained her balance and slowly picked up the cover and threw it back over the statue. Tears were hot in her eyes and blood warm on her lips, and she thought she would be glad to be going away and leaving the manor and the D'Avencourt family behind her.

CHAPTER 20

She said nothing about the incident to Roldan as he drove her home and said she had accidentally bitten her lower lip when she slipped in the snow, though she hated deceiving him.

He reined the pony in before they reached the cottage and took her in his arms and told her how much he loved her and how he would spend his life trying to make her happy.

"I know it," she whispered, close to tears again because of the gentleness of his love and trust in her when she was refusing to let him kiss her where Robert's hungry mouth had so recently set fire to hers.

"Darling, bathe your lips in salt water," he told her as he left. "I won't be able to hold myself back next time!"

The pile of mending was still in a heap on the table when she returned to the cottage and she was glad to be bent over it so that nobody could see her flushed face and sore lip.

Noah arrived home from searching the forest for their pig.

"No luck," he said. "The children must help me look for it tomorrow. Most of our neighbours have found theirs. They all look well fattened up, ready for the Christmas table. I'm famished. Ingaret, is the pottage ready?"

"We were just waiting for you to come home," said Gunnora. "Alice, lay the table."

"Roldan took me up to the manor this afternoon," Ingaret said, "and showed me the fireplaces he had built."

"They're very fine," nodded Noah, sitting himself at the table and grasping his spoon in readiness for his meal.

"And have you seen the statue in the rose garden?" Ingaret asked.

"No, but I have heard that it is an exceptional piece of sculpting and very life like."

"It's me," Ingaret said, the words tumbling out of her mouth. "Roldan has sculpted me."

"Nonsense!" exclaimed Alice. "You only think it looks like you."

"It *is* me!" Ingaret stated. "If you don't believe me, you can ask Roldan – he's coming here this evening."

"Again?" asked Alice.

"Yes, he wants to speak to father."

"What about?" Gunnora asked.

"We will no doubt find out," said Noah. "Now let's have more eating and less talking, if you please."

The family relapsed into silence for the remainder of the meal and the children were getting ready for bed when there was a knock at the door.

Ingaret jumped to her feet, upending her chair, and rushed to the door before anyone else could get there. With her hand on the latch, she paused and took a deep breath. Tonight would change her life for ever – because Roldan loved her. And she…

Without further intropection, she flung open the door.

"Come in, Roldan," she greeted their visitor, somewhat breathlessly. "Father is waiting for you."

Roldan entered, his shoes leaving wet patches on the rushes.

"Now, what's all this about?" asked Noah, standing and righting Ingaret's fallen chair.

"Sir, I have come to ask you for Ingaret's hand in marriage," Roldan said, his face flushed and his eyes shining, going straight to the point and not embarrassed to have the family present.

"Marriage?" repeated Alice. "You and my sister?"

"Yes, she's said she'll have me."

"Come in and sit down," Gunnora said. "Children, off to your beds and one of you bring the young man a stool."

James offered Roldan a stool and the four children sat on what had been Jethro's bed and huddled together, waiting excitedly to see what would happen next. Ingaret, her parents and sister joined their visitor by the fire.

"Sir, I will be able to support her, and any family that comes along, as I am earning well. We would live with my mother and sisters at first but I will build her a house in the city, and we will be very happy."

"This is a surprise," said Gunnora, not sounding at all pleased at the prospect of losing Ingaret's labour. "When did all this happen? Are me and her father the last to be told?"

"It happened this afternoon," Roldan explained. "I was showing her the statue I had sculpted in her likeness for her ladyship's rose garden. It is being unveiled tomorrow."

"Will you give her a ring?" asked Alice.

"Yes, I will give her anything she wants," he replied.

"That's all very well," objected Gunnora, "but we can't afford to pay the merchet tax on the marriage. His lordship will insist on it, I have no doubt."

"My wife's right, Roldan."

"It is all arranged, sir. As soon as I knew that your daughter would have me, I sought his lordship's permission for the marriage and he has given it. I have already paid him the tax."

"And a dowry. She hasn't got a dowry," persisted Gunnora.

"That is of no consequence. I'll marry her with or without a dowry."

"You are obviously determined to have my daughter," said Noah, standing up.

"I am, sir," replied Roldan, also standing, "indeed I am."

"Then you have my blessing," said Noah.

Gunnora just grunted.

"Thank you, sir, thank you. I promise I will do what is right by her."

"I'm sure you will."

"Thank you, Father," said Ingaret.

"When will you come for her?" Gunnora asked.

"The day after tomorrow. We have the unveiling of the statue tomorrow and I must be there. I will be leaving the manor on the morning of the day following."

"It is well," nodded Noah. "Now you should go."

"Come and see his pony and cart, Father – all of you. Come and meet Patches."

Excitedly, the children ran out into the yard, where torches had been lit, followed by the adults, to admire Roldan's acquisition. Attracted by the noise, several of the neighbouring families also came out into the cold to gawk and learn of Ingaret's good fortune, so there was a crowd to wave him on his way back to the manor.

Next day, Ingaret undertook all her chores in a happy mood and did much more than she need have done, knowing that this was her last day in the only home she had ever known. Her one regret was leaving her father.

She took the children into the forest and they found their pig, rooting about for fallen acorns and anything else he could find in the snow. After a chase in which the children were squealing as loudly as the pig, they managed to corner him and grab hold of his back legs while Ingaret tied a rope round his neck to walk him home for slaughter, ready for the Christmas meal.

"It will be strange to be spending Christmas with Roldan's family," she said.

She finished the mending and swept the rushes out of the door and strewed fresh ones over the floor.

Alice disappeared towards the end of the afternoon and did not reappear until late in the evening, with her own news.

"Ingaret, you're not the only one to have cause for happiness. Father, after Ingaret has left, Elis wants to come and see you. I told you all that we would be getting married and he asked me this evening. Will you also let him speak to you?"

"Of course, Alice. Jethro, Ingaret and now you. All three of you gone," Noah mused. "The cottage will seem empty."

"I won't be far way," Alice reassured him, "just living at the mill. And Elis is also willing to pay the marriage tax. Ingaret's Roldan isn't the only one to have money put by for the future."

"May I wish you both every blessing," Ingaret said, hugging her sister. "I hope you will both be very happy."

In the depths of her heart, though, she had her doubts. *Alice is not right for him*, she thought. *He needs someone more like – more like – well, more like me.* But she had had her chance in that direction and had thrown it away, and now Elis would be her brother-in-law.

Roldan came for Ingaret on the following morning. Noah stayed away but the rest of the family was gathered to say good-bye to her.

"To set your minds at rest," Roldan said, "and so you know that I mean to wed Ingaret, we will take our vows now in front of you all."

"If that is what you both wish," agreed Gunnora. "It makes no difference to me."

So Roldan took Ingaret by both hands and, looking steadily into her eyes, said slowly, "I, Roldan, take you, Ingaret, to be my wife. Now you must say the same to me, my love."

Ingaret repeated the vow to Roldan and he kissed her briefly.

"Now we are husband and wife," he grinned, "before witnesses. I promise that we will have the Banns read as soon as we can. You should have no fear, she is mine now and I will spend the rest of my life looking after her."

Ingaret hugged and kissed Alice and her young brothers and sisters and asked that they would say goodbye to her father and John at the forge. She could not bring herself to pretend to be sorry to leave her mother.

"You have done well," admitted Gunnora. "You are very lucky to have brought him to your bed. You will be missed around here."

"Only because she has lost her skivvy," commented Ingaret as she clambered up next to Roldan on the driving seat.

Turning, she waved to her family and the neighbours who had come out of their cottages to wish them well as they set off for their new life together.

Ingaret slipped her hand through his arm.

"Roldan – husband –" she said.

"Let me hear you say it again."

"Husband, my dear, there is something I must show you before we leave this place for ever. It's something I have hidden away since I was a child. Follow that path to the right. It won't take long then we can be on our way to Fortchester."

Intrigued, he followed her instructions and guided Patches along the path she had indicated. It was not long before she asked him to stop the cart and he helped her down, kissing her lightly as his arms went about her.

"Over here," she said, "by the stream. I know this place well as this is where I always come to draw water."

She led him to the oak tree with its twisted and gnarled roots and began to dig in the earth. Here was only a light dusting of snow as the ground had been protected by the overhead canopy.

The first object to surface was the chip of limestone Roldan had given her on their first meeting.

"Do you remember this?" she asked him. He took it from her and nodded. "It is the only gift I have ever received."

"From the ceiling of the cathedral," he said. "I remember. But is this what you brought me all this way to show me?"

"No, there's something else."

She continued to dig until her fingers touched what she had been expecting, and up came the button, covered in dirt. A quick swirl in the stream and it was sparkling as brightly as ever.

He looked at it in amazement.

"Where did you get this?" he asked.

"I found it on the high road many years ago," she explained. "It must have fallen from a lady's gown. I kept it because it was so pretty. I liked to pretend that the coloured glass was real, valuable jewels –"

"But I think they are," said Roldan. "I have seen real jewels, sewn into the robes of the Blessed Virgin in the cathedral, and they look just like these."

"Are you sure?"

"No, I'm not sure, but we can find out once we get to Fortchester."

"Then I might be bringing a dowry with me after all," she laughed and he replied, "Indeed you might."

She carefully placed the button in the leather purse hung from a chain round her waist, together with the limestone chipping.

They then returned to the pony and cart and set off on their journey to Fortchester and, by the time they reached the great walls of the city, Ingaret was no longer a virgin.

PART II

FORTCHESTER

CHAPTER 21

Roldan drove them to the centre of the city, across the square and past the cathedral.

Ingaret was still lying on the soft woollen blankets where he had left her after his gentle love making, when they had started getting to know each other's bodies.

"It will be even better next time," he told her. "We have all the time in the world."

She was still getting used to being Roldan's wife. It had all happened so quickly, in three days only.

He was now driving them through a less populated area. Curious, Ingaret sat up. Here there were cottages standing in their own plots of land, more like the cottages in the vill. However, here the walls were built of flints, not wattle and daub, and the thatch of the steep roofs almost touched the ground on both sides, keeping them very warm in winter and cool in summer.

Patches was reined in at the gate of one of these cottages and Roldan helped Ingaret from the cart. He kissed her on the lips again.

"Come and meet my family. I know they will love you almost as much as I do."

There was a post and rail fence all round the plot and he opened the gate for her to pass through. As she walked along the path to the door, she noticed that there was a small, thatched building to one side. A black and white milking cow was standing in the doorway, eyeing the newcomer, ignoring the chickens running about her hooves.

Ingaret looked up at the cottage and thought it must contain more than one room because of its size and the sight of shutters covering a tiny unglazed window on a second level, over the doorway and beneath the thatch.

Roldan took her hand, opened the door and led her inside.

Her first impression was of a homely room with a side board, a scattering of stools and chairs and a wooden settle by a proper stone fireplace, obviously the work of Roldan.

In the centre of the room, a dumpy little woman with pure white hair pulled back into a tidy bun at the nape of her neck was rolling out pastry on a table. She looked up as they entered and Ingaret saw a round face with red cheeks and intelligent blue eyes.

Seated on the settle and chattering and laughing together were three young women, who all jumped to their feet in surprise.

"Roldan, son!" said his mother, vainly trying to rub the flour and pastry off her hands and not succeeding. "We weren't expecting you!" She came round the table and gave him a hug, covering him in flour.

He kissed her on the cheek and tried to dust himself down, then looked across to the three girls.

"Mary!" he exclaimed, addressing the tallest of the three. "I didn't expect to find you here."

"She often comes to visit," explained the elder of the other girls. "It's so good to see you, brother, after all these months!"

She too came to give him a hug, as did his younger sister, but the girl he had addressed as Mary said simply, "Welcome back, Roldan."

"And who have we here?" asked his mother, turning to Ingaret with a smile.

"Mother, all of you, this is Ingaret – my wife."

Ingaret heard Mary gasp and watched as all the colour faded from her face. Oblivious of this, Roldan laughed at the onslaught of excited questions from his sisters.

"Son, when did this happen?" asked his mother, going to Ingaret and taking her hands and regarding her keenly.

"We took our vows before Ingaret's family this morning. I will arrange to have the Banns read as soon as possible."

His mother continued to study Ingaret for a few moments longer then said, "My dear, if you are Roldan's wife, you are also my daughter, and you are very welcome here."

"Thank you," Ingaret replied, relaxing, "that is so kind of you – er – I don't know what to call you."

"I'm known as 'Mother Mason' but 'Mother' will be very pleasing to me."

"Thank you – Mother," said Ingaret and wondered whether she had at last found a mother she could love.

Mary had not spoken and had not moved. "I'll be going now," she then said in an unnaturally strangled voice and hurried from the room, closing the door firmly behind her. As they looked at each other in surprise at her sudden departure, they heard an anguished scream that sounded like an animal in pain.

"Roldan," admonished his elder sister, whose name Ingaret had not yet learned, "you know she expected you would ask her to marry you!"

"I didn't know any such thing!" he expostulated, reaching for Ingaret's hand.

"Then you must be blind, deaf and stupid!" his sister exclaimed. "I'm going after her!"

"No, Joanna! Let her go!" said her mother. "Give her time to herself. She has to get over any expectations she had towards Roldan. He never gave her any reason to think he was going to propose marriage –"

"I certainly did not!" he intervened vehemently, shaking his head.

"So you see, it was all in her imagination," continued Mother Mason. "Go and see her tomorrow, if you must, but stay here now – we need to welcome Roldan home with his new bride and get to know her."

Roldan led Ingaret over to his sisters and introduced her to Joanna, the elder of the two, and Marjery. They all sat by the fire to chat while their mother went back to the table to finish preparing the savoury pie, which she explained was to be cooked over the fire on the following day. The meal for that evening was the stew bubbling in the cauldron that hung from an iron arm over the blaze.

She listened with interest while the sisters questioned Ingaret on where she had lived, how many were in her family and who was their lord and whether he was a Yorkist or Lancastrian. She told them about the fire that had brought Roldan to the manor to work for Lord and Lady D'Avencourt.

Roldan expressed concern about future sleeping arrangements. "We will sleep in the room upstairs," he said and turned to Ingaret with a smile. "We're used to climbing ladders, are we not?" Then, by way of explanation, "I took her and her father up into the roof of the cathedral."

"Upstairs among the barrels of apples?" asked Joanna.

"We will manage for tonight," he said, "and tomorrow I will set about making it more comfortable for us. I intend to build Ingaret a cottage of her own but that will take time and I hope we may live here with you all, Mother, until then?"

"Of course," said his mother, concentrating on the pie. "Where else would you go? And speaking of the morrow, the clerk of works at the cathedral wishes to meet with you. He has more work for you."

"That is good. I need the work even more now, with a wife to support as well as this family. I will go to see him tomorrow."

"I am fortunate to have such a son, Ingaret," his mother said, looking at him with pride and affection. "His father would have been proud of him."

"I worked hard at home," Ingaret told them, "and will work hard here, so that you can rest a little, Mother, and Joanna and Marjery – my sisters now – need not work so hard. You have only to tell me what you would have me do and I will be happy to do it."

"I think we are going to bless the day Roldan brought you to us," his mother said.

As they chatted by the fireside, with the contents of the cauldron bubbling above the embers, Ingaret studied her new family.

Joanna, the elder girl, with a round face and blue eyes like her mother's, had long, dark, straight hair. She was shorter than Marjery, who was much lighter in colouring and resembled Roldan with a face that was square in shape.

Ingaret was to find out that their characters were quite different but she came to love both of them, and their mother, more than she had ever loved her family in the settlement. The only exception was her father, whom she was missing, and Jethro, but she hoped one day to find her brother and Thomasyn somewhere in this big city.

True to his word, a few days later, Roldan arranged for their Banns to be read in a side chapel in the cathedral. As no one put forward a 'just cause or impediment' why they should not be joined together as husband and wife 'until death us do part', they were now truly married in the eyes of the Catholic church and the community.

Ingaret had never enjoyed Christmas in the settlement. There was little money to spend on extras, no presents were exchanged and Gunnora treated the day like any other once they had returned from early Mass in the parish church.

Christmas spent with Roldan's family was quite different. Early on Christmas Day morning, they all attended part of the day-long service in the cathedral, until Mother Mason complained that standing among the crowd of worshippers was making her legs ache. Then they walked home in the few inches of snow that had fallen during the night, relaxed and happy together, chattering all the way.

After breakfast, the old lady had a little gift for everybody. Roldan's sisters received ribbons for their hair and she gave Ingaret a pottery cooking pot, the first utensil her daughter-in-law had received for her new home, yet to be built. His mother had lately learned to knit and Roldan received a scarf she had laboured over for hours, which pleased him greatly.

For their Christmas Day meal, Roldan had rung the neck of one of their chickens and his mother had slow cooked the carcase accompanied by a vegetable stew, with apple pie to follow, eaten with their own fresh cream, thick and yellow. Ingaret had never known such a happy day.

She was content to keep herself busy in the cottage and on the smallholding. She learned how to milk the cow and make butter and cheese in the dairy built onto one side of the cottage. She also took her share of the cooking, using recipes new to her and more venturous than any the women in the settlement used, with the sole desire to please the family, knowing that it would stand her in good stead when she and Roldan inhabited a cottage of their own.

This would be happening much sooner than either of them had anticipated, because of the 'dowry' Ingaret had brought with her – the button she had found.

Roldan had taken it to the cathedral and had shown it to the curator of the jewel house, who confirmed that what Ingaret thought were pieces of coloured glass set in a common metal were, in fact, chippings of precious jewels mounted in high-carat gold. Roldan had been able to sell the button to a jeweller in the city and, with the money received, had bought from the cathedral a plot of land not far away from his mother's cottage.

"There's even some money left over to start building," he told Ingaret. She was so excited at the prospect of owning their own home and together they went to look at the plot on the following Sunday.

"Which way do you want the house to face?" Roldan asked her.

"This way, to the south, looking out over open countryside," she said decisively. "Roldan, I've been thinking a lot about the plan."

"Tell me," he said with some amusement.

"It should have a large kitchen with a proper fireplace with hearth and a bread oven built into one wall, and a separate sleeping room – perhaps two – and, across a passageway, a byre for the animals. That way, they will stay warm and I won't need to go out in the cold to milk the cow. The dairy and cold store should be on the north side of the house. Then upstairs –"

"Upstairs?" queried Roldan.

"Of course – there must be a floor above – with two more rooms for sleeping, a glazed window in each, and space for overwintering fruit and vegetables. There! What do you think of that?"

"I think it will cost four times as much money as we have left," he chuckled and kissed her cheek.

"Perhaps we could manage with only one sleeping room on the second floor," she offered helpfully.

"I know someone who will draw a plan for us," Roldan said. "Something we can afford and move into before winter sets in."

Ingaret clapped her hands together delightedly then took her husband's arm.

"You must speak to him about our plan without delay," she said as they walked back to his mother's cottage.

Roldan did. A suitable and more economical design was drawn and costed and work began, sometimes in spurts of great activity and sometimes at a frustratingly slow pace, when they had to wait for Roldan to be paid for his commissions before he could afford to hire labourers.

He was now working for the cathedral again, but on the outside of the building. Some of the statues in their niches at the main entrance had weathered or had been damaged by nesting birds and needed repairing or replacing.

"I am happy that he is not working at the top of the scaffolding," his mother confessed to Ingaret. "I am worried all the time he is up there."

Ingaret and Roldan enjoyed their nights together as they grew more experienced in their love making and more aware how to please each other. He was a gentle and caring lover and Ingaret learnt to respond to him without shyness or embarrassment.

She reflected that she had not known that family life could be so fulfilling and, although she still missed her father and had not yet found Jethro and Thomasyn, she had never been happier or more content.

CHAPTER 22

With winter past, Roldan took her with the rest of the family to the May Day celebrations. The cathedral square was vibrant with the large number of citizens who gathered as dawn broke to join with the choir as they sang the old hymns from the top of the tower. Then the bells were rung, so that no one in the city could have remained asleep, and a band of Morris men danced to entertain the crowd until it was time for everyone to return to their homes for the day's work. Ingaret had never heard such singing or seen Morris dancers before and was captivated.

Joanna noticed Mary in the crowd and went across to speak to her. Ingaret thought that her mother-in-law looked displeased.

"I don't like that girl," she heard her mutter to Roldan.

"She's harmless," Roldan replied. "I don't think that friendship will last for long. Let's start walking home. Joanna will catch us up."

They hadn't gone far, however, when Ingaret heard her name being called and, turning, saw a young man waving frantically.

"It's Jethro!" she exclaimed. "It's my brother and he's got Thomasyn with him and is that – is that – yes, she's carrying a baby!"

They waited as the young couple hurried towards them. Jethro threw his arms round his sister then brought Thomasyn forward.

"Ingaret, you know Thomasyn – she's my wife now," he said proudly, "and meet baby Edwina."

"A girl!" Ingaret exclaimed. "She's beautiful! Roldan, come and see."

Roldan came over dutifully to admire the baby, as did his mother and sister Marjery. Ingaret had already told them the story of the young couple.

"She's ours," Jethro stated emphatically, "and no one here knows any different. But what are you doing in Fortchester, sister? Have you and Roldan married, too?"

Then there were many explanations and Roldan's mother extended an invitation to the young couple to visit at any time.

"We will always have fresh milk and eggs for the baby," she said.

Ingaret thought that life was getting better and better. Jethro would be a free man if he stayed hidden for another six months. He said he had plenty of labouring work and was saving hard so that they could leave the family with whom they were lodging and rent something more suitable.

Thomasyn quietly said she didn't mind at all as long as they were together. Ingaret liked the new Thomasyn, now wife and mother, better than the rather brash girl she had met sometimes in the vill, and was delighted to see how happy Jethro was with his new family.

So the days passed and the timber arrived on site for cutting into beams for their new cottage.

One morning, Joanna came home from the fruit and vegetable market with news that she sprung on them as they were clearing the table after breakfast.

"I have heard some worrying rumours today," she began. "It seems – though I know it is hard to believe – that the two young princes who were imprisoned in the Tower escaped to Ireland and one of them is now challenging the King's right to rule."

"Young King Edward V?" asked Roldan, greatly surprised.

"No, his younger brother, Richard, Duke of York."

"But that does not seem possible," said Roldan.

The family were curious and wanted to know more.

"The young duke has taken sanctuary in the Benedictine monastery of St. Peter at Westminster," said Joanna, "and men are travelling to London from all over the country to support him. It means we will be at war again."

"Who told you this?" asked her mother.

"Mary heard it from the Yorkists," said Joanna.

"Oh," said their mother dismissively. "Mary. I might have known. You can't believe anything that young lady says."

"But they are gathering in the forest," said Joanna. "Mary says there are a crowd of them already and more are joining all the time. They are bent on causing trouble and are threatening disturbance and worse –"

"Worse?" echoed Ingaret. "What worse?"

"She said something about setting fires to Lancastrian property."

Roldan came across and put an arm round his wife's shoulders.

"Joanna, this is very irresponsible talk," he admonished her.

"It's not just talk," said Joanna. "I believe they mean it. Mary certainly does."

"Joanna, you should be careful what rumours you are spreading," Marjery said. "Can't you find out for sure? Ask some questions."

"And be caught as a spy?" countered Joanna, sounding very anxious. "I can't be seen showing too much interest in what they're planning."

"I can find out at the cathedral whether there *is* a young man seeking sanctuary in the monastery at Westminster," Roldan offered.

He returned from work later in the day to say that yes, there was a young man of about the right age in sanctuary at the monastery in Westminster and a crowd was beginning to gather in the vicinity. The Benedictine abbot was unable to refuse sanctuary unless the King intervened. Roldan explained that the King was unlikely to refuse sanctuary as he would want to keep his enemies where he could see them – "or so the bishop says," he added.

"Could I help?" asked Marjery. "Everyone knows Joanna but they don't know me. Perhaps I could join the rebels and find out what they intend to do."

"No, Marjery, I won't allow it," said her mother. "I won't have either of you girls putting yourselves in danger. We know they mean what they say – the fire at the D'Avencourt manor has shown us that."

Ingaret suddenly had an idea. "Jethro!" she said. "Nobody knows Jethro. He can mix with the crowd and find out what's happening."

"Would he do that?" Joanna asked.

"D'Avencourt is his home, too," said Roldan, "and his father and his family are there still. I will call at his lodgings."

"No, Roldan, you're too well known," objected Ingaret, unable to hide the fear in her voice.

"I repeat, I could go," Marjery offered.

Her mother was adamant. "You can't go out on your own at this hour," she said.

"I know the back ways. I'll be very careful. No one will see me. I can do this, Mother."

Her mother looked very doubtful.

"It's true what she says," said Roldan. "She could be there and back in no time. This is a very serious situation or we wouldn't ask her."

Their mother said no more so Marjery committed to memory directions to the lodging where Jethro and Thomasyn were staying and the message she should give them. She fetched her black shawl and wrapped herself in it.

"I'll go with you, at least part of the way," offered Roldan but Marjery said she would be less obvious on her own and left.

The family tried to occupy themselves while she was away but finally gave up the pretence and sat together round the table, waiting for her return.

She came home about an hour later.

"What news, sister?" asked Roldan, jumping up and taking the shawl from her shoulders.

"Jethro was greatly concerned," said Marjery.

"As well he might be," nodded Ingaret.

"He said he would go straight away into the forest and try to find those who are meeting there – it shouldn't be difficult – and learn all he could. He will come here if there is anything to report."

The family was preparing to retire when there was an urgent knocking at the door and Jethro burst into the room without waiting for an invitation. He was greatly agitated.

"It's true!" he told them. "There were about a hundred people gathered there with more joining all the time. They intend to spread out in all directions and attack and set fire to any Lancastrian properties on the way."

"How far will they travel?"

"Some will be on horseback, some will travel by horse and cart and the rest will be on foot. They will be setting off as soon as it gets light, which of course is very early at the moment. We haven't any time to lose!"

"No time to lose before we do what, Jethro?" asked his sister.

"One of the targets they mentioned was the D'Avencourt manor house," Jethro explained. "Someone remembered setting fire to it before."

"Then we must warn them!" exclaimed Ingaret, turning to her husband. "Roldan, we must do something! They're in great danger!"

"Of course," he said at once. "I will go with Jethro. We will travel in the cart."

"Then we must set out straight away, get a head start!" Jethro said.

"Roldan, you'll be missed if you don't turn up for work at the cathedral tomorrow morning and people will start asking questions," Joanna warned him.

"Then I'll go," said Ingaret. "No one will miss me. Jethro and I will go together."

"But didn't you say that Jethro is still bound to Lord D'Avencourt?" asked Marjery. "If they catch him, he won't be allowed to leave."

"She's right," said Ingaret. "Jethro, it will be too dangerous for you. Thomasyn and the baby need you here."

"Then I just won't have to get caught," said Jethro. "I will drive you there and back and we will ask our father to go with you to Lord D'Avencourt. No one need know how you got there. Once they hear our news, no one will bother to ask how you got there."

So it was settled. While Jethro slipped back home to let Thomasyn know where he was going, their mother prepared some bread and eggs and cheese for them to take with them, then Roldan drove Ingaret to the cathedral square.

They had tied sacking to Patches' hoofs and drove slowly so that they made as little sound as possible. Jethro arrived and changed places with Roldan on the driving seat.

"Thomasyn didn't want me to go," he said ruefully once they were on their way. "She said she didn't care if the whole house burnt down and everyone in it, but then she thought of her ladyship and changed her mind."

After their first stop to let Patches drink from a small stream by the road, where they had something to eat, Jethro suggested to Ingaret that she should get some sleep as it was likely to be a busy day once they arrived at their destination.

She climbed into the back of the cart, where she made herself comfortable on blankets that Roldan's mother had thrown there, and when she awoke, dawn was beginning to break and she recognised that they were on the high road not far from their one-time home.

Jethro sensibly avoided the vill and drove Patches into the forest near the settlement and tied him to a tree. The pony was happy grazing on the grasses and ferns at his feet and Jethro promised the animal to return with water as soon as he was able.

They wrapped themselves in cloaks so that they would not be recognised and walked to the cottage. People were already up and about and their sudden, mysterious appearance did not go unnoticed, but they decided that everyone would soon know who they were and why they were there and took a chance on their loyalty not to report Jethro's return.

They walked into the cottage as the family was preparing to go about their daily chores. The children had grown during the seven months Ingaret had been away and little Megge seemed to have taken charge of her three siblings and was organising them into having their faces washed and hair combed.

Noah and Gunnora were standing by their bed, arguing about something.

They all gaped as Jethro and Ingaret walked into the room.

"Son! And Ingaret!" exclaimed their father. "This is a surprise!"

Gunnora sniffed. "Come back home both of you? Been thrown out by that young mason, Ingaret? I wondered how long that would last! And Thomasyn? Walked out on her and her bastard have you, Jethro?"

Ingaret threw the hood off her head and took another step into the room, her whole body tingling with thorough dislike for this woman who she had had to call 'Mother' all these years! Well, now she knew what it was like to have a real mother and hatred rose as bile in her mouth. She surprised herself by actually spitting on the floor. Jethro laid a restraining hand on her arm. She realised that he too must be experiencing something of what she was feeling. Now, however, there was no need to even talk to this woman.

Then she looked at the children, at their vulnerability, remembering her own childhood, and her loathing subsided. She looked at Jethro.

"No, Gunnora –" he said.

So, thought Ingaret, *he too will no longer call her 'mother'.*

"– neither of us have abandoned our families in Fortchester and, if we had, this is the last place we would come back to. We have come to speak to our father most urgently."

"What about?" Gunnora demanded.

"I would like to say that it is none of your business," Jethro said, "but I regret very much that it is."

"Jethro, what's all this about?" Noah asked, coming towards them and offering them two chairs. "Sit down, both of you. You look exhausted."

They removed their cloaks and sat.

"Gunnora, bring them ale and bread," Noah said and Ingaret was glad that little Megge had not been ordered to wait on them. Now eight years old, she was a pretty little girl with soft fair curls and Ingaret had a sudden vision of what Gunnora must have looked like when she was young, and shivered.

While they drank the ale and gratefully nibbled the bread served to them with such ill grace, Jethro reported everything he had heard at the gathering in the forest yesterday evening.

The children listened, sitting on their parents' bed on the raised platform. Noah and Gunnora remained silent until he had finished.

"Are we all to be burnt alive in our own homes?" cried Gunnora.

"And you've come to warn his lordship?" asked Noah. "But Jethro, you are not yet a free man, not for several months more."

"Father, Lord D'Avencourt mustn't see Jethro," Ingaret said. "You must go with me to tell his lordship. There is no need for him to know who drove the cart here."

"There is no time to lose," Jethro urged his father. "They will have set out by now. Those on horseback could be here in a few hours."

"But they won't start an attack until the main force arrives," reasoned Noah. "Very well. You stay here, Jethro, and don't let anyone see you. Children, you must all carry out your chores as if nothing was amiss. Gunnora, see to that."

Gunnora nodded.

"Come, daughter, we will take the cart and go and warn the D'Avencourt family. Then it is up to his lordship what action he takes."

Together, they left the settlement, returned to the cart where they had left it in the forest, with a bucket of water for Patches, then made their way towards the manor house. They entered by a back door.

Noah asked a young footman to tell the seneschal that he needed to speak to him urgently. The young man hesitated but, recognising Noah, disappeared, reappearing moments later with an invitation to attend the seneschal in his office. He then led the way to that exalted man's room on the ground floor at the back of the house.

The seneschal received them genially, as Noah thought he would, having established a good working relationship with him since the night of the fire. He introduced Ingaret and she dropped a curtsey, overwhelmed by the luxury of polished wood and woven carpets she saw about her. The seneschal looked flattered as well as amused and invited them to sit in leather chairs on the other side of his desk.

Smiling, the older man regarded Ingaret closely as she took off her cloak and sat down.

"Have we met before this morning?" he asked.

"No, sire," she answered.

"Yet your face is most familiar."

Noah smiled. "The statue in the rose garden," he said. "It was sculpted by her husband, the young master mason, in her likeness."

The seneschal laughed. "You're right!" he agreed. "An amazing likeness! Now, what is so important that you had to see me so urgently?"

He listened intently to all that they had to say, occasionally interrupting them to ask a question. Noah often referred him to Ingaret and, if she did not know the answer, she said so. On one occasion, however, she added, "but Jethro will know –" then, in confusion, covered her mouth with her hand. Noah tried to pass off her blunder, in vain.

"Jethro is with you?" the seneschal enquired.

Noah could see no point in lying and asked Ingaret to relate the part her brother had played both last night by joining the meeting in the forest and then by driving Ingaret to speak to Lord D'Avencourt.

The seneschal stroked his beard and regarded her thoughtfully. "He is not a free man," he said. "I could send for him to be arrested."

"I beg of you not to do that, sire," cried Ingaret. "He came here of his own accord, knowing the risks, but he still came."

The seneschal rose from his chair.

"Wait here," he said. "I will relay all you have told me to his lordship."

He left Noah and Ingaret speculating on whether they should have kept quiet about Jethro and whether at this moment, as they fidgeted in their seats or wandered around the room, men were being sent to arrest him.

An hour later, the seneschal returned and said Lord D'Avencourt was very grateful for the information and he and his sons had decided on a strategy to keep their property safe from fire and attack.

"I will not reveal the details," he said, "but, as we speak, messengers are on their way to the settlement and the vill with his lordship's instructions."

Noah said he was concerned for the welfare of his family.

"They will be kept safe, as will all the women and children," he said. "Noah, take your daughter to the kitchen and ask cook to prepare food for the journey back to Fortchester. Then you should return to your home as speedily as possible so that she can be safely on her way."

He had made no mention of Jethro.

They rose to leave and the seneschal held out his hand to shake Noah's and kiss Ingaret's.

"Amazing likeness," he commented and led the way to the door.

Once outside, Ingaret paused.

"Father, you go back to the cart," she said. "I just want another peek at my statue."

"Don't be long!" he said.

"I won't!" she replied.

CHAPTER 23

She left the house by a back door and hurried out to the rose garden, anticipating the pleasure of seeing the statue again and admiring her husband's handiwork that so clearly revealed his love for her.

She approached the circle where all the paths met among the rose bushes, which were just coming into blossom, and saw the black marble basin, but the pedestal in its centre was unadorned. The statue of herself had disappeared!

Noticing a shiny black object at her feet, she bent with some difficulty to retrieve it and saw it was a chip of black marble. Wondering, she stared at it in disbelief but nervously dropped it when a voice she knew well spoke from behind her.

"I thought I'd find you here."

Swivelling round, she confronted the owner of the voice.

"Robert!"

"Ingaret!" he said, mimicking her surprise.

"Where is it? The statue? What's happened to it?"

"Oh, that," he said, shrugging as if it were of no consequence. "It toppled off – in the storm. Smashed to pieces."

Ingaret remembered the rolls of thunder, the vivid forked lightning and torrential rain one night about a week ago. They had discovered a leak and had to put a bucket beneath it to catch the rainwater until Roldan had time to climb onto the roof and repair the thatch.

"But it couldn't have fallen," she objected. "Roldan is careful. He would have fixed it very firmly. I don't believe you."

"It doesn't matter to me, what you believe," he said roughly. "What happened, happened."

She did not know what else to say so did not reply.

"How are you, Ingaret?" he asked, a little more kindly. "Is he treating you well, your young master mason?"

"Very well," she said stiffly. "We are very happy."

"I'm glad to hear it. Obviously, married life is meant for you. You are looking more desirable than ever."

There was an awkward silence.

"And thank you for coming all this way to warn us about the danger we are in. We will be prepared."

"And you will stay safe?"

"We will. I am gratified by your concern. Our seneschal told me that Jethro drove you here and not your husband."

"We didn't want to attract attention. Roldan would have been missed. Jethro offered."

"He put himself in that danger?"

"Yes, he did. We also have family here."

"Of course. And he guessed that my father would turn a blind eye in the circumstances. How is she, that little tramp? Has she been delivered of father's bastard yet?"

"You knew then?"

"Everyone knows – except my mother. No one will tell her. It is well that she lives in her own little world."

"Yes, she was delivered of a healthy little girl. And Thomasyn is not a tramp," Ingaret objected. "You are such a powerful family –"

She wanted to add that Thomasyn probably had no say in the matter of her relationship with his father, but decided against it. Robert probably read her thoughts and just grunted.

Then he looked at her, just looked.

"Dear God, Ingaret," he breathed softly, "does he know how lucky he is? When he holds you in his arms, does he thank all the gods for his good fortune?"

He took a step towards her and suddenly she felt light headed and grabbed hold of the top of the pedestal to keep from falling.

"What is it?" he asked, concern in his voice. "Are you not well?"

"It's natural, it will pass," she said.

"Natural? What's wrong with you?"

"Robert, I'm with child," she told him though, truth to tell, she was not sure if her early months of pregnancy were the only reason for her faintness. She was still very nervous of the charm and masculinity he exuded without trying.

"Are you telling me he's let you travel all this way through the night, in a cart, on these roads, in your condition? What is the man thinking about?"

"Hush, hush," she soothed him. "He doesn't know. If he did, of course he would never have let me come. You're the first person I've told."

"Oh, my dear girl," he said.

He picked up her cloak that had fallen from her shoulders and gently put it round her.

"Wait here and I'll send Mistress Aldith to you. Don't move. I'll be as quick as I can."

Then he left her.

Suddenly, Ingaret felt drained. She wanted the comfort of Roldan's arms around her. She sank to the ground and clung to the rim of the basin, breathing hard, and it was there that Mistress Aldith found her.

"My dear lady," she said, wrapping her arm round Ingaret's waist and helping her to stand. "Young master Robert told me you are with child.

Here, lean on me and I'll walk you back to your father. He is waiting for you, in the yard."

"Thank you, Mistress Aldith."

They began to walk slowly towards the gravel path that led to the courtyard.

"I understand we have you to thank," said the older woman, "and your brother. I hear that Jethro drove you through the night. Please thank him, too. You have probably saved our lives by coming to warn us of the danger the manor is in."

After a few more steps, she continued, "Tell me – in strict confidence, of course – has Thomasyn been delivered of a healthy baby?"

Ingaret nodded. "A girl."

"And Jethro will stand by her?"

Ingaret nodded again. "They're married."

"Thomasyn was not a bad girl," Mistress Aldith said. "Just unfortunate. It could have happened to any number of others. But I talk too much."

She was quiet for a few moments then sighed. "At least, my dear lady does not know – though sometimes I do wonder. I think she comprehends much more than she would have us believe."

"She is fortunate to have you to look after her," said Ingaret.

"His lordship will send her away to safety, to his sister's, just for a few days, as soon as I have packed a few things to take with us. We will travel with her two daughters-in-law and their attendants. It will give us a welcome few days away."

"And the other women in the house? The servants?"

"They will have to take shelter in the cellars until the danger is passed."

"And how will the danger pass?"

"His lordship will rally men like your father to his side and be ready to fight from the grounds of the manor house. Others from the vill will gather at the river bank, under the command of his two eldest sons, and so surround the attackers and cut off their flight."

"And what of master Robert?" Ingaret asked.

"His lordship will keep young master Robert by his side."

"How do you know?"

"Their strategy was planned in my presence. I had to know so that I could make decisions as to what is best for her ladyship."

They saw Noah in the courtyard, waiting by the cart and holding Patches' bridle.

Ingaret had one more question to ask. She desperately wanted to know the truth.

"Mistress Aldith – the statue that was on the pedestal in the rose garden."

Mistress Aldith nodded. "Your likeness," she said. "So lovingly carved."

"It is missing. Master Robert told me it had been blown down in the storm but –"

"What nonsense!" interrupted her companion. "I saw from a window what happened to the statue! He was at great pains to topple it off the pedestal then took a war hammer to it and smashed it to smithereens. I saw him with my own eyes!"

"Thank you for telling me," said Ingaret. "I had to know."

CHAPTER 24

"Father," said Ingaret as they left the manor grounds and crossed the bridge over the river, "the seneschal did not mention the mill. He said they were sending messengers to the vill and the settlement but he didn't mention the mill. We cannot leave without warning Elis and his family."

"They will have remembered the mill, I'm certain of it," her father said.

"But we can't be sure. We can't take the chance. The mill would be one of the places the rioters make for."

Noah nodded agreement and, once across the bridge, he turned the horse to the right and, at a canter, they reached the mill in minutes.

One of the mill workers came out to discover who had clattered into the yard in such great haste.

"Good morrow, Noah."

"Good morrow, Simon. Is the miller here?"

"He's in the house. I'm sorry, but I'm forbidden to go in there in my working clothes. The mistress is very strict about that!"

"Can't have you upsetting the mistress!" Noah laughed, jumping down from the driving seat. "It's all right, I'll go in by myself. You stay here, Ingaret."

"Good morrow, little lady," Simon called. "Good to see you. How's Fortchester?"

"Fortchester is home, now," she responded.

He smiled and nodded and went back into the mill.

She sat there for a few minutes, wondering whether she should follow her father into the house, when Elis came out with Alice in tow.

"Ingaret," he said, approaching the cart with a wide smile. "This is a pleasant surprise!"

"For me, too," she said, hoping that only she could hear her heart thumping. "Hello, Alice."

Alice acknowledged her presence with a nod of the head and didn't seem as pleased to see her as her husband was.

"You've heard what my father has come to warn you about?"

"Yes, and we're very grateful to be told. His lordship's messengers seem to have forgotten about us, but we'll be ready if the need arises. The men won't let anything happen to the mill – their livelihoods are at stake. Any interlopers will get what they deserve!"

"Take care, Elis. Don't put yourself in any danger."

"I won't. Now I must get back inside to support my father. It's been good to see you!"

He turned and went back into the house, to Ingaret's intense disappointment. Alice was about to follow but Ingaret asked her how she fared.

"I'm settled here," she replied. "All the family work hard. There's little time here for anything other than work. I must say, I expected more from this marriage than skivvying around the place."

"But you and Elis are happy?" Ingaret pursued.

"Oh, we're all right, especially in bed," she said. "We're very much in love."

"Of course," Ingaret agreed, wishing she hadn't heard all that and knowing that her sister was staking her claim on ground they had fought over.

"And how are you and Roldan?"

"The same – in love with each other."

"That's all right, then, though I must say, I envy your life in the city."

"Don't think that we don't have to work hard."

"If you say so, but there must be so many other distractions to enjoy."

"I can't deny that," Ingaret said.

"It is good to see you, sister."

"And to see you."

As Alice went into the house, Elis's mother came out. She clasped Ingaret's hands. "I am so pleased to meet you again, dear," she said and thanked her for coming all that way to warn them about possible danger.

Noah returned then and climbed back onto the driving seat. The family clustered in the doorway to wave them off and, as they left the yard, Elis and his father were heading towards the mill.

Ingaret's arrival home in Fortchester late that evening was welcomed with great relief by Roldan's family and he pumped Jethro's hand up and down as if he would never stop.

"I am so grateful to you for bringing her safely home," he said in several ways over and over again.

Jethro was anxious to get back to Thomasyn and their baby as quickly as he could.

"Ingaret will tell you all there is to tell," he said as he left to walk the short distance home.

Roldan took her cloak and hung it up on a hook behind the door then sat her down, holding her hands in both of his while his mother busied herself dishing up a savoury stew and his sisters brought stools to sit on either side of them and hear all the news.

She told them how grateful everyone was, of course, to be forewarned of the danger threatening them.

"If everything goes according to his lordship's plan," she said inbetween taking mouthfuls of bread dipped in the steaming mixture of rabbit and vegetables, "the mob will be met by himself and three of his sons and the strongest men who live on the manor, such as my father. His two eldest sons and other men from the vill and settlement will approach from the river so that the attackers are surrounded. All are ready to fight, though they hope it won't come to that."

"And Lady D'Avencourt?" asked their mother.

"His lordship has sent her and his two daughters-in-law away to his sister's country house for safety."

"The streets here have been very quiet all day," said Roldan.

"We met some of the mob as we drove back," Ingaret informed them, "in carts and on foot and I am sure there were many others in the forest. They seemed in high humour and called out greetings to us as they passed."

"Just as well they didn't know where you had been," commented Joanna.

"And we must make sure they never find out," said Roldan.

Later, in bed, after he had made repeated love to her, "to make up for missing you last night and because you are so ravishing," he said, she told him that she had some important news to impart.

"I'm listening," he said.

"Darling Roldan," she said, "I am with child, our child."

He raised himself on one arm and looked down at her.

"Are you sure?"

"Yes, quite sure. I have seen and felt changes in my body and I have missed my monthly flow for the second time. Had you not noticed?"

He admitted that he hadn't kept count of the weeks and should have noticed but hadn't.

Then he took her in his arms and kissed all of her that he could easily reach and said how wonderful this news was and he was the happiest and most fortunate man in the whole wide world.

"If I had known this, I would never have let you travel all that way in that bumpy cart," he added.

"I know that," she said. "That's why I didn't tell you. But I haven't suffered because of the journey."

"Tomorrow, we will tell everybody," he said, "but tonight we shall be the only two people in the world who are privy to the secret!"

Ingaret lay awake long after he had fallen asleep, feeling a tinge of guilt, knowing that they were not the only two people in the world who were privy to her news. She had not mentioned becoming faint in the rose garden and Robert's concern and certainly had not told him of the breaking up of the statue he had so skillfully carved in her likeness.

She stroked her stomach, still flat, though she had noticed a thickening of her waist. Content and wondering about whoever was hiding in there, she fell asleep.

Next morning, when the family was told the news, Joanna and Marjery were delighted and hugged and kissed Ingaret and discussed their forthcoming roles as aunts and what a fuss they would make of their nephew – or would it be a niece?

"And what do you think about being a grandmother?" Roldan asked his mother. She smiled and took hold of Ingaret's hands.

"It has come as no surprise to me, my dear," she said.

"You knew?"

"How did you know when I didn't?" asked Roldan, mystified.

"I know the signs," she said. "Haven't I had three children of my own? To be a grandmother pleases me very well."

Jethro came to see them two days later to ask if Ingaret and Roldan would be godparents to Edwina at her christening. He told them that he would be presenting himself as her father.

He was also happy to be told that he was to be an uncle.

"A playmate for little Edwina," he said.

They were all anxious for news of the uprising but heard only unreliable rumours. The streets of the city were very quiet once all the protesters had disappeared back to where they had come from.

They questioned some of the travellers who came into the city but they all said that there had been no trouble to Lancastrian property out in the countryside, as far as they knew.

Joanna tried to find out from Mary what had happened but she did not seem to know other than the mob had left to cause mayhem but she had been too afraid to join them. There was, though, one surprising piece of news that seemed to be true.

"The young man in sanctuary, who said he was duke Richard of York, was a fraud."

The Benedictine abbot at Westminster said he had granted sanctuary to the Duke of York, as he thought. Once he discovered this was not so, he released the imposter to the King's men, who escorted him to the Tower.

CHAPTER 25

Throughout her pregnancy, Ingaret insisted on taking her share of the household chores as usual but, as she grew larger and found difficulty in sitting on a stool to milk the cow or bending over to pull up vegetables, she was told to leave it to Roldan's sisters and go indoors and rest.

Roldan took great care of her. He had completed his work at the cathedral for the time being and, by the autumn, was working on renovating granite floors in a house a few miles distant. He sometimes took her with him to show her his work but she was finding it increasingly difficult to heave herself up into the cart and both laughed at her now clumsy efforts.

They were very happy as the time for her confinement drew ever nearer and, although frightened by her coming ordeal, Ingaret was confident to be in the capable hands of her mother-in-law.

"My grandchild will not be the first baby I've brought into the world," she said proudly, "and not one mother or baby lost."

Then Roldan would wrap his arms about his wife and ask his mother not to speak of such things. She confided to Ingaret that he had said he would not want to live if he lost her.

Early one afternoon at the beginning of winter, as the days were shortening and there was a nip of frost in the air, while Ingaret and her mother-in-law were alone in the cottage, they were surprised to see from the window a well-dressed young man in a blue cloak rein in his horse at the gate, pass the reins over one of the fence posts, and stride up to the door. Her mother had opened it before he had time to knock.

"Is this the cottage of Roldan, the master mason?" he asked.

"It is," she answered.

"I have a message for his wife."

"I am his wife," said Ingaret, coming to the door. "What message have you brought for me?"

"From Lady D'Avencourt," he said. "She is coming to the cathedral on Friday of next week to give thanks for their deliverance from the Yorkists, and would be pleased if you would wait upon her, at three of the clock, in the chapel of the blessed Virgin Mary."

"She wants to see me?" asked Ingaret in surprise.

"Yes, mistress, if you would be so kind."

"Of course I'll wait on her," said Ingaret. "It will give me great pleasure to see her again. Please tell her that I'll be there."

"Yes, mistress." He hesitated then said, "I understand that we all have you to thank for preparing us for the arrival of the mob."

"Was anyone hurt or any damage done?" asked Ingaret. "We have heard nothing since."

"No damage and no one hurt," he confirmed. "I am sure her ladyship will relate all that happened. Heartfelt thanks again, mistress."

He bowed to her then returned to his horse and was soon mounted and away.

"Well, fancy that!" said her mother.

"Well, fancy that!" said Joanna on her return from delivering eggs to a neighbour.

Marjery said much the same on her return and Roldan was also delighted.

"You deserve their gratitude," he said.

Friday afternoon of the following week was cool with intermittent showers. Their mother made sure that Ingaret was wrapped up warmly in her cloak and sent Marjery to accompany her to the cathedral.

"I won't go into the Lady Chapel with you," Marjery said, "but you won't mind, will you, if I stay hidden somewhere at the back, just so I can get a peek at your lady?"

"Of course not," Ingaret replied.

They arrived ahead of three o'clock. Ingaret left Marjery and went to the Lady Chapel, where she saw that several chairs had been brought in for them. She was unable to kneel at the altar rail so sat on one of them and spent a few moments in prayer, but turned her head as she heard footsteps on the stone flags and stood as her ladyship approached on the arm of Mistress Aldith.

Ingaret was pleased to see them and remembered to drop a curtsey and refrained from speaking until Lady D'Avencourt had greeted her.

"Good morrow, Ingaret," said her ladyship, holding out her hands in welcome.

Ingaret recognised her though she had not seen her since the night of the fire. This afternoon her silver hair was hidden beneath the swathe of white linen covering her head, chin and neck. Ingaret was again mesmerized by her sad grey eyes though today she was smiling. Her light green gown that peeked out from wrists and ankles was enveloped in a cloak, the colour of the forest's dark green foliage.

"Good morrow, Lady D'Avencourt," Ingaret said. "Good morrow, Mistress Aldith. There are chairs here for you. Please sit down."

They seemed relieved to sit and it was then that, for the first time, Ingaret noticed behind them the third member of the party.

"Robert!" she exclaimed in surprise. "I-I mean, Master Robert."

"Good morrow, Ingaret. So we meet yet again. My day has brightened considerably."

"Ah yes, I remember," said her ladyship, looking from her son to Ingaret and back again. "You two know each other. How is that, do you think Aldith, that they know each other?"

"Yes, your ladyship, I was aware of their acquaintance," replied Aldith.

"Sit, child," said Lady D'Avencourt. "You, too, Robert." As Ingaret did so, her cloak fell away, plainly revealing her condition.

"I see I have to congratulate you and master mason on your forthcoming event."

"Thank you, your ladyship," Ingaret replied, flustered and not looking at Robert. "We are very happy about it."

"And when is the baby due?"

"Early Spring."

"Then I wish you a safe confinement. But to come to the reason for my asking you here."

"I am so pleased to see you again, my lady, and hope you have kept well."

"Very well, thanks to you, Ingaret – may I call you Ingaret?"

"Of course. I would be honoured."

"Your warning to Lord D'Avencourt gave us time to leave the manor house and escape to my sister-in-law's home further north – myself and my two daughters-in-law. We are very grateful to you, my dear. You – and they tell me that your brother came with you – saved the lives of my husband and sons." She turned to Robert. "Robert, my dear, tell Ingaret what happened."

He swivelled in his chair and turned towards her.

"Your father, mistress, is a very brave man. He brought men with him, strong men, his neighbours and friends, prepared and spoiling for a fight. My father and my two younger brothers and myself, with the men your father brought, stood guard inside the curtain walls and in the courtyard, with torches lit and weapons to hand – hammers and mallets, some with pikes – ready to ward off any attack – with our lives if need be – and waited for the mob. It was an anxious wait, but eventually they arrived, quietly across the grass slopes, to the wall. A few scrambled over the wall or came through the gateway, but we were able to deal with them quickly. They were surprised to see us and raised the alarm, and soon the whole rowdy mob was baying and whistling and shouting, but they had no leader, no orders to follow, and were just an unruly rabble.

"Then other men from the vill, led by the blacksmith, came up from the river and surprised the attackers from the rear, and soon they were surrounded. Our supporters were also without direction or orders and there was a lot of shouting and fisticuffs and wielding of hoes and spades, axes and cleavers. There were some injuries and two of the attackers paid with their lives and, seeing this, suddenly the mob just disappeared into the shadows, as quietly as they had arrived. They just drifted away back into the forest. We stood guard for the remainder of the night but all was quiet and we realised that the danger was over." He laughed. "They certainly received a drubbing and I doubt that we shall have any more trouble. The young man in London who claimed to be Richard of York was found to be an impostor and will no doubt be hanged, and perhaps drawn and quartered, and that will be the end of it. There is no doubt, my lady, that the courage of yourself and your brother saved the family from a very nasty incident and we are most grateful. My father has sent a gift, in appreciation."

He took from the belt around his waist a leather bag and offered it to Ingaret. She shook her head.

"Jethro and I did not bring you warning from a sense of duty but from concern for your family and our family and our neighbours in the settlement and vill."

"Yes, we learned that the mob rampaged through the vill but, finding only women and children there, left them alone."

"Please take it, my dear," urged Lady D'Avencourt. "It would please me greatly if you would accept it. We cannot possibly repay you fully what we owe you. It is very little."

When Ingaret still hesitated, she took the bag from Robert and placed it in Ingaret's lap.

"Thank you, my lady. My husband is building a cottage for us and the baby and this will help with the cost. Of course, I will share it with Jethro and –" She stopped abruptly, suddenly realising that she should not finish her sentence by naming his wife.

Lady D'Avencourt nodded and Ingaret wondered how much she knew. She so hoped that her ladyship was ignorant of the facts but could not bring herself to look into those grey eyes, where she might read the truth.

She was relieved when there was a gentle cough behind them and they turned to see a priest standing at the wrought iron door of the chapel.

"Yes, reverend?" asked Lady D'Avencourt.

"I am prepared to hear your confession, my lady," he said quietly, "and to grant absolution. If you are ready, please follow me."

Lady D'Avencourt stood and reached for Mistress Aldith's arm. Robert and Ingaret also stood.

"I have to leave you now, Ingaret, my dear, but we shall always be in your debt. Robert, stay here and wait for me. I have much to confess."

"What possible sins has your gentle mother to confess?" Ingaret asked when she and her companion had gone.

"I cannot imagine," he said.

"And I must go, too," she told him, turning towards the now open door, but he laid a hand on her arm.

"Not yet, Ingaret," he said. "Stay awhile and talk to me."

"We have nothing to say to each other," she replied, turning back, "and Roldan's sister is waiting for me," but she made no attempt to leave.

"I did not expect to see you here today," she said to relieve the silence that followed.

"I would not let my mother travel on her own," he replied, "and I could not let pass an opportunity to see you again. How are you faring?"

"I fare well," she said.

"I'm glad – and the baby?"

She felt her face brighten. "The baby has quickened," she told him, "and kicks so hard I think it must be a boy."

He looked at her distended stomach so longingly that she pulled her cloak around her.

"You have no need – I would not hurt either of you," he said. "You do realise that it could have been mine – your baby?"

"There is no way it could have been yours, Robert, when we have never slept together!" she replied tartly. "It is Roldan's baby, his and mine."

"You let him into your bed but you ran from me."

"That's different," she said. "He offered me marriage. Were you able to do that?"

He said nothing.

"Of course not!" she answered for him. "You and I are worlds apart. You know that. You will never be in my bed!"

He looked at her for a long time, in the way he always did, which unnerved her so, and neither of them spoke.

"My little serf with the violet eyes," he said at last. "You're right, of course. We are worlds apart. We will never spend a night together and you will never know what you have missed – though I strongly suspect that I am the loser."

She took a step towards the door but he spoke again.

"Before you go, I have something to tell you."

She waited but he was silent.

"What is it? What do you have to tell me, Robert?"

She had to ask him again. "Robert?"

Ingaret was not prepared for what he then said.

"I am to be married."

She turned to face him, conscious of a stab of pain in her heart – *was it because of loss or just jealousy? What did she honestly feel for this would-be lover? Was she being a dog in a manger again? Whatever she was feeling, she had best get over it.*

"Married?" she repeated. "When? To whom?"

"Christmas Eve," he said. "To some girl my father has picked out for me. She's the daughter of a friend of his. Her father's an earl. I have no other prospects and my father is giving me a chance to rise in the world."

"Do you love her?"

He shrugged. "Of course not, but I'm told that will come. I've only met her a couple of times. She's a pleasant girl, I think."

"And this daughter of an earl – what does she get out of it?"

"This 'daughter of an earl' has a name. It's Helewise."

"Helewise – what does she gain from the union?"

"She told her father she is in love with me. It was he who approached my father, who agreed to the match. Of course, it is of no concern to my father where my heart lies. His gratitude to his one-time informer would not extend that far."

Ingaret ignored his last remark.

"She has fallen in love with you after only a couple of meetings?"

"Is that so hard to believe? Am I that repulsive?"

"Robert, I didn't mean that. You are not at all repulsive – the very opposite, in truth."

"Then why did you run from me?"

"I ran from you because you are not at all repulsive."

"Then why –?"

"We have been through all that. You know why."

There was silence between them again which Ingaret felt she had to break.

"I hope you will be very happy."

"I'm sure you do. As happy as you and your master mason, no doubt. Oh, we shall be happy – for a while – and I will be faithful – for a while. Anyway, I am just letting you know that this is the last time we shall meet like this. Probably the last time we shall meet at all. I will be going to live in her father's castle and will be subject to him as I have been subject to my own father, he who holds the strings of the purse. Come, let us shake hands and part as friends."

When she made no move, he said again, "Come, peasant girl, give me your hand."

Slowly, she held out her hand but, instead of taking it, he clasped her by the shoulders and kissed her hard on her mouth before releasing her.

"Goodbye, little peasant. I will never forget you."

"Nor I you," she said and hurried from the chapel, determined not to let any tears fall.

She found Marjery behind one of the pillars at the back of the cathedral, chatting with one of the vagabonds who frequented the building, especially in the inclement weather. These unwanted visitors had to be found and ejected every evening when it was time to lock up, although sometimes they evaded capture and spent a dry night in the cathedral, undiscovered.

"Quick, let's go!" said Ingaret, wondering whether her sister-in-law had seen what had just passed, although she gave no indication of having done so.

Outside, they saw her ladyship's carriage with two restless white horses in the traces and the coachman and footman lazing on the grass.

"Let's go home, Marjery," said Ingaret, handing her the leather bag to carry. "I want to go home."

CHAPTER 26

Lady D'Avencourt had described the contents of the leather bag as "very little" but it was a fortune to Ingaret and her husband, even after equally sharing the gold sovereigns with Jethro.

Roldan no longer had to build their cottage in stages, paying for each stage as he earned enough money to buy the building materials, and he and his hired labourers were able to finish it in record time. The young couple then filled it with furniture built locally.

Ingaret was delighted with her new home, which was facing south as she had asked. The ground floor room looked very much like Mother Mason's with a trestle table and benches, a few stools, a side board and a settle beside the plain stone fireplace Roldan had built. Ingaret made sure he had remembered the bread oven. The room contained two recesses for mattresses if required. A dairy and cold store faced north at the back of the cottage.

He had not included a connecting byre for the animals, which were housed in sheds in the yard, and Ingaret forgot that she had ever asked for one.

However, the solar above (only one), which was reached by a substantial ladder, was more elegant than the apple storage space in her mother-in-law's cottage and boasted a small glazed window beneath the eaves. It contained a four-poster bed with a canopy so that, in a heavy rainstorm, they were not pelted with any creature seeking shelter in the thatch above.

Next to the garderobe, where their few changes of clothing hung, and overhanging the floor below, was the wooden seat with a chute that sent all human waste into a pit dug in the earth. Their clothes would benefit from the odours from the privy which, hopefully, would kill any fleas and other unwanted insects.

The inner recesses of the second floor provided ample space for storing potatoes, apples and the like.

The day Ingaret and Roldan moved into their new home was a very proud and happy one for the young couple. At the gate, he lifted her up in his arms then carried her over the threshold and kissed her, "for the first time in our new home".

His mother, Joanna and Marjery followed them in and they uncorked a bottle of home-made dandelion wine to celebrate.

Brandon, a young weaver, had recently set up a small factory in the city and Ingaret had bought from him a length of rich brown woollen material so that all three women could make themselves serviceable new kirtles. There were also a few coins left over to hide in a hole dug in their earth floor beneath the rushes.

Jethro bought a plot of land not far away and begn to build a cottage for Thomasyn and Edwina and himself.

Thomasyn had not wanted to take money from the D'Avencourt family but Jethro said it was not a guilt payment – indeed, no one believed that his lordship felt any guilt for fathering her child, even if he remembered he had done so. It had also been the wish of her ladyship that Ingaret should take and share the gift. Thomasyn knew that her ladyship of all people was innocent of any wrongdoing and was most probably unaware of the true facts. No, the money had been given in gratitude for Jethro's and Ingaret's service in saving D'Avencourt lives and property, and was nothing more sinister.

One morning, in the early part of March 1502, while Ingaret was visiting Roldan's family and was sitting talking to his mother about the only subject on her mind now that her time was drawing near, suddenly she jumped up from her chair in alarm to find a trickle of water pooling on the rushes at her feet.

"Oh, Mother, I am so sorry," she apologised. "It seems my waters have broken!"

"No matter," her mother-in-law said calmly, "we can soon strew clean rushes. It means your time is near. Shall Joanna take you home?"

"May I – may I stay here, with you? I would rather be with you all than alone at home. Of course, if it is not what you wish, you must say."

"My dear child, we would be delighted to have you stay!" Roldan's mother assured her and her daughters looked equally excited at the prospect.

"You should not be climbing ladders," Joanna smiled. "You can have my mattress down here. I'll have clean bedding on it in no time."

So saying, she threw open the lid of a large wooden chest and began to rummage about in its depths.

"Meantime, come and sit down again," Marjery advised, taking her arm and helping her into the chair she had just vacated. Ingaret began to gently massage her stomach.

"Are you in pain?" asked Mother Mason.

"No, not pain exactly. It's like the ache I feel every month but it comes and goes."

Mother Mason's wide smile lit up her face.

"That's your contractions starting," she said. "The baby's in a hurry."

For the remainder of the morning and throughout the afternoon, Ingaret's contractions grew in intensity. They were doubling her up more often and lasting longer each time. Joanna helped her down onto the mattress, now covered in a clean sheet, and one or other of the sisters sat with her, holding her hand, counting the intervals, until the pain became too strong and it was no longer a game. Then they wiped her perspiring face with a cold cloth and spoke gently to her, helping her through each onset with their love and sympathy.

Soon, though, she was screeching in pain. Suddenly thoughts of her mother assailed her.

"Am I going to die?" she asked, clutching someone's hand. "I want to live! I don't want my baby to kill me!"

"You're both going to live," Roldan's mother consoled her, feeling inside the birth canal. "All is well. Your baby is exactly where it should be. Don't fight the pains. Let your body take control. It knows what it has to do even if you don't. It won't be long now."

"I want to push!" Ingaret suddenly exclaimed after being contorted by two further contractions. "I need to push!"

"Then push, dear girl, push hard. Push the little one out into the world. There's a clever girl! Push! Push!"

Ingaret tried. "It's like being on fire!" she exclaimed.

"I can see the baby's head!" Marjery told her excitedly.

"Another push and it will all be over!" Joanna predicted.

Ingaret made an extreme effort and it took two more exertions with her face screwed up and low grunts being forced out of her, relieving the tension, before the baby and all that had been supporting it slipped out into the world.

"It's a baby boy!" Mother Mason announced jubilantly, expertly cutting the chord with a kitchen knife and tying a knot. "I have a beautiful grandson!"

Joanna was beaming but Marjery was somewhat tearful as they came to inspect their new nephew.

"Has he got all his fingers and toes?" Ingaret asked anxiously, quiet now after all her exertions.

"Yes, have no fear, they're all there!" Joanna replied.

"He's just perfect!" enthused his grandmother. "Just perfect!"

She gently handed him to Marjery to wash in a bucket of warm water that was standing by and sent Joanna to the cathedral to bring Roldan home. Marjery wrapped the baby in a soft woollen blanket and placed him in Ingaret's arms. Ingaret was completely unprepared for the sudden rush of maternal love that overwhelmed her. She was singing quietly to her baby son while Mother Mason and Marjery were tidying and cleaning up when Roldan rushed in.

"I hear I am a father!" he said and tripped over the bucket in his haste to reach Ingaret, sending it flying and the water splashing everywhere.

"Roldan, son, I know you're pleased, but do look where you're going!"

"How are you Ingaret?" he asked, ignoring his mother and bending over to kiss his wife. "And here he is – my son! Haven't we been clever?"

"It's Ingaret who's done all the hard work!" Joanna reminded him.

"May I hold him?"

"Only if you sit on a chair and quieten down!" his mother said.

Chastened, he did so.

"What are you going to call him?" asked Marjery.

Ingaret said they had decided on the name of Allard if he was a boy and the three women nodded in agreement at the choice.

Ingaret was persuaded to stay where she was and rest for two more days before returning home, by which time her milk had come in and Allard was feeding lustily and making his presence felt.

She had greater difficulty than she anticipated in adjusting to motherhood, which surprised her as she had seen Gunnora dealing with the births of all her younger brothers and sisters – but then, Ingaret had been around to carry out all the household chores.

She struggled with the new routine of regular breast feeding and caring for her son while finding time for all her usual duties and the extra washing. All this, when every night her rest was disturbed when Allard would not sleep or would not feed or lay there crying for no apparent reason. Then she relied on the experience, wisdom and comfort that Roldan's mother gave her.

When the baby was six weeks old, after Ingaret had been churched, giving heartfelt thanks for her safe delivery, they took him to the cathedral for his christening ceremony.

Jethro and Thomasyn had consented to become godparents and Ingaret promised Roldan's disappointed sisters that she would ask them to become godmothers to their brother's first daughter, a promise she was able to keep eighteen months later when baby Philippa was born. Another bottle of dandelion wine was uncorked and drunk with relish.

Baby Philippa was placid and slept a great deal and Ingaret, now experienced, became less anxious and enjoyed being the mother of her two children.

CHAPTER 27

Roldan was much in demand now, not only for repair and restoration work but for his carving of ornamental statues for gardens and terraces, and he was able to employ two young apprentices.

The money he was earning paid for many luxuries such as bed hangings, curtains for both windows and padding for the wooden benches, stools and lavatory seat, and he was able to give an acceptable dowry when Marjery married Brandon, the young weaver.

On 2nd April of that year, 1502, the eldest son of King Henry VII, Arthur, Prince of Wales, died of the sweating sickness, leaving as widow the Spanish Princess Catherine of Aragon. Both were fifteen years old and had been married for only five months. This meant that ten-year-old Prince Henry became heir apparent.

Then in February of 1503, Henry's Queen, Elizabeth, died of childbirth complications; their baby predeceased her. On both occasions, the cathedral bell tolled all day to mark the sorrow of the nation.

So everyone was looking forward to the Feast of Corpus Christi, celebrated with great enjoyment every year during one of the long days in June.

This year, as usual, there were markets in all the streets in the centre of the city and a great deal of drinking and feasting took place all day. Groups of musicians and singers settled themselves at street corners, thanking passersby as coins were thrown into their hats and instrument cases, and companies of Morris Men and folk dancers roamed the city, performing wherever there was space enough to do so and an audience to applaud.

"Come, partner me!" called one of the young women, provocatively hitching up her skirt and beckoning to a man who was gyrating at the edge of the crowd, ale slopping down the sides of his tankard. "For a penny dropped in my shawl, you can ring one of my bells!"

"If it's a penny you want, I'll drop it somewhere warmer!" he responded as he staggered up to her and proceeded to pour ale down the inside of her bodice. She gave his exploring hand a hefty slap that sent the tankard spinning away into the crowd. He then received a thwack! across the back of his shoulders from a stick wielded by one of the Morris Men, which sent him sprawling among the dancers' feet, bringing their figure eight to an untimely end, to the delighted roar of the onlookers.

It was during the Feast of Corpus Christi that actors presented their mystery plays to one and all.

Each craft guild was responsible for presenting one of the popular stories from the Bible. In the Old Testament cycle, the guild of husbandmen acted out the story of Adam and Eve in the Garden of Eden; the water carriers the story of Noah and the ark; the sheep farmers the story of Abraham and Isaac, using a live ram for Abraham to pretend to slaughter instead of his son Isaac; and the story of Jonah and the whale was presented by the fishmongers.

The stonemasons' guild was responsible for the story of Jacob, who used a pile of stones as his pillow in the desert and dreamed of a stairway reaching up to Heaven with angels ascending and descending.

In the New Testament cycle, the goldsmiths presented the story of the three wise men bringing their gifts to the baby Jesus; the woodworkers showed the young Jesus helping his father in his carpenter's shop; the surgeons' guild presented several of the miraculous healings; and the metal workers, the Crucifixion, holding up iron nails for the audience to see.

The actors had been rehearsing for several days previously by rising at about half past four. They used for their performances the floors of carts which had been sluiced down in preparation. The carts would move from place to place so that everyone who wished could see all the performances; as soon as a cart left one venue, the next cart would take its place for the following part of the cycle.

The performances lasted till midnight and were greatly enjoyed by their audiences, who clapped and cheered, catcalled and whistled, their increasing consumption of ale making them more rowdy as the day wore on.

Roldan was a respected member of the Fortchester stonemasons' guild, and had been elected to serve on the city council. He protested that he was no actor but was happy to lend two of his horses and carts, which were usually pressed into service to transport blocks of marble, granite and limestone.

The family was looking forward to the day's holiday although Ingaret was concerned for Mother Mason, whose eyes were watering and her nose 'running' and she was sneezing more than usual.

"I'm used to this," she said. "It happens every year, this summer cold. Take no notice."

Joanna, too, said that her mother was so afflicted every year, but came to no harm, and the cold cleared up in a few days.

Everyone dressed in their best clothes, if they had a change of clothing. If not, their one set of clothes was freshly washed or brushed down and hung on a line to freshen in the warm June air.

Ingaret was wearing a new blue kirtle with lace-up bodice over her white shift. Joanna and her mother were also wearing new kirtles in soft grey.

Baby Philippa, a wriggling toddler now ten months old, was being carried by either Ingaret or Joanna, and Mother Mason had tight hold of Allard's hand. He was not yet two and a half years old and liable to run off exploring, if he had a mind.

As dawn broke, they walked with the crowd to the cathedral square for the first play, the story of Adam and Eve, then missed most of the Abraham and Isaac play because Allard and Philippa wanted to stroke the sheep that the shepherds had brought with them to entertain the children, who often became restless and disturbed the actors with their noise.

They were quiet for the stonemasons' presentation. An overhead platform had been constructed so that the muscular angels who were ascending the ladder could miraculously disappear into Heaven.

Roldan led his horse and cart away when that drama had been played to the end, and the family waited as the next cart took its place.

The words of the Joseph drama, presented by the weavers, were familiar. They watched as the story unfolded, their excitement increasing as one of the actors raised a hand to shade his eyes and peered into the distance, above the heads of the crowd.

"Behold! Here comes our young brother, Joseph, that weaver of dreams."

"Brother, how can you be sure?"

"Do you not see that he wears the coat our father gave him? Its many colours glow in the sunshine."

Another of the brothers came forward and also peered into the distance.

"'Tis him, no mistake. See how the peacock struts! 'Tis Joseph, right enough."

Another of the actors spoke.

"Brothers, let us away with the upstart! He boasts that our mother and father and all of us will one day bow down before him. Let us, instead, see him bow down before us in supplication for his life."

"Nay, brothers, 'tis against all that is holy to kill one's own flesh and blood!"

"Reuben, your head is as soft as your heart!"

"Perhaps but you will bring down our father's grey head in sorrow to the grave if you kill Joseph. Look, here is a pit dug by some poor wretch searching for water. Let us throw him in there and leave him a while without food or drink, to bring him to his senses."

At that point, the actor playing Joseph sprang on to the cart and, while he was explaining that their father had sent him to make sure that all was well with them and the flocks and to report back, his ten brothers set upon him. Fisticuffs ensued and he was overcome. They dragged off his coat of many colours and tied him up with rope. The audience began shouting encouragement or vilification.

Ingaret looked for Allard, to lift him up so that he could better see what was happening, but he was not by her side.

"Mother Mason, where's Allard?"

"He's here –"

But he wasn't.

"Mother, where is he?"

"He was here a moment ago. I had to let go of his hand when I started sneezing again. He could not have disappeared in that time."

"But he has! He has!" Ingaret could hear her voice rising on a wave of alarm. "Mother, take Philippa from Joanna and don't move in case he comes back. Joanna, you go that way, and I'll go this. Hurry! Hurry! He can't have gone far!"

Joanna set off at a run in one direction and Ingaret turned towards the main thoroughfare, shouldering her way through the crowds, ignoring the oaths of those she pushed aside in her desperation to find her son. The side streets were less crowded but afforded no sight of him.

Now she was really beginning to panic, her heart thumping at an alarming rate and a throbbing pulse in her temples making her dizzy. *Where was he? He couldn't have got this far! Not on those little legs! Someone must have taken him! No, no, no, she wouldn't think about that!*

She arrived at an open space in one of the markets and thankfully saw her husband there with his horse and cart. The actor playing Jacob was just about to climb on board. She shouted Roldan's name several times before he heard and came to meet her.

"Ingaret, what are you doing here? What's the matter?"

"It's Allard, he's run off. Joanna and I are both looking for him. He's nowhere to be seen!"

"All right. Don't cry. I'm sure we'll find him. Where's mother?"

"With Philippa, back in the cathedral square."

He spoke urgently to the manager of the players' company and handed him the script and the horse's reins then took Ingaret's hand.

"Come, let's go back. Joanna may have found him."

Still holding her hand, he pushed their way through the throng to the square. They saw his mother with Philippa waiting on the edge of the crowd. Joanna was there but no Allard. Jethro was with them.

Joanna shook her head as they approached.

"I haven't seen him but I found Jethro and family and he has something to tell you."

Jethro nodded. "I think I saw him. A woman had him by the hand. I thought at the time that it looked like Allard but they were at a distance then were swallowed up by the crowd and I decided it couldn't be."

"A woman?" cried Ingaret. "What woman?"

"I think I've seen her before," he said, "but I can't be sure. Do you remember when you asked me to join the Yorkist trouble makers in the forest? I think she was one of the young women standing on a barrel, who had a lot to say, but that was nearly three years ago and I can't be sure."

Roldan and Joanna looked at each other.

"He means Mary!" said Joanna. "She's getting back at you, brother."

"Roldan, do you know where she lives?" Ingaret asked.

"Yes, I do."

"Then we must go after her!"

"No, not you, darling. Leave it to me and Jethro. Joanna, take them home and wait for us there. We'll be back in no time, Allard with us. Is that not so, Jethro?"

"But –" began Ingaret.

"In no time," Jethro agreed. "Leave it to us, Ingaret. Go home."

She was not inclined to move but Joanna took her by the arm.

"Come, sister, come home. We'll wait for them there."

As Roldan watched them leave, he was heard to say, "Right, Jethro, let's go and get my son!"

It took them some time to reach home as everyone else seemed to be headed in the opposite direction. When they did, Mother Mason was glad to sit down, leaving Philippa to play in the rushes with a clay doll Roldan had fashioned for her. While Joanna filled three pots with ale, Ingaret paced round the room until she was prevailed upon to sit on the settle. Joanna brought her cushions to make her more comfortable.

After about an hour, during which they had little to say to each other apart from words of encouragement, they heard Allard's excited voice outside, the door was flung open and in he rushed.

"Mummy!" he shouted and Ingaret swept him up in her arms and burst into tears. He was followed by Roldan and Jethro.

"You must never, never again go away with a stranger!" Ingaret scolded her son, kissing him all the while.

"She was a kind lady," Allard protested.

"No she wasn't, she was taking you away and we might never have seen you again!"

Jethro grinned. "I seem to remember that you went off with a stranger when you were about Allard's age," he said. "A tinker, wasn't it?"

Ingaret did remember. "That was different," she said.

"Tell us what happened," Joanna urged them.

"I knew where she lived –" said Roldan, " – in one of the little streets behind the cathedral. It was a hovel. We didn't knock, we went straight in."

"What if the woman Jethro saw hadn't been Mary?" asked his mother.

"We took a chance and Jethro was right, it *was* Mary."

"We gave her such a fright," continued Jethro. "She was stuffing Allard full of strawberries."

"Kind lady," Allard said again, struggling to get down. Ingaret put him down and he ran off to find his hobby horse.

"She came at us with a knife!" Roldan told them. "She was screaming that Allard was her son, hers and mine, and she wasn't going to give him up."

"She wasn't making any sense," said Jethro, "just screaming and jabbing the knife at us."

"I was afraid she was going to hurt our boy," Roldan added. "Jethro got the knife off her, I grabbed Allard, and we left. Fortunately, the man she is living with wasn't anywhere around."

"This is your fault, Roldan," Joanna accused him, "letting her think you were going to marry her, then bringing Ingaret home, surprising us all."

"That isn't a good enough reason for taking Allard away," said Mother Mason. "Anyway, Roldan never made her any promises, did you, son?"

"I certainly did not, as I keep saying," he confirmed. "It's all in her head."

"So how do we get it out of her head?" asked Ingaret. "If she's taken him once, she may try again."

"I will speak to the city fathers," Roldan decided, "and ask that she be given a warning to stay away from my family or she'll be locked up. Perhaps that will calm her down."

"And we must never let him out of our sight," added Ingaret. "Never!"

As promised, Roldan placed his complaint about Mary before the city fathers at their next meeting in city hall, an imposing wooden framed building opposite the cathedral in the square. They questioned him closely about the incident and agreed that the requested warning should be given to her without delay. This had the desired effect and from that day she stayed away from the stonemason's family. If they chanced upon her in the market or anywhere else in the city, she would either turn her back and walk in the opposite direction or scurry down a side street. Ingaret hoped that was the end of the distressful matter.

CHAPTER 28

"I have a fancy for fish today," Ingaret announced one morning in September, three months later. "It's Thursday and the fishmonger should be in the market today."

Now almost nineteen years old, she was pregnant again. Both she and Roldan were happy at the prospect of the birth of their third child in the following April.

"I'll come with you," Joanna offered. "There were another twelve eggs in the coop this morning. I'll take our surplus to sell to the egg woman."

Leaving the children with Mother Mason, the two young women had plenty to gossip about on their way to the market and, once there, went their separate ways, agreeing where to meet an hour later to make their way home.

Ingaret decided to leave buying the fish until she was ready to meet Joanna and was happy inspecting the fruit and vegetables on the stalls, buying what they needed. The weather had been kind all year, with days of hot sunshine but also a deal of timely rain, and the harvest was plentiful.

She then wandered round the haberdashery stalls with their displays of buttons, leather laces, thread, coloured ribbons, brooches and pins, all ornamentation for plain dresses. At a mercer's stall she fingered the linens and silks, tried on a pair of kid gloves that were very expensive, then passed the time of day with a woman selling straw hats. She had worn such hats to shield her face from the sun when working on her father's strips of land.

The time came for her to find the fishmonger so she wandered back into the food market and bought a block of salt and fillets of sole for the recipe she had in mind.

On her way to the meeting place with Joanna, as she was passing a stall selling grain and sacks of flour, she heard her name called by a voice she knew. Turning her head, she looked straight into the blue eyes of Elis. He was beaming at her, his smile lighting up his face, *his dear face*, thought Ingaret.

"Elis! I never thought to see you here!" she exclaimed as he came round the stall to give her a big hug, his long yellow hair brushing her cheek.

"Nor I you – though I hoped I might," he said, releasing her.

"You look different."

"How, different?"

"You've grown up – you're a man now."

"A man with responsibilities," he said, laughing. "See the wrinkles?"

"Nonsense!" Ingaret laughed too. "You're still only twenty one. But the beard has grown!"

"It *is* good to see you again," he said. "How are you? You look blooming! And if I'm not mistaken?"

"You're not," she said.

"Your third?" he asked and she nodded.

"And how is my sister?" she asked. "Is Alice well?"

"Alice is Alice," he said with a grin.

"And do you have children, Elis?"

"Just one, a daughter, Constance. Alice finds child bearing and being tied down –" He searched for the right word. " – inconvenient."

Ingaret smiled. "She never was one for hard work. And how is my father? I miss him greatly."

"And he misses you, he has said so. That didn't go down well with Gunnora. Her tongue is as acid as ever it was."

"Tell me about the family."

"John is taking on a lot of responsibility at the smithy and is happy living and working there. James, Megge, Henry and Lizzie are thriving and, with Jethro, John and you gone, Noah dotes on them. He finds little happiness with Gunnora, I think."

"And your family?"

"All in good health, I'm pleased to say. My father is feeling his age, though, and more and more is leaving the day-to-day running of the mill to me and my brothers, but that suits us well."

"You always did have a happy family, Elis."

"It's a family you could have been part of," he reminded her.

"I know," she said.

"But, looking at you," he remarked, "it is obvious that Roldan is caring for you and making you happy. I see him at work in the manor from time to time and I hear his name mentioned as I go about my deliveries. I believe he is very well respected in the area."

"He is," Ingaret said, "and in all matters is climbing ladders." They laughed at her unintended allusion to his work.

"So, Ingaret, you have everything you always wanted."

"I have," she said though, looking at him then, memories stirred her heart, and suddenly she wasn't so sure.

A customer approached and Elis returned to his place behind the stall. Ingaret said she must leave to meet Joanna. He was busy and she said 'goodbye' and left, glad that there was no opportunity for a formal farewell.

Suddenly she was missing her home at the settlement, missing the family, missing her father – and missing the close bond she had had with Elis. Alice was in that place now, she thought, and Roldan was in the place where Elis had once reigned – or was he? Ingaret wasn't sure. Seeing Elis again had shaken up her complacent acceptance of life, as comfortable as it was.

"Are you feeling all right?" Joanna asked with concern on their way home. "You're very quiet."

"I'll feel better once I get home and have a pint of ale," she said, and hoped she would.

CHAPTER 29

11th June 1509

The cathedral bells began pealing at dawn, calling the population to early Mass, and rang throughout the day until nightfall.

Roldan and Ingaret with their three children, Joanna and Mother Mason joined the throng of excited worshippers, who had been given a national day's holiday to celebrate the marriage of King Henry VIII to the Spanish Princess Catherine of Aragon. The young king's father, Henry VII, had died only six weeks previously and the period of mourning had been set aside so that the nation could rejoice with the royal couple.

It had been a foregone conclusion that the 18-year-old, handsome, talented, well-educated and virile Henry would take as his wife the widow of his brother Arthur, the previous Prince of Wales, although she was his senior by more than five years. He had been granted dispensation by the Pope to marry his brother's widow; she swore that her first marriage had never been consummated, the couple being so young, only fifteen years of age, and the marriage lasting for only five months.

Ingaret was overawed at the splendid appearance of the cathedral within – at the thousands of candles flaring in the draughts as the entrance doors opened and closed, lighting up the colours in the stained glass windows; at the beautiful lilies and roses and other summer flowers in silver and gold containers on every altar and overflowing from the font; at the banners, pennants and gonfalons flying from poles all the way along both sides of the nave; and, permeating the whole building, the perfume of the incense as acolytes swung the incense burners.

From somewhere high up in the galleries rang out the pure, sweet voices of the boy choristers, accompanied by musicians hidden behind grilles.

"Where are the angels? There must be angels!" exclaimed Mother Mason.

The Latin words of the service were being intoned by priests at the high altar, who remained unseen behind the carved wooden chancel arch. The arch gleamed a burnished chestnut in the flare of flames from beeswax candles in silver candlesticks that stood taller than any man present.

The family did not stay long as the children were restless, especially the youngest, five-year-old Lora, but the worship would be continuous till sunset and Roldan said they could return later in the day if they had a mind to do so.

In spite of it being a national holiday, Ingaret was as busy as ever even though Mother Mason and Joanna were spending the day with the young family, helping with the chores.

Roldan had been teaching Ingaret to read and write and calculate, so that she could help him with his business records, and his tuition had proved very successful. She needed to spend an hour or so that morning catching up with entering transactions in the leather bound books he provided but was feeling very tired, due to the imminent arrival of their fourth child.

After their mid-day meal, she slept a while, then felt restless and said that she would like to walk, and perhaps would return to the cathedral because it was unlikely that she would ever see such a spectacle again. Roldan looked anxious and his mother offered to go with her, as she herself would enjoy hearing the music again.

The crowd had thinned slightly and they were jostled a little less as they approached the cathedral. At the entrance, they saw a carriage waiting, its two white horses contentedly munching fodder from their nose bags.

"I recognise that carriage!" Ingaret exclaimed. "It's the D'Avencourt carriage!"

"From your home manor?" asked Mother Mason, and Ingaret nodded.

They were about to enter by the main door when they met Jethro and Thomasyn with their three children hurrying out.

"You've seen the carriage?" he asked, giving Ingaret a hug. "They've just arrived."

"We had to walk out," said Thomasyn, kissing Ingaret then Mother Mason on the cheek. "His lordship nodded to Jethro but he looked straight through me as if I wasn't there – a thing of no value, an empty space!"

"My dear, he could hardly do otherwise," reasoned Ingaret.

"But there was a flicker of recognition from Master Robert, before he looked away," she said.

"He's here, too?" asked Ingaret.

"Yes," answered Jethro, "with his wife."

"What's she like?"

"I didn't take much notice. I could see that Thomasyn needed to come out, so we left. If you want to find out, go in and see for yourself."

"I will. Did they see Edwina?"

"No. Thomasyn shielded her so that they wouldn't. We're going home now. Children, say 'goodbye' to Aunt Ingaret."

The three of them, Edwina, Gregory and Rudd, did as their father had bidden and Ingaret promised that she would send them word when her baby was born and then they must come to play with their cousins and see the new member of the family.

After they had left, Ingaret and her mother-in-law passed through the entrance door into the cathedral.

123

They stood, spellbound as before, listening to the choir and joining in with the responses as best they could. However, Ingaret's mind was not on the service, as much as she tried to concentrate, and her eyes were wandering around the congregation, looking for the D'Avencourts, hoping to see Robert's wife and hoping, if she were honest, to see Robert.

Very few in the congregation were standing still. Most were on the move, trying not to miss a single occurrence. She and her mother-in-law were standing before a chapel dedicated to the Sisters of Mercy, admiring the vibrant blue of the blessed Mother Mary's robes, which matched the sapphires in her crown, when she felt she was being watched. Turning, she looked across a gap in the crowd and straight into the gaze of Robert D'Avencourt.

He looked away immediately and spoke to the woman by his side, presumably his wife, Helewise. A diminutive person, she was no beauty but had an interesting, intelligent face. Ingaret could not see the colour of her hair as it was enclosed by cauls on both sides of her ears, pearls entwined at the intersections of the wires, and kept in place by a gold circlet across her forehead that was also studded with pearls.

She could not help thinking that Robert had certainly fallen on his feet by marrying this daughter of an earl. She displayed a placid demeanour and Ingaret hoped that she was making Robert happy. She had the feeling, however, that he had too much of an adventurous spirit in him to endure a placid wife for very long.

With them were Lord D'Avencourt and his lady wife, on the arm of Mistress Aldith, as usual. None of them had changed very much, though Ingaret thought that Robert's mother looked a little more frail than when she had last seen her.

She decided, having seen the D'Avencourt party for herself, that she was now ready to make her way out. Also, the clouds of incense were making her feel sick.

Outside, she paused to breathe the fresh air and then was chatting happily to Mother Mason as they prepared to cross the square, but their progress was interrupted when the old lady saw a friend and wished to greet her.

With nothing better to do for the moment, Ingaret wandered over to the D'Avencourt carriage and reached out to hold the bridle and stroke the muzzle of the nearest horse when suddenly she was struck by a rain of gravel, which also hit the horse. She turned in surprise, only to receive another handful of gravel in her face, then another aimed at the horse.

With her eyes painful and watering because of the grit in them and feeling blood trickling over an eyelid and down her cheek, and not understanding what was happening, she stood stock still as the horse whinnied in fright and reared, followed a heart beat later by its companion.

Ingaret, who still had hold of the bridle, was pulled off balance and fell. The horse's hooves narrowly missed her as they landed but then it plunged and reared again and she looked up in fear to see its hooves above her and beginning to descend.

She screamed but could not move and thought her last hour had come when suddenly she was pulled clear of the danger, then blacked out.

As she came round, she could hear a babble of voices, reaching her from a very long distance away. She lay quite still, afraid to move.

"Someone get the old lady a chair!"

"Ingaret! Ingaret! Speak to me!"

"Stand back! Let her breathe!"

"I saw everything that happened!"

"Here, take my cloak! Put it beneath her head!"

Ingaret felt her head being lifted gently then laid back down on something soft.

"Ingaret! If you can hear me, open your eyes!"

Ingaret moaned. "Roldan?"

"No, it's not Roldan, it's me, Robert. Someone's gone for your husband. Can you open your eyes?"

She made a supreme effort and opened her eyes, to see the blurred and anxious face of Robert hovering above her.

"Robert? What happened? Where am I?"

"You're with me, darling. You had a nasty accident but don't worry, I've got you now. I'm going to take you to the hospice in our carriage. The Sisters of Mercy will look after you."

She felt herself being lifted up in strong arms and carried a few steps, then nothing more.

When she regained consciousness, she was in a single cot with the comforting smell of lavender and clean linen sheets around her. A nun in a grey habit was looking down at her, then her face disappeared and its place was taken by the kindly face of Mother Mason. Someone was holding her hand on the other side of the cot.

"Robert?" she asked.

"No, it's me, Roldan. Robert brought you here in his carriage but he left. I'm here now."

He kissed her on the forehead.

"How are you feeling?"

"Very tired and my eyes are sore. Roldan, why are my eyes sore? What happened?"

"We're not sure. Something frightened the horses and you were nearly trampled but he pulled you clear. If it wasn't for Robert, you might not be talking to me now."

"Gravel! Someone was throwing gravel at me and the horses. A storm hit me in the eyes, like hail stones. I couldn't see! The horses were terrified!"

"Ingaret, my dear, dear child, we have something to tell you." Mother Mason's voice conveyed all the anguish she was feeling.

"You need not be so anxious for me, mother. With rest, and Roldan's help, I will be on my feet again in a few days."

"Yes, you will, dear heart," said Roldan, "but this is not about you."

His mother took hold of Ingaret's other hand and held it tightly aginst her breast.

"Ingaret, dear, it's about the baby. The sisters did all they could, but you lost her. She was stillborn."

For a heart beat Ingaret could not comprehend what they were telling her, then she let out a wail of anguish and turned her head towards Roldan.

"Tell me that's not true, Roldan! Please tell me it's not true!"

"What mother says is the truth," he confirmed, gathering her up in his arms and holding her tightly as tears began to run down her cheeks, wetting his shirt.

"But why, Roldan, why? Gravel in my eyes doesn't kill a baby!"

"No, but there were more serious injuries, darling. You fell heavily and awkwardly and one of the horses' hooves landed on your stomach before Robert could get to you. Then you had to be brought in the carriage to the hospice. Everyone did their best to keep you lying quietly but you were terrified and would not lie still – and it was all too much for your body and the baby came too soon!"

"Where is she? I want to see her!"

"She was damaged, Ingaret, and the sisters took her and buried her."

"But they can't have had time to bury her already."

"She was born three days ago. You've been asleep for three days."

"But we will have other babies, Roldan! We will have more babies!"

Sadly, he shook his head and that was the final blow.

"Cry, Ingaret, cry. The sisters say you must cry."

And Ingaret did.

She came home from the hospice three weeks later and was put straight to bed. Having visited their daughter's grave in the grounds of the hospice, she had been having nightmares on the occasions she had been able to sleep but now, surrounded by her family, she felt the healing process beginning to take effect, though she still grieved deeply.

"Mummy, don't you love us any more?" asked Lora one day when she said she was too tired to play with them.

"Of course I do, darling," Ingaret was quick to reply.

"But you are always so sad," added Philippa, now seven years old.

Ingaret ruffled Allard's dark hair.

"Then you must make me laugh," she said. "Tell me the joke about the ducklings."

While Allard was telling his childish joke and she was waiting for the laughter line, she reflected that she must not neglect the children she had for the one she didn't have and resolved to try to put the past behind her.

Several days later, when she had resumed her household chores and had put the children to bed and was sitting in the front yard, enjoying the evening sun with the rest of the family, they fell to discussing the accident. Roldan did not try to stop her talking. The Sisters of Mercy had said she should talk about it as often as she wished.

"My memory of what happened is hazy," Ingaret said. "Mother, you were there, coming out of the cathedral with me. Did you see what happened?"

"Not all of it. I was behind you, talking to my friend, and the first I knew that anything was amiss was when the horse reared."

"I remember that I went over to stroke his muzzle," said Ingaret uncertainly, "but don't understand what happened after that. All I remember was the hail of gravel."

"There was someone there who saw it all," said Mother Mason. "He kept saying, 'I saw what happened! I saw it all!'"

"Who was that?"

"Just a bystander."

"Tell Ingaret what he said," Roldan prompted her.

His mother paused. "Well?" asked Ingaret. "What did he say?"

"He said," she reported, "he said that there was a wild-looking young woman picking up handfuls of gravel and throwing it at the horse while you were talking to it. When you turned round, she threw a handful at you. A stone hit you on the forehead, hence the scar there now. She kept on throwing until the horse reared."

"But why would she do that?" asked Ingaret.

"There's more," added Joanna.

"This witness," continued their mother, "said that the woman's companion, a man, was trying to stop her and was saying over and over again, 'Drop the gravel, Mary! Drop it! Come away home or we'll both be in trouble!'"

"Mary?" echoed Ingaret.

"That's what we were told. I wish now that I had asked his name but I was too shaken up to be that sensible."

"Then you must talk to the city fathers straight away, Roldan. What she did amounts to murder. She murdered our daughter!"

"That's what *I* said," Joanna interrupted, "but there's no proof that it was the Mary we think it was. It could have been another Mary or that man could have misheard. Anyway, we don't know who he was."

"I would warn her again," said Roldan, "if I thought it would do any good. She's acting like a mad woman! But I will speak to the man she lives with and put the fear of God into him, to see if that has any effect."

"I'm terrified of what she might do next."

"So am I," he agreed. "You must never go out on your own in future, do you hear me? We must arrange it so that there is always someone with you."

"I had intended visiting the hospice tomorrow to thank the Sisters for their kindness," Ingaret told him.

"Then I will come with you," Joanna offered.

"Roldan, I would like to take them a thankoffering."

"There's no need," Roldan told her. "Your stay there has all been paid for."

"That was thoughtful of you."

"Not by me, it was Robert D'Avencourt. He gave them a large donation before he left. He informed me of that fact when we met on my way in and his way out. I offered to repay him, of course, but he wouldn't hear of it. It has made me uncomfortable that we are so deeply in his debt."

Ingaret, too, was embarrassed but she took Roldan's hand and said he shouldn't worry about it. Robert had plenty of money and a kind heart, in spite of all his efforts to make people think he was a hard-bitten man of the world.

Roldan grunted. "I suppose so."

He said no more but Ingaret knew there was more to come. He waited till they were in bed.

"Ingaret," he said, "was there ever any – understanding – between you and him? I mean, did you ever –"

"No, Roldan. You cannot have forgotten our journey to Fortchester in the cart! You know I was a virgin when you married me."

"But did he ever –?"

"To him, I was just one of his father's serfs, only a peasant. That's what he always called me – peasant girl."

"Sorry, sweetheart, but I have sometimes wondered."

She put her arm across him and kissed his cheek.

"Roldan, I love you. I would never betray you."

To try to set his mind at rest, she rolled on top of him.

"Never!" she repeated.

He allowed her to make love to him then held her very close.

"You remember the sculpted figure I made for the rose garden at the manor house?" he said as she was drifting off to sleep. "It was destroyed – blown down in a storm years ago. Her ladyship has asked me to replace it."

"And will you?"

"There could only ever be one original. I could never make a copy of you. I told her ladyship that and she understood. I replaced you with an urn."

Ingaret laughed and soon fell asleep.

CHAPTER 30

June 1517

Everyone had decided that Joanna was a confirmed spinster and would never marry but then she met Kolby, a carpenter with his own business and three apprentices. His wife had died in childbirth a year earlier. He proposed to Joanna not long after they met and she had accepted, sure she was equal to the task of mothering his four sons. The family believed so too and was delighted for her.

They had all been to the cathedral early to hear the Banns read and were now in the yard in front of Roldan and Ingaret's house, preparing for a mid-day meal together.

The men had brought out trestle tables and benches and now the women were employed in carving the goat meat and serving the vegetables while the children were in and out of the house, transporting dishes and large trenchers of bread, earthenware drinking vessels and flagons of ale and mead.

Kolby's four sons were a delight to everyone. They seemed to fill the house and yard with their energy and laughter. Tall, well-built and sturdy, it was difficult to tell them apart at the outset as they were all topped with the same coloured hair as their father, apart from the streaks of grey, in various shades of red gold, pale to bright orange. The two eldest, Matthew and Mark, were handsome lads of sixteen and fifteen, adored by their younger brothers, Luke, John and Peter.

The young members of the family sat at one table. As well as Kolby's sons, there were Marjery's four children, Jethro's three – Edwina, Gregory and Rudd – and Allard, Philippa and Lora who were Ingaret's three.

Ingaret had been told by the Sisters of Mercy that it was unlikely that she would be able to bear more children because of the damage done to her after her accident, but the family was still growing as Marjery was big bellied with her fifth pregnancy.

Ingaret was amused to notice that Matthew and Mark were greatly taken with Edwina, whom they managed to seat between them, engaging her in animated conversation throughout the meal and making sure she had everything she needed. Allard, at the head of the table, looked a little grumpy, Ingaret thought, as the brothers monopolised his cousin. He and Edwina had always been happy companions but for once no one seemed interested in anything he had to say.

Edwina was a striking young woman, now sixteen years old. She was tall and as dark as her mother but with the D'Avencourt features that sometimes took Ingaret off guard and reminded her uncomfortably of Robert.

Mother Mason, now nearer eighty than seventy, sat at the head of the adults' table, Roldan and Ingaret at the other end, with Thomasyn, Joanna and Marjery on her right side and their husbands seated opposite.

Looking at this large family, her family, Ingaret thought that she could not be happier and, in passing, bent to give her mother-in-law a kiss on the top of her head. Mother Mason half turned and squeezed Ingaret's arm.

After everyone had eaten and drunk their fill, Roldan stood and said a few words, welcoming Kolby and his boys to the family and saying how delighted they all were to see Joanna so happy, then asking everyone to stand and drink a toast in honour of the family that had joined theirs.

After the meal had been cleared away and the tables removed, the adults sat and discussed what was happening in the city at that time. The children meanwhile played in the yard, chasing each other or playing team games, demonstrating their skill in running while bowling wooden hoops, the younger ones bouncing a ball backwards and forwards or throwing it into the air and spinning round several times before they caught it again.

When it was time for the gathering to break up, there was general confusion of sorting out cloaks and hats and a great deal of laughter.

"Ingaret, have you seen Edwina?" Thomasyn asked her.

"Not recently. She was playing with the little ones the last time I saw her," said Ingaret.

Thomasyn sent Rudd to find his sister and he returned with her a little later, saying she had been in the outhouse.

"The ball rolled in there," she explained. Ingaret saw her pink cheeks and wondered how much mead the Kolby brothers had inveigled her into drinking.

When the guests had left, the house seemed very quiet. Mother Mason helped to clear up and wash the dishes then left to go home. Roldan and Ingaret had asked her to come and live with them now that Joanna had moved out but she had declined, saying that her health was robust enough at the moment to enable her to live on her own but one day she might be glad of their offer.

Allard, now fifteen years old, brought in a clean bucket of water so that they could all wash their hands and faces before retiring to bed.

For some time he had been assisting his father and learning the skills and art of stonemasonry. Roldan had told Ingaret proudly that he was a fast learner.

On the morrow, he was going to the cathedral with his father and was anxious to rise in good time so as not to keep Roldan waiting. Their commission was to refurbish a third layer of supporting pillars high up in the roof where the columns, instead of being plain or fluted, were in the form of holy women from the Old Testament, the mothers and wives of the prophets. They were deteriorating under the smoky residue of thousands of burning candles and the grime of centuries.

"Your father is very happy to have you with him tomorrow," Ingaret told Allard as she absent-mindedly picked straw out of his hair and wished him good night. "It reminds him of the time he used to work beside his father. We are both so proud of our tall son!"

One evening, about a month later, Jethro paid a surprise visit, walking in unannounced and sniffing the aroma in the kitchen.

"Hello, brother," Ingaret greeted him, laying down the woollen hose she was darning. "This is an unexpected pleasure."

"What can I smell? It's making my stomach rumble, whatever it is."

"Honey biscuits," she said. "They're not ready yet but will be before you leave. I trust all is well at home."

"All is well, sister," Jethro replied. "I need to speak to Roldan privately, though."

"Ale?" He nodded and she got up to pour him and herself a pot of the dark brown liquid.

"He and Allard have gone for a swim in the river," she said. "Their work covers them in dust, head to foot. They should be home soon. What do you need to talk to Roldan about?"

"I need his advice. I'm sure he'll tell you about it after we've spoken. You have no secrets from each other, have you?"

Ingaret laughed. "None that I know of," she said. "Tell me now, have you heard anything of father?"

"Not for a year or so. I have determined to go back to the vill soon to see how they all are. As you know, all the children are married and Gunnora is dead, God rest her soul. Father was living on his own."

"And Alice?"

"Still leading Elis a merry dance, I hear."

"And children?"

"Still only one daughter. Alice told Thomasyn a long time ago that she had tried childbirth once and had no liking for it!"

"Poor Elis."

"Maybe. I hear that he has greatly enlarged the mill now that his father has passed on and he is the owner."

Ingaret was silent.

"You know, sister, that once I had the notion – the expectation and the wish, even – that you and Elis, one day, would –"

"That was a long time ago," she interrupted him, "but it was not to be."

Jethro looked at her quizzically. "Because you married Roldan."

"I did and I have no regrets. He has been very good to me and has given me our children."

They were chatting and laughing together about this and that when Roldan and Allard returned, their hair still wet, their faces scrubbed and shining following the vigorous administration of lye soap. Roldan slapped Jethro on the back.

"Glad to see you, brother-in-law," he said. "To what do we owe this unexpected pleasure?"

"I was enticed here by the aroma of Ingaret's honey biscuits," Jethro laughed.

"There's a reminder I can't ignore," she said and crossed to the fire to remove the tray of square biscuits, losing one on the way to the table as Allard stole one and promptly dropped it on the rushes.

"That was hotter than I was expecting!" he exclaimed, retrieving it and throwing it into the fire. Philippa and Lora left their play and came over to sample a couple each before being sent to bed in the corner of the room. Allard drank a pot of ale before retiring to his bed in another corner.

"Take your ale outside if you wish to talk," prompted Ingaret. "I've got this pile of sewing to do while it's still light."

The two men went out into the yard, leaving Ingaret wondering what was so important that it had caused Jethro to come to see them this evening.

She did not have long to wait before Roldan opened the door a little and called to her.

"Ingaret, my love, we need you out here. I want you to hear this."

She put down the hem of Philippa's kirtle that she was shortening for Lora and went outside. The men made room for her between them on the bench.

The nights were drawing in and the sun was setting, throwing fiery red and orange banners across the sky to the west. The men's expressions were grave and she wondered what news could cause them such anxiety on such a beautiful evening. She was soon to find out.

Roldan took her hand.

"Jethro is concerned about Edwina," he said.

"In what way?"

"*You* tell her, Jethro."

"A week or so ago," Jethro began, "I received a visit from Kolby, Joanna's husband. He suggested that we went for a walk together along by the river, which we did. He said again how grateful he was for the feast Roldan and you, Ingaret, had arranged for his and Joanna's wedding day and how pleased they were to see how his boys – their boys now – had mixed so well with the other children in the family and that they had been especially taken with Edwina. In short, he had come to make a proposal that Matthew, their eldest, or perhaps Mark, the second eldest, should ask for her hand in marriage."

"Marriage?" repeated Ingaret. "Marriage already?"

"She is sixteen," Jethro reminded her, "and old enough for marriage, and those boys are sixteen and fifteen."

"They have been well brought up," observed Ingaret uncertainly, "respectful and well behaved. It could be a good match, I see that. So what is the problem? What did Thomasyn think about it and why are you involving us?"

"Thomasyn was very much in favour. Of course, Joanna would become Edwina's mother-in-law – one big, happy family."

"Have you spoken to Edwina about it?"

"We have –"

"And?"

"She erupted like a volcano!" said Jethro. "Said she was in love with someone else and he was in love with her and she wouldn't marry anybody but him and, as they couldn't marry, she would never marry, and might as well go into a convent, and that was the end of the matter! Then she ran out of the house. I went looking for her but couldn't find her and she didn't come back until the middle of the night. We were worried sick."

"That doesn't sound like the Edwina I know," said Ingaret. "She's usually so calm and happy. Do you know who this boy is who she says she's in love with? Did you ask her?"

"Of course they did," said Roldan.

"And did she tell you?"

"She did," Jethro said.

He stood and paced a couple of steps away then came back and looked down at her.

"I think you will be as surprised as we were. It's Allard."

"Allard? Our Allard?" repeated Ingaret.

"Yes, our Allard," Roldan confirmed.

"But – but – didn't she say they couldn't marry? I consider it a perfect match. I would be very happy about it. Why can't they marry if Allard feels the same way?"

"Because they think they're cousins!" said Jethro.

"Have you still not told her who her natural father is?"

"No. We have never found it necessary – until now."

"Then tell her!" exclaimed Ingaret. "Tell them both and surely all will be well!"

"But everyone thinks they're cousins," Roldan said, "and to say otherwise would shame Thomasyn."

Ingaret nodded and fell silent while she thought about the problem.

"So, what's to be done about it?"

"There's more," said Roldan.

She looked at her brother. "What more?"

"Next morning, at breakfast, she told us that she had been thinking about it all night, and didn't want to go into a convent, but there was someone else who she thought loved her and she would marry him and live in misery for the rest of her life – her words, not mine."

Ingaret was feeling confused. "So who is this mysterious someone else?"

"She wouldn't say," volunteered Roldan.

"We couldn't get it out of her," confirmed Jethro, "but she showed us a brooch he'd given her, a red enamelled rose. Thomasyn confiscated it and has since sold it and we have forbidden her to see him again, whoever he is."

"Do they meet often?"

Jethro shook his head. "She says – and I've never known her to lie to her mother and me – that their meetings are always by chance, in the market or the cathedral or the cathedral square."

"What's to be done about it?" Ingaret asked again. "In truth, there is no problem. I, and I am sure I speak for Roldan, would be delighted for Allard to marry Edwina."

"But not possible if we stay in Fortchester," Jethro said. "The only way is for us to move somewhere else, where no one knows us, wait a while, then arrange the marriage."

"But where will you go?"

"That is for Jethro and Thomasyn to decide," said Roldan. "But I do think that Thomasyn is the person to explain the truth to Edwina and put her heart at rest. Our young couple must wait a while and exercise patience. It will be easier if they are not seeing each other so much."

Jethro nodded. "I have asked Roldan to explain everything to Allard as soon as possible. He may come with you all to say goodbye to us when we move away, but other than that, I ask that they do not meet until the marriage is arranged."

"I will make sure that he has plenty of work to do until that time," said Roldan, "which will not be difficult. The cathedral is keeping us both very busy. Now will you join me in another pot of ale?"

"Thank you, no. I will go home to Thomasyn. She will be waiting to hear how you have responded to the situation. Then tomorrow I must visit Kolby and explain to him what he will not wish to hear."

Ingaret smiled and hugged her brother.

"If Kolby still wishes to have his sons marry into our family," she said, "remind him that, if they will wait a few years more, our Philippa and Lora will be eligible."

"I will indeed," laughed Jethro and left.

CHAPTER 31

Roldan and Allard left for their work at the cathedral as usual the next morning. As Ingaret kissed them both goodbye, Roldan whispered to her that he would tell their son all that had been discussed the previous evening and ask him not to meet with Edwina, unless in company, until their marriage could be arranged – if, indeed, he wished to marry Edwina, which she assured her parents he did.

Ingaret could not settle to her chores after they had left and decided to go to the market to buy what she needed for their family meal that day and to visit the cathedral afterwards so that she could be shown their work on the depiction of Hannah, the mother of Samuel. Roldan had explained that, as mentioned in the Bible story, she was holding a robe which she had made for Samuel and would be taking with her on the annual pilgrimage to the Temple in Jerusalem, where she had dedicated him to serve the old priest, Eli.

She arrived at the square to find a large, noisy crowd gathered at the entrance doors, and realised that something unusual was happening but did not know what.

"What's going on?" she asked a woman who was fingering the beads of her rosary and murmuring a prayer, "What's to do?"

"They say there's been an accident," a man beside her said. "They've locked the doors so no one can get in."

"What sort of accident?" choked Ingaret, a touch of premonition causing her heart to thump and fear to constrict her throat.

"They haven't said," replied the man.

"I must get in," Ingaret said in desperation. "My husband and son are in there. They'll know what it's all about."

"It may only be that someone's stolen something and they're not letting him escape," offered the man, hopefully.

Ingaret knew the cathedral well and left the crowd to circumnavigate the outside walls until she came to a small insignificant-looking door that led into the chancel, through which Roldan trundled the blocks of stone so that he did not have to convey them through the nave among crowds of worshippers and visitors. Fortunately, she found it unlocked.

She slipped inside and shut the door behind her. Ahead in the chancel she saw a bevy of monks and clergy standing in a huddle, all talking animatedly with lowered voices, with none of them seeming to be listening to anyone else or giving any answers to questions.

With relief, she noticed her son among the cathedral brotherhood and called to him. He didn't hear her above the hubbub so she went nearer and called again. He turned and saw her and immediately came towards her, roughly pushing his way through the crowd.

"Mother! Stay there! Don't come any nearer!"

As he parted the way between the monks' cassocks and clergy vestments, she saw a green cope lying over the tiles. Then he was by her side and she was crushed in his arms.

"Allard! What is it?"

He turned her round so that her back was towards the crowd and that green cope, and he pressed her head against his shoulder.

"It's Father," he said, his voice choked.

"Father? No! No! No! Not that!" she pleaded, looking up into his face. "No, there must be some mistake! It can't be your father. He'll be around somewhere. Go and find him, Allard, and tell him we need him here. Tell him that someone has –"

"Mother, dear, you have to be brave!"

"It's someone else, I tell you. I'll go and have a look and we'll find out who it is."

She made as if to leave Allard's arms but he held tight hold of her.

"There's no mistake. One of the brothers saw it happen, the fall. There was nothing anyone could do."

"He fell from up there?" she asked, as if it mattered where he had fallen from. "I want to see him!"

She struggled in his arms and tried to break free again but he held her fast.

"Trust me, trust me, you don't. You need to remember him as he was."

She was not conscious that the chatter had subsided. No one was speaking. One by one they had realised that she was present.

She turned her head and saw again the green cope someone had thrown over him. *But he could not be lying beneath it because the brocaded material lay almost flat against the tiles, although blood was spattered all around it.* Ingaret screamed.

She heard someone say that the Bishop had been sent for and Allard said that he had despatched an altar boy to fetch Jethro.

Someone brought a chair for her and a priest brought a silver chalice of water for her to drink; he said it was holy water, saved from the sacrament, and it would help her.

But nothing could help her. Not the expressions of love and respect and sympathy that flowed into the house from neighbours, friends and Roldan's colleagues, nor the administration of the sacrament of Holy Communion by the Bishop, nor the flowers laid at her door, nor the arms of those who loved her, nor the burial service. Roldan had been her lover and her support, the father of her children, during seventeen years of happy marriage, and now he had left her.

Also bearing this great sorrow was Mother Mason, for whom it had now happened twice in her long life. Her decline into senility started from that day and she died a year later, in spite of all the devoted love Ingaret, her daughters and her grandchildren could show her – the mother Ingaret had always longed for since childhood.

There was an investigation, of course, ordered by the Bishop. It transpired that one of the boards high up on the scaffolding, which were always placed so carefully with each one overlapping its neighbours, had been moved so that it would be upended by anyone who stepped on it. That unfortunate soul had been Roldan and he had been hurled to the floor below.

How this came about was a matter of conjecture. Allard swore on the Holy Bible that the boards had been carefully placed when he and his father had descended the scaffolding on the previous evening.

One of the Benedictine monks reported that he caught a fleeting glimpse of a shadow when he came to lock the cathedral doors that evening but he had made a thorough search of the building and had found no one.

The family had their suspicions but Ingaret had no energy or desire to pursue the matter. Her dear Roldan was dead and no witch hunt would bring him back. They were thankful that Allard also had not fallen, as he could have done so easily.

"How is it that you weren't with your father?" Jethro asked him.

"God forbid!" exclaimed Ingaret.

"I was praying at the altar of the Blessed Virgin," explained Allard. "That morning, Father had sat me down on the low wall in the square and had told me the truth about Edwina's birth."

"Of course," said Jethro, "it was the morning after I had visited your parents. The subject has not been referred to since your father's death."

"But it has to be addressed," Ingaret commented, "sooner or later."

"I needed time to think about it," Allard explained, "to thank the dear Lord that Edwina and I could marry after all, when we had thought we could not commit that mortal sin and endanger our souls in the hereafter. I needed time to think about the consequences and her move to another town. I was praying there when I heard – when I heard that bang that will haunt me for the rest of my life." He choked and could not continue.

Ingaret changed the subject.

"Allard has suggested that we follow your family, Jethro, when you move away, so I will be near you after they are married, but I am not sure I want to move myself and my girls out of our family home. I have to think about it carefully. The Bishop is allowing me a pension so I should be able to support Philippa and Lora until they marry."

"Only you can decide," agreed Jethro. "We will not pressure you either way."

"But I do not want to delay Allard's marriage to Edwina. He has had enough sadness in his life of late. He deserves to be happy. I want this for them."

"And so do we," agreed her brother. "I can work anywhere and we just have to decide where to move to."

CHAPTER 32

Ingaret's period of mourning lasted a year, during which time she did not wear any colour other than black. However, she would not allow her daughters to do so for more than three months.

They were all very busy during that time, taking on Roldan's chores around the house and yard as well as their own, and assisting Mother Mason as much as she needed.

At the end, as she approached death, the old lady was bedridden and unable to feed herself or do anything else for herself, but it was a great joy to Ingaret to be able to nurse her and repay some of the love and care she had always received from those loving hands. Her eventual passing was a great sorrow to all the family.

Allard, meantime, continued the work his father had left unfinished, which took him many months to complete. Jethro and family had moved to the small town of Brocklebury, some twelve miles distant, where Allard was a frequent visitor.

The young couple were impatient to be married and their parents allowed them to take their vows in the presence of the family, promising to have their Banns read as soon as Ingaret felt she could relinquish her mourning.

Since making their promises, they had been living with Jethro and Thomasyn and family but Allard had been able to buy an old wattle-and-daub cottage and was engaged in repairing and renewing it, as necessary.

Marjery, her weaver husband, Brandon, and their five children were frequent visitors to Ingaret and made sure that she and her two daughters were among the best dressed women in the neighbourhood.

This did not go unnoticed by Kolby's four sons when their family came to share a meal; on those occasions, Ingaret provided chicken or goat meat, always a luxury.

Noah came to visit the family occasionally, usually on Lord D'Avencourt's business, and brought all the news from the manor. Ingaret was pleased to learn that her ladyship was still well, under the care of Mistress Aldith, and was a grandmother many times over.

When she diffidently asked about the welfare of Master Robert, Noah said he had little news but rumours were rife about his philandering, the earl's displeasure, and that he had not fathered any children, at least legitimately. When Ingaret expressed her surprise, Noah said that Robert's wife was a weakly creature and had had several miscarriages and one stillbirth.

Ingaret put aside her black mourning attire on the anniversary of Roldan's death and came down from the solar that morning in a white shift and green kirtle. She had plaited her hair into thick braids that circled her head but had left one long strand curling on each side of her face.

"Mother, you look – you look – so young," Philippa approved.

"Don't sound so surprised, darling," Ingaret laughed. "It felt good to cast aside the black. Your dear father is dead and there is nothing anyone of us can do about it – and I am only thirty two when all is said. You both know what today is?"

"The anniversary of Father's fall," answered Lora.

"Yes, God rest his soul. I have sent word to Allard and asked him to join us in the cathedral for the service of Terce, to give thanks for the life of your father. Your aunts Joanna and Marjery will also join us."

"That will be a good thing to do," said Lora quietly.

"I thought so," said Ingaret. "And then, soon, Jethro will arrange for the whole family to gather in Brocklebury parish church to hear the Banns read for Edwina and Allard. You have probably heard that Edwina is already with child and is thinking of asking you both to be godmothers." The two girls smiled at each other and nodded enthusiastically. "But first, my dears, we will have breakfast together, then Philippa, you will take your turn at going to market while Lora and I clean up here."

Philippa returned from the market in a state of excitement. She shut the door behind her with her foot and banged the basket on the table.

"Mother, I have such news!" she said.

Ingaret came to the table to help her unpack the basket.

"Careful, or you'll be spilling oats all over the floor. What news?"

"The watchman fished a body out of the river early this morning."

"Oh dear, poor soul."

"Whose body?" Lora wanted to know.

"Do they know whose body it is?" asked Ingaret.

"Yes – it was Mary's!"

"Mary's?"

"Yes, the Mary who has been causing us so much grief. Don't you see, Mother? It can't be a coincidence that it is the anniversary of Father's fall."

Ingaret stayed silent for a while. Her daughters looked at her, not knowing what more to say.

"So," she said at last, "her guilt must have been too heavy a burden for her to bear. Let's hope that she repented before she took her own life. Come now, girls, it is time for us to meet Allard at the cathedral, where we will pray for her immortal soul."

"Curse her, Mother, don't pray for her!" exclaimed Philippa.

"Hush, hush," Ingaret said. "What is done is done and there's no changing it. Cursing her will only damage your own soul, not hers."

"Then you forgive her?" asked Lora, surprised.

"Not yet I can't," Ingaret answered, "but I hope that will come in time."

Allard was waiting for them at the main door of the cathedral and Joanna and Marjery arrived not long afterwards. Together, the family walked together along the nave and into the Choir stalls, with the monks facing them.

Ingaret remembered sitting here with her father on the day she had first met Roldan, and tears came to her eyes. She reached into the silk bag that hung from her girdle and fingered the broken piece of limestone rose leaf that he had given her on that occasion and felt overwhelmed with her grief for that kind young man who had loved her so much. Instinctively aware of her distress, Allard drew her arm through his and she was comforted.

The service was simple, mainly recitation of psalms, and the rhythm and flow of the words acted as a balm for her soul. The celebrant gave thanks for the life of Roldan and for his work for God in this building, and prayed for his family. To this, Ingaret silently added the words "and Mary", believing that that young woman's anguish in the knowledge of the evil she had done to the family on three dreadful occasions must have greatly surpassed all that she, Ingaret, had suffered.

The service over, the rest of the family left the cathedral to go about their business but Ingaret said she would stay for a while to soak up the peace she found there.

"Are you sure you'll be all right, Mother?" Allard asked her anxiously. She smiled at him and was about to ruffle his hair, as she had always done, but stayed her hand. She had to remember that he was now head of the family and no longer her little boy.

"I shall be quite all right, dear," she assured him. "You get back to your work – laying a pathway, did you say?"

He nodded. "Bread and butter work," he said.

"But safe," she added.

He left her then and she wandered along the side aisles, stopping to admire each small chapel, so familiar now that she was living in Fortchester but once so awe-inspiring.

"Hello, Ingaret."

She had just walked around a pillar and there he was, standing in her path.

"Robert!" she gasped in surprise. "What are you doing here?"

"Waiting for you," he replied.

"But – but – I don't understand. How did you know where I was?"

"I knew that it was the anniversary of Roldan's death and guessed you would come to the cathedral to remember him – and you have."

"And I have," she repeated, not having the wits about her to say anything else.

"You have a fine son and two lovely daughters," he volunteered.

"Have you been spying on us?" she asked sharply.

"Not spying, exactly – just observing," he replied.

"So how long have you been here?"

"I made sure I was here when they opened the doors. I was prepared to wait all day, if necessary."

"Oh."

"You look radiant!" he said.

She remained silent.

"Will you walk with me?" he asked her. "For old times' sake. Down by the river."

When she hesitated, he added, "Ingaret, I promise I won't touch you. Just walk with me."

"Robert, you're married now."

"You've no need to remind me. I know it well enough. Please, Ingaret. I just want to talk to you. I promise."

Ingaret knew she should refuse but had not the strength to do so – and he had promised.

"All right," she said. "By the river."

It was not far to the river, just along a side street, and they reached it in a short time, walking together in silence. Once there, they set off along a path formed by the passage of thousands of feet over the centuries. The water was clear as it bubbled over its stony bed, which afforded a crossing when the water was low during dry summers. After leaving the stones, it flowed fast and evenly through fields of wheat before entering a copse in the far distance.

For a while they stood and watched the antics of several ducks, the males with their iridescent green heads and white collars and curled tail feathers.

"They found a body in the river this morning," Ingaret said, "a woman's. Her name was Mary."

"You knew her?"

Ingaret nodded and told him all that they knew and surmised. Her story included, of course, the occasion when Mary had thrown gravel at the D'Avencourt horses and Ingaret had been injured and lost her baby. He interrupted her then and said how sorry he had been to learn that news.

"I have never had the opportunity to thank you for helping me that day," she said. "You saved my life."

"I'm so glad I was there."

"I have often wondered," Ingaret said, "how you came to be there, so close, when the last I had seen of you was in the cathedral with your family."

"I followed you out," he said, "and glad I was that I had done so."

She asked him about his wife, Lady Helewise. He was non-committal in his reply, just said that she was well for a change and not with child, thank God, as that had been a fruitless exercise and not worth the little effort he had taken.

"Be kind to her, Robert," Ingaret said. "It is a terrible pain to lose a baby."

"I know," he reluctantly agreed. "I know it."

They stopped to admire a pair of swans with their cygnet, its brown feathers just beginning to turn white. Absentmindedly, he picked the head off a yellow iris then cursed and rubbed his hand when he accidentally brushed it against a patch of stinging nettles.

"Ingaret, now that you are out of mourning –"

"This is my first day."

"So be it but can we be friends again? Just friends – I'm not asking for anything more."

"I don't think that's appropriate, Robert."

"There is no one else?"

"That's none of your business! But no, there is no one else."

"Then may we not meet, now and again? Where's the harm in that?"

"Your wife –"

"She won't find out."

"That's not the point."

"Her father is more to the point – but he won't find out either, if we're discreet."

Ingaret shook her head and could not help herself smiling.

"Oh, Robert, Robert, you haven't changed, not one little bit."

"Not when it comes to you, Ingaret, no, I haven't."

"I am still a peasant, as you've always reminded me."

"But you've come up in the world, my little serf with the violet eyes."

He took a step towards her and she backed away.

"Robert, you promised."

"Sorry."

"We should go back now. I have work to do at home."

"You will let me see you again?"

"I don't think so."

"I'll walk you home."

"There's no need. Once we reach the ford, I can make my own way."

They walked back in silence, he with his head down and shoulders slumped. When they came to part, he ignored the hand she held out to him, took her face between his hands and planted a hearty kiss on her lips.

Ingaret felt the beginning of a response in her body and regretted the brief duration of the kiss. To cover her confusion, she chided him.

"What happened to your promise?" she asked.

"What promise? Oh, that one. You didn't really expect me to keep it, did you? Farewell, my lady." He bowed and turned and strode along the side street on his way back to the centre of the city.

Ingaret could not help smiling as she followed him. If she was honest with herself, she had known in her heart that he would never keep his promise.

That night, she was aware for the first time since Roldan's death, how lonely she was and how cold and empty her bed and that she wanted – needed – to see Robert again.

PART III

D'AVENCOURT MANOR

CHAPTER 33

He arrived only two days later, knocking at her door.

"Robert," she exclaimed in surprise, "you're back!"

Out of respect for her reputation, he had dressed less flamboyantly than usual, in cream and brown under a brown cloak, and he looked like any city merchant.

"Couldn't stay away," he answered matter-of-factly. "Well, are you going to keep me standing at your door or will you let me in?"

"Come in," she said, moving aside so that he could pass her. She shut the door, first glancing up and down the street to see if anyone was watching, but no one was.

Philippa and Lora were indoors, Philippa preparing vegetables and Lora sweeping the hearth.

"Girls, I would like you to meet a friend of mine, Master – er – what should we call you?"

"Robert does well enough," he said.

"Robert then," she continued. "Robert, this is Philippa and this is Lora."

They both dropped him a curtsey and he smiled, amused.

"Now, young ladies," he said, feeling in his purse and handing them each a coin, "I'm sure you can find yourselves something pretty to buy in the market. Off with you now! I want to talk to your mother."

They were fulsome in their gratitude and could not get out of the door fast enough.

"Robert, you shouldn't," Ingaret remonstrated.

"They're lovely girls but I just wanted you to myself."

"Ale and honey biscuits?"

"Heavenly," he replied, taking off his cloak and laying it across the bench as she busied herself bringing to the table a pitcher and mugs and a plate of biscuits.

"So, why have you come?" she asked, glad that he was sitting at her table in her kitchen in a cottage of which she was very proud.

"I wanted to see you again. I've missed you all these years."

"But your wife –"

He sighed heavily. "That again! Helewise is a dear girl, a pleasant companion, and we rub along well enough most of the time, but there is no fire in her belly! She has not been able to give me a son or even a daughter, and now we have stopped trying. So I look elsewhere for comfort."

"If that's all you've come for, you can leave straight away!" Ingaret told him.

He was amused. "Huh! That's not what your lips told me when I kissed you by the river!"

"You are greatly mistaken," said Ingaret stiffly, though she guessed it was the truth.

"Have it your own way."

He helped himself to two more biscuits.

"Her father threatened to horse whip me once. I probably deserved it. I'd had too much to drink and brought one of them home. Rubbed my wife's nose in it. I wouldn't have done it if I had been sober."

Ingaret felt nothing but pity for Lady Helewise.

"Can you not divorce her?"

"No chance of that – no grounds, you see. We can hardly plead that the marriage has not been consummated after all the failed attempts at producing an heir. No, we both have to bear it, her in her way and me in mine."

"What is her way, Robert?"

"She spends time with her embroidery and gossiping with her lady-in-waiting, or in the chapel or visiting the peasants on the manor with food and clothes and herbal medicines and anything else they need. They despise me, I have no doubt, but everyone loves her."

"Except you."

"Oh, I love her in my own way. Actually, I love her enough to keep out of her way. I only make her unhappy."

Ingaret gulped down a mouthful of ale. It felt unusually hot for an autumn day and she was perspiring.

"You should not be here."

"I know that but I couldn't stay away after that kiss."

He stood and prowled round the room, inspecting the gleaming copper pans lined up on a shelf, the pottery vases full of chrysanthemums, the furniture.

"Roldan was a good provider, was he not?" Ingaret asked him.

"He was a well-respected young stonemason," Robert agreed then came and sat at the table again.

"I have a confession to make," he continued, not looking at her.

"About what?"

"The statue of you that Roldan carved for our rose garden. I smashed it to smithereens."

"I know," she said. "Mistress Aldith told me."

"The devil she did!"

"I saw it was missing and asked her. She would not have told me, otherwise."

"I was so angry that I had lost you to Roldan that I was beside myself. I was sorry afterwards. It was all I had left of you."

They had finished the pitcher of ale and she offered to top it up again but he shook his head.

"I have spent time in Fortchester over these years, you know, always hoping to see you in the market or the cathedral or the square, but I never did. I didn't waste my visits, though. I found a friend – met her in the market. Sweet child – much younger than me, but there's no harm in that. It's fun showing the young ones the power they possess to pleasure a man. Haven't seen her recently, though. I think her family must have moved away."

Ingaret stared at him.

"Her name?" she asked. "Robert, what was her name?"

"I don't know that I remember – began with an E, I think. Edith? Eleanor? No, that wasn't it. It was – Edwina! Yes, that was it. Edwina."

Ingaret looked at him, aghast.

"Robert, you didn't? You can't have!"

"Didn't what? Can't have what? We didn't, as a matter of fact. I hadn't got that far. Beautiful girl, though, very dark, and two years past the age of consent. Strange, but she looked somewhat familiar, though we hadn't met before, as far as I could remember."

Ingaret continued to stare at him, not knowing for the moment what she should say.

"Don't look at me in that accusing way. What did the difference in our ages matter? So, she was only fourteen but you were fourteen when I fell in love with you – or have you forgotten?"

"The day you crashed your horse into our cart in the forest."

"Yes, that day. You were such a beauty – and still are, Ingaret, in spite of all you've been through, though now you have a maturity you didn't have then."

"Don't change the subject. Her age is not the reason. Robert, haven't you realised?"

"Realised what?"

"Edwina is your sister."

"What? What are you saying?"

"She's Thomasyn's daughter, your father's bastard."

"I don't believe you."

"She is now my son's wife."

Robert looked at her, long and hard, then doubled over and put his head in his hands.

"By all the gods," he said, "I would have been indulging in a mortal sin and on my way to hell for the rest of eternity."

Ingaret regarded the top of his head

"Yes, you would have."

He moaned. "You see, I need you, madam, to keep me out of trouble."

"And keep you from bedding all your father's and brothers' bastard daughters? I wouldn't know where to begin! I'm not your mother, Robert; you're not my responsibility."

"But I could be," he mumbled.

"What?"

He raised his head.

"Live with me, Ingaret. Become my wife in all but name. I swear to God that I'd never look at another woman for the rest of my life. I love you, my lady. I always have since you first looked at me and entangled me in those eyes."

"But your family would never accept me. I am still of peasant stock. I could never hold my head up in the company of your brothers' wives."

He swore then and stood and took her hand. "You're more of a lady than the whole gaggle of them tumbled together. Not one of those marriages comes even close to the joy we would have in each other. You shall have everything I can give you, everything you want. Come, live with me, Ingaret. I'll die if you don't."

"All right, Robert, I will," she heard herself saying, much to her own surprise. "I will – but not before my two girls are married and happily settled in homes of their own."

He groaned. "They're beautiful girls but that could be years away."

"I don't think so. They already have suitors and a couple more years will pass quickly."

"It's a lifetime," he complained.

"Nonsense. We've waited all this time. Another two years or so won't make much difference. Anyway, those are my conditions."

"Then I must accept!"

He took her in his arms and laughed and kissed her and pulled her close to him. Then he quietened and she felt his body shudder and his desire for her rise, and they would have loved each other there and then except that they heard her daughters returning and had to push themselves apart and compose themselves before the girls came in, laughing and wanting to show their mother the ribbons and laces they had bought from the stalls in the market.

That night, Ingaret was no longer lonely. She looked ahead to her future and wondered how she had come to this point in her life when she would become the mistress of the youngest son of Lord D'Avencourt. She wondered at her lack of modesty and temerity in accepting his proposal but thought it had always been their destiny from their first meeting in the forest when she was a dirty little girl with bare feet and only six years old. She would become his wife in all but name and was very glad about it.

And Elis? Ah, Elis. She would be living very near the mill once she had been installed in the manor house. Very near. Perhaps she would see him on occasions. Probably she would. But her dear Elis was married to her sister. She hoped that Alice was making him happy but doubted it, knowing Alice. Elis, of course, would never leave. He would always be close by.

However, that was not her concern at this time in her life. Robert would be her concern and she looked forward to that moment, however far in the future it might be.

CHAPTER 34

Following that visit, Ingaret did not see Robert for three months, until after Christmas. He sent her gift after gift by messenger, items of jewellery, with letters expressing his love but saying that he would not be able to meet her without fulfilling their union, which was not in the best interests of either of them at this time. He wrote that he was working hard (doing what, she was never sure) to tire himself out and trying not to think about her, which was impossible. He wrote many more words of love, seducing her by letter, so that she had to destroy them in case they were found by her daughters. She was reluctant to throw such sentiments in the fire but knew that there would be another letter in a few days' time.

Her daughters, however, were much engaged with their own affairs. First came the reading of the Banns between Edwina and Allard in the parish church in Brocklebury and then Kolby's son Matthew began to court Philippa, at first gently but then more urgently. Ingaret said they should wait to marry until Philippa was 15 years old in the Summer but they would not, so she relented, but insisted that they allow Edwina's baby to be born first so that neither event should overshadow the other, and the young couple agreed to that.

Once the snow and ice had melted and the snowdrops that had been brought over to the cathedral garden from France were hanging their heavy heads towards their frozen nursery, but before the primroses brought sunshine into the woods, a baby son was born to Edwina and Allard. He was christened Roldan in the ancient stone font in the cathedral, a privilege allowed because the baby was the grandson of the first of that name. Philippa and Lora became his godmothers and the brothers Matthew and Mark, as prospective husbands of the baby's two aunts, his godfathers.

Philippa and Matthew were married the following month and Lora and Mark followed their lead a year later when Lora had reached her fifteenth birthday.

Ingaret gave Philippa and Matthew her cottage and to Lora and Mark sufficient money to buy a plot of land and build their own. Both daughters were now happily settled in their own homes and the way was clear at last for Robert to claim Ingaret for himself – "My prize for waiting so long," he told her, "and I will not wait a heartbeat longer!"

During the months of waiting, Ingaret had had time to acquaint her family with her intentions and the delay had given them all time to become used to the idea, whether they liked it or not. Her own children were most opposed to what she was suggesting, but all were happily following their own paths and, whatever their scruples, were well pleased that their mother seemed happy at the prospect and would no longer be on her own. She promised that she would not lose touch and they could visit at any time, with Robert's agreement, whether he was around or not. The only aspect of which she was certain was that Edwina and he should never meet and that none of Jethro's family should ever guess how close all those involved had come to a disaster that was none of their making.

Late one evening, Robert brought Ingaret to D'Avencourt manor. His father had carried out an extensive building programme during the time she had been away and had allocated Robert and his brothers various rooms in the newly-built west wing, which was well distant from the main house.

Robert had assured Ingaret that it was unlikely she would ever meet his father, but if she did happen to do so along some corridor or other, he would think she was one of Lady D'Avencourt's young ladies, her hairdresser or seamstress or some such. In that case, she should not be surprised if his father tried to fondle her but she would have to tolerate that and escape as best she may.

As for his mother, whom he loved dearly, she was gradually succumbing to the decay of mind that plagued old women. Ingaret said that she liked his mother very much and hoped they would have occasion to spend time together. Robert replied that his mother did not remember from one day to the next whom she had or had not seen, and no one took any notice of her ramblings, so there was no reason why they should not have discourse from time to time, if Mistress Aldith allowed it.

"The servants will know I am living with you," she said.

"They do as they're told or they lose their positions here," Robert replied. "If they are told that you are not living in my rooms, then you are not living in my rooms. It is that simple. Just keep out of the way of my father – and my brothers and their families when they come visiting."

"What of Lady Helewise?" nagging guilt pushed her to ask.

"I will have to go home sometimes," he answered, "but I won't be able to stay away from you for long. However, it will be natural for me to want to visit my mother at times and the earl and his daughter will have to accept that I am a most dutiful son. She will probably be relieved, anyway, not to have to share her bed with me as a dutiful wife." He paused and smiled wryly. "It has always been duty with Helewise and me. It will be different for you and me, I know it."

Ingaret was sorry to leave the city but was excited at the prospect of living as the nobility lived, though she recognised in her heart that she was still the same peasant girl whom Robert had fallen in love with and whom Roldan had married. She did not know the ways of the nobility but would have to learn quickly if she was to survive this new life.

The carriage, pulled by black horses so as not to be so conspicuous, arrived in the manor courtyard after their long journey. During those hours,

Robert had not ceased kissing her, his hands straying all over her body on top of and beneath her shift, and they would have taken matters further but the speed and swaying and jolting of the coach prevented it.

They were met by two menservants, ready to carry Ingaret's trunk to wherever they were directed.

"My solar," Robert instructed them and they disappeared through a door.

Robert helped Ingaret from the carriage and, holding her hand, led her through the doorway and up two flights of winding stairs. They stepped out onto a landing. The two men were emerging from an open door ahead of them. Robert ignored them and they disappeared down the stairs. The staircase continued up to other floors above.

Robert, still holding her tightly by the hand as if he were afraid she would disappear, drew her into the room and shut the door behind them. Candles were alight on tables but Ingaret had no time to appreciate her surroundings because he was pulling her through an inner door and into his bedroom, where more candles were burning.

She hardly had time to take breath before he was pulling at the laces of her bodice then tugging at her skirt.

"Robert, wait! Wait!" she gasped. "Let me!"

His breath was hot against her skin as together they undressed each other, throwing aside their clothes, and she was lying naked on his bed before she had time to think about what was happening.

He fell on top of her and the fire that was erupting inside him was not quenched until he had possessed her again and again. Ingaret had never known anything like this violent need and responded with a need of her own that she hardly recognised.

When their hunger had eventually been satiated, both lay exhausted.

"Ingaret," he said at last, when his breathing had eased, "what was all that about? What happened there? I have never –"

"No, nor have I," she said.

"I need a drink," he decided and slid off the bed. He found a silk robe across the back of a chair and put it on and disappeared into the next room. Ingaret found her shift and put that on then followed him.

There was a silver pitcher on a tray on a side table with two tankards and he filled both with mead.

"Hungry?"

She nodded and he rang a small bell on a side table.

"Best go back into the bedroom," he said when there was a knock at the door. She did so and heard him order another pitcher of mead and bread and cheese, and breakfast for two at noon next day.

Ingaret sat on the bed and hugged herself in amazement and delight. She had never slept in till noon in all her days.

After they had finished the bread and cheese and drunk more mead, they sat for a while in companionable silence. The shadows cast by the candle flames flickered around them. He sighed.

"If we go on like this," he said, "you will send me into an early grave." He grinned. "Though I can think of worse ways to die!"

He stood. "Come, my beautiful peasant, my Ingaret – and you are mine now, at last. I've waited long enough!"

He drew her back into the bedroom.

"We've probably ruined the bedcover. Let's make sure the sheets go with it to the washerwoman!"

CHAPTER 35

Those first few weeks passed as if in a dream with Ingaret feeling only half awake. She and Robert drew closer in minds and bodies as they made love as often as they pleased, relieved of any fear of pregnancy.

Inbetween whiles, they walked in a side garden or down by the river or in the forest or across the fields; they laughed at each other's jokes and talked about many aspects of life in general, and he taught her how to play chess and cards and games of dice.

If he ever thought about his wife, he never mentioned her. At times, a shadow crossed Ingaret's heart, a shadow named Helewise, but then she would hungrily seek out Robert's lips and rid herself of it.

These tinges of guilt caused the only faint disturbance to her love for him. But was it love on her part? She wasn't sure but it hardly mattered as they were both very happy and she could see no reason why their life together should not last until – old age? But neither of them was going to get old – at least, it was too far away to think about.

Robert went home once during that time and took with him a black puppy, one of a litter born to his mother's pet Labrador, to give to his wife. He confided to Ingaret that everything she wanted was supplied by her father and there was nothing he could give her, except babies – and that hadn't happened – but he thought the puppy would please her.

"And did it?" asked Ingaret on his return four days later.

"She was more pleased to see the puppy than she was to see me," he admitted.

"Is she well?"

"Yes, and I think – though I can't be sure – that she has a lover."

"Really? Who?"

"One of the young under gardeners. I arrived unexpectedly, of course, and I was told that she was in the kitchen garden – a strange place for her to be, I thought – and I caught them together in a greenhouse. By the time I entered, they were admiring some plant or other, but it seemed to me that there was a distinct nervousness about her and he was talking too loudly and with too much animation – about leaf mould – and she was showing too much interest – but, as I say, I can't be sure. If her father knew, he would turn her out of the castle and have the young man horsewhipped and dismissed. Anyway, she adored the puppy, and it hardly seemed to matter to her when I said I was leaving again. She knows where I am if she needs me."

Selfishly, Ingaret hoped that Lady Helewise had found herself a lover as it would relieve herself of any feelings of guilt.

She began to settle into her new routine, not that she had much of a routine to follow. Relieved of all the chores she had known since a child, all she had to do was please herself and Robert.

He had found her a young lady-in-waiting from among the daughters of a merchant who travelled the continent and brought back fine silk to sell in Fortchester. Ostensibly, she had come to the manor to serve her ladyship but found herself whisked away to wait upon Ingaret and was living in a room next door to the solar.

Her name was Beatrix and she was a plump, happy and efficient girl of twenty years, and a comforting companion when Robert was away. It was she whom Ingaret sent to Noah to let him know where she was and he visited often, being someone who had been at the manor on many occasions for many reasons throughout the years so that no one thought to question his presence.

The two rooms in which Ingaret was living were opulent but very plain in masculine fashion and Robert gave her permission to change anything she wished. So she and Beatrix began introducing many improvements, starting with the bed hangings and coverlet, and engaged Beatrix's father to design and produce hangings in the new damask weave, in dark red. She laughed when she saw the canopy being tied in position, knowing that she no longer had to fear creatures dropping onto their heads during the night as there was no thatch above them but solid wood, bricks and slates.

Now there was no need for the constant replenishment of rushes as oak floorboards replaced the hard-baked mud floors she had known all her life.

She then commissioned matching drapes for the windows, covers that reached the floor for the flat-topped chests, cushions for the chairs with arm rests, padded seats for the settle, and screens to keep away the draughts. She ordered cheerful rugs for the floors and scented candles for the side tables. Finally, she sent Beatrix to the garden to bring back greenery or an armful of flowers to fill bowls and pots.

Robert indulged her fancies and only remonstrated when the cover over one of the chests got in his way when he was looking for a belt or hat or a heavy ornamental chain to wear round his shoulders or waist.

The stone fireplaces in each room had been designed and built by Roldan, she was sure, but she never asked.

She felt great pride in the beauty of the stone carvings and initially a heart stab of loss when she remembered her dear husband, but she was still young and life had to go on. She knew that she would not be here in the manor if he had not died but she had mourned him for a year and could not wear black for the rest of her life. That was then and this was now and she resolved not to let her new life with Robert become haunted by ghosts.

Sometimes she would visit his mother in her solar or in the great hall. Before entering, she was always careful to ask Mistress Aldith if her ladyship would be pleased to see her that afternoon. Sometimes the answer was no, her ladyship was sleeping or was not in the mood to receive visitors, but usually the answer was that her ladyship would be delighted to talk to Ingaret and hoped she would take refreshments with her.

On the first occasion, she had become lost in the maze of rooms as she left the west wing and ventured into the main part of the manor, trying to keep to the passageways that the servants used. She arrived at the door of the great hall, where Mistress Aldith sat, busy with her embroidery, at the same time keeping her eye on Lady D'Avencourt, who was dozing in a chair in front of a lively fire.

Ingaret was at a loss what to say to explain her presence in the manor, making the lame excuse that she was visiting her father and had hoped to have an audience with her ladyship to renew their acquaintance.

"No explanation is necessary," Mistress Aldith reassured her. "Little happens in the manor of which I am not aware. Come."

She led Ingaret forward.

"Her ladyship always feels the cold," she explained as they approached the recumbent figure by the hearth.

Ingaret thought that Robert's mother had lost weight since she saw her last. Her silk gown was loose over breast, shoulders and arms, though she was still a striking figure, her silver hair drawn into two plaits and curled into a wheel over each ear, her head covered with a soft white cloth. Her gentle face was more lined than previously and her grey eyes were still as sad as Ingaret remembered.

"My lady," Mistress Aldith said, "you have a visitor. Do you remember Ingaret who came to warn us that the Yorkist rabble was on its way here, intent on burning us all in our beds? She has come to see you."

Ingaret stepped in front of her ladyship and dropped a low curtsey.

Lady Margaret looked puzzled.

"It was a long time ago, your ladyship," said Ingaret, "about twenty years, but you came to Fortchester to thank me and my brother."

Her ladyship's face cleared. "Yes, of course, I remember you, my dear," she said, "and glad I am to see you again. Come, draw up that chair and sit beside me. Aldith, some mead if you please and send down to the kitchen for some sweetmeats."

Aldith left to carry out her wishes.

"So, my dear, what brings you to D'Avencourt manor? I heard that your husband had been killed by falling in the cathedral. I am so sorry."

She reached out and touched Ingaret's arm lightly.

"But you are not here to talk about sad happenings, I am sure. There are so many sad happenings, are there not? Better to speak of happy times. Tell me, have you any children to bring you comfort?"

"I am blessed with three children and one grandson," Ingaret replied.

So, while sipping mead and enjoying candied fruits, sugarplums and honey and nut paste served on a silver dish, they talked of family. Lady D'Avencourt said she had seventeen grandchildren and recited their names with the help of Mistress Aldith but on subsequent visits the number changed and the names changed and Ingaret pretended that she was being told for the first time.

Her ladyship presumed that Ingaret was still living in Fortchester, where she had last seen her, and asked her about the dress and hair styles of the women there and the religious ceremonies in the cathedral, then asked how her husband was and what work he was engaged in, and remembered the statue of Ingaret in the rose garden that had been blown down in a storm.

"What was your name again?" she asked for the tenth time.

"Ingaret, your ladyship."

"I shall never remember that, far too complicated. How well do you know your Bible, my dear?"

"Not well enough," Ingaret admitted.

"The angel Gabriel came to warn our Lady that she was to experience a virgin birth. You came to warn us that the Yorkists were about to attack."

Ingaret nodded.

"Yes, you came to warn us. You were our angel Gabriel. I shall call you – no – Gabriel is a young man's name. I shall call you Gabriella. How does that sound? Our angel – Gabriella."

Ingaret laughed and forebore to mention that the name Gabriella contained one more syllable than her given name, and said, "I am honoured, your ladyship, to be regarded as your angel. Gabriella pleases me well."

"So, Aldith, how does that sound to you?"

"Very holy, your ladyship, but will you remember it?"

"Of course. When do I ever forget anything?"

Mistress Aldith exchanged an amused glance with Ingaret and answered, "Very seldom, your ladyship."

So, Ingaret became Gabriella to Lady D'Avencourt from that day forwards, when she remembered.

Sometimes one of Robert's brothers and his family came to visit for a week or so. They stayed in the rooms prepared for them and, on those occasions, Robert forbad her to venture out of his suite of rooms. She heard the sound of children's shouts and laughter echoing around the walls and watched them as they ran and played with their sticks and hoops out in the courtyard or rolled down the grassy slope or splashed in the river. She would have liked to have joined them in their games but had to stay content with watching and listening.

When he was at home, Lord D'Avencourt was much engaged with hunting deer or foxes, shooting game birds especially bred for the sport or fishing in the river for barbel and chub. However, he seemed to spend a great deal of time away from the manor and Ingaret never met him during her discreet wanderings about the house and grounds until one occasion when she came face to face with him in his wife's solar.

She and her ladyship were deep in animated conversation, with Mistress Aldith guarding the entrance to the solar as usual, when he unexpectedly strode into the room.

He was still a handsome man although showing signs of age, his dark hair and beard turning grey and lines wrinkling his forehead and cheeks, but he exuded energy.

He was across the room in a couple of strides to where his wife sat in her chair and bent over to kiss the top of her head, then took her hand and kissed that.

"Margaret, my love," he beamed at her, then noticed that they were not alone and there was someone who had just jumped to her feet, knocking over the stool on which she had been sitting beside his wife.

"So, who have we here, my lady?" he asked, then turned to Ingaret.

"We have not met before, I believe – I would have remembered," he said. "And what is your name?"

He obviously thought that she was one of his wife's companions and Ingaret was happy to let him think so.

She dropped a curtsey, wondering how to reply. She did not want to give him her name or any other personal information about herself.

"You do not answer," his lordship said. "You need not be afraid of me, madam. I just want to know your name."

"Her name is Gabriella," said his wife with great certainty. "She is an angel, do you not think so, sir?"

"I do indeed," said his lordship, looking Ingaret up and down so intensely that she felt uncomfortable. "An angel, no doubt of it. And where does this angel live?"

"In Fortchester," replied his wife again, greatly pleased with herself that she had remembered.

"So why is she here?" he asked, still looking at Ingaret. She looked down in embarrassment but he reached out and put his hand beneath her chin and lifted up her face and looked into her eyes.

"Such eyes," he breathed. "Such eyes."

Ingaret stepped back a pace and dropped another curtsey, not knowing what else to do, trying to break the intimacy he was building between them.

"May I send for refreshments for you, my lord?" asked Mistress Aldith from the doorway, coming to Ingaret's rescue.

He turned then. "If you would, Mistress Aldith, thank you," he said.

He took off his cloak and threw it over the back of a chair and sat in another.

Aldith rang a small hand bell and gave instructions to the servant who appeared. All Ingaret wanted was to escape from this subtle entanglement. She had Thomasyn very much in mind.

"Then I will leave you, my lady," she said.

"You don't need to leave on my account," her husband said.

Oh, but I do, she thought but said aloud, "I will visit her ladyship again some other day, with your lordship's permission."

"You are welcome here any time," he replied, "any time. From Fortchester, eh? 'Tis a long journey just to keep my wife company."

"I have friends in the vill," she said.

"Then I am certain we will meet again. You should not be difficult to find – should her ladyship wish you to keep her company again."

He stood and bowed his head. She kissed her ladyship on the cheek, curtseyed again and made for the door but he called her back.

"Gabriella, it has come on to blow a cold wind out there and you are likely to be chilled on your way back to the vill. Allow me," and he gathered up his cloak and held it out to her. She did not move so he had no option but to bring the cloak to her. He turned her round so that her back was towards him and put the cloak round her shoulders. Then he turned her round to face him and tied the cord at her neck, his face close to hers, smiling at her as he did so. The cloak was much too long for her so she bunched it up in her hands. He completed the arrangement of the cloak by smoothing it down over her breasts. She shuddered at his unwelcome caress but he obviously thought it was a shiver of delight.

"Until we meet again, Gabriella," he breathed into her ear. "Be sure I will find you."

Then she was out of the door and away down the passageway, returning to the west wing by the route she had come. When out of sight of the solar, she stopped to remove the cloak and would have discarded it on the floor but thought that might be unwise so bundled it up in her arms and eventually arrived back at Robert's rooms, vowing never to leave herself open to his father's advances again. She did not tell Robert and hid the cloak in a coffer, hoping to get rid of it at the first opportunity.

CHAPTER 36

Robert strode into the solar one afternoon informing her that a messenger on horseback had arrived from his wife, saying that she needed him at home urgently. He and Ingaret discussed at length the reason for the message but could offer no plausible explanation for her request.

"I'll leave at first light," he said.

"Can't you let her wait for a day or two?" Ingaret pleaded. "You know I miss you when you're away."

"No. I pay her little enough attention without ignoring her urgent summons."

Ingaret pouted and he laughed.

"You're getting so possessive of late," he said. "That's not like the Ingaret I knew."

"You would prefer that I play difficult to seduce?"

"It's certainly more fun that way."

She knew it, but had so little to engage her energies these days except their love for each other. She missed her children and her growing family of grandchildren and sometimes felt that life had little meaning any more.

As for her family in the vill, Ingaret had kept in distant touch with all her half-brothers and half-sisters while she was ensconced in the manor but her brothers' wives and her sisters were embarrassed by her position as Robert's mistress and seldom let it be known that they were related to her in any way. Everyone in the vill knew it but it was never discussed and certainly not in front of Noah.

At first, this disapproval distressed Ingaret but, after a while, it ceased to concern her. She wondered who among them would not jump at the chance to become the mistress of Robert D'Avencourt if they were given the choice and were not forced into a liaison, as had been Thomasyn. Perhaps young Megge would refuse, maybe Lizzie, but she wasn't sure even about them. So she shrugged off their silences and continued along the path she had chosen and, when all was said, it was a path she enjoyed immensely.

Having shown her no affection when she was a child, since their journey to Fortchester with the sheep, Noah now would not hear a word said against her.

He knew what no one else did, how much she had been able to ease the lives of members of the family with small gifts and sometimes a little coinage, or had secured for them paid work at the manor over and above the days spent as dutiful serfs.

Noah still served Lord D'Avencourt in many ways but the work demanded of him was lighter than when he was a younger man, especially as he was supplying so many days' service through his sons and grandsons.

"Such a long face!" Robert chided her. "Come, it was just an observance. I don't want you to play hard to persuade at this moment. Come, share this bottle of red wine with me and then we'll make such love that neither of us will be satisfied until we are back in bed together again!"

He kept his word and she was reluctant to let him go next morning and interfered with his getting dressed until he was inside her again, but finally she had to let him go. Her last sight of him from the window was as he rode out through the archway on Son of Pendragon, and down the slope to the river, which she knew he would follow past the mill and church, and up onto the high road, where he would turn left on his way to the hilly country and cross the ancient Ridgeway.

This time, he was away for three weeks, and sent no word to explain his delayed return. Ingaret fumed every day he was absent and would not be mollified, no matter what cause Beatrix suggested might be keeping him away so long.

"He could be dead," Ingaret railed at her, "and I wouldn't hear of it! Who is there to tell me when no one knows I am here?"

"Everyone knows you're here," retorted Beatrix, "at least everyone except his lordship and Lady D'Avencourt. I am sure that Mistress Aldith would let you know if there was bad news."

"My body aches for him, Beatrix," Ingaret complained. "Do you know what that's like? Have you ever ached for a man's arms around you? For his organ to be inside you? Have you?"

"No, my lady, not yet."

"You will one day then you will understand what I am talking about."

She was angry with herself for feeling so much in need of him, but it was a desire she could not control, an overwhelming desire that had crept up on her during the two years she had been living with him. She did not want to be so dependent on this physical contact but there was nothing she could do about it – nothing she wanted to do about it.

So she and Beatrix played endless games of cards and chess and she visited Lady D'Avencourt two or three times each week, having made sure that Lord D'Avencourt was away, but nothing satisfied her restless wanderings through their two rooms in the west wing.

Then, suddenly, he was back. He strode into the solar one evening in his usual way, his cloak mud-spattered from his ride, his riding crop in one hand and a bottle of red wine in the other.

"Where is she?" he asked Beatrix, who was collecting up Ingaret's clothes where she had dropped them on the floor.

"My lady has just gone to bed."

161

"Good answer!" he said, putting down the crop and bottle on a table. "Help me off with my cloak then you can go. We won't be needing you again till morning – and not too early, mind."

Beatrix helped him off with his cloak and hung it on a hook behind the door, then folded Ingaret's clothes over her arm, curtsied, and left with a wide smile on her face.

Ingaret came to the communicating door in her night shift. She also had a wide smile on her face.

"Robert!" she exclaimed. "I've missed you so. What kept you away this long? Oh, I've missed you!"

"Come here," he said and threw his arms around her and nuzzled her ear and kissed her full on the mouth.

"So, why did you not come home sooner?"

"Wine first," he said, "then bed, then I'll tell you all about it."

He poured them both a drink.

"This is excellent wine," she said appreciatively, raising her silver goblet until it reflected the light from the flame of a nearby candle.

"I visited the cellar before I came up," he told her. "Thought you'd like this one. Would you play the part of my mistress and take my boots off – and anything else you've a mind to take off?"

She had a mind to take everything off him then pulled him into the bedroom. She pushed him down on the bed and took pleasure in just gazing at him, lean and muscular as he was, his desire for her evident, then she laughed, took off her night shift and straddled him.

"You must be tired," she said. "Let me do all the work."

When they once again had had their fill of each other and she was lying quietly in his arms, she said, "So tell me. What was all the urgency?"

He took a deep breath and said, "My wife is with child."

"She is?" Ingaret was astounded. "How did she allow that to happen?"

"The usual way, I imagine," he said. "She admitted that it was the gardener's bastard. She pleaded with me not to beat her, as I had the right to do, or tell her father, who would turn her out and have the lad horse whipped across his bare back then dismiss him so that he would never get another position."

"So, did you beat her?"

"I may be many things, Ingaret, but I am not a wife beater."

"Sorry, darling," she apologised and kissed him where her hands had just stroked his cheek. "So, what's to be done?"

"She has missed her bleeding only twice so is not far along in the matter but she was in a great state of agitation and had eaten nothing for several days. She –" He paused to cough. "She – er – well, she asked me if I would bring the baby up – if I would bring the baby up as my own, when it is born, if it is born."

"What an idea! What did you say?"

162

"I thought about it long and hard and finally said yes, I would."

"Robert!"

"We both thought that she would probably not bring it to full term and, if she did, it would probably be another stillbirth."

"And if it lives?"

"I will say that it is mine. If it's a boy he will be my heir – not that I will have much to leave – but what's the harm in that? It doesn't worry me what happens after I've gone. It won't matter to me that he doesn't carry my blood. Of course, I won't have much to do with the child. My mother will love it. My father will be delighted that at last his youngest son has done something right for a change. And Helewise will be the happier for having a child to think about. As for the gardener, he will keep his mouth shut if he knows what's good for him. I've told her, though, that this is the one and only time. I can't keep on fathering her bastards."

Ingaret raised herself on one arm and looked down at him. "But to be yours, Robert, you would have had to have been there, and you haven't been there for months."

He coughed again and threw back the coverlet and sheet and sat on the edge of the bed. Ingaret came up behind him and knelt and put her arms round his waist and leant her head on his shoulder.

"Isn't that so?"

"Yes, it is so. That's why I stayed longer this time, to make feasible her claim that I am the father. With her history of pregnancy, no one will think it strange that the baby arrives several weeks early."

There was silence between them. Finally, Ingaret plucked up courage to ask the question that was uppermost in her mind, "Robert, did you sleep with her?" When he did not answer, her voice rose almost to a screech. "Did you sleep with her?"

His tone of voice as he answered her was rough. "Yes, I did, most nights, if you must know – her story had to have some credence in the minds of her ladies of the bedchamber."

Ingaret drew back and let her arms drop.

"Robert, how could you? You swore to me that you'd never look at another woman for the rest of your life!"

"Ingaret, don't be cross. She is my wife, after all. And she and I didn't reach anywhere near the heights that you and I reach – though she had got better at it. I could tell she'd been practising!"

"And you're willing to bring up another man's child as your own, to perpetrate this lie? Robert, you're insane!"

"What would you have me do? Send my wife to some charlatan to kill both the baby and probably herself as well? To let her die in her shame? Is that what you want? Do you think then that I would marry you?"

Ingaret was ashamed of the dark imaginings that crossed her mind as she thought about his last question and answered too quickly, "No, of course not!" That poor girl had done little amiss except fall in love with the wrong man.

"I couldn't think of any other safe answer to her problem. It's the best solution."

"And what about us?"

"What about us? So I made you a promise. You know I never keep my promises for long – and she is my wife, after all. Now go to sleep Ingaret. You'll feel better about it in the morning."

"No, I won't. I'm going to sleep in the solar."

So saying, she picked up her night shift from the floor and, with as much dignity as she could muster in her nudity, walked through into the next room. In a moment of sweet revenge, she opened the coffer and found his father's cloak, which she had not yet had the courage to consign to the river, wrapped it round herself and lay down on the settle by the hearth. The cloak smelt of his father's shaving creams and of his sweat and his horse's sweat, but she didn't care.

After a while, Robert came to the door and found her curled up on the settle.

"Oh well, have it your own way," he muttered and went back to bed.

CHAPTER 37

Ingaret woke early next morning after a restless night's sleep. Lord D'Avencort's cloak had fallen to the floor and she scooped it up and returned it to the coffer, hoping that Robert had not noticed it.

She went into the bedroom and sat on the edge of the bed, watching him as he slept. He was still the handsome man whose proposal she had accepted against all her own scruples and those of her family. After all, he was proposing to do for his wife exactly what Jethro had done to save Thomasyn from disgrace, and Jethro had been applauded for his compassion. Jethro, though, had been a full-time father to Edwina and now a full-time grandfather to little Roldan, whereas Robert intended to be a father in name only.

His left arm lay on top of the coverlet and she looked at the gold band on his finger. She had been a fool to forget that he had a wife who could have become pregnant at any time. He had not fathered this baby, although he had agreed to bring it up as his own, and she knew she would have to get used to the idea and not lose him by becoming as petulant as a spoilt child.

She lay on her stomach beside him, on top of the coverlet, and stretched her arm across his chest. His night shift was unbuttoned at the neck and she slid her arm beneath it, intertwining his dark chest hair round her fingers, content in the knowledge that they were still together and would be together far into the future. How far, she did not let herself speculate.

The movement of her fingers woke him and she withdrew her hand. He sighed contentedly, turned towards her and laid his arm across her. They lay there quietly for a while then she said, "I'm sorry, darling. That was foolish of me. Forgive me?"

"Nothing to forgive," he said. "I should have expected it. It was a natural reaction."

"I will get used to the idea. It's not as if it's going to make any difference to us, is it?"

"None at all," he replied. "Oh, by the way, whose cloak was it that you covered yourself with last night?"

"I hoped you hadn't noticed it," she said and told him about her meeting with his father. Instead of being angry, he roared with laughter and pulled her close and kissed her.

"I heard him asking his seneschal if he knew a young lady, a companion of his wife, by the name of Gabriella. He told him to make enquiries in the vill. He even asked me if I had met a Gabriella around the manor, companion to my mother. I should have known when he said he had been bewitched by her eyes." He roared with laughter again, then became serious.

"You are not to leave these rooms when he is home, do you hear me, Ingaret?"

"Yes, Robert."

"I mean it." She was nuzzling his chest. "Ingaret I mean it. Are you listening?"

"Yes, dear, I'm listening."

A month went by, his father was home again, and Robert decided it was time to tell his parents that his wife was with child again and it was due after Christmas, if she went full term, which was doubtful, as they knew. He told Ingaret that they were happy to hear the news but thought it surprising as he spent so little time with her. He reminded them that he had been at home with her for three weeks back in the Spring and his father nodded and said he hoped they managed a live birth this time.

Robert did not go home again, knowing that Helewise had care enough from her parents and her ladies, and it would probably be necessary when he received news of her miscarriage.

He was, therefore, greatly surprised and everyone with him when a messenger arrived during November to say that she had had a baby boy, a live one, and mother and baby were thriving.

"I have to go," he told Ingaret when he heard the news. "It is my duty – as a delighted father – to make sure she has everything she needs and is in good health, and see the baby. A boy, eh? And my heir! Who would have thought it?"

"Of course you must go," Ingaret agreed, knowing that this moment had to come and he would have to appear as delighted as any new father, "but don't stay away too long. Just make sure they are all right then come back to me."

"Of course," he said. "I'll come straight back. Strange, though, I didn't expect to feel as excited as I do."

He was so preoccupied that he reached the door before he remembered he had not kissed her goodbye. Offended, she grabbed hold of his codpiece, just to make him sure it would be worth coming back as soon as possible. He laughed, kissed her again, and was gone.

Once more, she watched him from the window as he left her to go to his wife, and this time it was a month before he returned.

Becoming more and more angry as the days went by and there was still no sign of him and no messages, she decided to visit her family in Fortchester, and arranged for herself and Beatrix to take one of the carriages, only telling Mistress Aldith of her intention.

They arrived in Fortchester without mishap. Ingaret bid Beatrix farewell as she left her outside the girl's family home in the centre of the city, then continued to the cottage she had shared with Roldan, now in the ownership of Philippa and Matthew. They were surprised to see her but made her very welcome. They had been married for more than three years and had a toddler christened Ingaret after her grandmother, and there was another baby on the way.

Ingaret stayed with them for a week and, in that time, met all the members of her growing family.

As yet, Mark had not given Lora any babies but Ingaret was not sorry as her daughter was still so young and there was plenty of time.

Jethro and Thomasyn still had their sons Gregory and Rudd at home and were also the proud grandparents of Allard and Edwina's sons Roldan, now three and a half, and two-year-old Noah.

Ingaret did not tell Thomasyn of her encounter with Lord D'Avencourt. Neither did she mention that Edwina's suitor, the older man she had boasted about, had been her half-brother, Robert.

When she thought about it, Ingaret was surprised at the way in which the lives of the D'Avencourts and those of Noah's family, her own life and that of her brother Jethro, had become inextricably interwoven, like a tapestry designed by a mad artist.

She also spent time with Marjery and her husband, Brandon, and was shown round their weaving mill, which was very busy. She met again their five children as well as Joanna and Kolby and their three youngest sons – Luke, John and Peter – who were still at home.

After a very busy week, during which she felt more like her old self, she decided it was time to go back to the manor, as Robert would be impatient for her return. So, reluctantly, she said her goodbyes, paid the bill of the carriage driver, who had stabled the horses and himself at a fairly respectable tavern, collected Beatrix from her home and they were on their way back to the manor.

In anticipation, she hurried up the two flights of stairs to Robert's rooms, only to find that, far from pacing the floors with impatience and in frustration at her absence, he had not returned. Next morning, she enquired of Mistress Aldith, who informed her that there had been no messages from him.

He came back a week later. She happened to be passing a window and saw him ride into the yard. He slid off Son of Pendragon, handed the reins to two of his servants from the stables and strode across to the doorway, with a surprising spring in his step after his long ride.

She waited for him expectantly, hovering by the door, two drinks poured in readiness, but he did not come. She was undressed and ready for bed before he finally entered the room.

"Robert! Where have you been?" she asked. "I saw you arrive. Come here!"

He did not hesitate but came to her and threw his arms about her, pulled her tightly to himself and kissed her soundly on the lips.

"Sorry, sweetheart, I'll make it up to you," he promised, "but not tonight, I'm exhausted."

"But where have you been?"

"I had to go and see mother. I knew she'd be anxious for news. Then I ate with her and sat with her until she said she was tired and I should leave. Oh, Ingaret, he's beautiful!"

"Who is?"

"Little Robert, my son."

"*Your* son?"

"Yes, my son. You should see him. I've never seen anything so perfect."

"Every baby is like that," she said, but he was hardly listening.

"You should just see his tiny fingers and toes, and his tiny finger nails. I couldn't be more obsessed with him if he were my own."

"What of his real father?"

"I had him dismissed – with a reference, of course. Helewise let him see the baby secretly before he left, but he'll cause us no trouble."

"She is well, then, Helewise?"

"Blooming! And she won't have a wet nurse. Insists on feeding him herself, in spite of everyone's entreaties. And he's thriving on her milk. Quite something to watch, isn't it, that breast feeding? I've never thought much about it before."

"You watched her breast feeding him?"

"Of course. Father's privilege."

"But you are not –" but he wasn't listening to her.

Ingaret felt the first premonition of a subtle change in their relationship and determined it should not happen.

"I'm sure she was glad to have you there with her, Robert. A first baby is a worrying but special time for any woman. But you're here now, with me, and you won't be seeing them again for months."

"Not so. As soon as she feels able to travel, I will send for her and baby Robert to come and meet my mother, and father if he is around. Then you can see this little bundle of perfection. Her ladies are saying that he looks like me."

"They would, wouldn't they?"

"And why not? There are only four people in the world who know I am not his natural father, and one has been forbidden to see him again."

"Come to bed, Robert. I've missed you. We will make love whatever way you wish."

"Not tonight, Ingaret. You'll still be here in the morning, won't you? Of course you will. Ask me again then."

"Ask you?" she almost screeched. "Am I a supplicant to be coming to you, begging bowl in hand, pleading for you to take me?"

Robert looked nonplussed and quite uncomprehending of what he had said or done to upset her.

"Ingaret, hush, hush. It's just that I need to sleep now. I promise you that, in the morning, I will make you forget that I have been away a couple of weeks."

"Four weeks!" she fumed.

"Four weeks, then," he conceded. "But I'm back now. I've come back to you, have I not? I'll make it up to you, I promise. We will stay in bed all day tomorrow, if you've a mind."

Mollified, Ingaret helped him undress and put him to bed, then climbed between the sheets herself. Once again, she despised herself for being so obsessed with him. She knew only too well what power a young baby could exert over a doting parent, but had not been prepared for this baby to have affected Robert so strongly.

She determined that, by tomorrow evening, he would have forgotten that he was a new father.

CHAPTER 38

That was not as simple as Ingaret had planned. News was received frequently about the healthful progress of Helewise and her baby and, after each messenger had left, Ingaret was appraised of every detail of little Robert's development – he was feeding well and gaining weight, he seldom cried, he slept through the night or not, and finally he had begun to smile. His mother would have no one caring for her son except herself, day and night.

Robert showed Ingaret one of the letters Helewise had scribed herself in which she asked him to come to stay so that they could try once more to live together harmoniously as a family and baby Robert would grow up with a father who was present in his young life.

"Is that so important?" he wondered aloud. "My father was not present when we boys were growing up."

Ingaret remembered her own father and thought it was very important, though he had never paid her much attention, but she did not say any of this to Robert. Anyway, he seemed to come to his own decision.

"I'm not ready to do that yet," he announced.

"Yet?" she enquired, raising an eyebrow and beginning to panic, sensing a very real threat to their relationship.

"Not while I've got you waiting for me here," he added quickly. "This is the second time she has urged me to go back. She said in a previous letter that we could try again to start a family. She said she had at last been able to bring a live baby into the world and felt sure she could do so again."

"Start a family? You?" laughed Ingaret. "I should have thought that was the last thing you wanted, being tied down to a wife and family."

"I would still have you here, little peasant girl," he teased her but she would not be patronised.

"And do you think I would hang around, waiting for you to throw me the crumbs left over from your feast with her?"

"Ingaret, my love, where else would you go?" he asked.

Where indeed? she thought. He was right. There was nowhere else for her to go.

Disagreements like this were always brought to a conclusion in the only way they knew how, and for days afterwards they would find again the love they had shared when she first came to live at the manor, but Ingaret worried that these arguments were becoming more frequent and more spiteful. She looked back to the less exciting but stable life she had once shared with Roldan, secure in his love, and tried to prepare herself for the day that Robert's love, that he had vowed would last a lifetime, might fail her.

Helewise and her baby came to visit Lady D'Avencourt when he was eight months old. Robert could not contain his excitement at the news and told Ingaret that his mother wished them to live in the main part of the house while they were here, but promised he would try to steal away on occasions and come to see her. She thanked him with ice in her voice and again he seemed hurt as if he did not know what he had said that displeased her, then repeated the sentence that always made her want to scream, "She is my wife, after all".

On the day they were expected to arrive, he said he would come back to his rooms in the afternoon so that they could be together, but he did not come, explaining later that he had been too busy overseeing arrangements for the rooms that they would occupy as a family so that Helewise and the baby would lack nothing that they needed.

From a window above the entrance door, Ingaret watched the carriage arrive, knowing that almost the whole household had been summoned to line up in the main hall to welcome master Robert's wife and baby.

Ingaret saw two footmen open the door of the carriage and help Helewise descend. She was as diminutive as Ingaret remembered seeing her at a distance in the cathedral. No longer wearing cauls on each side of her head, her hair, rich brown in colour, was braided in a circlet above her forehead. Whereas, before, Ingaret had thought her pale and uninteresting, today she was flushed and looked the picture of health. She was wearing a cloak and was carrying her son.

A young nurse followed her out of the carriage and took the boy from her mistress so that Helewise had her hands free to greet Robert, who came forward, arms outstretched, and kissed her on both cheeks. He was followed by his mother and, surprisingly, by his father. Ingaret did not know that his lordship was at home. Helewise dropped them both a curtsey, a courtesy as she outranked them.

Robert then took her arm and escorted her to the entrance to the manor, where the seneschal, bailiff, the housekeeper, head cook and head gardener were presented to her, then they all went into the hall, presumably to meet other members of staff.

Ingaret guessed rightly that she would not see Robert for the next couple of days at least, and tried to settle down with Beatrix as a companion until he could slip away and come to her.

As before, she was restless without him. She continued to despise herself for being so vulnerable to his favours and caught Beatrix sometimes looking at her sideways, showing little understanding and no patience with her mistress's weakness. The girl said nothing but occasionally her attitude was less than respectful and she did not always overly hasten to do Ingaret's bidding.

Helewise seemed in no hurry to go home.

"My mother will not hear of her returning to the castle yet," Robert reported to Ingaret one afternoon when he had managed to slip away. "She dotes on that baby, as we all do. No expense is spared and nothing is too much trouble. Beatrix, bring me some ale, girl."

"Robert, send her away."

"Assuredly. Beatrix, bring me the ale then disappear. Did I tell you, Ingaret, that he is nearly crawling? He can raise himself onto his hands and knees and starts rocking backward and forwards. It won't be long."

Beatrix poured the ale into two goblets and brought them over.

"Thank you, Beatrix," Ingaret said. "You may go now."

The girl curtsied and disappeared into her own room.

"How have you managed to get away?" Ingaret asked him.

"Robert is asleep after his feed and Helewise is resting. We have about an hour."

"Darling, that's not long enough!"

"I regret it's all I can spare. Someone or other will be looking for me. Sweetheart, it's long enough."

Ingaret was conscious that, in spite of the usual excitement of their union, he did not display his usual hunger for her.

"Robert," she asked, "are you still sleeping with Helewise?"

He hesitated a moment, which was not lost on her, then rolled out of bed and began to get dressed.

"Yes, I am," he said, pulling up his braies. "I told you, she wants to try for another baby and –"

Ingaret finished the sentence for him. " – and, after all, she is your wife. I know that."

"And there's only one way to accomplish what she wants," he said, pulling his shirt over his head.

She could not stop herself asking, "And you enjoy it now with her?"

"I always enjoy it," he said, patiently, as if explaining the facts of life to a questioning child, "but not in the same way that I enjoy you."

He leant over her where she still lay naked on the bed and nuzzled and kissed a nipple. She reached over for him but he scooped up his boots and was gone, still half dressed, knocking on Beatrix's door on the way out to alert her that Ingaret needed help to dress.

That was the last that Ingaret saw of him for the next two days so her heart leaped when there was a knock on the door at about the same time on the third day. She stopped herself from hurrying to the door and asked Beatrix to open it instead.

"Robert!" she cried delightedly as the door was opened, "I've been waiting for you to –"

Her greeting came to a startled halt as the words died in her mouth. Standing there was not Robert but Helewise with her baby sitting up in her arms.

Beatrix was dropping a curtsey and Ingaret followed with a curtsey that almost overbalanced her.

"My lady!" she managed to stammer and stared at her.

"May I come in?" Helewise asked.

"Yes, yes, of course. Beatrix, pull up that chair for her ladyship. Please, my lady, do sit down."

Helewise did so. No one spoke. The baby was gazing about him. He was, as Robert had said over and over again, a handsome little boy.

"So this is where my husband escapes to while I take my afternoon rest," she commented. "Now I understand. Is your name Ingaret?"

"Yes, my lady," said Ingaret and lapsed into silence again.

"I thought so," Helewise said, without rancour. "It's the name he speaks in his sleep."

"My lady –" Ingaret began, not knowing what to say in explanation.

"No need to explain," Helewise said. "You are very beautiful. I can see why – I was so afraid that you would be just – well – ordinary, but you are beautiful and I understand why he prefers to be with you rather than me."

"Is there anything I can get for you, my lady – or little Robert? Beatrix here will bring you anything you need."

"No, there is nothing, thank you."

"Then, Beatrix, you may leave us."

Beatrix did as she was asked but Ingaret had no doubt that she would be standing with one ear to the communicating door. Ingaret pulled up a chair and sat facing Robert's wife.

"How did you find me?" she asked.

"I followed him last time he came," Helewise said. "He is always most careful to return before he thinks I have awoken."

"He dotes on the baby," Ingaret said and Helewise nodded.

"Of course, he has told you who is the natural father? You must have known that it was not him as he spent so little time with me."

Ingaret nodded and answered the unasked question. "Of course, I would never say –"

"Of course you won't," agreed Helewise. "It would not go well with you if you did."

Ingaret heard the threat and wondered what mishap would befall her if she ever told the truth, but she had no intention of doing so and the threat did not worry her.

"I wonder, my lady, if I may hold him?"

"Of course, though he will probably wish to get down."

His mother was right. He wriggled to be put down on the floor then raised himself onto all fours, as Robert had described, and began to rock backwards and forwards.

"It won't be long before he starts crawling," Ingaret said, "and then you will never know where he is. You will have to keep your eyes on him all the time."

Helewise looked at her enquiringly.

"I have grandchildren of my own," Ingaret said. "I do miss them."

They watched little Robert for a time, as he tried to crawl, collapsed, then tried again.

"I'll fight you for him – my husband," Helewise said. "I may not win but it won't be for the want of trying."

Ingaret did not reply for a while then said, with an honesty that surprised herself, "My lady, you'll win, especially if you get pregnant again – but you won't win yet. Not yet. I will hold onto him for as long as I am able."

"Then we will have to share him for a while," his wife said, "for a little while. That will content me as it is more than he has given me in the past, till little Robert came along. He has something to prove now, you see. Something to prove."

Ingaret nodded and realised that she liked this woman who Robert had married, who strangely did not seem to resent her at all as long as she did not outstay her welcome.

The subject of Robert was then dropped and they proceeded to discuss other matters such as all that Helewise saw on her drive south and the beauty of the countryside hereabouts, and the prospects of a good harvest, and Ingaret's family and the latest miscarriage of Queen Catherine and the miracle of the birth of six-year-old princess Mary.

They were fully interested and engaged in their conversation when the door was flung open and Robert strode in.

"Ingaret!" he exclaimed. "I've lost my wife and baby! I have no idea –"

He stopped short as if he had been kicked by his horse and looked just as amazed.

"Helewise!" he said on seeing her. Then his eyes strayed to young Robert, now on his stomach on the floor.

"Hello, husband," Helewise greeted him.

"Hello, Robert," echoed Ingaret with less enthusiasm.

"I've met your mistress," Helewise enlightened him, "so you've no need to introduce us. We are getting along very well, aren't we, Ingaret?"

"Yes, my lady," Ingaret agreed.

"And we seem to like each other," Helewise continued, "which is most unfortunate as I came prepared to hate her. We have agreed to share you for the time being, until you make up your mind which one of us you choose to stay with for the rest of your life. You will have to choose one day, Robert, and that day is not very far away – I think you agree with me, Ingaret?"

Ingaret nodded, too humilited to speak. She realised only too well that she was no match for this clever young woman who had all the winning cards in her hand. And Helewise should win. There was no room for Ingaret any longer in this marriage. But she intended to hold on for as long as she could. She wasn't going to give him up yet and there was the slight chance, the slightest chance, that she may not have to give him up at all.

Beatrix had emerged from her room when she heard Robert come in and was listening to this conversation and looking in amazement from one speaker to the other.

"Well," said Helewise, rising from her chair. "It is time for us to leave. I will not trouble you any further, Ingaret. Are you coming, Robert?"

"Yes, of course," he said. "Hello, young man." He picked the child up and held him firmly in his arms. "Let's take you back to your grandmother. I am sure she has some special sweetmeats for you." He turned to Ingaret. "He's being weaned off his mother's milk now. Starting to eat more solid food."

"The doctors say that it is unlikely I shall conceive another baby while I am breast feeding Robert," Helewise told Ingaret confidentially, "but, of course, you know all about that."

Ingaret watched her leave, feeling unutterably miserable.

As he followed, with his wife ahead of him and her back turned to them, Robert kissed Ingaret surreptitiously on the cheek.

"I'll be back," he promised, but as both knew now, he was not very adept at keeping his promises.

CHAPTER 39

He did come back two evenings later and, surprisingly, stayed the whole night. He looked tired and hadn't the energy that had always exploded once he was in her arms. He did make love to her, just the once, then seemed content to lie quietly with her next to him.

"I nearly forgot," he mumbled sleepily, "but Mother asked me to find you and tell you that she would like to see you in the morning."

She cuddled up to his back and put an arm over him.

"Do you know why?" she asked but, by then, he was already asleep.

It was good to wake up in the morning and find him still there with her. She smiled and stretched and kissed the back of his neck then tickled him there and woke him. He turned and contemplated her.

"Dear God, Ingaret," he said, "those eyes of yours will haunt me for the rest of my life. How can I leave you?"

"Leave me?" she repeated in alarm. "How, leave me?"

"Helewise and Robert are going home today," he told her, "and I have said I will follow them in a few days. I shall be going for good this time. We are trying to patch up our marriage." He paused. "Tonight was meant to be a farewell but I don't know how I can leave you."

"Then don't."

"My son needs me. She needs me."

"So do I, Robert, so do I," Ingaret cried in desperation, not knowing what to say or do to make him change his mind.

"No you don't, my love," he said. "Not really. You have your family. I am all they have. You'll do well with or without me. She won't."

"Robert, make love to me. I'll show you how much I need you."

He shook his head and sat up. A thought struck Ingaret.

"Does she know you're here, that you've been with me all night?"

He nodded.

"Yet you still came?"

"Yes, to tell you our decision."

Ingaret stared at him. "You mean that you came because she allowed you to come?"

"It wasn't quite like that –"

"Oh, I think it was. How clever she is, your wife! Don't you see it?"

He looked perplexed.

"Just go, Robert! Go!"

She scrambled from the bed and gathered up his clothes from a chair, from the floor, from the end of the bed.

"Take your clothes and get out! Beatrix! Beatrix!"

Beatrix came hurrying from her room, still in her night shift.

"Open the door!" she screamed, thrusting the bundle of clothes into his arms. "Master Robert is leaving! Open the door! And prepare a bath for me. I have an audience with her ladyship!"

Robert was hovering by the foot of the bed, speaking words to calm her, but she picked up a heavy silver candle stick, with the candle still in it, and raised it above her head. He backed out of the door and she threw it after him, followed by a boot he had dropped on the way, and he disappeared down the staircase.

She did not cry. She could not cry. Perhaps she would later. She lay back on the bed and waited while Beatrix dressed hurriedly and went down to the kitchens to organise servants into carrying up hot water, then watched as the girl busied herself laying out towels and sweet-smelling oils and lye soap on a chair by the side of the tub. She brought a sheet to place carefully over the base and sides, so that Ingaret would not catch her skin on any splinters.

When the tub was full of water, still hot enough to steam up the glazed windows, she dismissed Beatrix, saying that she had always bathed herself and would do so now, and asked her to return in an hour.

On the last occasion she had had a bath, before All Saints' tide at the beginning of November, Robert had been there to help her and hinder her and all had been happiness between them and it was all she could do not to have him climb in on top of her, fully dressed as he was. He had, of course, been drinking a great quantity of red wine all evening.

She smiled at the memory then closed her eyes tight shut so that the tears would not flow and lay her head on the back of the tub, and tried to concentrate on the reason that her ladyship should wish her to visit, other than that they always enjoyed each other's company.

By the time Beatrix returned, Ingaret was sitting on a chair, wrapped in towels, drying her hair. The girl helped her dress in a clean white shift with long sleeves, draped at the wrists, her dark blue kirtle tied on the shoulders, the bodice laced and the skirt divided at the waist so that it fell away on each side to reveal her shift, blue against white.

Beatrix twisted her hair into one long plait then expertly wound the plait into a tidy bun at the nape of her neck.

Her stomach was cramped up so tightly that she could not eat breakfast and departed, leaving Beatrix to organise emptying the tub and tidying up the room.

She found the candlestick on the floor outside the door and left it there. She had thrown it with such force that it had splintered wood on the staircase. It was as well that it had missed Robert's head.

She hoped that Lord D'Avencourt was not anywhere around as she negotiated the passageways and arrived in the main part of the manor, but her ladyship was alone in her solar, except for Mistress Aldith, on guard as always.

"Come in, come in, Ingaret," said Mistress Aldith on seeing her. "Her ladyship has an errand she wishes you to carry out for her."

Mystified, Ingaret approached Lady D'Avencourt, in her usual chair by the hearth, where a blazing log fire was sending orange sparks exploding up the chimney.

"My lady," said Ingaret, dropping a curtsey. "You wished to see me?"

"There you are, Gabriella," her ladyship greeted her. "Yes, I did. Aldith, bring up a chair for my angel."

"There's no need," Ingaret said, embarrassed, recognising the age difference between herself and Mistress Aldith, "I can do that myself."

When she was sitting by the side of Robert's mother, her ladyship reached over and placed a hand on Ingaret's thigh.

"My dear, I have an errand for you to perform for me, if you will."

"Of course," said Ingaret, wondering what errand this could be. Reading to her from the Holy Bible, as she did sometimes? Singing one of the folk songs popular at the time? Ingaret did not have a special talent in this direction but she used to sing to her babies and could manage passably well.

Painting on wooden panels was another pastime that they had enjoyed together. Her ladyship had great skill in this direction and often sent Ingaret to the kitchen to bring back ground pigments – charcoal, white lead, mercury – that a travelling merchant had brought to the manor, or lavender and the stamens of lilies, and greenery picked in the gardens. One of the scullery boys was trained in mixing the powders with egg yolk or oil from poppy seeds to furnish her with the coloured paints she used, some of which were more successfully mixed than others.

But no! It was none of these that her ladyship required of Ingaret this time.

"My dear," she began, "Robert tells me that you have seen his son, little Robert, so you will know how very special he is to Lord D'Avencourt and myself and the family, especially as dear Helewise has had such a sad history of loss."

Ingaret nodded, wondering what was coming next. She looked across to Mistress Aldith, but she was engaged in playing a solo game of cards at a small table and did not look up.

"My husband and I feel that we would like to make a thankoffering to our dear Lord and Heavenly Father for the precious gift of this grandchild and wish to give it personally to the Bishop at Fortchester. Do you not think that this is a worthy gesture?"

"Most certainly," agreed Ingaret, beginning to have an inkling of where this conversation was headed.

"We wish to entrust you to take our offering to the mother church, Gabriella."

"To Fortchester, my lady?"

"Indeed. I will send Mistress Aldith with you as companion for the journey and you will travel in our carriage, of course. You will stay at one of the taverns in the city and the driver and his companion will sleep in the stables along with the horses. My dear Aldith will carry the purse to cover your expenses and also the purse containing the thankoffering, so you need have no worry about that. Will you do that for us? It would please me greatly."

Ingaret's only thought at that moment was that Robert would be leaving the manor before she could return. Her ladyship was still talking.

"You will be supplied with several changes of clothing, so you need not worry about your appearance. You will be our representative and must be dressed accordingly. Is that to your liking?"

"You are most gracious, my lady," said Ingaret. At any other time she would have enjoyed the prospect of a journey to Fortchester, making time to see her family, to worship in the beautiful cathedral and see again the stone artistry of Roldan and Allard, their son. But all she could think about was that Robert would be leaving without giving her another chance to entice him to stay with her.

"Have you informed master Robert of your intention?" she asked.

"Yes I have and I have asked him not to leave us, his father and me, until your safe return with news of your reception by the Bishop and the handing over of the offering."

So! He would still be here on their return. Ingaret knew that she could now enjoy the few days away from the manor, as he would have to pass the time without her in his bed and would surely come to his senses and realise that he couldn't leave her.

"It would be an honour for me to take the thankoffering to Fortchester for you," she said.

"Good," said Lady D'Avencourt. "Aldith will arrange it all. You need have no concern about anything other than meeting with my seamstress."

Ingaret looked out at the heavy grey skies above the rose garden.

"My lady, it looks like it's going to snow," she observed.

"Then there should be no delay. You will both leave in two days' time."

Ingaret hoped to see Robert again in that time but was so busy helping Lady D'Avencourt's seamstress produce several changes of clothing for her that she would not have had time to entertain him even if he had arrived at the bedroom door.

Some of the gowns were newly sewn and some were altered from her ladyship's own wardrobe of gowns that were probably three decades old, they were so slim fitting.

Robert did not put in an appearance and she had to leave without seeing him.

CHAPTER 40

She awoke on the morning that she and Mistress Aldith were due to leave for Fortchester to find that it had been snowing during the night and was still snowing.

The flakes were small and light and melted as soon as they settled on the gravel of the courtyard but, even so, the drivers of the carriage were cussing and swearing as they placed the step to help the two women clamber inside and loaded their bundles and bags on the floor beside them. The men wore mittens and were enveloped in heavy woollen cloaks with broad-brimmed hats that encouraged the melting flakes to drip down away from their faces.

"Not the weather to be driving to Fortchester!" grumbled the man with the bulbous nose and heavy eyebrows, his breath turning to vapour in the cold air.

"Try telling his lordship that!" rejoined his co-driver as he removed the step and stowed it away.

The driver clambered onto the driving seat, still grumbling. "Why it has to be today of all days, I don't know."

"Nor do I, but he's not going to tell us, is he? Best get on with it. The sooner we get there the sooner we'll have a potful or two of ale in our bellies, without being charged for it!"

Inside the carriage, the women wrapped themselves in their cloaks and blankets. Ingaret was agile enough to remove her shoes and curl her feet up under her skirts, comforted by a brick that had been heated in the fire and wrapped in cloth. Mistress Aldith rested her feet on a low stool on which had been placed another heated brick, and wrapped them and the brick in a blanket.

She bemoaned the fact that baby Robert had not been born in the summer, but they hoped that the journey would take no more than four hours, even allowing for both horses to be rested by letting them walk for a while.

As they set off, they were glad of the canopy above their heads and the high sides of the carriage, though the icy wind funnelled its way between and around them. As the driver had complained, it was not the weather in which to be travelling.

Once on the high road, the carriage set off at a smart pace and afforded a smoother ride than any Ingaret had experienced so far along the highway.

Her companion was soon dozing but Ingaret's mind was too busy with her thoughts and her heart too tight in her chest to allow her to relax and sleep.

It was ironic, she thought, that she had been chosen to suffer this miserable journey to take a heavy purse of gold sovereigns to thank God for a baby who, unknown to the donors, had no blood ties with them and who was the cause of her losing, perhaps for ever, the man she loved. How she detested that baby – except that she didn't. He was a dear little fellow and it was no wonder that everyone loved him, and the way in which he was being used was no fault of his. But he certainly had become a tribulation.

She closed her eyes. No, she wouldn't think about it all not making any sense. She would take the opportunity to see her own family, and Robert's mother had said that he would still be at the manor when she returned.

They arrived at the tavern cold, wet, weary and hungry. Mistress Aldith made all the arrangements for their stay then the drivers unloaded their luggage and led the tired horses to the stables to feed and water them. They would groom them and clean the filth off the wheels and sides of the carriage in the morning.

Ingaret and Mistress Aldith were shown to a room at the back of the building that looked out over the stables and part of the city centre, the jumble of roofs gradually being overlaid with a white coverlet.

Taking up most of the room was a double four-poster bed. There was also a washstand, chairs and a bench, a chest and a small table bearing a lit candle. A very welcome fire blazed in the hearth and a pile of logs was stacked there.

They removed their cloaks and spread them out across the backs of chairs in front of the fire to dry them then washed their hands and faces in cold water.

When their baggage arrived, brought up by two servants, Mistress Aldith opened the bundles and very carefully laid out their changes of clothing in the chest.

"I don't expect you to wait on me," Ingaret told her.

"Force of habit," said Mistress Aldith and smiled. "How else would I fill my time?"

That accomplished, they went down the stairs to find something to eat and drink.

They were not the only guests and the room on the ground floor was noisy, the servants being kept busy serving sustenance to several travellers who looked as hungry and tired as they were feeling.

Directed to a table for two, after they had had their fill of ale and slices of cold meat pie with pickled onions, cheese and bread, they visited the candle-lit privy in the yard at the back then were more than ready for bed.

Neither of them found any difficulty in sleeping in the big bed until the late dawn and woke to find that it had been snowing all night and a thick white sparkling mantle was covering the ground.

After a hasty breakfast eating up some of the leftovers from the previous evening, Aldith summoned the carriage to take them to the cathedral, where they sought an audience with one of the priests on duty.

A short, wiry little man with thinning grey hair, in a priest's black cassock, came hurrying to meet them and escorted them into a side chapel dedicated to one of the saints and asked their business. After explaining the reason for their visit, he asked them to wait while he consulted the Bishop, who was in his office. He said he was sure his reverence would be pleased to welcome them and please not to leave until he returned.

They waited for some time, leisurely inspecting the memorials and paintings, and were beginning to think that they had been forgotten, when they saw the priest hurrying towards them, rubbing his hands together and looking very pleased.

"My dear ladies," he beamed. "His reverence welcomes you to the cathedral and is very gratified to receive the thankoffering sent by Lord and Lady D'Avencourt, whom he has met in the past."

Ingaret did not know how much gold was in the bag but guessed, as the Bishop must have done, that it would be a not inconsiderable sum.

"Tomorrow is the Feast of St. Nicholas, 6th December," the priest continued, "so tonight there is a midnight mass. His reverence will be very pleased to accept the gift at that service during the giving of alms by the congregation. In fact, he will be delighted to announce the giving of the offering and the reason you have come. Will that be pleasing to you? I myself will receive you at the door and escort you to the front of the congregation."

He beamed again while awaiting their reply.

"Thank you, reverend," said Ingaret, "that will suit us very well. We will see you tonight at a quarter to midnight."

"You will know," the priest continued, "that the legend of St. Nicholas tells how he left a bag of gold for each of three sisters whose father could not provide dowries for their marriages. He has always been known as a follower of Christ who helped the poor and sick. This thankoffering will be used for the same purpose."

"We are glad to know that, reverend," said Ingaret, "and will convey that message to Lord and Lady D'Avencourt on our return."

After leaving the cathedral, while sheltering beneath Roldan's carvings of flying angels above the main entrance door, Ingaret said she wished to visit her family. Aldith said she preferred to return to the tavern to rest as they would be losing sleep that night, and she would take the opportunity to lay out their gowns for the evening.

She climbed into the carriage, leaving Ingaret, at her own wish, to walk the short distance to her old home, the cottage she had given to Philippa and Matthew.

She was wearing strong leather ankle boots and did not find the walking too difficult as the snow had compacted over the filth in the streets and beneath hundreds of feet as their owners hastened about their business. She enjoyed the crunch! crunch! crunch! as her boots negotiated the frozen snow.

Philippa opened the door to her knock, a baby in her arms and three-year-old Ingaret clinging to her skirt.

"Mother!" exclaimed Philippa, delighted to see her. "What are you doing in Fortchester in this weather? Come in! Come in!"

Ingaret followed her daughter inside and looked around the familiar room. It was much as she had left it although the young couple had made a few changes such as removing a couple of chairs to make room for a cradle, and there were winter berries in a vase on the window sill and another on the table.

"Mother, meet baby Matthew!" said Philippa, putting her son into Ingaret's arms. "The time has passed so quickly and he's now three months old."

"He's a handsome little lad," said Ingaret, looking down and giving him a finger to grab.

Philippa pulled her daughter from behind her kirtle, "Ingaret, you remember your grandmother, don't you?"

Little Ingaret did and her grandmother bent down to draw her close with her free arm. They then sat together on the settle by the fire.

Ingaret explained the reason for her visit, without going into any unnecesssary details. Robert was not mentioned except as the father of the baby being honoured during the Mass that night, and Philippa did not ask any questions.

She was nineteen years of age now and had matured into a capable young mother with busy hands, square tipped and practical like her father's. Her light brown wavy hair, also like his, was kept tidy in a plait wound into a bun at the nape of her neck.

Ingaret talked animatedly to the baby she was cuddling then handed him back to his mother so that she could sit little Ingaret on her lap. The child had hair the same colour as her father's, a copper-coloured red, but Ingaret was unprepared to see wide eyes whose colour had deepened into violet, and became anxious that they would one day lead her into as much trouble as had her own.

"Her eyes," she said to Philippa.

"I know, Mother," her daughter replied, laying Matthew in his cradle and covering him with a blanket, "they're just like yours. There's no mistaking the two families she comes from."

While they were chatting together, Matthew arrived. He was hoping for something to eat before he returned to work and consumed a large bowl of stew. Philippa asked him to make a detour to tell Lora that her mother was here.

He grinned. "Work always takes second place to family," he said with resignation. "It will make me late back."

"He's not at the workshop today," Philippa explained. "He's constructing a beautiful display cabinet in the customer's own home."

When he had left, Ingaret asked her daughter whether there was any sign of pregnancy for Lora.

Philippa shook her head, her foot on the rocker of the cradle as she tried to lull Matthew to sleep. "Not yet, but don't mention it. She is very sensitive on the subject."

Lora soon arrived. Now seventeen years old, and without a family, she had time to sew all her own gowns and was very prettily dressed in a grey shift over which she wore a green kirtle with a great deal of lacing and gathering and a green silk plaited cord over her hips. Ingaret smiled to see Philippa looking with envy at Lora's tiny waist although she knew that babies and tiny waists were not compatible.

It was not long before Lora bubbled up with the latest gossip.

"Mother," she said, playing with the tasselled end of the cord, "I don't suppose you've heard the news about Alice."

"Alice?" asked her mother. "My sister Alice?"

"Yes, aunt Alice."

"What about her?"

"She ran away a week ago. She's left Elis and has run away."

"Surely not!" exclaimed Ingaret.

"Where to?" asked Philippa.

"No one knows where," Lora replied, "but gossip says she had met a merchant from Antwerp with plenty of money – Mother, you know what Aunt Alice is like – and she has just disappeared."

"How do you know?"

"Elis drove over to see Jethro, to ask if he had seen her in the city, and Jethro came enquiring at the workshop. Father-in-law, as master of his guild, said he would send a description round to the carpenters' and joiners' and cabinet makers' guilds to keep a lookout. He could do no more than that. No one has seen her."

"Poor dear Elis," murmured Ingaret. "Is Jethro still in Fortchester?"

"No, he has gone back home."

"I will spend an extra day in the city and call on him tomorrow," Ingaret decided, "then I can meet the rest of the family. How are they all?"

"Well," nodded Lora. "They will be pleased to see you."

The day passed happily for Ingaret, and Matthew walked her back to the tavern after his day's work, in the dark of the early December evening. It had stopped snowing during the day but was still treacherous underfoot.

At the entrance door, he kissed her on both cheeks.

"It has been a pleasure, mother-in-law," he said, "to see you again, as always. We hope it will not be so long a time until your next visit."

"Matthew, dear, I am not sure what the future holds," she replied, "but family will always be family, no matter what."

He nodded and waited until she had gone inside before turning to walk back home.

CHAPTER 41

Aldith had enjoyed her restful day and had laid out their gowns in preparation for their visit to the cathedral that night. Ingaret gasped when she saw hers.

"It's much too splendid," she remonstrated.

"My dear, you are dressing to attend our Lord's supper, not dressing for yourself. My lady personally chose the gown and wimple."

Aldith offered to send down for some sustenance before they left but Ingaret refused, wishing to fast before taking Holy Communion.

A large wooden tub had been delivered to the room and Aldith went downstairs to order hot water to be brought up. When she had prepared the bath for Ingaret, much as Beatrix had done, and the hot water had arrived, Ingaret slipped into the tub and luxuriated in the embrace of her second bath in a week.

"I will be washed away," she laughed.

"But my first for a long time," replied Aldith, who was wrapped in copious towels, waiting to get into the tub when Ingaret got out. "Don't try to dress yourself, wait for me to help you."

Ingaret had dried her hair and was in her undergarments by the time Aldith emerged, plump and flushed from the warmth of the water. Ingaret waited for her to also dress in her undergarments – a cloth band to keep the bosom in place – more difficult for the elderly Aldith than for Ingaret's still firm breasts – white hose secured to a band round the belly and a white shift that reached her ankles.

"Now I will help you with your gown," said Aldith. "Raise your arms."

Ingaret did so and Aldith slipped over her head a shimmering silk gown in oyster cream with a wide band at the waist, white lace at the wrists and a panel of white lace across the bodice that reached up to her neck.

She was told to stand quite still while Aldith buttoned her up at the back.

"How many?" asked Ingaret.

"Twenty four," Aldith replied.

Suddenly, Ingaret had a vivid memory of another button, the bejewelled button she had found on the high road all those years ago.

"Aldith, dear," she said. "You will think I am going mad but will you loosen one of the buttons? Just snip the thread that holds it in place."

"But why?" asked Mistress Aldith, greatly mystified.

"I will tell you later, but I have a very good reason."

"If you wish," agreed her companion, "but you may lose it before the night is out."

She did as Ingaret had asked her.

"Now for your shoes," said Aldith. "Raise your feet one at a time," and she slipped on her feet a pair of cream leather shoes.

Ingaret's light chestnut hair was wound in two cartwheels about her ears and held in place with two wire cauls studded with pearls.

"Fixing your wimple can wait until we leave, as can your train. Sit on the bed and don't move."

Ingaret did as she was told, feeling quite unlike herself and hardly daring to breathe in case something dislodged. Aldith smiled, amused, and proceeded to dress herself much less flamboyantly, as befitted her age and station in life.

Over a white shift that reached up to her neck, she donned a long brown woollen gown with black lining and a black band beneath her bosom. Her shoes, also in leather, were coloured brown. She pulled her hair back into a bun.

Ingaret blushed at the comparison in their clothing, knowing that she was dressed as someone she wasn't. She said as much to Aldith, who remarked that she was there, not on her own behalf, but as representative of a noble lord and lady. Ingaret grimaced when she thought of Lord D'Avencourt and his unwelcome advances but she wanted to be at her best for her ladyship.

Soon it was time to leave. Ingaret had never worn a tower wimple before and a double one at that.

"Just remember to duck when you go through low doors," Aldith reminded her, covering the wimple with a finely woven veil that hung down her back in two drapes. She gave her another veil to use as a shawl if she wished, which Ingaret draped round her waist and over her arms.

"I'll clip the train to your dress when we reach the cathedral," Aldith said. "I ordered two pages to meet us at the entrance. They will carry it for you over the dirty ground."

"You have thought of everything," said Ingaret appreciatively. "Her ladyship is so blessed to have you serving her."

"And I am blessed to be able to serve such a dear lady," rejoined Aldith as she struggled to put on her own wimple over a white cloth that covered her head. It was also a double wimple with a draped veil, like Ingaret's, but less ornate, and she had a black woollen scarf round her neck to keep the cold away from her 'old bones', to quote her own words.

The taverner had learned of their mission and had passed on the news to his customers and there was a crowd of guests and local people crowding the lower room and the street outside as Ingaret and Aldith descended the stairs, bending their necks beneath low beams to make room for their wimples.

When the crowd saw the two ladies, dressed as they were in all their finery, there was a concerted sigh from the women and a few whistles from the men and the waving of tankards. There was also a lewd remark or two but neither woman could look to right or left in indignation as both were nervous of moving their heads in case something should fall off.

The carriage was awaiting them – again due to Aldith's forethought – and they left for the cathedral.

On their arrival and before the drivers helped Ingaret from the carriage, Aldith clipped the train to the back of her gown. Waiting for them were two young page boys in red tunics, hats and hose, who knew what to do and ran behind her to each pick up a corner of the heavily embroidered silk train.

The priest they had met that morning was waiting for them at the west door. Worshippers who were crowding into the cathedral, on seeing Ingaret approaching with her elderly attendant, and obviously presuming her to be some great lady, moved aside and cleared a pathway. A man ran to open one of the doors and the small party entered the great edifice.

Once inside, the jostling crowd also made way for them and the priest led them to the crossing of nave and transepts. Ingaret ventured to ask for a chair for her attendant and two were brought immediately. Aldith was greatly relieved to be seated, and Ingaret also took advantage of the thoughtfulness of the priest.

The Right Reverend Bishop of Fortchester, in his magnificent golden vestments and a mitre almost as tall as their wimples, conducted the service. During the Thanksgiving, he gave especial thanks for the birth of Robert, the grandson of Lord and Lady D'Avencourt. The bag of gold sovereigns, relinquished by Mistress Aldith, was laid on a gold collection plate and conveyed to the altar for blessing. His sermon was about the widow's mite and how the smallest amount, if given sacrificially, could also be used by God to usher in his kingdom on earth.

Ingaret was comforted to accept the bread and wine for the first time since arriving at the manor, as she had been unable to join Lord and Lady D'Avencourt and the household while living as the mistress of Robert, and had had to content herself with slipping into the manor chapel to pray when she knew that no one was about.

At the end of the service, the Bishop came to speak to Ingaret personally, to ask her to convey his thanks and blessings to the donors for their generous gift.

He looked at Ingaret thoughtfully.

"My child, have we not met before?" he enquired, a frown furrowing his brow. "I cannot quite place –"

His face cleared and he regarded her with something approaching affection.

"Were you not – I do not forget a face – in my memory, I see you standing with –"

Ingaret helped him out. "Roldan," she said.

"Yes, our much loved and greatly missed master mason. You were his wife?"

"Yes, your reverence," said Ingaret. "Your memory serves you well."

"Then you are doubly welcome here," he said, extending his hand so that she could kiss his bishop's ring, at the same time looking puzzled, but he asked no further questions.

The priest came to escort Ingaret, with Aldith at her elbow, back along the nave to the west door. Having seen the exchange between their Lord Bishop and Ingaret, a scene they had looked upon with awe, the worshippers again stood aside to allow them to pass, some women curtseying and some of the men bowing to Ingaret, which amused her greatly, then thronged after them as they left the building.

Those who had escaped into the square before them were already clustering outside, awaiting her arrival, and torchboys had their torches lit and raised high to light her passage back to the carriage.

"My lady," said Aldith, in mock courtesy, "delay a moment and let them look at you. Most of them will not have seen a noble lady before. Let them have their moment of privilege and awe."

"But Aldith –" protested Ingaret.

"No buts, my lady," insisted Aldith. "We are not in a hurry. You and I know what we know but give them a moment to savour, a story to tell their children and grandchildren. You owe them that."

So Ingaret paused and looked behind then around her. The two pages were greatly enjoying their role and were giggling together, mindfully holding her train above the slush. Ingaret thought that she was keeping them up and they should be safely tucked into their beds. She was surprised to see behind her another young page bearing a cushion with boxes and bottles on it, probably containing holy water, gifts from the cathedral.

All others in the crowd were adults, as befitted the hour, now the morning of St. Nicholas' Feast Day. She saw Cistercian monks, their black hoods pulled over their tonsures and faces to keep out the icy cold. Here were faithful men and women of all ages, some nuns among them.

Ingaret remembered being told by a nun during her childhood that Jesus called his disciples to follow him, but the women came anyway.

She noticed an elderly man leaning on a tall staff and thought that he too should be home in bed and she should not dally too long.

To her right, in front of the stone cross on its stepped base and tall column, waited another group, mostly elderly, but there was a younger man among them, standing slightly forward of the crowd, a man of about her own age, a man with yellow hair to his shoulders –

"Elis!" she breathed and was aware of a pleasurable warmth deep inside her, too deep even for Robert to reach, and she remembered the close friendship they had shared when they were young.

"Pardon, my lady?" Aldith asked.

"It's Elis," Ingaret repeated, with a tremor in her voice. "Aldith, you see the young man who looks like an angel, the young man with yellow hair?"

Aldith nodded.

"Please ask him to join me in the carriage," she said and proceeded on her way towards the vehicle, the crowd following at a respectful distance.

The drivers already had in place the little wooden platform to help her climb in, which she did, forgetting to lower her head so that her wimple was knocked sideways and had to be adjusted before she sat down, whereupon she decided to take it off and was much relieved to do so.

"Leave the little step," she instructed them and soon Aldith and then Elis climbed into the carriage, Aldith sitting next to her so that Elis had to sit on the opposite bench.

It was snowing again.

"Elis, my dear, dear Elis," said Ingaret, "what pleasure it gives me to see you again. Aldith, please lean out and tell the drivers to move forward."

"Yes, my lady," said Aldith, obviously puzzled at this strange turn of events.

"You may stop calling me 'my lady' now, Aldith," said Ingaret, "and take your wimple off. They are so unwieldy."

"Thank you, my – Ingaret," she said and removed her wimple.

"So it is you, Ingaret," said Elis. "I could not believe that it really was you. But how – ?"

"It's a long story and I will tell you in time, but now you must let me know your news. I saw my daughters this afternoon and have heard part of it. My sister has run away?"

"Yes. I had hoped to find her in the city but have not been so fortunate. I came to midnight mass to ask our Lord to help me find her."

"Where are you staying?"

"In Brocklebury, with Jethro."

"Then we will take you there."

"I have Jethro's horse and cart stabled on the outskirts of the city."

"I plan to visit Jethro this afternoon. It will be a simple enough matter to collect it on the way and I will ask one of our drivers to follow our carriage with Jethro's horse and cart. I doubt Jethro will need it before then, in view of the weather."

Having stopped the carriage and spoken to the drivers, they were then on their way to Brocklebury at a distance of twelve miles, which the two men were none too pleased about, considering the weather and the lateness of the hour.

Ingaret found that she liked making decisions and giving orders, expecting them to be obeyed. She saw Aldith looking at her quizzically in the gloom of the torch-lit carriage and smiled, reminding herself that she was a lady only for the next two days and after that would have to revert to what she actually was – mistress of the youngest son of Lord D'Avencourt. At the thought of Robert, she clenched her hands, then dismissed the thought and held them out to Elis, who took them in his. He held them for a while then released them and she returned them to her lap.

"Elis, we are still dear friends, are we not?"

He nodded.

"Then tell me all about Alice."

"Ingaret, she is my wife. I cannot –"

"Elis, dear, I would not have you reveal the intimacies of your marriage – I can guess that, with Alice, you have had to – never mind. Just tell me what has happened now – if you can."

"He turned her head," Elis replied miserably. "He was a merchant from Antwerp, dealing in German copper and silver. He was on the high road from London and one of the shafts of his carriage had split and someone sent him to the vill to find the carpenter. He stayed there for a couple of days and in that time he met Alice. She visited the vill a great deal to gossip with the old wives and the young, unmarried girls. She knew most of them, of course, and used to come home with all sorts of tales, usually not true, I daresay, but Alice believed them all."

"How do you know all this?"

"That was the first place I looked for her, in the vill, and the girls she called her friends tittle-tattled about him and her together. He was on his way to Fortchester to sell his wares and was boasting that, when he returned to Antwerp, he would join a group of young men like himself who were starting to deal in diamonds."

"Diamonds? Do you believe that?"

"I don't know. I never met the man. But Alice believed him. The young women I spoke to said she was mesmerised by him and his stories but they didn't think she would actually go away with him. He certainly left on his own, but that means nothing. Alice could have met him somewhere between the mill and the high road. They could be anywhere."

He looked so worried that Ingaret's heart went out to him and she thought again of the friendship they had once shared and the speed with which his marriage to Alice had been announced after she had accepted Roldan's proposal. But that was a long time ago.

"What will you do now?"

"Just wait and hope that she comes home. I have people looking out for her in Fortchester but she may be on her way to London by now and thence to Antwerp."

"She would go with him to Antwerp?"

"The girls said he had asked her to go with him as far as that but they thought he was playing a game with her and she would never in her right mind trust him to take her with him. They had met only a couple of days previously, after all."

Ingaret stayed silent and so did Elis. Aldith was already asleep.

When he jumped down from the carriage, having reached Jethro's cottage, Ingaret asked him to tell them that she would be calling later that day to return their horse and cart.

Then the carriage left to take her and Aldith back to the tavern.

Before Ingaret undressed for bed, she asked Aldith to inspect the back of her dress.

"It has dropped off, that button," Aldith said. "I knew it would!"

"Good!" said Ingaret. "I hope whoever finds it will appreciate it. And I was quite unaware that I had lost it, quite unaware. Just as it should be."

Aldith shook her head, lacking comprehension, but was too tired to question Ingaret and soon both were in bed and fast asleep.

CHAPTER 42

They slept in until mid-day, when hunger drove them downstairs to find something to eat and they were served in the tap room with a steaming, thick vegetable soup tasting of onions and salted beans.

Once replenished, Ingaret asked for the carriage to be brought round to the front of the tavern and they set off for Jethro's cottage, collecting his horse and cart on the way, which the second driver was instructed to take in hand and follow them.

Ingaret was surprised to find, now that she could see clearly by daylight, that her brother's home was not a cottage but a half-timbered construction on two floors, with a thatched roof. There was a small vegetable garden at the side of the house and a large workshop where, she presumed, he kept all his tools. There was also a small barn for the cart and a stable for the horse.

Inside, Thomasyn kept the living room neat and tidy, and the enticing aroma of baking bread wafted from the bread oven built into the wall at one side of the fireplace. A long-handled wooden peeler was propped up against the adjoining wall, well away from the log fire that was burning lustily in the hearth.

Jethro was so happy to see his sister, as was Thomasyn. Elis had told them that she would be calling so they were expecting her and Jethro had stayed at home purposely. His son, Gregory, who partnered him in their contracting work, was engaged in building a pig sty for a farmer out in the country and could not be present. Jethro's younger son, Rudd, a sensible lad approaching twenty years, had walked Elis back into the city to continue their search for Alice.

Allard and Edwina, with their sons Roldan, almost five years old, and two-year-old Noah had set up home in a house of their own in the centre of Fortchester. Jethro had sent them a message and Edwina had promised to bring their sons to see their grandmother. Allard, however, was working some distance away, building a stone summer house in the form of a Greek temple on a manor estate south of the city, and could not leave his work.

When Edwina arrived, Mistress Aldith was delighted to meet this part of Ingaret's growing family and spent time sitting in a chair in a corner of the room, the children on the wooden floor at her feet, looking up, wide-eyed as they listened to the stories she was weaving. This left the adults to talk together.

"Jethro," Ingaret began as they sat at the table, "tell me about Alice. How has our sister been treating Elis? Have they not been happy?"

Jethro pulled a face. "It's no use asking me, I don't understand the humours of a woman's heart and brain. Ask Thomasyn. Alice used to confide in her."

Ingaret turned to Thomasyn, who shrugged.

"It's too long a story to tell all and it changed by the day, but she has not been faithful to Elis. It seems that any handsome face –"

"Or handsome purse," Jethro interrupted.

Thomasyn nodded agreement. "It is as Jethro says. Elis has had a lot to endure but he has taken her back every time, I think because of their daughter, Constance, whom she has largely ignored, leaving Elis and his parents to raise her."

"None of this would have happened if you had married Elis when he asked you!" Jethro accused her.

"How did you know that?"

"He told me."

"That was a long time ago, Jethro. Twenty three years. It was not to be. Perhaps in another life –"

"We are only given one life," Thomasyn said quietly, "but sometimes we are given the chance to put things right."

She put her arm round Jethro's neck and kissed him but then the boys began to squabble and their mother had to intervene and apologise to Mistress Aldith.

"Please don't fret on my account," the older woman said. "I spend little enough time with children, which I regret."

Edwina had already taken her sons home by the time Ingaret thought she and Aldith should return to the tavern. Elis and Rudd had not yet returned from their search.

"I've had another very happy day. Thank you so much," she said as she kissed her brother and sister-in-law goodbye. "Please tell Elis that we will call for him at dawn. He has no need to travel in discomfort when he can ride in the carriage with us. Our man will make sure that his horse and cart arrive safely back at the mill."

CHAPTER 43

Dawn next day saw them on the road home. It was no longer snowing and, as the sun rose higher and the clouds were burned away, the surface of the ice-packed road ahead glinted and glittered and the foliage around them, bowed beneath the weight of its snowy burden, began to drip, drip, drip.

Ingaret and Aldith were both tired and Elis was listless and disinclined to talk, though he brightened as they neared home and spent the last hour in conversation about mill matters and asking questions about Robert's baby son, the reason for their visit to the city.

Then Ingaret became reticent and his questions were answered briefly by Mistress Aldith. She had never spoken to Ingaret about the baby's parentage, but Ingaret had the feeling that her elderly companion suspected the facts as presented to Lord and Lady D'Avencourt and that their generous thankoffering to the bishop was misplaced. However, Ingaret was not about to stir up mischief, especially as her ladyship doted on the baby.

"I would like to meet Constance," said Ingaret, changing the subject. "She is my niece, after all – or should it be 'half-niece' as she is Alice's daughter?"

"I would like that, too. I am sure you would get on well together," Elis replied with enthusiasm. "We will arrange it when Alice comes home."

Ingaret wished that they could be alone together so that she could talk to him as they used to talk, but she was inhibited by the presence of Aldith.

"What a pleasant young man," Aldith said when they had left him at the mill and were on their way to the manor.

"Yes, he is," Ingaret agreed. "We were inseparable when we were young."

Aldith looked at her enquiringly but said nothing more. What a wise woman she is, thought Ingaret.

Arriving at the manor house mid-afternoon, Aldith instructed a servant to unload all their bags and take them up to her room, so that she could sort them later, and they went at once to find Lady D'Avencourt.

They found her in her solar in the east wing, looking as elegant as always, but Ingaret thought she appeared very tired and – what was the word? – diminished. She greeted them from her chair with arms stretched towards them. Ingaret curtseyed and Aldith was about to do the same but her ladyship prevented her.

"Please don't, Mistress Aldith – your bones are much too old. It is enough for me that you are back safely."

"Thank you, my lady," Aldith replied, with evident relief.

She invited them to sit on the couch facing her then rang the bell on the table beside her and sent a servant for wine.

"Now," she said, "I want to hear every detail of your visit to the cathedral, and the service, and an explanation of why you are home one day late."

As they sipped the dark red liquid that sent strange sensations into Ingaret's brain and interfered with her thoughts, they relayed the gratitude of the Bishop and described every detail over and over until her ladyship's head began to loll forward onto her chest. Then Mistress Aldith said she must take her lady to her bed chamber and send for something to eat and her nightly pot of ale then begin the lengthy routine of preparing her for bed. Sleep, however, came fitfully to her lady and she said she expected to be disturbed several times during the night to attend to her.

"Then I will remember with longing the bed in the tavern," she smiled, "and four nights of uninterrupted sleep."

She supported her mistress as they slowly left the solar with Ingaret following.

"What will you do for the rest of the evening?" Aldith asked her.

"Go to the kitchen and find something to eat," decided Ingaret, "then refresh myself and make ready for bed. And you?"

"What I do always depends on what my lady needs," said Aldith. "I thank you, Ingaret, for your company over these last few days and for introducing me to your family. You are to be envied."

Ingaret replied that it had been a pleasure for her, too, and an experience she would never forget.

"Nor will I ever forget those wimples!" she added and both women laughed.

She left them then and walked through the manor's great hall and into the kitchen, where she scrounged some leftovers from the mid-day meal, then made her way through the passages to the west wing and Robert's rooms. She wondered whether he would be there and was surprised to find that she did not much mind whether he was or not.

This change of heart she blamed on being travel weary and on the effects of the wine, but came to the uncomfortable conclusion that there was more to her reluctance than that, something deep inside her that she was not able to locate or did not want to locate.

She hoped that seeing Robert would concentrate her thoughts. She guessed that he would want to take her to bed as soon as she set foot in the room, if he were there, and if thoughts of Helewise impeded his desires, she knew how to seduce him into ridding himself of them. After all, he had been without her for four days and that was a long time for Robert to remain celibate.

Of course, that was if she wanted him in her bed tonight and she wasn't at all sure that she did, which was a strange new experience. So she was in a quandary of emotions when she opened the door to his rooms and announced loudly, "Robert! Robert! I'm back!"

There was no reply and the room was empty, though candles were burning. Surprised, she called again, "Robert?" There was still no reply but she thought she heard a sound from the bedroom.

Silently, she tiptoed across the room and threw open the bedroom door, announcing as she did so, "Robert, it's me, I'm back!"

There was a quick movement from the bed as Robert threw back the coverlet and slid from beneath the sheet and came uncertainly towards her, tousled and naked.

"Ingaret," he said, "I didn't hear the carriage – I didn't know you were –"

She stared at his fever-bright eyes and flushed face then her eyes travelled down his body and what she saw there caused her to look at the bed again and at the lump beneath the bedclothes.

He reached out a hand to stop her but she was too quick for him and had the coverlet and sheet pulled back to reveal a young pair of breasts and thighs.

"Beatrix! Beatrix!" she gasped and whirled round to face him again. "My serving girl? How could you?" She was shrieking now and calling him a string of names that she blushed to remember in the days that followed. "How long has this been going on, under my nose?"

"It hasn't," he was quick to respond, "but you stayed away –"

"Four days!" she shouted at him. "Four days!"

"Ingaret, my love, Beatrix means nothing to me – nothing at all."

Now it was the girl's turn to scream and he clapped his hands over his ears as they both railed against him.

Ingaret was about to tell him to get out but realised in time that these were his rooms and, if anyone went, it had to be her.

"Robert, you can have Helewise or Beatrix or anyone else you've a mind to humiliate – anyone else – anyone! But it won't be me! This is it, Robert. This is the end of you and me! I'm going – for good!" and so saying, she ran out of the room and down the stairs.

She needed to find Aldith and tell her what had happened, she owed her that, and ask her to think of some untruth to tell her ladyship, to explain her future absence, but then she would leave the manor and never return. But where could she go?

There was only one place where she could feel safe – to Noah, her father.

So late that night she found herself half running and half walking on her way to the vill. Aldith had made sure she was wearing the sturdy leather ankle boots and had a cloak and a blanket about her shoulders, and it was dressed thus that she was knocking on her father's door and fell into his arms when he opened it.

PART IV

THE VILL

CHAPTER 44

Noah was now sixty years old. He still worked his three strips of land with the help of Ingaret's half-brothers, James and Henry, and their children.

Her half-sisters Megge and Lizzie were also married and lived in the vicinity, all four families working their own land as serfs to Lord and Lady D'Avencourt as did their father, his forebears and their forebears, stretching back further than anyone could remember.

John had stayed with the blacksmith's family after working out an unpaid apprenticeship in return for his board and lodging and, on the death of Thomasyn's father, had married one of her sisters and taken on responsibility for his new mother-in-law and the forge, the only blacksmith for many miles.

Noah had now left the settlement and lived in a half-decent cottage in the vill, still wattle-and-daub with a thatched roof, but larger and more sturdy than the old family home.

It was to this cottage that Ingaret fled on the night she left the manor.

"Ingaret, daughter, what brings you here? What has happened to you?" he asked as he wrapped his arms around her and drew her into the warm room. "You're shivering with the cold. Come over to the fire. Sit here. Let me take your boots off. My dear, you're frozen!"

Ingaret tried to explain but he cut her short.

"You can tell me later. Now we must get you warm. I will bring blankets. Your blanket and cloak are wringing wet."

An hour later, with her hands wrapped round a bowl of hot carrot soup thickened with bread, her feet on a stool near the fire, which he had replenished, she was feeling much better and was telling him the story of her flight.

He listened patiently then commented, "Young master Robert was never going to remain faithful to you forever. I am surprised that you lasted as long as you did. And he should go back to his wife, Ingaret, you must see that. Every child needs a mother and a father."

"But the baby is not his," Ingaret said, and relayed the true facts of the birth then went on to describe her visit to Fortchester cathedral with Mistress Aldith – and meeting Elis – and hearing about Alice.

"That is enough for one evening," her father said, taking the bowl from her and putting it on the table. "There is time for all this in the morning. You must sleep in here tonight on my platform, near the fire."

"But where will you sleep?"

"There is another room beneath the rafters. I will sleep there. My legs are not so old that they can't climb the ladder."

Ingaret slept well in the warm room. She awoke to the aroma of porridge bubbling away in a cauldron over the fire. As they ate, he smiled as he said, "Daughter, you must stay here with me while you decide what you are going to do with your life."

"Father, may I?" she asked quickly. "I will keep house for you, like the old days, and will look after you as you grow older."

"That will suit me well," he replied happily. "I admit I have been lonely since the family left. That will suit me very well."

During the days that followed, Ingaret relayed to him all the family news she had gleaned in Fortchester. Both knew that they were avoiding the subject of Alice's disappearance but they had to talk about it finally when everyone else's welfare had been debated.

"So, Father, what's all this about Alice?"

He sighed. "She is my daughter but she always favoured Gunnora's family rather than mine, being so wayward. I think we have been made aware of only half of what Elis has had to tolerate over the years. He never should have married her – we all knew he was building for himself a house that had no foundations and that one day it would come crashing down around his ears. He married her on the rebound, of course. You have to bear responsibility for that."

"That's not just," Ingaret protested hotly. "Roldan came along and he loved me and offered me a better life, and we would still be together were it not for his accident."

"I know," her father placated her. "He was a good man and I was pleased to welcome him into the family. He has been a great loss to all of us."

"What a mess!" Ingaret said. "Life can dish up such a mess!"

"So now it is just you and me," said her father. "Perhaps it's not as good as it could be but neither is it as bad. We still have each other."

"We will always have each other," Ingaret stated with certainty.

CHAPTER 45

So Ingaret settled down to living in the vill and looking after her father. She missed the exuberant physicality of Robert, whose attentions she had enjoyed and whom she had come to love without being in love with him, but was well content with the quieter and less traumatic life she now lived. This was not to say that she did not sometimes long for his ardour during the night but then she reminded herself that she had on occasions had to share him and had never been quite sure, after his absences, whether or not he had been in someone else's bed. In time, she was able to forgive him his weakness and smile at the happy memories when she had him all to herself.

Her father, meantime, seemed to flourish and looked and seemed happier than she had ever known him to be.

Noah had been able to live comfortably on his own and Ingaret had a little money saved and, if they became anxious about their living expenses, she was willing to go to Fortchester and sell the few pieces of jewellery that Robert had given her and that she had been wearing when she ran from the manor.

One stormy afternoon in early January, after their mid-day meal, when they were sitting by the fire, Noah dozing and Ingaret planning their meal for the following day, there was a knock at the door. Noah woke with a start.

"Stay there, Father, I'll open it," she said and was surprised to find Elis on the doorstep.

"Hello, Elis," she said, "come in. Is it Father you want to see?"

"Hello," he replied, stepping inside and shaking the rain from his hat, "I heard you had left the manor and were here looking after your father." He looked at her enquiringly.

"It's a long story," Ingaret told him, "but I'm here to stay now."

"Take off your cloak, lad, and come and sit by the fire," Noah said. "Lay it over the back of the chair. Do you wish to stable your horse?"

"Thank you, no, he'll be all right for a while and I don't intend to stay long."

"You'll join us for a drink of ale?" Ingaret asked.

"I will, indeed, thank you," Elis said and she went across to the side board to fill their pots.

"Now tell us why you're here," Noah said, "though, of course, we are always pleased to see you, whatever the reason. "

"I came to tell you that Alice is back. She has come home!"

"That's wonderful news, son. How is she?"

Elis shook his head. "Not good, not good at all."

"Sit down and tell us," Noah said. "What has my daughter been up to this time?"

While Ingaret brought their pots of ale to the fireside and they drank together, Elis told them that this unscrupulous merchant had taken her to London on their way, as she thought, to the coast and eventually to Antwerp but, after a week spent in a lodging house, he had paid the bill and walked out, leaving Alice stranded. She had no money and the landlady had turned her out into the street, with just the clothes she was wearing, which he had bought her.

"How did she get home?" Ingaret asked.

"By any means she could," Elis said. "Walking, begging lifts, sleeping in woods –"

"But it's been so cold," Ingaret said.

"She couldn't tell me how she got home, not all of it – says she doesn't remember. Anyway, she's home now – repentant, of course, but then she always is."

"You've taken her back?" asked Noah.

"Of course. She is my wife and she looked so ill. I put her straight to bed and my mother has been nursing her and feeding her. She is a little better, I think."

"I'm glad to hear it," Noah said. "How long has she been home?"

"Two nights ago. I thought you would want to know."

"Of course, thank you, lad."

"I should go back. She frets if I am away too long."

Ingaret took his cloak from the back of the chair, shook it out, then handed it to him.

"Thank you," he said. "I will listen to your story one day when I have more time. I'm glad I've seen you."

"'Tis little worth the telling," Ingaret replied. "Will you give Alice my father's love, and mine."

Elis smiled for the first time since he had been in the house.

"I'll give her Noah's, certainly, but not yours, I think. Alice is very sensitive when it comes to talking about you, even though you are sisters. I always have to think about what I am about to say before I say it – you understand?"

Ingaret nodded and longed to throw her arms round his neck and tell him how sorry she was that her sister was causing him so much anxiety, but she just said, "Whatever you think is best."

"Please let us know how she fares," Noah said. "I will come to see her as soon as she is well enough."

"Rest assured, I will keep you informed," Elis replied then put on his hat and left the cottage.

"There seems to be nothing we can do to help," Ingaret said forlornly.

"There has never been anything anyone could do to help," Noah said with resignation.

"We should let the rest of the family know that she is safely back."

"Yes, I'll make the rounds tomorrow morning," said Noah, "and put their minds at rest."

CHAPTER 46

Elis kept Noah abreast of Alice's progress, slow though it was, and sent a messenger to Fortchester to let Jethro know the latest news so that he had no further need to continue searching.

Winter gave way to early Spring and ploughing, sowing and harrowing kept everyone in the vill busy, including the children and dogs, who were engaged in scaring off the persistent birds.

One morning, the neighbours were gossiping that Lord D'Avencourt was at the farrier's, having his palfrey shod. Ingaret had no wish to meet him accidentally and told her father that she would take a walk in the forest. He looked at her strangely, she thought, but he said nothing and she set off along the paths she had known since childhood, avoiding the centre of the vill where the farrier's barn stood next to John's smithy.

There was a light breeze to ruffle her hair as she made for the spot she loved best, where she had first met Robert when she was six years old, near the oak where she had buried the button she gave to Roldan on their wedding day, among the bright yellow celandine, the pale primroses and retiring violets.

Reaching the tree, she sat among its roots and leaned back against the old trunk and closed her eyes. She thought about Alice, her impulsive and foolish half-sister, and tears came unbidden and slipped down her cheeks, but she knew she was shedding them for Elis, who had looked so confused and vulnerable when he came to tell them that his wife had returned. He had not been near them since but sent one of the apprentices from the mill if he wanted to give them any news.

In the distance, a woodpecker was tap, tap, tapping on a tree trunk.

She dozed off for a while and awoke with a thirst that she could easily quench at the stream. Lying on her stomach, as she used to do as a small child, she lapped up some of the clear, cold water then splashed handfuls over her face.

It was probably time to return home as she had the mid-day meal to prepare and it was with some reluctance that she retraced her steps back to the vill, passing along the main street on her way to the cottage. There was no sign of his lordship's palfry and she sighed with relief.

Entering the cottage, she removed her light shawl from around her shoulders and hung it on the hook behind the door. Her father was sitting by the fire, absentmindedly whittling a piece of wood.

"Hello, Father," she greeted him, "are you starving? I'm sorry if I've kept you waiting but the meal won't take long."

Her father looked up.

"Ingaret, before you do anything else, I need to talk to you."

"About what?" she asked. "You are looking very serious but it can't be that important or you would have spoken to me before I went out."

He sighed and indicated the settle.

"Come and sit down," he said. "It *is* important."

Mystified, she came over, put her arm around his shoulders and kissed the top of his head, then sat down.

"So tell me," she said. "I'm listening."

He threw his piece of wood into the fire, paused for a moment then began.

"I had a visit this morning – from Lord D'Avencourt."

"Lord D'Avencourt?" she echoed. "What about?"

"About you."

"Me? Surely not."

"It seems, my dear, that he has become – what shall I say? – interested in you. He said that he had met you occasionally in the manor and had come to the conclusion that you were a companion of Lady D'Avencourt. Her ladyship said your name was Gabriella for her own obscure reason, and since then he has been, at intervals, making enquiries, trying to locate you, but of course he was asking about someone who didn't exist.

"When her ladyship wished to send someone she could trust to Fortchester with Mistress Aldith, he suggested that she sent you. He hoped to approach you on your return but you disappeared like a spirit into the air, leaving no trace."

"Where is this leading, Father?"

"Patience. Hear me out. He was so frustrated that he questioned Mistress Aldith, who professed ignorance, saying you lived in the vill, which he thought not to be the case because he had already made exhaustive enquiries here. So then he questioned the servants minutely and gradually pieced together the whole story."

Ingaret felt her heart beginning to beat alarmingly fast and heat rising in her face.

"Father, what are you saying?"

"He is making us an offer, Ingaret. He is desirous of installing you in the manor as his mistress. You would have your own suite of rooms, your own ladies-in-waiting, and you would want for nothing, and neither would I."

"He wants you to sell me to him?"

"I suppose it amounts to that, yes."

"But why? Why is he so interested in me? He can have anyone he wants any time. Why me?"

"He spoke of his desire for you but I think it also has something to do with his son. Now master Robert is out of the way – he has gone back to his wife, as you know – it seems to me that he has to convince himself that anything his son can do, he can do as well."

"Until he also tires of me. What did you say, Father?"

"I said the decision was not mine. It was yours. You must do whatever you think right."

"And what do you think is right?"

"Ingaret, it is for you to decide. I do not wish to sway you in any direction."

She stood and came across to him and sat at his feet and laid her head on his lap.

"You need never work again if I agreed to what he is suggesting, Father, but please forgive me – I couldn't, I couldn't, never, ever. He is an old man – but that's not the reason. I've been Robert's mistress, but he and I were good together, we liked each other – and then there's her ladyship, that dear lady. I couldn't do that to her. No, it's out of the question and he had no right to ask it of you – of me –"

"My dear, he has every right. It is the likes of us who have no rights. Your refusal will damage his pride but I don't think he'll take any action. You're right. He is an old man and he knows it."

"How will you give him my answer?"

"I will go to see him tomorrow. No one need ever know why he came to see me today. Now, how about that meal? I'm hungry. I'll help you prepare the vegetables."

CHAPTER 47

Spring blossomed into summer and the wheat in the fields was growing apace and promised a heavy harvest.

Alice continued to make slow progress physically but Elis confided to Noah, who visited often, that he was more concerned about her humours. There were nights when she slept not at all, days when they could hardly wake her, others when she didn't speak and yet others when she refused to eat anything.

Constance, now twenty years old, was being courted by a cordwainer in the vill, whose shoes sold well in Fortchester, but she would not marry him and leave her mother while she was so ill. Both husband and daughter were at a loss to know how to help her.

As forecast, the harvest was plentiful and the community breathed a sigh of relief to know that there would be ample food for all during the winter months ahead.

Ingaret decided that she would like to see her grandchildren again and left Noah to fend for himself for a few days while she stayed in Fortchester. He arranged for her to travel with a local carrier as a paid passenger and said she should ask Jethro to make the same arrangement for her return journey.

As before, she arrived unexpectedly at the home of Philippa and Matthew and enjoyed just as warm a welcome. Her granddaughter Ingaret, now nearly four years old, and little Matthew, who had just had his first birthday and was walking, straightaway took her out into the yard to watch them ride their hobby horses.

"I do wish you lived nearer, Mother," said Philippa wistfully. "The children miss so much by not having you living close by."

Ingaret spent several contented days with the family, during which time Lora and Mark, who seemed resigned to remaining childless, came to see her.

She then walked to visit Allard and Edwina and their children, Roldan and Noah, both of whom she helped make mud pies and crudely-moulded figurines of the first Noah and some of the animals who lived in the Ark.

"I have to say, I can't recognise some of these strange creatures," Edwina laughed, "but one day, they'll be carving them in stone, just like their father and grandfather."

Finally, Ingaret called on her brother Jethro. Thomasyn invited her to stay with them for as long as she wished and Ingaret gratefully accepted.

She debated with herself whether to tell Thomasyn about the proposal made to her by Lord D'Avencourt, and decided she would, glad to talk it over with someone who understood.

Thomasyn thought for a moment on being told. "He must be feeling his age if he no longer expects young women to come running as soon as he looks their way," she said and added, "At least he gave you the choice. I was never able to refuse."

Ingaret said slowly, "I remember something my father told me a long time ago. Life is like a maypole dance. We are each given a ribbon to weave into a perfect pattern with the other people in our lives, but few succeed. Most of us tangle our ribbons but, somehow, in spite of the entangling, we still create something beautiful."

Thomasyn looked at her. "You always were the thinker, Ingaret. That's too deep for me to understand."

Ingaret laughed and told her the story of how her father had met her mother beneath the maypole and that she and her brother Jethro would not be alive were it not for the entanglement of the ribbons. Thomasyn laughed, too.

"So how about you, Thomasyn?" Ingaret continued. "Lord D'Avencourt entangled your ribbon, did he not? But he fathered Edwina – a lovely daughter for you and Jethro, a wife for my son, a daughter-in-law for me and a mother to the children, and none of us would want to be without her."

Thomasyn nodded. "I understand. So much happiness from so much shame."

"I only wish the same could be said for Elis," mused Ingaret. "My sister heaps sorrow upon sorrow on his head and he doesn't deserve any of it. She entangled him into marrying her and this is how she repays him."

"How is she faring since coming back home?"

Ingaret relayed all that Noah had seen during his visits.

"No one seems able to help her and Elis is exhausted, trying to look after her and run the mill."

Thomasyn laughed. "Still your angel," she said.

Ingaret sighed. "That was a long time ago but, yes, still my angel."

Nobody expected to find Elis on the doorstep two mornings later, dishevelled and anxious, his hair falling over his face and with dark rings under his eyes. Thomasyn brought him indoors at once.

"Ingaret, you here?" he asked on seeing her.

"Yes, visiting for a few days" she explained. "Come and sit down, Elis. You look done in."

"I've come to see Jethro," he said as he sank onto the settle. "I've been driving all night."

"Unfortunately, my boys aren't here, they're at the workshop with their father," said Thomasyn, "but I'll ask the little lad next door to run and fetch Jethro home. Trouble, Elis?"

"She's gone again," he said. "Alice has run away again!"

"I'll call next door," said Thomasyn and hurried out.

"I'm so sorry, Elis," sympathised Ingaret, wanting to put her arms round him but he was too vulnerable and she refrained. Instead she asked him if he would eat something.

"There are slices of chicken breast left over from our last meal, and bread and cheese, washed down with Thomasyn's elderflower wine."

"Perfect," Elis mumbled, leaning his head against the wooden back of the settle. "I wish I could just rest here for hours."

Thomasyn returned and helped Ingaret prepare the meal for him. He had finished eating by the time Jethro hurried through the door.

"What's the urgency?" he asked then saw their visitor. "Elis – what are you doing here?"

"I've come to ask for your help once more, Jethro."

Jethro raised his eyebrows. "Alice?"

"Yes, I regret to say it's Alice. She's run away again! Constance discovered her missing early yesterday morning. Her bed hadn't been slept in. She must have crept out after we all retired for the night."

Jethro came to sit by him and poured himself a tankard of wine and topped up Elis's tankard. Thomasyn and Ingaret cleared away Elis's trencher and busied themselves within earshot.

"We hoped she would come back during the day but she didn't," Elis continued. "She was in no fit state to go anywhere!"

"And the reason this time?" asked Jethro.

"No reason that I know. She has had all the love and attention that Constance and I and my mother could give her – all the love I could give her. But she hasn't been eating very much and wasn't sleeping, in spite of the deadly nightshade we gave her – though in small doses – and she was so thin. I don't think she could have travelled as far as Fortchester but there is just the chance she found someone to bring her here."

"Did she give no warning of her plans?" Thomasyn asked.

"None."

"We'll keep a lookout for her," Jethro promised, "but there's no need for you to stay. Sleep here tonight, if you don't mind sharing the upstairs room with the boys and me. Thomasyn and Ingaret are sleeping down here."

"Thank you. I would benefit from a good night's sleep."

"What are old friends for if not to help each other?" Jethro asked. "If you do decide to drive back tomorrow, perhaps you would take Ingaret with you. She came with the carrier and I was going to pay him to take her back."

"There's no need for that. Of course I will take her home."

Ingaret dropped the knife she was drying and it fell on the rushes. She stooped to pick it up and wiped it again, her head bent low to conceal any sign of the wave of pleasure that was sweeping through her. But what was she thinking? Alice was missing. Alice, his wife and her sister. Now it was shame that was flushing her cheeks.

When she finally raised her head, Thomasyn was looking at her but made no comment.

"Don't worry," Jethro was saying. "If she's in the city, we'll find her. I should be getting back to the workshop now, we're very busy, but you must rest, Elis. Thomasyn will look after you."

"My horse –"

"I'll stable your horse and cart so you've no need to worry about that."

"Thanks, Jethro."

"You won't be disturbed upstairs," Thomasyn told him. "You can sleep as long as you like."

Elis repeated his thanks and climbed the ladder.

"Ingaret –" Thomasyn said when he had closed the trap door at the top of the steps, "Ingaret – be careful."

"I know, I know. You've no need to warn me. I am quite aware of the situation. He is my sister's husband. I am not about to do anything foolish."

She did not add that she had been bowled over to discover that her feelings for Elis had not changed. They may have been repressed all these years but they had not changed and were beginning to resurface.

I'm still in love with him, she acknowledged, but only to herself, *the same as I always was. I'm still in love with him!*

CHAPTER 48

Jethro kissed his sister then helped her up onto the driver's seat, next to Elis, as they made ready to set off for home on the following morning. As they gained the high road, a light breeze was rustling the leaves on the trees and freshening the air, which was dry and warm.

Elis set the pace of the horse to a brisk trot.

"There's no rush," Ingaret said, hoping they would slow down and the drive would last a little longer.

"There is for me," Elis replied. "Alice may have come home while I've been away."

"I'm so sorry that my sister has brought you to this," Ingaret sympathised with the utmost sincerity, conscious that somehow it was her fault – everyone seemed to think it was.

Obviously, Elis had no such thought in his head as he answered, "It's not her fault. Alice is Alice and always has been. I knew her well enough when I married her."

They drove on in silence, he seemingly lost in reverie and Ingaret with thoughts and emotions churning in her mind and heart that she would be embarrassed to reveal.

The traffic on the high road was light and mostly travelling in the opposite direction. They had little else to say to each other for the remainder of the journey but Ingaret felt well content to be at his side, as companionable as they were when young, and Elis seemed to be at peace, too.

He dropped her off at her door and waved to Noah, who came out to greet them, then was on his way home to the mill.

Ingaret was very conscious that he had not touched her once throughout the journey, not even to steady her when the cart negotiated the holes in the surface of the road, and he had left her to scramble down without his help. And she had so wanted to feel his touch again.

Noah brought her into the cottage and sat her down and poured two pots of her blackcurrant cordial while he listened to her news. He sighed and said much the same as Elis had said, that Alice had always done as she pleased without regard for anyone else, and repeated yet again that she took after Gunnora's side of the family.

A week went by and still she had not returned, which Ingaret felt gave herself the freedom to visit the mill and renew her acquaintance with Mistress Edith, Elis's mother. She was nearing seventy years of age but in good health and her mind was still very alert. They had always enjoyed each other's company and she was delighted to see Ingaret again.

However, the reception from Constance was cool, which grieved Ingaret, who was acutely aware that her niece made every effort not to leave her and Elis alone together for a moment. She wondered what Alice had told her about their past.

Elis never paid her any particular attention when she visited but always seemed pleased to see her; at least he never seemed displeased.

She was there in conversation with his mother, Alice having been missing for two weeks, when he came in from the mill, dusting down his working clothes so that he entered in a cloud of flour. Usually he discarded his white hat, overalls and shoe coverings as soon as he left the mill, but not today.

"Mother," he began breathlessly then said, on noticing Ingaret, "Hello, Ingaret. Mother, one of the woodcutters has just walked to the mill to see me, with this."

He held out a small moleskin purse on a yellow ribbon. Both ribbon and purse were smeared with mud.

"Oh? But isn't that Alice's purse?" his mother asked.

"Yes."

"So where did he find it?"

"Hanging from a branch of a tree in the forest, on the bank of the river."

"How strange but perhaps it got caught up during one of her wanderings. Did she say she had lost it?"

"It wasn't lost. There's a letter inside it, from Alice, to me."

"What has she written? Does she say where she has gone?"

Elis looked at his mother very strangely and bit his lip, then looked at Ingaret.

"Ingaret, would you mind giving me time alone with my mother? I'm sorry, but this is a private matter between Alice and myself – would you mind?"

"No, of course not. I'll wait outside."

She closed the door firmly behind her and went out into the mill yard, where the woodcutter was waiting, then wandered into the mill. She had known most of the men there since childhood and they greeted her above the noise of the machinery with nods of the head and broad smiles. It was not long before Elis's mother came to find her. She had his work clothes over her arm.

"Ingaret, you should go home now. Elis has gone with the woodcutter. He is going to show him where Alice's purse was found."

"Has she said in her letter where she was going?"

"Not exactly. Please tell your father that Elis will let him know if he finds her."

"Of course. And if there is anything we can do –"

"We know, dear," she said and turned away to speak to the foreman.

Disconsolately, Ingaret walked home. Whatever Alice had written in the letter, it was obvious that Elis did not want her to know – and why should he? Ingaret asked herself. It was no business of hers, though Alice was her sister – half-sister. She would learn more when Elis came to speak to Noah.

He did not come that day nor the days that followed and they presumed that he had no news to give them. Noah said that Ingaret should not go visiting the mill but should leave the family to deal with the situation, whatever it was, as they thought best. He was sure that Elis would let them know if there was any help they could give.

It was Noah who came home with the first report. He had been working in the river, checking crayfish traps, and had heard that a body had been found caught up in weeds not far from Fortchester, having been washed down river by the current.

"Some vagabond, I expect, fallen in the river and too drunk to climb out," surmised Noah. "Not reported as missing because there was no one to report his loss."

The next day he arrived home at noon.

"Hello, Father," Ingaret greeted him in surprise, "I wasn't expecting you home. Are you hungry?"

He came in and slumped down at the table.

"No, I'm not hungry but would you pour me a pot of ale, and pour one for yourself."

"Of course." She crossed to the side board to pour the drinks and brought them to the table. He looked very seriously at her.

"Bad news, I'm sorry to say, my dear," he said. "Take a drink before I tell you."

She did and looked at him expectantly.

"Tell me."

"The body they found yesterday, it's a woman's. They think it's Alice. Elis has gone to identify her but it seems there is little doubt."

"Oh, Father!"

"I know." He reached across the table and grasped the hand she held out to him. "Our Alice."

"It must have been an accident," Ingaret said. "She was very weak. She could have fallen in."

"I don't think it was an accident. I spoke to the water bailiff who found the body. He said that Elis seemed to expect this news, or at least he wasn't greatly surprised."

"But why would she do an awful thing like that?"

"I don't know. She couldn't have been in her right mind. Why didn't she ask someone for help? My poor little girl."

"We still don't know what was in that letter to Elis."

"No, I don't think he has told anyone."

"He told his mother. I was there when the woodcutter brought it to him, as you know. When he asked me to leave the room, I am sure he told his mother."

"All I can see is a little girl standing at the kitchen table, her hands covered in flour, kneading the dough."

"And complaining that it wasn't her job, it was mine." Ingaret smiled. "There was only ever one Alice, God rest her soul. Should I go to the mill to express our sorrow at the news? There's not only Elis but Constance to think about."

"I don't think you'd be welcome there, Ingaret. If the body is Alice's – and it may not be – as her father, I should be the one to share their grief."

Ingaret readily agreed, knowing that she could not trust her own feelings at the moment. Her thoughts and hopes and dreams and sorrow were entangled and did not bear probing too deeply. In any case, perhaps the body was not Alice's.

The corpse had been difficult to identify but Elis confirmed that it was Alice.

He himself came with the news to the cottage.

"Come in, lad," Noah said, on opening the door. "Ingaret is out, blackberrying in the field. Come and sit down. I can guess why you're here. Your face says it all."

Elis nodded as they both sat at the table. "It's as we feared. It *is* Alice. No mistaking, in spite of – in spite of – I recognised some fragments of her skirt and there was her hair, although it was matted with weeds and mud – that lovely light brown –"

His voice broke as he rested his elbows on the table and cradled his face in his hands. Noah reached across and touched his arm.

"If you'd asked, I would have gone with you, son."

Elis murmured his thanks but said the gruesome task had been his responsibility.

"She is a loss to us all – " Noah grieved, " – the most wilful of all my children – always knew exactly what she wanted and would not rest until she possessed it. She had loved you, Elis, since she was a young girl. It was only you she ever wanted."

Elis raised his head and nodded miserably. "I know it." He stood, ready to leave. "Please tell Ingaret."

"As soon as she comes in," Noah promised.

Ingaret shed tears when she was told. She did not remember life without her younger half-sister. Alice had always been there to play with, to fight with, to fight for on some occasions when neighbouring children stole her toy or pulled her hair.

Gunnora had always given her the best of everything – new laces or a length of ribbon Noah had brought home from the fair, the stickiest piece of honeycomb – and Alice was seldom willing to share anything with her brothers and sisters.

Then Jethro had brought home his new friend, the boy from the mill – Elis – and their lives had changed. Alice had captured Elis… Ingaret cut short her train of thought. She would not follow it, not today.

Noah led their large family of mourners, walking behind Elis and Constance and her suitor as they followed the coffin. Bringing up the rear of the procession was the equally large company of Elis's mother and his brothers and sisters and their families.

After the funeral service at the graveside, they watched in silence as the old priest murmured the words of committal and Alice was reverently laid to rest in a plot that Elis had bought for her in consecrated ground behind the east end of the ancient church.

No one had said a word about the letter, even if they knew of its existence. Certainly the priest had been kept ignorant of any letter. He would have refused to bury Alice in consecrated ground if there had been any hint of suicide.

The accepted version was that, being very weak in mind as well as body, she had wandered from the mill and into the forest and had tragically fallen into the river.

Throughout the entire proceedings, Elis did not speak to Ingaret, had not even looked her way or acknowledged that he knew she was present. Ingaret felt she had become invisible to him and found his coldness towards her very hurtful when all she wanted to do was speak words of comfort to him and Constance.

She slipped her arm through her father's as they walked sadly home. Jethro had travelled from Fortchester and was staying with them that night, and they spent the evening talking about the old days and the exasperation and laughter Alice had caused when she was growing up, just by being Alice.

Not long afterwards, Constance married her cordwainer and moved into a cottage in the vill.

CHAPTER 49

Ingaret supposed that she would not be welcome at the mill and stayed away. But her longing to see Elis, to talk to him or just be with him grew stronger as the days came and went. She was concerned that one day she would explode like fermenting wine and would take matters into her own hands, would trust in their one-time friendship, leave her dignity at home and go and see him.

But she didn't. Instead, she cleaned her father's cottage from top to bottom, dug manure into the vegetable garden and planted spring cabbages and onion sets for an early crop. And the year died and 1525 reigned in its place.

One morning in late April, she was on her own in the cottage sorting undergarments to take to the river to wash, when there was a knock on the door and, on opening it, she saw standing there an unexpected visitor.

"Robert!" she exclaimed in great surprise.

"Hello, Ingaret," he said with a wide smile, as if nothing untoward had taken place between them.

"Why are you here?" she asked suspiciously.

"I've come to see you. Aren't you going to ask me in?"

She stood aside and he entered the room, looking round with curiosity.

"Won't you sit down?" she asked and he nodded and made for the settle.

"So," she said, and could not help smiling at the memory. "It has taken you all these years to accept my invitation and come to visit me in my hovel."

He grinned up at her apologetically. "I was very discourteous – full of my own importance. I had no idea then how much that little peasant would come to mean to me."

"Will you have something to drink?"

He shook his head. "I've had more than enough already this morning. So, how is my peasant girl? I must say, you look blooming. The years are dealing gently with you, Ingaret."

"You, too, look well, Robert." His features had softened and there were only a few lines wrinkling his eyes. She pulled up a chair to sit opposite him. "How is Helewise and little Robert?"

"Robert is a joy. I forget that he is not my own. Helewise keeps well and is expecting again – in the autumn."

"I hope all goes well again."

"We pray so. I'm here visiting my parents for a few days only. I don't ride over as much as I used to." He smiled at her slyly. "I wonder why that is. Also, of course, my father-in-law keeps me very busy helping him manage his manor. I think he is determined to keep me out of trouble."

"And how is your mother?"

"No better, no worse. Mistress Aldith says she has her good days, when she is in the real world, and bad days, when she is in a world of her own imagining. That is the reason I am here. She misses you."

"And I have missed her. We always enjoyed our time together."

"Then will you come up to the manor sometimes, to be with her? You always did lighten her mood. She still thinks you were her companion, in my father's employ, and doesn't understand why you are no longer there."

"And that is my fault?"

He self-consciously twisted his hat around in his hands and lent forward.

"I'm sorry about what happened, Ingaret. It was very stupid of me. You have been the best thing in my life, do you know that?"

"It had to end sometime, Robert, if not that way, some other way that hurt just as much."

"You could always come back, you know, on the few occasions I'm here. That would give me great pleasure."

Ingaret laughed but without malice.

"The same old Robert! No, my dear, it's over for good."

A knowing smile lit up his face. "I heard that you had an even better offer – from my old man."

"How did you find out?"

"Mistress Aldith told me that you refused him. Probably the first to do so. He must have been surprised."

"I could never betray your mother like that."

"Mistress Aldith was supposed to come to see you today but I said I would come in her stead. She sends the message that she hopes you will forgive much and visit my mother sometimes."

"Yes, I will. I shall be glad to do so."

He stood. "Thank you for your compassion. Is tomorrow convenient?" She nodded. "I will tell her – not that she is likely to remember, but Aldith will remind her."

He walked towards the door with Ingaret following him, then turned.

"Until tomorrow."

She nodded. "Tomorrow," and shut the door after him.

As soon as Noah returned from work, Ingaret told him of Robert's visit and her promise to visit his mother on the following day.

"It will give you something to do," he said. "It concerns me that you spend your days cooped up here. You very seldom go out and never further than the vill. You should have your family around you."

216

"I'm content here, Father. Yes, I do miss my children and grandchildren but I would rather be here than living in the city again, and I do manage to visit them at least once a year."

She was looking forward to seeing Lady D'Avencourt again, and Aldith, and was in high spirits as she walked to the manor house on the following afternoon.

The servant who opened the door showed her into the solar in the east wing, where she was greeted warmly by both women. Wine was ordered by Aldith, and sweetmeats and gingerbread.

Ingaret sat beside her ladyship and held her hand and said she was sorry that she had been away but she was back now and would come to see her any time – Aldith need only send a message. And, yes, she was living now with her father Noah – did her ladyship remember Noah? – in his cottage in the vill.

The refreshments arrived from cellars and kitchen and, while the wine was being poured into silver goblets, Ingaret gave them the news from the vill – the births, marriages and deaths.

Aldith said they were sorry when they heard what had happened to Alice then asked about the wedding of Constance.

"Her new husband makes and mends my lady's shoes," Aldith told their visitor, "and is often at the manor. We know him well." Lady D'Avencourt nodded agreement.

"Shall we see you here on May Day?" Aldith asked.

"You must come and watch the maypole dance!" said her ladyship. "I do so enjoy watching the children weaving their ribbons round the pole, so pretty!"

"I never miss it!" Ingaret replied.

"Now tell me how the river is looking, my dear."

"My father and his gang of workers are cutting back the weeds now," said Ingaret, "and I saw a kingfisher on my way here. It was sitting on a branch, preening its feathers. There are primroses on the river bank and the trees are dressed in that bright Spring green that you only see in April. The hawthorn is blossoming, the mayfly are hatching out and the trout are rising. The countryside is looking so beautiful as it always does at this time of year."

The afternoon wore on and her ladyship's eyes closed and her breathing became slow and regular. She murmured in her sleep.

"It is time for me to go," Ingaret decided, rising from her chair.

"Please come as often as you are able," Mistress Aldith said.

Ingaret hesitated. "I don't want to meet his lordship."

Aldith nodded. "That would be most unfortunate." She thought for a moment then exclaimed, "Ah, I have an idea! Always come through the rose garden. When he is home, I will tie a ribbon round the neck of the urn that replaced your statue on the pedestal. If you see the ribbon there, just turn round and go home again."

"You may forget."

"I won't forget, trust me."

Ingaret smiled. "I do. Thank you, Aldith."

Ingaret kissed her on the cheek and left, smiling to herself as she walked across the grass down towards the river, appreciating the intimacy they shared and Aldith's simple plan for warning her of Lord D'Avencourt's presence.

"So, what is amusing you and making you smile so delectably?"

Ingaret jumped and looked round.

"Robert!"

"Yes, it's me again. Thank you for coming to see my mother. I'm here to walk you home."

"I am quite capable of walking myself home."

"I know you are but I wanted to see you again to say goodbye. I'm riding home tomorrow and don't know when I'll be back."

Ingaret hesitated.

"Come now, what harm can it do for me to walk with you? I promise I won't lay a finger on you."

She laughed good naturedly. "Oh, Master Robert D'Avencourt, I know all about your promises."

He laughed too and fell in beside her as they crossed the bridge over the river and walked in single file along the track leading across the marsh, chatting all the time in the easy way they had always been able to converse together.

The pathway widened across the heathland and he walked beside her. When they reached the edge of the forest he stopped.

"What is it?" she asked.

"Ingaret, I have a mind to see again the place where I first met you. Do you know where that is?"

"Yes, of course."

"Will you take me there?"

"But why?"

"This is 'goodbye' – you know that, don't you? I just had a fancy to say 'goodbye' where we first said 'good morrow', where I first met my little peasant girl."

"You seemed to me like a god."

"Then you looked at me and I became your prisoner for life. Will you take me back there?"

Why not? Ingaret asked herself silently and said aloud, "Of course. It's this way."

After threading their way through the trees and bushes for about a quarter of a mile, Robert exclaimed, "I recognise this. It's where William announced that his stomach had declared war and he couldn't wait till we reached the privy at the manor." He laughed at the memory. "He almost fell off his horse and ran off into the trees and told me not to go away."

"But you did," said Ingaret as she went further into the trees.

"Of course I did, and how glad I am that I disobeyed him, otherwise I would never have met you."

"This is the place," said Ingaret. "I heard you thrashing at the bushes as you came and hid behind one of them."

"And would not come out, as I remember."

"So you threatened me, saying you were a Lancastrian and I had to obey you. I didn't know what a Lancastrian was but it sounded very important so I thought I had better do as you said."

"Then you looked at me with those violet eyes and I was done for."

Both fell quiet, then, remembering the time when they had been so young and so innocent.

"Ingaret, may I kiss you?"

"No, you may not – I know all about your kisses."

"This one will be different. I can't leave without kissing you goodbye. This time you can trust me, I swear it."

Ingaret did trust him, perhaps for the first time, and came into his open arms. His kiss was long and gentle and loving and she wanted to cry. Then he released her lips and drew her closer to him and she rested her head on his doublet.

"I can find my own way back," he said. "Don't forget me. I will never forget you. And thank you for loving me."

Then he was gone.

Ingaret sank down on the ground among last year's fallen leaves and the wood anemones, disturbing their musky smell, feeling as if a great void had opened up beneath her. She had never been in love with Robert but he had always been there throughout her entire life, in the background, and now he was gone. She knew he had gone for the best possible reason, to be with his wife and son and his baby-to-be, if Helewise was able to bring a second live baby into the world, but her gain was Ingaret's loss.

She stood and brushed herself down then heard the crunching of approaching feet among the leaves and thought that Robert must have returned but, to her great surprise, saw Elis among the trees.

"Elis! This is a surprise!"

"I was taking a walk, there's no harm in that."

A sudden suspicion made her ask, "How long have you been there?"

"Long enough."

"Did you see –"

"I saw," he said. "It was most edifying."

"You were spying on us?"

"Not really. The whole episode sickened me. I was too embarrassed to make myself known."

"We were saying 'goodbye'."

"That's not what it looked like to me."

"He's going home to his wife and family tomorrow."

"That's noble of him! It's none of my concern, Ingaret, what he and you do together. Why do you think you need explain?"

"Because we are friends –"

"*Were* friends, but that was a long time ago. I'm going now. No, to hell with both of you! If he can say 'goodbye' to you in that way, then so can I!"

Before she could remonstrate, he had grabbed her arm and pulled her roughly towards him. His other arm went round her shoulders then both arms supported her as he bent her backwards under the pressure of his lips, kissing her again and again, moving his mouth so roughly all over hers that it brought tears to her eyes. Then he released her.

"Now I am going," he said. "I too can find my own way home."

He turned and scuffed his way through the trees, angrily pushing aside the branches that got in his way, stooping beneath others.

Ingaret was left panting for breath. She licked her sore lips and tasted salt and found that her bottom lip was bleeding. She was too shocked to think straight. She had never known Elis in such a rage.

An uncertain hope began to rise but she squashed it as too fanciful. She had lost Robert today and it seemed she had also lost Elis.

CHAPTER 50

Noah was working in the vegetable patch, planting seeds for summer vegetables, when Ingaret arrived home. He looked up as she passed him without a word and went into the cottage. Moments later, he followed her in, wiping his hands on a cloth.

"What's the matter?" he asked. "You look as if you've lost a golden guinea and found a groat. Have you been crying?"

"I think I have just lost two golden guineas, Father."

"Then I have some news that will bring a smile to your face."

Ingaret slumped down on a chair at the table.

"Try me," she invited him.

"Elis was here, not long ago."

"Elis? What did he want?"

"He came looking for you. I said you had gone up to the manor to see her ladyship and I didn't know when you would be home but he could wait for you if he'd a mind. He said no, it wasn't important and he would call another day. He left to take a walk in the forest."

"He found me in the forest and we had an almighty quarrel."

"You and Elis quarrelling? That I don't believe. Do you know what I think?"

"So, old wise one," Ingaret teased him, "what do you think?"

"I think he's in love with you, daughter, and always has been and, what's more, I think you've always been in love with him though you wouldn't admit it."

"Father!" she reproached him.

"Am I right?"

"The second part may be true but I'm not sure about the first part."

"Why don't you get up to the mill and sort it out with him? Life's too short to waste a heart beat. Go on, off with you!"

"If you're wrong –"

"You won't know unless you ask him."

Ingaret threw her arms about her father's neck and kissed him on the cheek.

"If you're wrong, don't be here when I get back!" she called to him, hurrying out of the door and banging it after her.

As she ran, until she was out of breath, then walked, her resolve to speak to Elis began to evaporate like morning mist that burns off when the sun rises. Suppose her father was wrong and Elis now hated her? She could not turn back, though, and she needed to know how things stood between them, one way or the other.

She walked purposefully into the mill yard and into the noisy engine room. One of the men looked over and smiled.

"Will, have you seen Elis?" she shouted at him.

"He came in a while ago, looking like a thunderstorm about to break over our heads. He said he was going for a swim."

"Thank you," she said, making for the doorway.

"Sing before you get there!" Will called after her. "Give the man some warning!"

Ingaret knew where Elis liked to swim, below the mill, in what was known as the 'rose pool' because of the depth of the water at that point and the dog roses that grew alongside the bank, perfuming the air with their sweet fragrance. Trees on the further bank overshadowed the water, making it cool in summertime and giving shelter when it was raining.

Ingaret reached the river and saw Elis's clothes and boots discarded on the grassy bank then saw him ducking and diving at the far end of the pool just before the river bed climbed a slight incline and the water became shallower.

He was forty three years old now and not as slim as he once was but, because of the hard physical work in which he was engaged every day, he still had a muscular body and she sat and watched him for a while with great pleasure.

When she thought she had enjoyed the view long enough and was beginning to feel slightly uncomfortable about spying on him – although it was exactly what he had been doing to her a couple of hours ago – she called out to him. He heard her after her third attempt. She waved and he began to swim towards her. She stood and picked up his towel and waited for him.

When he was a little distance from the bank, he started treading water and asked her what she was doing there.

"I came to find you!" she called back.

"So we can have another argument?"

"No, I came to find out why you called at the cottage."

"Oh, that! Throw me the towel and turn your back and I'll come out!"

"I'll throw you the towel but I won't turn my back!" she answered.

"Don't be a tease!" he called to her. "Throw me the towel!"

She threw it a little distance from her then stood, feet apart, hands on her hips, looking at him. He continued to doggy paddle.

"I'm getting cold," he complained.

"So, what are you going to do about it?"

He paused for a moment then swam towards the bank and began to wade out of the water.

Suddenly Ingaret felt that she had taken matters a little too far. It was not the first time she had seen Elis naked but they had been children then and this was different. She lowered her eyes and, when she looked up again, he had the towel wrapped around his waist and was rubbing himself dry.

He looked at her then with an expression that sent a hot flush through her body and it was as if a sheet of lightning had suddenly revealed to both of them the truth they had been hiding from each other throughout the years.

"This is what I am going to do about it," he said and pulled her down on the grass with him and, discarding the towel, rolled on top of her and, after a frantic scramble, there were two piles of clothing scattered over the grass and his kisses were covering her body.

"Elis, oh, Elis," she gasped while she was still able to speak, "you've come home. At last you've come home."

When it was all over and they were lying panting in each other's arms, Elis told her how much he loved her, he had always loved her, and she had almost destroyed him when she refused him then had married Roldan.

She, in turn, said that her love for him had never gone away but she could not regret marrying Roldan, he had been a good man and had cared deeply for her and had given her their children and grandchildren.

"Then you smashed me into the ground again when you went to live in the manor with that philanderer, Robert D'Avencourt – how could you do that, Ingaret?"

"How could I not, Elis, with you married to our Alice and having Constance to support? But now there is nothing to stop us loving each other and getting married, is there?" she asked, her body pressing to his of its own accord and longing again for the fusion they had just shared.

Elis made no reply. She pulled away from him a little and looked into his troubled eyes. "Is there a law that says two people should not be so happy? Should we now be feeling guilty because our love is too deep, too strong, too consuming?"

Unexpectedly, he removed his arms from around her and sat up.

"My darling, I can't marry you, not yet – I just can't!"

Alarmed, she also sat up.

"Why not, Elis? Tell me why not! What is there to stop us if we love each other? You do, don't you? You said you did!"

He scrambled up, tied the towel around himself again, and walked over to where his clothes lay scattered and found the leather purse that he wore on a chain round his waist.

"This is why not!"

He extracted a small roll of parchment and handed it to her.

"Read that!"

It was a letter inked in an untutored hand, but readable. It was Alice's letter.

"Dearest Elis," Ingaret read aloud, "I am leaving you for the last time. Tell Constance I love her though I have never been the mother she deserved. I have always loved you but you never loved me. You never loved anyone but my sister, Ingaret. I know you can never forgive me for what I have done and the way I have treated you but you are a good man, the best, and I ask you to try. Now I no longer stand in your way. Always, Alice."

Ingaret looked up at him. He already had his shirt on, tucked into his breeches.

"So there is no doubt," she said. "It *was* suicide. She intended to kill herself."

He took the letter from her and helped her up, trying to avoid looking at her, then picked up her shift and handed it to her.

"She didn't kill herself. I did. Because I didn't love her and she knew it. I killed her. That knowledge has been eating away at me, day and night, since receiving this letter. I can't marry you, Ingaret, at least not yet. I need time, time to acknowledge my part in her death, time to repent, and I can't go to the priest for confession or he will rebury her in unconsecrated ground. Get dressed, Ingaret, and I will take you home."

"So, alive she came between us and dead she still comes between us. Oh, how clever you were, sister mine."

"Surely you can't think she contrived this?"

"I don't know what to think, Elis. All I know is that you will not marry me."

"I'm not saying for ever, sweetheart, just not now. I need time."

"Then time you shall have, Elis, as long as you come back to me. I will wait. I have nowhere else to go."

They finished dressing and she picked up his towel. "It's better than nothing," she said and hugged it to her. "It smells of river water and of you."

When they reached the mill, she said there was no need to take her the rest of the way.

"It's May Day in two days' time," he remembered. "Will I see you at the festivities at the manor?"

"Never miss it," she said.

"Please forgive me, my darling," he pleaded. "I will see you there."

Noah was waiting for her return.

"Well?" he asked. "Have you two reached an understanding?"

"Yes, but there won't be any wedding bells yet."

He looked puzzled but asked no more questions. Ingaret, however, needed to make sense of all that Elis had said, needed to explain it to herself as well as to her father.

"It's the ghost of Alice coming between us."

She told him the content of the letter her sister had left behind.

"Elis thinks he killed her because he had never stopped loving me and didn't love her enough. The guilt is eating away at him. Father, she was your daughter. Do you think she knew what she was doing when she wrote those words? Was she that spiteful?"

"I don't know. I can't think that it was her intention to take such revenge, but I don't know and we shall never know."

That night, Ingaret went to sleep with the towel, damp with her tears, crushed to her breast and all her thoughts and imaginings were only of Elis.

CHAPTER 51

There was a shower of rain on the morning of May Day, just sufficient to wet the grass so that the maypole dancers had to be told to be careful not to slip. One little girl did slide and fall on the wet grass and was taken away in tears, which brought the dance to a standstill for a few moments, but her place was taken by another child and the dance continued where they had left off.

Ingaret could not summon her usual enjoyment and enthusiasm for the annual fair but did frequent the stalls and bought bread, a length of lace, some hair ribbons, and a charm bracelet for her granddaughter, little Ingaret.

She and Noah tried their skills with a bow and arrow, throwing balls into a bucket, and knocking from their iron rings the strange coconut fruit that had newly arrived in the country, whose white inner crust, that could be eaten, enclosed a sweet refreshing liquid.

They threw dice and turned up cards, without winning any of the fortunes guaranteed, and Noah tested his strength on a machine that sent the ball almost to the top of the chute.

All the time she was there, Ingaret was looking for Elis, but could not find him.

However, they saw her half-brother John and his family and James, Megge, Henry and Lizzie and their families, and watched with much enjoyment the children juggling eggs in the egg-and-spoon race, repeatedly tumbling over in the three-legged race, and John's son winning the prize of a toffee apple after reaching the winning post first in his sack.

Having eaten their way through savoury and sweet pies and sweetmeats, Noah said he would spend an hour with his sons and workmates under the canvas awning, testing the home-made beers and ales, and all the children wanted to visit the stables and pat the horses, so they parted company.

Having noticed that her ladyship and Mistress Aldith had left the fair some time ago, Ingaret decided that she would invite herself to the solar in the east wing and ask if her ladyship would enjoy her company, if she was not too tired.

Remembering that Aldith had suggested that she enter by way of the rose garden, she headed in that direction. Many of the roses were in bloom and the garden was a picture of scarlet and crimson, yellow, white and sunset orange.

She reached the pedestal at the meeting of the paths and stopped. Round the neck of the urn that Roldan had sculpted, she saw a bright blue ribbon tied and, remembering Aldith's warning, with a smile she turned on her heel and left the garden.

When she returned to the fair, she spied Elis in the distance and joined him. Thankfully, his face lit up when he saw her and they kept each other company for an hour.

He decided to take part in the arm wrestling contest and she watched him arm wrestle her brother John. Each contestant was trying to win at least two of three attempts.

John won the first bout after a fierce show of muscular strength and the crowd round the table roared their approval and clapped the winner. Having assessed the strength and tactics of his opponent, and John having relaxed minutely, which he acknowledged afterwards, Elis won the second bout. Determined, John regained his position on the third attempt, and won the prize of a free flagon of beer poured from one of his lordship's barrels.

It had been a foregone conclusion that the blacksmith would annihilate the miller, but Elis had put up a creditable fight and was slapped on the back for his endeavours and treated to a free beer by the organiser of the competition.

John had to repeat his challenge later that afternoon but lost to the eventual champion, a burly woodsman who felled trees in the forest and stood a head higher than all his opponents.

It had been a very happy day for everyone, made happier for Ingaret when Elis accompanied her home and gave her a loving kiss at her door.

"Careful," she warned him, "my lips haven't healed since your kiss in the forest."

He was apologising yet again for his shameful treatment of her on that occasion when Noah opened the door from within and feigned surprise at seeing them there.

"Oh, hello, you two," he greeted them good naturedly. "I hoped you would be home, Ingaret, before I left. I'm spending the night at Megge's. One of her boys wants to show me some of his woodcarvings – birds and horses and the like. Megge says he is very skilled. I'll see you in the morning."

He walked away with what Ingaret could only describe as a spring in his step. She looked at Elis in surprise.

"I didn't know he was spending the night at Megge's."

Elis smiled. "I don't think she knows, either. I think he has left the cottage to us for the night."

"He's not usually that devious."

"Shall we stand here discussing his motives or take advantage of the chance to spend the whole night together?"

"He is full of surprises," Ingaret said as she led the way indoors.

CHAPTER 52

She found difficulty in settling to her chores on the following day and her head and heart were so full of Elis that she made her way to the mill early afternoon. He was very busy scooping milled flour into bags and loading the cart for delivery but made time to whisper in her ear words that made her blush.

"I hope you thanked your father," he said with a grin, kissed her on the cheek and went back to his work.

Feeling restless, Ingaret decided to visit the manor to ask whether her ladyship would like her company. She wanted to thank her for once again hosting the May Day fair and chat about the day's enjoyments.

Today, there was no ribbon round the urn so with confidence Ingaret made her way through the rose garden, picking a yellow rose on her way, and went through the door into the east wing, intent on making her way to her ladyship's solar.

However, as she rounded a corner in the downstairs passage, Lord D'Avencourt was idling at the bottom of the staircase as if waiting for her. Ingaret's immediate thought was that Mistress Aldith had forgotten to warn her that he was at home, until she saw a length of blue ribbon dangling from his lordship's veined hand.

"Good morrow, mistress," he said as he leaned against the newel post of the banister rail, looking at her with great amusement. "You seem surprised to see me. Now I wonder why that is." He toyed with the ribbon, slipping it this way and that between his fingers. "A pretty ribbon and a clever plan, was it not? A warning not to come visiting because I was in residence?"

"How –?" Ingaret began then stopped, realising that she should have denied his accusation.

"How do I know? I didn't, not really, but I happened to be looking out of a window yesterday and saw you in the rose garden, seemingly intent on your way here but, when you reached the pedestal, you suddenly turned round and walked away. I was intrigued, then noticed the ribbon tied round the urn. So today, when I saw that the ribbon was still there, I decided to remove it and see what happened – and you happened. A most pleasant occurrence, my dear – a ripe plum fallen into my waiting lap, just as I hoped."

Ingaret stared at him with an incredulity that quickly turned to trepidation when she saw the intensity of his scrutiny, his eyes locked in hers, luring her into his schemes, preventing escape. She had never noticed the natural colour of his eyes but now they were black, fathomless black.

Then, suddenly, he looked away, releasing her.

He's playing with me, Ingaret thought.

"My dear wife, by the way, is dozing – I looked in on her not an hour since – and she won't be needing your companionship this afternoon. So, I have you all to myself. Whatever shall we do to pass the time?"

Ingaret said nothing, her fists clenched. He discarded the ribbon and changed his stance so that he was standing on the bottom step, arms folded, feet apart, preventing her from passing him.

"Nothing to say? Then let me offer a few delights. We could take a stroll in the rose garden or play a round of cards or a game of chess – I'm sure you have spent many an evening playing with my youngest son – or we could spend a delectable hour or two in my very comfortable bed. I think that's the best suggestion of them all. You won't refuse me, my lamb, will you? Not again? You are just what I need to keep my manhood performing as it should these days, just what I need."

Ingaret continued to look at him, now with horror, and started backing away, unclenching her fists, ready to repulse him. But he was too quick for her. He closed the gap between them, trampling the yellow rose she had dropped, and grabbed her, putting his arms round her in such a vice-like grip that she couldn't move. He brought his flushed face close to hers, his beard rough against her cheek, and she could smell the alcohol on his breath. She would have screamed but did not want to be found in so compromising a situation that could be misconstrued and have an account of it reach Lady D'Avencourt's ears. He tried clumsily to cover her lips with his but she turned her face away.

"You disgust me!" she spat at him.

Abruptly he stopped trying to kiss her but did not release his grip. She looked up at him in defiance and with fear watched his eyes change colour again and knew that she had gone too far and his revenge would be swift and total.

"So!" he came back at her, his face above hers, his lips a thin line, his voice a growl, still not releasing his hold on her. "My lady thinks she is too good for me, this scabby peasant, my son's dregs, daughter of a serf – one of my own serfs. Do you think I am so enamoured that I will not have you and your father thrown off my manor? Your property confiscated? Your cottage demolished?"

He released his grip on her but took her chin in his hand, holding it fast and hurting her jaw, mouthing his next revelation with great relish.

"Your sister had no such scruples!"

"My sister? Do you mean Alice?"

"Of course I mean Alice – Alice who welcomed the kisses of his lordship wherever his lips pleasured him. She wasn't too proud to give herself to me – in the forest, in the fields, even on a pile of sacks in the barn in the mill yard, under her husband's nose. She knew how to please her lord, that hussy!"

Ingaret clapped her hands over her ears.

"No!" she shouted at him. "No! I'll not hear another word!"

"Oh, yes, you will if I've a mind to tell you!"

He pulled her hands away from her ears and held them rigidly down by her sides. She was not prepared for what he then whispered in her ear at great length, words that she would never repeat to another living soul.

He raised his voice slightly, menacing her, terrifying her.

"And we will play that same game, madam, whether you like it or not!"

She had heard enough of his filth and reasoned she had nothing more to lose. He lunged for her again, roaring his lust, his anger and humiliation at being rebuffed, but the roar finished in a howl of pain as Ingaret jumped on his foot then brought her knee up against his cod piece with all the strength she could muster. He lost his balance and collapsed on the stairs, clutching himself where he hurt most, raining down dreadful oaths and curses on her head.

She turned to run but had only gone a few steps when a strange gurgling sound caused her to turn round to look at him, terrified that she had killed him.

What she saw brought her back to his side.

"Is this one of your tricks?" she asked suspiciously, "Because if it is, it won't fool me!"

Still clutching his groin with his right hand, he was trying to lift his left towards her in supplication but it flopped back by his side. He was trying to say something but saliva was running down his chin from a mouth that seemed somehow lopsided.

"What's the matter with you?"

Then someone was coming down the stairs and taking hold of her arm.

"Go, Ingaret, go! It's apoplexy! I'll deal with it."

"Aldith!" Ingaret exclaimed in amazement. "What are you doing here?"

"I saw the ribbon had been removed and was coming to warn you. I've been standing at the top of the stairs."

"Then you saw –?"

"Everything," she confirmed, nodding. "Now go, child!"

Ingaret turned again and ran as fast as she could out of the side door, through the rose garden, across the grass, over the bridge and through the forest. She needed to reach home and tell her father in what danger she had placed the two of them.

She stumbled through the door of their cottage but Noah was not at home so she ran through the vill to the blacksmith's and found her brother at his anvil. He called to one of his men to continue hammering the weather vane he was working on and took Ingaret outside. There, he sat her down at the table under the trees and listened to her garbled story.

"I know where father is," he said. "He has gone to visit old Mother Sharples in the forest and take some logs for her woodpile. I'll ask Eleanor to come and sit with you. I'll bring him back with me. I won't be long."

John's wife brought a drink of water from their well and held Ingaret's hand while she related all that had happened.

"He'll evict us for sure," Ingaret wailed, "and it's all my fault."

"I don't see what else you could have done," Eleanor sympathised. "Anyway, if he is suffering from apoplexy, he won't be able to give the order to evict you."

It was not long before Noah and John arrived and Ingaret related her story yet again.

Noah was nonplussed and could not think clearly but John told him and Ingaret to go home and pack up their belongings, and he would go to the mill and ask Elis whether they could stay there if they were evicted.

"Don't tell Elis what Lord D'Avencourt said about Alice," Ingaret pleaded. "If he's got to hear that, it should come from me."

"Understood," John said. "Now back to your cottage and make ready to leave. And I hope that he doesn't vent his anger on the rest of the family!"

Noah and Ingaret hurried back to their cottage and began to bundle up everything they thought they would need if they were thrown out.

Lord D'Avencourt's revenge was swift. In spite of his incapacity, he had managed to whisper instructions and four men soon arrived and threw open the cottage door.

"Out!" they shouted. "Out! We are evicting you on the orders of Lord D'Avencourt. You are to leave at once and not return!"

So saying, they roughly pushed Ingaret and her father out of the door, banged it shut and proceeded to nail two planks obliquely over the doorway, barring re-entry.

"If you are found anywhere on Lord D'Avencourt's land by this time tomorrow, you will be thrown into the lockup, both of you!" they warned them. "Be off with you!"

The men departed and Ingaret and her father were left standing helplessly in their yard, each clutching a blanket wrapped around their goods.

"I am so sorry, Father," Ingaret began but he silenced her.

"I don't see that you could have done anything else. And all that about Alice? Do you believe him?"

"I think I do. But –" She shook her head to try to rid herself of the suggestion his lordship has whispered in her ear.

As they stood there, John returned.

"I've spoken to Elis. He says of course you must go to the mill but try to attract as little attention as possible. He says you can stay in one of his barns until the dust has settled and his lordship's next move is clear. Come! We won't go by the usual paths but will approach the mill from downstream and hopefully nobody from the manor house will see us."

Elis and his mother were anxiously waiting for them and quickly ushered them into what had been a stable but was now being used for storage. They were made comfortable on a large stack of hay. Later, Mistress Edith brought them peas mashed with bacon, bread and ale, which they consumed hungrily and felt better for it.

Elis came to see Ingaret after they had eaten, to ask her exactly what had happened to make Lord D'Avencourt so angry, and Noah left them alone till he was ready to sleep.

Ingaret decided she had to tell Elis the truth and have the whole episode out in the open so that there were no secrets between them. However, she found it very difficult to know what to say and was very upset and hesitant in the telling. When it came to those words mouthed with such relish in her ear, she knew she could not repeat them, not to this man she loved so much, who had trusted and cared for her sister, and her lips clammed shut and stayed that way.

In the silence that followed, Elis clasped his head in his hands and his voice was hardly above a whisper.

"You are telling me that Alice – my Alice – the whole time, was deceiving me and that she and Lord D'Avencourt – ? I cannot believe it of her."

"It seems so," said Ingaret miserably.

"So that is what she meant in her letter about being ashamed of what she had done and the way she had treated me. I thought she was referring to her suicide."

"It does seem that she regretted everything," said Ingaret. "Oh, Elis, I am so sorry!"

"I should have known," he said. "I should have seen what was happening. If I had been paying her more attention, I would have noticed that she was hiding something from me. It explains her frequent visits to friends in the vill – friends I never met and never asked about because I wasn't that interested. I have been such a fool!"

"No, my darling, never a fool," Ingaret comforted him, putting her arms round him and guiding his head onto her chest as they sat together in the hay.

"Constance must never find out," he said.

"She never will from my lips."

After a moment, she asked, "Elis, what if they find us here?"

"His lordship can hardly evict me," Elis reassured her, looking up. "Now I have bought the mill from him, it is my land and he should not be setting foot on it without my permission. And he could not touch you, if you had protection as my wife."

"What are you saying?"

"Give me a few hours, sweetheart, to think all this over, to get used to the idea that I wasn't wholly responsible for Alice's death. I don't think I could have saved her – that any of us could have saved her. Just give me a few hours, then you can ask me again what I was saying."

They were both silent as they thought about the tragedy that had been Alice's life and were brought back to the present when Noah entered with a lantern.

"I didn't realise how dark it had become," Elis said. "Good night, my love; good night, Noah. Ingaret will tell you what we have talked about. I'll see you both in the morning."

CHAPTER 53

For the next two days, the fugitives kept themselves out of sight. The men who worked for Elis knew they were there but he trusted them to keep silent on the matter when any of their customers were about.

On the third day, they heard the sound of a cart approaching the yard and scurried back into the stable until whoever it was had contracted their business and left. Both were alarmed, then, when the stable door was thrown open, and daylight streamed into their hiding place.

"Ingaret, let me handle this," Noah instructed her, preparing to confront anyone who tried to intimidate them, but they were surprised when Elis called out, "Ingaret! Noah! You can come out! You have a visitor!"

They both emerged from the gloom into the daylight to find Mistress Aldith there, a horse and cart from the manor, and its driver standing behind her.

"Aldith!" Ingaret exclaimed.

"Mistress Aldith," said Noah, "what brings you here? We are under the protection of the miller and you are trespassing on his land."

"Oh, fie!" laughed Aldith. "You can just get off that high horse, Noah, and listen to what I have to say."

"There is no advantage in standing out here discussing the situation," said Elis. "Come along inside the house and my mother will let you sample her maids-of-honour tarts, not long out of the oven."

He ushered them into the house, where his mother, though surprised, welcomed them warmly then busied herself serving the delicacies while Elis poured the ale, taking a pot out to the driver.

Ingaret was unsure and anxious at what was happening and, noticing this, Mistress Aldith began to explain.

"First of all, my dear, let me reassure you and your father that you are no longer in any danger from Lord D'Avencourt who, these days, is very ill and hardly has his wits about him. I am not here on his behalf but on her ladyship's. I will start at the beginning though you are aware of most of my story."

She paused, swallowed a mouthful of ale then began.

"As you know, Ingaret, I said I would tie a ribbon round the urn in the rose garden to warn you if his lordship was in the house. He was here on May Day, though he didn't attend the festivities, and I tied the ribbon round the urn as soon as he arrived."

Ingaret nodded. "I saw it on May Day so didn't go into the house."

Aldith continued. "I left the ribbon tied to the urn overnight. On the day following, in the afternoon, her ladyship was dozing and I was sitting at the window, working at my embroidery frame, when I happened to look down and saw you walking through the rose garden. You picked a yellow rose."

Ingaret nodded.

"Of course, I expected you to turn back on seeing the ribbon, but instead you continued towards the house. This surprised me greatly, then I noticed that the ribbon was no longer tied round the neck of the urn. My lady was still asleep so I left her there for a few moments to meet you on the way and warn you that his lordship was somewhere around, knowing that you wished to avoid an encounter.

"When I reached the top of the staircase, I saw him standing at the bottom. It did not occur to me that he was waylaying you until I saw the ribbon in his hand and realised that he must have removed it from the urn. I felt helpless, trapped as I was, and did not know what to do."

"Then I came in –" said Ingaret and Aldith nodded.

Elis came round to the chair in which Ingaret was sitting and laid his hand on her shoulder. She reached up and covered his hand with hers.

"Yes, then you came in and I heard every word and saw everything that passed between the two of you."

Ingaret continued with her account of what had happened. "After he fell, I started to leave but he was making such a strange sound that I came back, but I still didn't know whether he was playing a game. Then you came down the stairs and said he was having a fit of apoplexy and you told me to go and you would deal with it."

Everyone was looking at the storyteller, waiting to be told what happened next.

"I shouted for help," said Aldith, "and servants came and got him to bed –"

His very comfortable bed, Ingaret found herself thinking, remembering how his lordship had described it to her.

"– and his physician in Fortchester was sent for. By the time he arrived next day, the worst was over, his lordship had survived the apoplexy, though his speech was hesitant and slurred, but not so much that he could not warn me to keep my mouth shut about the circumstances of his attack. I did not know what to do so, like a coward, did nothing. The physician bled his lordship then men were sent out to find a pine tree to burn in the hearth, as he said that breathing in the smoke would help cure the condition. The physician left a diverse collection of pills and potions.

"Next morning, his lordship was in such a vile temper, and uttered such vile curses, dishonouring my dear lady, who had spent all night ministering to him, that I could keep silent no longer. So I told her everything – everything. I judged it was time she knew what sort of man she had married unadvisedly – but she had been very young. She seemed to know a great deal, anyway, and hushed me in the middle of my diatribe. However, she was very concerned about you, Ingaret, and what he could do to revenge himself on you, as ill as he was."

"He evicted us!" Noah declared.

"I know," said Mistress Aldith. "I saw four of his men ride out and guessed they had gone to evict you. My lady summoned the bailiff and questioned him about what was happening, if anything, and he told her that you and your father were being removed from your cottage and the door barred. Then she sent me to find out where you had gone. I went first to your brother, the blacksmith, and he said you had found refuge here, so that is where I came – and here I am."

"They are under my protection," Elis repeated. "I have asked Ingaret to marry me. She is to become my wife."

"Really, dear?" asked his mother. "Ingaret, I am so pleased to welcome you into the family at last. I don't know why it has taken my son so long to come to his senses."

"There will be time for celebrations," Aldith interrupted her, "but now I have to tell you, Noah, that my lady has given instructions for your cottage to be unbarred immediately. If you return, you will find that you can go back inside."

"That is indeed great news!" Noah exclaimed.

"But his lordship will put a stop to that, surely?" asked Elis.

"I am not privy to the conversation my lady had with her husband," Mistress Aldith said, "but I do know that their fortune came from her side of the family. He had nothing until he married her, which was one of the reasons he married her, I daresay. If she chooses, he will have nothing again."

There was silence in the room while her listeners registered all that she had told them.

"So," she said to Noah, "you both may return to your cottage immediately. You have nothing to fear from his lordship."

"I will go with you," Elis offered. "We will collect all your belongings, my love, then I will bring you back here. We will marry in the morning, if you've a mind. I will ask you again as becomes a suitor who is very much in love with his lady, when we are alone together."

"And do I have no say in this serious matter?" asked Noah, feigning offence.

"I will marry Elis whether you give your consent or no," Ingaret laughed and went to him and put her arms round his neck and kissed him on the nose.

"Then it is just as well that I give my consent," he said and clapped his future son-in-law on the back and shook his hand then kissed Ingaret and Elis's mother and even Mistress Aldith, and everyone laughed.

She was then helped back into the cart to return to the manor and report to Lady D'Avencourt all that had happened.

"Elis and I will visit her soon, to thank her," Ingaret promised.

Then Elis drove Ingaret and Noah back to the cottage, where they found the door jambs splintered where the wooden bars had been roughly levered off.

"'Tis no matter," said Noah, "I will have it fixed in no time."

While Ingaret piled her few possessions by the door for loading onto his cart, Elis left to tell John and his family, then Constance and her husband, about the news of his marriage next morning to Ingaret.

He reported that his daughter received the news with resignation but, of course, he had said nothing about the relationship between her mother and Lord D'Avencourt.

On his return, he loaded up Ingaret's belongings and, after her farewell to her father, drove her back to the mill house, where Ingaret and Elis shared his bed for the first night of many nights stretching away into their long future together.

They took their marriage vows next morning in the downstairs room of the mill house. With great solemnity, Elis slipped his mother's wedding ring onto the third finger of Ingaret's left hand, witnessed by his mother Edith and Noah, Ingaret's brother John and his wife, and the mill workers. Then the couple drove to the church to ask the priest to read their Banns at the morning service on the following Sunday.

On the return of the wedding party from church that Sunday, a messenger from Mistress Aldith was awaiting them to advise that Lord D'Avencourt had taken a turn for the worse and was unable to move or speak. His physician was being summoned again and messengers had been sent to inform his sons, but it seemed doubtful that his lordship would survive until they and his physician arrived.

It was learned later in the day that he had passed away.

"Oh, Elis, did I kill him?" Ingaret asked him in panic. "Did I murder him?"

"No, no! You must not think that!" he remonstrated. "Didn't he attack you first? Didn't he frighten and threaten and molest you? Did you have apoplexy? Of course not, because you were innocent. You were merely defending yourself, trying to get away! He killed himself, with his lust, his anger, his frustration, his violence and utter disregard for her ladyship."

Ingaret was not convinced that she hadn't caused his death until she remembered what he had whispered to her, followed by his threat, "And we will play that same game, madam, whether you like it or not!" and she knew then that he could have killed her and would not have turned a hair in doing so as long as he had satisfied his unnatural desires. With that thought, she was able to banish from her head the notion that she had murdered Lord D'Avencourt.

The messenger also brought a letter from Lady D'Avencourt, wishing Ingaret and Elis every happiness, and offering to waive the merchat tax on their marriage as her wedding present.

In bed that night, Ingaret confided to Elis her fancies about life being a maypole dance and both agreed that their tangled ribbons had at last been woven into a beautiful pattern and the deepest shared love that either had ever known.

EPILOGUE

The voices fade and I am fighting my way out of a tangle of coloured ribbons, fighting my way to the surface, to consciousness. I am lying on my back on the floor. What am I doing here? My head hurts. I gingerly feel a lump the size of an egg on my cranium.

I open my eyes and the first thing I see is the picture, reflecting back a garland of coloured lights. I turn my head and see the decorated Christmas tree in the corner of the room. I remember now! I remember falling…

Unsteadily, I raise myself onto all fours and crawl towards the couch. I push aside the newspaper wrapping and slump onto the cushions. I wonder that I haven't got the headache of all headaches, but I haven't. I contemplate that I am very fortunate not to have cracked open my skull. I will sit quietly for a while and try to remember where I have been since I fell.

Then I hear the sound of a key in the lock.

"Coo-eee! It's only me!"

Pam, my lodger!

"I'm in the living room!"

She dumps her shopping bag in the doorway and comes in.

"What's happened to you? You look as if you'd seen a ghost!"

"I fell off the stool. I'm all right, or will be once you've kindly made us both a cup of tea."

"Coming right up!"

While she busies herself in the kitchen, from where comes the chink of cups and saucers and the welcome sound of a boiling kettle, I begin to remember.

She bustles in with a tray and the tea things and a plate of digestive biscuits, my favourites.

"So, tell me," she says as she pours the tea.

"Feel this," I say, putting my cup on the coffee table and guiding her hand to the lump on my head. "You'll think me mad, but I've been back in the fifteenth century."

"You should go to the doctor about that lump," she says.

"I will if I feel ill tomorrow."

"So what were you doing, climbing about on a stool?"

"I was hanging that picture," I reply.

Pam puts down her biscuit, wipes her mouth with a tissue, and goes across to the fireplace to have a better look.

"It's a beautiful painting," she says. "Who's the lady?"

"Her name's Ingaret."

"Really?"

She stands, still staring at the picture, then says slowly, "I know her. Her name's Ingaret Miller."

This takes me aback. "Yes, I guess that's her name. But how do you know her?"

Pam comes back to the couch and sits beside me again, hands in her lap.

"There's a statue of her in Fortchester cathedral. She was one of their benefactors."

I feel the hairs rise on the back of my neck.

"You've seen it?"

"Yes, several times. It's a beautiful statue."

I feel the strongest urge to see the statue for myself.

"Pam, would you come with me to visit the cathedral? I've never been to Fortchester."

"Of course. We could drive over at the weekend. Now tell me what you know about her."

On the following Saturday, the weekend before Christmas, we leave the house during the morning to drive the fifty or so miles to Fortchester. It is a beautiful day, coldly crisp and sunny, the air clear and bright, the journey breathtaking across the downs and through the fallow fields.

When we reach the city, Pam drives to the central public car park and parks her car. There are stretches of the old wall visible in places.

"The Romans built them," I tell her.

Together we walk the few minutes to the cathedral. Being Saturday, a Christmas market has been set up in the cathedral square. Children are playing round the fountain, splashing each other and laughing hilariously.

We negotiate the rows of stalls with their enticing, seasonally-packaged goods for sale, ignoring the aroma of locally-made cheeses, and pass through the west door into the cathedral. The sudden change from good-humoured noisy clamour to reverent silence is dramatic.

The stained glass west window is throwing pools of light on the tiled floor.

"Where?" I ask Pam.

"In the right-hand transept. This way."

I follow as if in a dream, past the familiar double columns, aware of the tiny chapels lining both side aisles, and up to the crossing where the transepts meet the nave. Above the high altar the colours of the east window glow. Not the fifteenth century windows, I read later in the guide book, as Henry VIII then Oliver Cromwell destroyed them, along with the chantries and many of the treasures of the church. The eighteenth century replacements depict angels but none of them has long yellow hair.

Pam leads the way into the south transept – and there she is! Standing alone on a plinth in the centre of this large area. Ingaret! Older than when I left her but unmistakably Ingaret, carved in limestone, wearing the shift and kirtle of her time and standing with a bag of flour at her feet and a child in her arms.

"Hello, Ingaret," I greet her. "How good to see you again!"

"Anything about her in your guide book?" Pam asks.

I flick through the pages until I come to a photograph of her statue.

"It names her as Ingaret Miller, who died in the sixteenth century of old age. She was the wife of a miller on a manor some distance away. The couple remained childless but she had three children by a previous marriage to the master mason who, it says, was responsible for much of the ornate carving we see around and above us. Tradition says that tragically he fell to his death from scaffolding while working high up in the roof."

I realise that this transept is where Ingaret first met Roldan and look up to the distant carvings of fruit and flowers in a swag that loops its way around the apse. Such beauty!

I go back to the guide book. "The statue," it continues, "was carved from memory after her death by her son, Allard Mason. He said in a document, which is in the cathedral library, that he found his mother imprisoned in a block of limestone and simply freed her. Mrs. Miller was a benefactor of the cathedral and left the mill to the diocese on her death. The cathedral is still in receipt of rent from the flats built on the site."

"And she's been here for close on five hundred years?" Pam asks. "What about Oliver Cromwell?"

"It says here that Henry VIII let her statue stay because of the money the mill was bringing into the cathedral's coffers, but she was spirited away during the years of the Commonwealth, when Cromwell stabled horses in the building, and was brought out of hiding after the Restoration."

I study her closely. Allard had been faithful to his mother's beauty – her hair falling in curls to her shoulders, her smile. He had tried to give an impression of her mesmerising eyes but, of course, the colour was absent. I realise that I am the only person alive today who knows that her eyes had been that piercing deep violet.

After a while, reluctantly I turn from my study of the statue, as we intend to have a look round the cathedral while listening to the hymns soaring up into the fanned roof as organist and choir began their rehearsal for the next day's services.

Pam is ahead of me and I am about to follow when I notice something on the tiles at my feet. It is a wonder I hadn't stepped on it. I bend to retrieve it and discover a chipping of limestone, a small rosebud. It is light and smooth and cool between my fingers. I gaze up into the roof, half expecting to see Roldan up there, smiling down at me. He isn't there but I smile anyway.

"Thank you," I whisper and pop the chip into my pocket.

THE END

AFTER MIDNIGHT MASS, FIFTEENTH CENTURY

THE STORY OF MY SEARCH FOR THE ORIGINAL OIL PAINTING

The following research was carried out during 'lockdown' occasioned by the Covid-19 pandemic of 2020/21, when non-essential businesses were closed and many of their staff were working from home. This explains why it was so difficult to make contact in some instances.

My ninth novel, *Dancing at D'Avencourt*, has been inspired by what is to me a fascinating and beautiful painting by George Henry Boughton, R.A. I own a framed print of it, which I found in some antique shop, I don't remember which, years ago. Pasted on the back of the picture are the following details:

"From the picture in the collection of W.K. D'Arcy, Esq.
Size of canvas 50 by 96 inches.
Exhibited at the Royal Academy, 1897.

This important work by the painter shows a congregation coming away from midnight mass in some Continental city in the fifteenth century. The eye is at once attracted to the lady of high birth, slender in form, youthful and elegantly clad, who is stepping lightly over the snow-covered ground on her return to her home. Torch-bearers make sure of her way, and by her side is an elderly attendant, while groups of respectful and interested spectators mark their sense of her importance. The rest of the congregation, who follow her through the spacious doorway, are all in quaint and picturesque costumes, that give in themselves a beauty and interest to the work, apart from the effect of the massive cathedral walls and the cold midnight air. The charm of the Mediaevalism of the scene is the attribute in the picture sought, and most successfully attained, by the painter."

My print, which measures 10½ by 6 inches, was framed by Wilfrid Coates of 25, Fawcett Street, Sunderland, who advertised himself as a Fine Art Dealer and High Class Picture Frame Maker & Gilder.

Wikipedia has the following information about Mr. D'Arcy:

William Knox D'Arcy was one of the principal founders of the oil and petrochemical industry in Persia. Concession to explore, obtain, and market oil, natural gas, asphalt, and ozokerite was given to him and the concession known as the D'Arcy Concession in Iran.

Born: 11 October 1849, Newton Abbot
Died: 1 May 1917, Middlesex
Spouse: Elena Birkbeck (m. 1872)
Education: Westminster School
Organisations founded: BP, National Iranian Oil Company

On contacting the Royal Academy, I discovered that they had no knowledge or information about the painting's present whereabouts.

So I wrote to the head office of BP in St. James's Square, London, asking if the painting was hanging in their board room, and received a most helpful reply by email from a member of the Group Press Office, to whom my letter had been passed:

"I've done some digging around on your behalf, to see where the painting is and whether we could be of help.

The original oil painting is owned as part of the Baker/Pisano collection out of New York, but has found its way into the archives of the Smithsonian American Art Museum in Washington D.C."

I contacted the Smithsonian and discovered that what they possess is a small study of the finished painting measuring 'only' 18½ x 36 ins.

They pointed me in the direction of the Heckscher Museum of New York, which had included the original in a catalogue of an exhibition held in 1983, so I contacted them.

Before receiving a reply, I obtained a copy of the Catalogue mentioned above. It did not contain an illustration of the finished painting but of the study, which is nothing like the final painting but includes elements of it.

I came to the conclusion that there is only one such study and not two and it is now at the Smithsonian Museum.

I then received an email from the Heckscher, telling me what I had already found out. They do not know where the original is.

So I wrote to Philip Mould of *Fake or Fortune?* TV fame, to ask if he has any ideas where I should search next. After sending a letter, phoning, sending an email and phoning again, one of their staff pointed me in the direction of Bridgeman Images of London. They replied to my email, suggesting I got in touch with M and J Duncan art dealers, whose website records the painting as SOLD but no date or purchaser given. I emailed twice and then wrote to Duncan's to see if they could help.

Success! A gentleman from M & J Duncan rang me on a Saturday morning, having just received my letter but not the two emails, as the company is in 'lockdown' because of the coronavirus pandemic.

He told me that he is the agent who sold the painting a few years ago. Obviously, he is not allowed to tell me the purchaser or the price paid but said it is now in a private collection and not on public display. Such a pity!

I have let everyone who contacted me know the outcome of my search and the Heckscher Museum say they will add the information to their file.

In this process, I have learned a little about the art world, and have discovered that the professional people who work there have been unfailingly courteous and helpful.

And I still have my framed print which, from the look of the pasted label on the back, may be contemporary with the painting's 1897 exhibition at the Royal Academy. To try to establish this, I am now researching the framer and have discovered that he closed his business in the 1920s.

Am I being too fanciful in thinking that my print could be the only one in existence?

Iris Lloyd

Lightning Source UK Ltd.
Milton Keynes UK
UKHW041459290421
382825UK00001B/5